WEB OF BETRAYAL

WEB OF BETRAYAL

BY

PETER S. BERMAN

AUTHOR'S NOTE

This novel is a work of fiction in its entirety. All characters, settings, dialogue, incidents and other story elements are wholly imaginary, as are the personalities of my characters. Following an old literary tradition, I have honored some of my friends by using their names to identify fictional characters, but there is no real connection between my imaginary characters and my real-life friends. Any resemblance between the fictional contents of this book and real people, companies, institutions or places, is strictly coincidental.

This story is dedicated to my wife, Renée.
Her great strength in the face of terrible adversity was my daily inspiration.

It is also dedicated to my children and their respective spouses:
Bryan, Jeremy, and Julie,
Jennifer, Amy, and Michael.
And my grandchildren; Maxwell and Charlotte

We have to distrust each other.
It is our only defense against betrayal.

-Tennessee Williams, *Camino Real* (1953)

A clean glove often hides a dirty hand.

- English Proverb

PETER S. BERMAN

WEB OF BETRAYAL

****

PROLOGUE

Darkness spread quickly over Belfast, Northern Ireland, plunging sections of the city headlong into a no-man's-land of existence. The deepening shadows enveloped what remained of the twilight while the anonymity of the coming darkness lured the city's disenfranchised Catholic youths from their neighborhood flats and out into the streets where they were free to dissent while protected by the security of their numbers.

Belfast is known as a city of enclaves. A large number of the residential areas are religiously mixed neighborhoods with Protestants and Catholics evenly distributed throughout the community. But over the years, the Protestant-dominated housing council made a conscious effort to see that many of the districts were completely segregated; and quite intentionally, the less desirable housing units were relegated to the Catholics. This gerrymandering was nothing more than a means of drawing the ward boundaries to limit the Catholic parliamentary seats to as few as possible, thereby protecting the Protestant stranglehold on government jobs and benefits.

Inside Belfast, near the banks of the *River Lagan*, there were a series of roads whose names were synonymous with violent protest. Known as *Shankill, Crumlin, Springfield* and *Lower Falls*, they separated the various enclaves like international borders.

The Catholics, in their gray slate, flat roofed row houses, lived amidst the squalor brought about by chronic unemployment and forced overcrowding. The cold and grimy streets were devoid of even the barest pretense of hope. It was a place where people were united together by an ever-present fear of Protestant sectarian violence.

History has demonstrated that the "troubles" periodically ebbed and flowed. The 1970's were considered by many to be a time of violent upsurge. It began with the random killing of a member of the Royal Ulster Constabulary (RUC), the Protestant dominated police force, and this brought about the usual governmental response. The Catholic enclave nearest to the killing was placed under a dusk to dawn curfew, and the reaction to this policy was sadly predictable;

demonstrations and marches designed to challenge the unfairness of the government's anti-Catholic bias.

Eventually, the violence would run its course, but in the meantime, night after night, an agonizing ritual was allowed to play out.

****

Jimmy Cassidy moved quietly down the stairs from his bedroom on the second floor when he could no longer ignore the shouts and laughter from the streets in front of the old, faded brownstone on *Springfield Road*, where he lived with his parents and his younger brother, Liam.

Grabbing a faded wool coat from the closet at the foot of the stairs, he walked quickly and silently to the front door, casting a wary eye sideways in search of his alcoholic father; a chronically unemployed factory worker with big, meaty hands which he frequently used to keep his family in line.

Jimmy could hear his father's deep nasally breathing as it rose unmistakably from the frayed and sagging parlor couch where he now seemed to spend the majority of his life in dreamless oblivion, lying comfortably among the remnants of empty bottles of ale.

Jimmy looked for his mother, but the vacant chair next to the couch signified that she had gone to bed as soon as supper was over. She preferred the solitude of her bedroom to an evening in the parlor where she would invariably become the target of her husband's drunken abuse.

It no longer mattered to Jimmy that his parents showed little or no concern for his welfare. In fact, he preferred it that way. With no one to set any limits on his activities, he could come and go as he pleased, unlike many of his classmates who would be forced to stay home, where they would miss the excitement of protesting in the streets.

Arriving at the front door, Jimmy was surprised to discover his little brother Liam already bundled in a tattered brown jacket that was several sizes too big for him.

At age eleven, Liam was physically small. He sported a mop of brown hair and a freckled face that was always quick to smile.

He stood up straight and reached for the knob while he tried to exude a level of confidence that he hoped would persuade his older brother to take him along.

"Are ya ready?" Liam said as he turned the handle.

"Yer not goin'. Get back in yer room."

Jimmy grabbed him by the coat and gave him a shove down the hallway and away from the door.

Liam tripped and fell, striking his knee on the hardwood floor, but he refused to cry. He got back up, his self-confidence now in tatters, and resorted to pleading.

"Please, Jimmy, I wanna go too!"

But Jimmy was not about to let his little brother get caught up in the troubles. For all intents and purposes, he had become Liam's surrogate father, so he shook his head and raised his fist for emphasis.

"I've tol' ya b'fore. Yer too little. Get yer coat off and stay in the house."

Liam whimpered, but it fell on deaf ears. Jimmy gave him a final shove towards the parlor, then opened the door and stepped outside. He loved his little brother and he dearly wished he could let him come along, but he didn't want the responsibility of having to watch out for him if things got out of control. Someday soon he would be ready to tag along, but tonight would not be the night.

After pulling up his jacket collar, he shoved his hands into his pockets and wandered out into the Belfast night. The dreariness of the ever-present winter fog always made him feel cold to the bone, and because the street lamps had all been broken out to prevent the residents from becoming targets for snipers, he had to wait a few moments for his eyes to adjust to the darkness.

Glancing about, he noticed several young people from his neighborhood carrying stones, sticks and metal construction bars which were hammered at one end into a point. Above him, on the roof of this block of flats, he could hear the scurrying about of the older boys who carried petrol bombs to the corner of the roof closest to *Falls Road,* where they would be stored in crates for use on the police if they were foolish enough to enter the enclave.

The bravest ones among the children had already begun moving towards the intersection at Falls Road, so Jimmy headed in that direction. He spotted several of his mates and ran to catch up with them. They waved and gestured, taunted each other, and urged the more timid ones still standing on the sidelines to join them in their spontaneous parade, and once the group had grown sufficiently, they began to move about and act as one.

As the lead group reached Falls Road, the first target of opportunity became an older model Rover that was parked at the curb. It mattered little to the demonstrators that it belonged to one of their own. The car had become an object of convenience. Using sticks and pavers, they smashed out all the windows, dented in the sides, and caved in the hood. Jimmy joined a few of the older boys and they pushed it out into the middle of the road where soon, with great fanfare, it was turned on its side and set ablaze.

Flushed with excitement, Jimmy's cheeks were rosy from exertion. At fourteen, he was still as thin as a rail and just beginning to show signs of a growth spurt that would manifest itself as the onset of puberty. His light brown hair was generally unkempt, and hung down into his eyes, causing him to continually flip his head to the side in order to see clearly.

Smiling broadly to his mates, and using a heavy piece of metal piping he picked up from the gutter, he took a swing at what remained of the driver's side door. The impact stung his hands, but the exuberance of the moment and the cheers from his peers outweighed the discomfort and pain.

As the wind shifted, blowing the smoke from the burning car into his face, Jimmy moved around to the other side of the Rover to continue his revelry. A few of his mates were singing the Irish Republic's national anthem, *A Soldier's Song*, and one of the older boys unfurled the Republican's tricolor flag.

Standing over by the curb, Jimmy spotted some of the girls from his class at school, and the fact that they were watching him made Jimmy act out even more. Emboldened by the limelight, he became a captive to the moment and was soon striking out at the car with even greater abandon.

The fire in the vehicle spread to several of the tires, and a thick blanket of choking smoke settled in a pall over the entire street, causing some of those in the crowd to begin moving up the road and back into the safety of their enclave.

Most of those who remained milling about were oblivious to the arrival of a snatch squad from the *Royal Ulster Constabulary,* (RUC). The men of this

Protestant dominated paramilitary force quietly pulled up nearby in lightly armored grey personnel carriers—known by the locals as *PIGS* because of their shape—and by not using their lights, they managed to arrive without detection to a staging area on *Grosvenor Road*, just around the corner from the intersection at Falls.

From the depths of the shadows of a row house porch stoop, Liam Cassidy peered out at the antics of his older brother with envy and pride. He spent the last two nights in this secret place of concealment, observing the battles unfolding in the streets, and he both enjoyed and feared what he knew would inevitably occur. For him, the game had an added factor. Once the police arrived, he would have to get home before his brother did, or face the prospect of a knocking about if Jimmy discovered he'd been outside on the streets. For this reason, it was no accident that Liam was one of the first to notice the PIGSs as they slowly inched forward in the darkness towards the intersection with the Falls.

Liam watched the vehicles intently, for his vision was not obscured by the smoke from the tires. He kept waiting for someone else to yell a warning, but apparently, no one else was yet aware of the presence of the police. He debated whether or not to sound the alarm, but at that moment, he was more afraid of his brother then he was of the RUC. When they sprang silently from the armored cars and ran quickly towards the intersection, Liam broke from his cover on the porch and ran away, towards the safety of his home.

He looked back over his shoulder and noticed that the police had almost reached the crowd which was still unaware and cavorting loudly in the road. Liam froze in his tracks, gripped now by fear for his brother's safety. He realized that Jimmy could not foresee what was about to happen, so he spun around on his heels and ran back. He darted around those who were meandering slowly in his direction, all the while screaming out Jimmy's name.

In the midst of the noise and confusion, Jimmy was still singing and posturing, oblivious to the imminent surprise attack. Liam finally caught up to him, grabbed him by the coat, and attempted to drag him towards the shadows and away from the light emanating from the burning car.

"*Run, Jimmy*," he screamed. "*Run!*"

Instinctively, Jimmy pushed at Liam, trying to loosen the grip that his little brother had on his coat, but when the warning sank in, Jimmy panicked and started to run.

Liam, who still had a death grip on Jimmy's jacket, found himself being dragged along.

Out of the corner of his eye, Jimmy could see a policeman emerging from the smoke and haze. Others now sensed what was happening, and a panic swept over the crowd. People screamed and ran in all directions, and Jimmy tried to dart away from his pursuer, but in his haste, his legs tangled with those of Liam, and both of them fell to the ground.

Jimmy scrambled to his feet and resumed his flight, but Liam had landed hard, striking his already sore knee. He was unable to easily get to his feet, and in that brief instant of delay, his chance to escape quickly disappeared.

An RUC trooper struck him unmercifully with a rubber truncheon. Liam screamed and rolled on the ground, trying to cover his face while kicking wildly to ward off the blows. The trooper continued to beat him, reigning blow after blow until Liam lay quietly by the side of the road. Only then did the trooper move on in search of another victim.

Jimmy had turned around when he heard his brother's first terrible scream. He watched in horror as the soldier struck Liam again and again. All around him was chaos, as people were caught and beaten by the troops.

A battle of sorts raged within Jimmy as he tried to decide what to do. In a moment of weakness, his fear won out and he fled up the street, lunging into the shadows of a nearby porch where he pressed himself against the cold stones of an archway that provided him with a measure of concealment.

Tears streamed down his face as he cowered on the porch, overcome by the knowledge that he'd betrayed his brother's unwavering trust.

A minute later, as the sounds of the battle moved farther up the road, he summoned up his courage and ran back to his brother. A neighbor had already picked up Liam's inert body and was rushing him towards a nearby flat. Jimmy ran after them, bounding up the porch stairs and catching up to them as they entered the house.

Liam was placed on the sofa where the neighbor's wife tended to his injuries with cold water and a towel. He was still unconscious, and his face was severely swollen and misshapen. There was a gash on the left side of his face, running from mid-cheek to his chin. Blood dribbled from his mouth; a dark space now visible where his two front teeth had previously resided.

At first, Jimmy could only stare in abject horror at the damage done to his little brother's face.

Still wracked with guilt, he somehow found the strength to move over to the couch. He gently cradled his brother in his arms; he looked so small and frail, and through tears of genuine remorse, he silently begged for his brother to forgive him.

Jimmy wiped his tears with the sleeve of his jacket, and he swore an oath to God—and to his still unconscious brother—that he would never leave Liam behind again.

****

ONE

Years Later, November 15

It had been raining steadily for hours and the gray sky over Belfast resembled a large, wet blanket. The effect was so gloomy that at two that afternoon, the city father's gave the order to turn on the streetlights. The highways were plagued by long delays resulting from the usual assortment of minor traffic accidents that the Irish had come to expect during this type of winter weather, and the bitter winds sweeping over the countryside from the west numbed all who were forced to go out. It was not a day for traveling, particularly by air.

At *Aldergrove Airport*, on a plateau northwest of the city, inside the *British Airways* waiting room, many of the passengers shed their rain gear as they adjusted to the warmth of the terminal. Puddles of water formed on the floor where umbrellas had been thoughtlessly shaken, and a maintenance man, mop in hand, worked tirelessly and without let-up to keep the mess under control. Most of the flights had taken off relatively close to their scheduled departure times, but as the severity of the weather increased, delays appeared inevitable.

By two forty-five p.m., activity was bustling around the check-in counter at Gate 21A. The flight listed on the board was for London's *Heathrow Airport*, and it had been scheduled to depart on time, but because of the weather, the plane was not yet ready for boarding, and the passengers milled about nervously in anxious anticipation as they waited to get started.

An in-house telephone buzzed at the gateway counter and was answered by a female passenger agent who was smartly dressed in a midnight-blue winter uniform. She signaled to another agent, and together, they walked over to the boarding ramp. Their movements attracted the attention of the passengers who began to stand up and collect their baggage.

One of the agents, a tall, attractive brunette with a milky-smooth complexion, picked up a microphone and announced the seating priorities. The gate became a sea of movement as passengers queued up to get on board.

Mairead Devenny sat at a nearby gate that was crowded with passengers who were waiting for a scheduled flight to Paris. From her vantage point across the room, and without drawing undue attention, she carefully studied the passengers and airline personnel who were waiting for the London flight. Nothing seemed out of the ordinary, but one couldn't be too careful. She forced herself to focus on the people without luggage. It was hard to be patient—she was anxious to get started—but she had no choice. She had to take it slow.

Once the boarding began for London, she pulled out her ticket and checked her seat number, 24A. Since the plane would be loaded from the rear, she knew her number would soon be called.

Should she wait until everyone cleared the gate? She rejected that option as far too risky. She would blend in better in a crowd, and besides, if the weather had created an overbooked flight, a delay in boarding might cause her to get bumped, and since she had to get to London before the storm shut down the airport, she opted to board when her group was called.

After taking a final look around the terminal, she stood up, picked up her carry-on bag, and quickly joined the queue at Gate 21A.

She followed an overweight, middle-aged businessman who struggled up to the gate with two small bags and a large stuffed animal.

Her auburn hair pulled into a bun, and her black, horn-rimmed glasses, gave her a severe look, a far cry from her usual appearance. In a knee-length trench coat, buttoned up against the cold, she was confident that she appeared sufficiently nondescript to avoid attracting any undue attention.

As the man in front of her cleared the gate, Mairead handed her boarding pass to the ticket agent—a statuesque blond with a wooden smile—who looked it over quickly, handed it back, then wished her a pleasant flight.

Mairead entered the conveyor that led to the plane. Once on board, she grabbed a pillow from the overhead, stowed her carry-on, and took her seat by the window.

The flight was only three-quarters full—the weather had scared off a number of passengers—and Mairead smiled to herself when the seat next to her remained empty. Once they were underway, she'd be able to stretch out in reasonable comfort.

The blond gate agent watched in silence for a few moments from the terminal window as the plane taxied out to the runway. She walked back to the desk, picked up a phone, then punched in several numbers.

"Orphan's on board," she whispered.

****

Wind drafts buffeted the plane during takeoff, but they abated as the flight reached a cruising altitude of 27,000 feet. Mairead fought to stay awake, afraid that the nightmares might return, but the medication she'd taken to calm her fear of flying overpowered her will and soon she was fast asleep.

She was lying in her cell in Crumlin prison, staring into the blackness of the ceiling above her small bunk. Her sense of smell was assaulted by the stench of human excrement, and she suppressed the urge to vomit by taking short, shallow breaths while she fumbled with a rag that she used to cover her face. With her nose and mouth filtered, she began to breathe more evenly. The others in the cell were still mercifully asleep.

As the early morning light filtered through a tiny barred window above her bed, she tried to muster the courage to face the hell that had become her daily reality.

She and her cellmates had called a strike as a means to get political recognition. They wanted to be treated as prisoners of war, and until they got their way, Mairead and the others refused to become involved in the ordinary prison work details. Their defiance was punished—confinement to their cells around-the-clock—and they were forced to make do with a chamber pot which was emptied only once a day.

At first, in anger, they refused to bathe or even clean their cells, calling it a "no wash protest." When this had no effect, they raised the stakes by emptying the chamber pot on the floor and rubbing the excrement on the walls.

Reaction to their protest was swift. In an effort to avoid political embar-rassment, the government restricted their access to the outside world. Their plight was ignored, and their visits from family and friends were curtailed. A Catholic chaplain brought them their meals—scaled-back portions of food— and because of the smell, even his visits grew shorter and shorter.

*The noise began as a soft, far-off rumble—like the sound of distant thun-
der—but suddenly grew deafening, and before she could open her eyes, she was
struck in the head by water from a high-pressure hose.*

*She was knocked from the bunk and her body bounced along the floor.
Gasping for breath and thrashing about, she felt as if she was drowning.*

"Are you all right?"

Someone was shaking her arm. She opened her eyes and was greeted by the
concerned looks of a stewardess and several of the nearby passengers.

She sat up abruptly and stretched her legs.

"I must 'ave been dreamin'. I'm sorry."

She lowered her glance and turned to look out the window. Sent to prison at
nineteen and released at thirty, she seethed at the loss of her youth, but the pending operation would settle many scores, and maybe put her demons to rest.

****

She entered the crowded terminal at Heathrow and walked past a young
chauffeur standing just inside the doorway with a small group of limo drivers.
He held up a sign that said "Harris," and as she walked by, he raised it up to
conceal the lower portion of his face.

She took a slow look around the terminal then headed for the baggage claim
area. He let her get comfortably ahead before he lowered his sign and blended
into the crowd that followed behind her. He watched as she passed through a
revolving security door that prevented her return to the main concourse area.
She would now have to leave the building through the baggage terminal doors.
Since other watchers were waiting in that area, he continued on through the
main terminal doors toward a black limousine that was parked in a nearby loading zone.

It had rained sporadically throughout the day and he had to dance on his
toes through several large puddles to keep his leather shoes from getting soaked.
He climbed into the front seat, shut the door, and spoke over his shoulder to the
two men sitting in the back.

"She's alone. No sign of anyone followin' her."

The two men did not reply. They were busy monitoring the surveillance reports which came in over their earphones from out in the baggage area. Orphan had already retrieved her bag, so the thinner of the two men, Piers Anders, opened a briefcase and flipped on a tracking monitor.

"The suitcase is coming out," he said.

The driver's vision was obscured by the drizzle that mixed with reflections from the terminal lights. He turned on the wipers, and a moment later, Mairead appeared at the doorway with a suitcase and her carry-on bag. She joined a queue of passengers who waited in the rain for the intermittent arrival of cabs.

Anders adjusted the volume on his tracking monitor. He extracted a power cord from his briefcase and plugged it into an elaborate communications console concealed between the front and rear seats. The car proved ideal cover for surveillance since darkened windows were not uncommon in a limousine.

They watched for a moment as she scanned the arriving cabs and slowly looked around.

"She's cautious," muttered Anders, "but she's been down too long. Technology has left her behind."

He was referring to the fact that her bag had been searched after she checked it in and a miniaturized tracking device with a battery operated transmitter had been inserted into the lining of her suitcase.

"Just don't lose her," said Colonel Nigel Ward. At sixty-three, he suffered from poor circulation, and to counteract the coldness in his hands, he forced his sweating subordinates to keep the heater running on high.

His slate gray eyes—his most arresting feature—were clear and cold, and they never revealed what he was thinking. His close-cropped gray hair gave him a military look that was almost old fashioned, but Nigel Ward was anything but that. As the Director of *MI-5* (Military Intelligence, Department 5), a group responsible for intelligence gathering within the country, he oversaw the activities of an elite counter-terrorist unit composed of operatives from the *Special Air Service Regiment,* (SAS), which was being augmented by members of his own division.

Ward was the one who authorized the planting of the tracking instrument.

He was technologically savvy, and he knew that the device would give off a signal which would enable his people to know the precise location of her suitcase by reference to a grid map on a laptop computer screen. The device was so powerful that his people could follow their quarry from more than half a mile away.

They watched with interest as Mairead entered a cab which pulled out and headed towards London. Ward reached for the transmit button on his two-way radio.

"Stay sharp, ladies and gentleman. They're on the M4. *Operation Sandman is in play.*"

****

The cabby dropped her off in front of the *Dorchester Arms Hotel* in the *Belgravia* section of Central London. An old, conventional hotel, the Dorchester catered primarily to well-heeled tourists. Set in a neighborhood of fashionable row houses, it was impeccably maintained in the white-and-black color scheme that characterized the rest of this upscale community.

She scurried through the rain to the front of the hotel, refused the assistance of a smiling doorman, then carried her own bags into the lobby. She walked slowly through the foyer, past the registration desk, and out the side door to the adjacent street. She opened an umbrella, then walked out into the rain, where she frequently glanced over her shoulder.

"She's looking for a tail," whispered a watcher into a microphone that was pinned to the underside of her jacket lapel. She was in her early thirties, but the dowdy clothing and makeup she wore helped her pass for a working class pensioner who was out on a shopping expedition. The streets were almost empty, so she kept her subject barely in view from the opposite side of the road.

"Orphan's heading for the tube," she said. "I'll need to switch-over once she reaches the station."

From an earphone concealed under her scarf, she received confirmation that the transfer would be made. She picked up the pace and shortened the distance between herself and her quarry.

When Mairead reached the station, two men made the switch-over. One was on foot, just inside the archway, in case she decided to use the tube. The second was positioned on the sidewalk, working on a chain that secured his bicycle to a wrought-iron light pole. If she jumped on a bus or took a cab, he would follow her until others could close in and resume a moving surveillance.

Mairead walked past the entrance to the Underground and proceeded to the bus stop on the corner. When one arrived, she climbed aboard and took a seat on the lower level where she could keep an eye on her bags. The man on the bicycle stayed just behind the bus and provided the others in cars with a running commentary concerning her location. Three stops later, a new watcher boarded the bus, while surveillance vehicles surged ahead to anticipate her moves.

She switched buses several times and ended up at the *Harrow and Weald-stone Station*, where she purchased a ticket for use on the *Bakerloo Line*. Two of the watchers closed in and followed her down the escalators and into the Underground. Before losing radio contact, they broadcast her proposed route to the other surveillance units up on the surface streets.

****

When it became apparent to Ward that the surveillance would be moving back towards London's city center, his hands began to perspire. All his life he'd been blessed with finely honed instincts, and given the direction this surveillance appeared to be going, he was quickly coming to the conclusion that it was time for Sean Clarke to take over the operation.

"Get Clarke on the secure line," he ordered.

His adjutant dialed a number then handed Ward a cell phone rigged with a scrambling device.

Captain Sean Clarke was a soft-spoken man whose intense dedication to his country commanded the respect of both his superiors and his men. A graduate of Cambridge, he made his mark in the military during the Falklands war when as the leader of an SAS expeditionary troop, he rescued several wounded men at great personal risk. After the war, in recognition of his valor, he was given command of an Intelligence unit stationed in Northern Ireland. He was later promoted to Chief of Operations for this SAS Counter-Terrorist Unit.

Clarke answered his phone on the second ring.

"This is Clarke."

"Sean, I think she's leading us directly to her contacts. I'm turning *Sandman* over to you. Good luck."

Clarke hung up the cell phone and spoke into his headset.

"One is now Control."

Consistent with the policy of never using names over the radio, each operative in the team was given a number for the purpose of identification, and as head of the unit, Clarke's number was *One.*

His men checked in and acknowledged the transfer of authority while he reached for a road map. His driver guided them at high speed through the city streets, and despite the rain, they closed in quickly on the *Baker Street Station* where Orphan would have easy access to four other lines.

Clarke fidgeted in his seat. If anything went wrong, he'd be held accountable, and failure would be costly. They'd received information from an informant in Belfast that Orphan would be joining an active service unit that planned to detonate a car bomb somewhere close to No. 10 Downing Street, the residence of the Prime Minister. They were told that she would be carrying the remote-controlled detonators, but her suitcase was searched and the devices were not found.

Were they on her person? Or worse, could the informant be wrong?

She'd traveled under an assumed name and there was no doubt that she was taking steps to avoid being followed. That led to only one logical conclusion; they were on the right track.

His driver pulled up at the station, and from the back seat, a plain clothes trooper who'd been monitoring the tracking device on a laptop, jumped out of the car and scurried briefly through the rain before hurrying down the stairs and into the subway station.

He reached the turnstiles and bolted over one, ignoring the shouts of angry passengers who resented the fact that he hadn't paid for a ticket. Spurred forward by the sounds of the trains below, he rounded the last corner, took the escalator stairs two at a time, and arrived at the tracks just as a train pulled up.

The doors slid open and a sea of passengers flooded the platform. He did not see Orphan get off, so he walked beside the train and stared in the windows in search of other agents he would know on sight. He finally spotted one, a young man with sandy blond hair who stood in an open doorway in the third car from the rear. He stepped aboard the subway car, took a seat near the back, and used the reflection in the windows to continue his search.

He found her seated quietly near the front of the car.

The young man he replaced slipped off the train and made his way upstairs and back to the street.

"She's still on the train, sir," the young man reported as he climbed in the back of Clarke's car. He opened the laptop and took over the monitoring duties.

"The radios are useless down there, sir," he said. "The Sergeant Major is seated one car in front of her, and Trooper Sanderson took my place in her car. Sanderson will get off and transmit from street level if she switches trains any-where father down the line, but if you don't mind my sayin' so, we better get some others down there in case she makes more than one switch."

Clarke had learned long ago to pay attention to his men. He turned to his driver.

"Get us closer to central London. I don't want to get caught short if she goes anywhere near Downing Street."

He hit the transmit button on his headset.

"Seven and Eight, join the train at Oxford Station. Make sure we get a broadcast if she changes trains."

****

The train made a stop at *Westminster Station*. Mairead gathered up her bags, and just before the doors closed, she stepped off and watched it pull away from the platform. She waited for the other disembarking passengers to leave the sta-tion before walking out the exit to *Bridge Street*.

Under an old, stone archway, she opened her umbrella and started her walk towards *Westminster Bridge*.

She found a bright red phone booth along the way and dialed a memorized number. It rang five times before someone answered.

"I'm home, darlin'," she said, then waited for the coded response.

"Is your cousin Charles with you?" the voice asked.

"No, he couldn't make it," she said, convinced that no one had followed her.

"Very well, we'll be over to get you shortly."

The rain stopped. She crossed the street and walked out onto the bridge. Halfway over the Thames, she pulled her coat tight against the chill. She moved near the edge of the street and anxiously watched the traffic from both directions.

****

Clarke flipped on the defroster switch to help clear the condensation from the windshield. His driver had parked about four blocks west of the bridge. Orphans' phone call meant she was soon likely to make contact, so he ordered his teams to set up on both sides of the bridge.

The radio chatter was constant as the units checked in and gave their positions, but Clark was only half-listening. He turned to his driver.

"Have you picked up any counter-surveillance?" he asked.

"Not yet, sir, but the Provos are awfully good."

Clarke sighed, his brow perspiring.

"Do your best. We don't want a nasty surprise."

A voice spoke up in his ear piece.

"This is Two. A vehicle just pulled up to her position."

"Can you see how many are in the car?" Clarke asked.

"Negative, sir. She's moving towards it; a white Cortina, four-door."

"Hold positions," warned Clarke.

"Three to Control," said another voice. *"I've got them in the scope. There's three in the car."*

Provos rarely used more than five operatives; the more there were, the greater the chance of a leak.

"This doesn't make sense, sir," said his driver. "Why would they expose the whole team?"

"Good question," Clarke replied. "If it is the whole team?"

"Do we take them on the bridge, sir?"

Clarke thought for a moment.

"Not yet. We've got them all in one car. Let's watch 'em for a time and see what they do."

He spoke again into his headset.

This is Control. Everyone stay alert. We may have 'em all, so don't take any chances. Three and Four, stay within reach.

****

After circling the area around the bridge to look for people seated in parked cars, the Cortina approached Mairead from the lane closest to the curb.

A man climbed out of the back seat. Tall and lanky, his dark hair and freckles made him look like a teenager, and his unshaven face did nothing to alter the impression. He pulled a key from his pocket, opened the trunk, and placed her bags inside. Together, they climbed into the backseat of the car.

"I'm Ryan Thomason," he said, extending his hand. He seemed pleasant enough, with a generous smile.

Mairead shook it, smiled, then looked over at the driver.

"Were you followed?" the driver asked.

"Not that I could tell."

"Well, we'll 'ave a little look around; see for ourselves."

Colin McCann used his rearview mirror to study her face in the glare of the oncoming headlights. Her eyes were flat and devoid of any spark. He'd seen that look before; a total lack of fear, and that meant trouble. Time in prison had certainly taken its toll. With no self-interest, and no fear of death, people made mistakes, and mistakes cost lives.

He was thirty-two years old and a long-time member of the Provos. Tall and sturdy, with a weathered face that made him seem much older, he wore his hair long on the sides in a somewhat vain attempt to cover some acne scars. There were premature wrinkles, the kind that went with life too long on the edge.

He drove down the highway while his practiced eye scanned the intersections. He doubled back and used side streets until he felt completely satisfied that they were alone.

He caught Mairead's eye in the mirror and motioned with his head to the man seated next to him.

"This is Riley."

Riley Meader looked back from over his shoulder and nodded in her direction. Full faced and also freckled, he kept his shock of red hair closely cropped like a soldier. He was big, just over six feet tall, with the build of a heavyweight boxer, and his single greatest talent was his skill with a handgun.

McCann drove for a few more minutes.

"Before we go to the loft, I want to do a walk-through while the streets are empty. We may not get a chance to do it tomorrow, so tonight we'll act like tourists and 'ave a look around."

He eased the Cortina through a roundabout while he stared at the headlights of a truck in his rear view mirror. Having followed behind them for the last several minutes, the truck finally left the round by a different exit. He relaxed once again; confident that they were not being followed.

He looked over at Meader and said, "Once we get there, you and Ryan split up and take the opposite sides of the street. Walk the backup escape routes and look for anything unusual."

He slowed the Cortina and made a left turn into a residential neighborhood. As he drove down the darkened street, he concentrated his attention on his rear view mirror. When no one made the turn behind him, he reversed his direction and headed back to the main road.

"I think we're okay," he said.

McCann caught Mairead's glance in the mirror. "Have you been briefed yet?"

"No, I was told you'd be lettin' me know what to do."

McCann was silent for a moment while he again studied the traffic behind him.

"We're goin' to take out the Prime Minister's residence usin' a mortar fired from a van. After that, we'll leave it with a delayed explosive charge to take out those who arrive on the scene."

Mairead smiled.

"What do you want me to do?"

"You'll be drivin' the van to the shoot. I'll fire the mortar while the others provide cover from the street. Once you're out of the van, you'll be responsible for clearin' the escape route. After that, we'll follow you through. We've got cars parked along the roadway, and we'll be switchin' several times before we separate."

"When do we do it?" she asked excitedly.

"In two days. We'll spend tomorrow teaching you how to use a MAC 10. In the meantime, you'll stay with me while we do the walk-through and I'll be showin' you what you need to know."

****

Clarke put the map down and cradled his face in his hands. The Cortina was now headed towards central London and it was time for a decision.

"What do you think?" he asked his driver.

"They seem to be heading towards the target, sir."

Clarke rubbed his forehead.

"They can't have the explosives with 'em. I wonder what they have in mind?"

"Maybe they're gonna look things over."

Clarke frowned.

"This is moving too fast. If we let 'em go, they may get too close to the Prime Minister. On the other hand, if we take 'em down now, we might never find the explosives."

"Better to err on the side of caution, sir. Besides, if we take 'em alive, we can always get 'em to talk."

Clarke thought for a moment.

"Let's tail 'em a little longer. As long as they stay away from the target, we can take a chance that they'll lead us to their base."

The young man in the back seat shook his head.

"No good, sir. They've just turned towards Downing Street."

"That leaves us no choice," Clarke said. He pressed his transmitter.

"Control to all units. They're heading towards the target. Three and Four, take the point. If they stop within the kill zone, take 'em down."

"Three affirmative."

"Four."

Satisfied that his team was now ready for any contingency, Clarke used a scrambled car phone to notify Downing Street to move the Prime Minister to an underground bunker.

****

About two blocks from the Prime Minister's residence, McCann started looking for a parking space. He slowed the Cortina when he spotted a vehicle pulling out from the curb. He then eased into the spot, killed the engine, and turned off the headlights.

"Luck of the Irish," he said, causing the others to laugh.

Due to the rain and the lateness of the hour, pedestrian traffic was almost non-existent.

"Right," said McCann. "You know what to do. You boys meet me back here in thirty minutes. Mairead, you come with me."

****

Three and Four sped ahead to within a half block of the Cortina. Double parked, they idled without lights, just close enough to watch Orphans car pull up to the curb. The rain had slowed to a sporadic drizzle.

Clarke's unit stopped a block away and the others set up around the area. The seconds seemed to drag while they waited for something to happen.

"Control," came a voice. *"They're getting out of the car."*

Clarke swore under his breath. They were almost on top of the Prime Minister's residence. What if the bomb was already in the trunk?

"Three and Four, get ready to move in."

His men pulled down their knit balaclava hoods.

21

Clarke watched the targets through his binoculars. They were out of the car and splitting up. Time had just run out.

"Control to Three and Four. Move in and take them down."

Simultaneously, the doors of both units sprang open and two men jumped from each vehicle. Wearing full body armor, the lead team ran silently up the sidewalk while the second pair followed close behind. All four soldiers used the line of parked cars to conceal their approach.

****

As they walked up the street, McCann was first to sense that something was wrong. He froze in his tracks and listened intently. The hair on the back of his neck stood up when he heard what sounded like running footfalls. He spun away from Mairead and tried to find cover in front of a parked car. From the corner of his eye, he glimpsed two shapes coming at him from the street. He reached into his waistband for his gun, but they were already too close for him to get to it in time.

The first burst of gunfire caught him in the chest and he was lifted into the air, limbs askew. His breathing had stopped before he hit the ground.

Mairead screamed and dove for cover, but she was silenced by a series of shots that tore open the side of her head.

Riley pulled a pistol from his jacket pocket, spun around and fired blindly, striking one of the soldiers in the center of his vest. Almost immediately, he was shot by one of the flankers who let loose with a burst from an Uzi automatic.

Thomason tried to run, but he was taken from behind by a series of shots that caught him in his back and lower skull. He pitched forward to the sidewalk and landed on his face.

****

Clarke ordered the men involved to return to their vehicles, while Units Five and Six moved in and secured the scene.

Clarke called in Scotland Yard and the neighborhood was evacuated for two square blocks, but no trace of explosives was found inside the car. Photographs were taken of everything before the bodies were removed to a makeshift morgue at a nearby SAS airfield. Within two hours, the scene was cleared and the local residents were returned to their homes.

Operation Sandman was over.

****

Two months later, the first edition of the Irish News, an inexpensive newspaper read widely by Catholics in Belfast, contained a front page article that recapped what was known about the official findings of the London Board of Inquiry:

"... according to the Home Secretary, a governmental inquiry was conducted into Operation Sandman amid allegations that soldiers were ordered to take no prisoners. Citing provisions of the Official Secrecy Act, many of the details were not released, but the Board of Inquiry determined that Operation Sandman was conducted with circumspection, given the information known at the time.

"Sources close to the investigation disclosed there was an imminent plan to strike at the residence of the Prime Minister with a mortar to be fired from a panel truck.

"Authorities confirmed that two weeks after the incident, sixty-four pounds of Semtex explosives and high explosive mortar shells were located in a safe house being used by the terrorist team. It is theorized that the explosives were to be placed in the vehicle and detonated with a remote controlled device as part of a plan to kill the police who responded to the scene.

"Captain Sean Clarke, publicly identified as the Officer-in-Charge, testified that his unit believed that the terrorists had explosives in their vehicle at the time they were approached. The terrorist were armed, and the four SAS personnel involved in the shooting testified in secrecy that they fired only in response to terrorist actions they deemed threatening to their lives.

"The Board concluded that Captain Clarke and his team acted in accordance with the seriousness of the situation. The order to detain the terrorists

near the Prime Minister's residence was proper, and no evidence was uncovered of any plan to kill the terrorists outright."

****

In the back room of the Iron Gate Pub in West Belfast, relatives and friends of those killed during Sandman gathered to discuss the results of the inquest. Most of those present were older, working class laborers.

Liam Cassidy finished reading a reprint of the article and threw it on the floor. Pint in hand, he faced the group at large.

"Hypocrites!" he yelled.

The noise level died down as heads turned to face him.

Liam had filled out nicely since childhood, and although he was just a hair shorter than six feet tall, he was all muscle, freckles, and charm, except when he was drinking. He kept his light brown hair cut short, which he hoped would disguise his working class background, but the jeans, scuffed boots and waist length black leather jacket were a dead giveaway that he was still nothing more than a product of his environment.

He downed his drink and slammed his glass on the bar. He was heavily intoxicated and it was obvious to everyone when he slid off the stool and nearly lost his balance.

"Bloody hypocrites, the lot a ya."

He stumbled forward, caught his balance, then shook off the hands of those who tried to help him keep his feet.

"Leave me be."

Those nearby stood back and gave him room. He staggered forward and glared from face to face through rheumy, bloodshot eyes. He pointed a shaky finger at the crowd.

"Yer a bunch of fuckin' cowards! Real soldiers are dyin' and all ya can do is stand around and gab." He waved a menacing fist. "I don't give a *shite* for the lot a ya. I'll do what needs doin', even if the rest of ya are too fuckin' scared."

Three men watched the outburst with surprise and concern. When he spoke of taking action, they slid from their booth and quickly approached him.

The eldest of the group, John Magruder, was solidly built with large, strong hands. He grabbed Cassidy's coat and pulled him face to face.

"We understand how you feel about Mairead's murder, but the drink has made you foolish with your tongue. Go home and sleep it off before you're a danger to yourself."

Without any thought, Cassidy brushed Magruder's hands from his coat and pushed him away. Several nearby men sprang forward, but Magruder raised his arm and held them back. Cassidy stared from face to face. When he fixed on Magruder's eyes, he knew that he'd made a grave mistake.

He held Magruders' stare for a brief moment longer, then he turned and walked out without looking back.

Magruder watched the door close behind Liam and motioned to one of his men.

"Follow him," he whispered, "and see if anyone else does the same."

****

TWO

September 10, Friday, Daytime

Anne Magruder hurried towards her dormitory room on one of the myriads of planted pathways that crisscrossed the UCLA campus. With her last class over for the day, she planned to do her laundry and finish some homework.

It was only mid-morning, and because of an early fall heat wave, the temperature was already at ninety-two degrees.

Blessed with classic Irish good looks, she sported a band of freckles that melted easily into smooth, creamy skin. Her thick auburn hair, shiny with crimson highlights, fell gently to the middle of her back. Her waist-tied T-shirt and cutoff jeans accentuated her long legs and hourglass figure.

She bounded up the stairs and headed for her room. When she got inside, she threw her book bag on her bed.

"Hey, Trace," she said.

Tracy Prescott, a short, blond transplant from Michigan, was sprawled on her back on her bed.

The two women shared a room containing twin beds, two desks, two closets, and a small flat screen TV. Having just come in herself, Tracy's face was flushed, and there were beads of perspiration on her brow. She waved one hand to acknowledge Anne, then let her arm flop back down on the bed.

"I can't take this damn heat," she whined. She looked over at Anne. "Aren't you dying?"

"I'm tryin' not to think about it." Anne sat down on her bed. "Are we still goin' to the movies tonight?"

Tracy smiled.

"Can't, Anne. I've got a date."

"Sweet mother of God! How'd you manage that?"

"You make it sound like it's a miracle?"

"It is a miracle, Trace. I just wish I could get one, too."

Tracy sat up and drew her knees up to her chest."I'm sorry if it leaves you hanging. We're going to a party at the Pike house. If you want, I can ask Paul to fix you up, and we can double date."

Anne shook her head.

"Thanks, but *no thanks*. I've made that mistake before. I'll just stay here and catch up on my readin'."

"Anne..?"

"It's okay, Trace. *Really*."

"You sure?"

"I'm sure." She stood up and started to undress. "Right now, I need a shower and a place to cool off."

Anne pulled her T-shirt off and unsnapped her jeans.

Tracy fanned herself with a pamphlet.

"By the way, there was a message for you on the machine. I accidentally erased it, but I think I got the number down right."

"Who was it?" Anne asked.

"Some guy. He didn't give his name, but he sounded cute. He had an accent like yours."

Anne walked over to the desk. The number written on the message pad was not familiar.

She sat down and picked up the phone. It was answered on the third ring.

"I was hopin' you'd call," said a warm, deep voice.

"Liam? Is that you? Oh, my God! Where are you?"

"I'm in town. Can we get together?"

Her mind started racing. *What was he doing in Los Angeles? Had he changed? Should she see him? What if her father found out?*

Then she remembered his smile.

"Of course I'll see you."

"Good. I'm stayin' at a place near the airport. Have you got a car?"

"I suppose I can borrow one, but you'll have to give me directions. I still don't know my way around too well."

He gave her the address of the *Radisson*, a large hotel near the Los Angeles airport.

"Come as soon as possible," he told her, "but don't say anythin' to anyone."

His admonition was troubling.

"Has anythin' changed, Liam?"

He was slow to respond.

"We'll talk about that when you get here."

****

By the time she was dressed and on the road, it was almost three-thirty in the afternoon. She'd borrowed Tracy's car, but it needed gas and that caused another delay. When she finally headed south on the freeway, she found herself caught in the rush hour traffic. A ten mile creep towards the LAX airport delayed her journey even longer, and it was almost five-thirty when she found the hotel and parked in the underground lot.

The Radisson Hotel was similar to many hotels in the area. Catering primarily to a business clientele, the lobby contained several darkened bars where a guest could get a drink and watch a sports game.

Anne walked through the door of the Mexican theme bar. Called *Francisco's,* its claim to fame was a generous margarita served in a goblet rimmed with rock salt. She stood for a moment just inside the doorway to allow her vision to adjust to the dimness of the lounge.

There were half a dozen men seated randomly at the bar, and one by one they turned, looked and measured their own chances for success.

In a knee-high, cotton, flower print summer dress, she knew she was attractive, but she dismissed them all with a turn of the head that signaled her lack of interest. Only one male bothered to make an approach, getting up from his seat in a darkened booth in the back. She saw him coming and ran to meet him half way.

They exchanged a tentative kiss, and she was surprised at how easily it rekindled strong feelings from the past.

"Ya look grand," he told her.

She smiled in appreciation.

"Let's go where we can talk." He took her hand and led her out into the lobby.

"Where are we goin'?" she asked.

"How about my room?"

She stifled a laugh. "And why doesn't that surprise me?"

They took an elevator to the sixth floor and entered his room. It was fairly standard for business hotels, with two queen-size beds, a mini-bar, a dresser, and a table with chairs.

He shut the door and reached for her, but she held him off at arm's length.

"Slow down, Liam. I just got here. Let me 'ave a look at you."

She gave him a once-over. He hadn't changed. He still looked fresh and boyish, and the hunger in his eyes spoke legions about what was chiefly on his mind.

"Ya look awfully tan. Have ya been on vacation?" she asked. Talking with him was causing her to slip into a Belfast accent.

He laughed. "I made a stop in Mexico. Do you like it?"

"It's very becomin'."

"Want to see more?"

"Not yet," she said with a smile. "Not till I know what's goin' on. Why're ya here?"

"We've unfinished business, Annie." His voice adopted a serious tone. "Why? Aren't ya glad to see me?"

"Ya know I am."

He pulled her close again and this time she let him kiss her, but she pulled herself away when he reached for her breast.

"Liam...not now."

His confusion was evident.

"You've changed Annie."

She smiled. "Considerin' what's happened since I saw you last, I'll take that as a compliment."

She moved over to a chair and sat down. "And you? Have ya changed?"

He sat on the edge of the bed and faced her. "I'm still with the Cause if that's what you're askin'?"

Her smile faded. "There's supposed to be a truce on now, or haven't you heard?"

"I heard, but it don't mean nothin'."

She studied his face for a moment and then looked down.

"You know it can't work between us. Those days are long past. My father is—"

"It could work if ya wanted it to," he said, cutting her off.

"Oh?" Her mouth tightened. "And what's that supposed to mean?"

"It means you can't always let others fight your battles. While yer here enjoyin' the sunshine and the good life—our people are still sufferin'."

"I'm not like you, Liam. I'm not a soldier."

"Everyone needs to do their share, Annie."

"Listen to yourself." She wanted to laugh. He sounded like a politician. "How can ya be so narrow-minded? A peaceful solution is the only way the North will ever survive. You and your mates only know how to kill, and violence doesn't solve anythin'."

He studied her carefully. "You're probably right." He got to his feet and gave her a smile. "Can I get ya some wine?"

Not waiting for an answer, he walked over to the mini-bar next to the table and produced a small bottle of Chardonnay. He poured her a glass and grabbed a beer for himself.

They sipped their drinks in silence, and Anne found her thoughts drifting to the first moments she set eyes on Liam Cassidy.

They'd met at a party in Belfast. He was brash, worldly, and older than his years, and he'd regaled her with tales of intrigue and the actions he'd taken against the hated British. His passion had moved her, and it made her easy prey. She'd shared his bed often—when they'd had the chance—and as the affair progressed, he drew her into the Cause. Soon she was running errands for the IRA.

Anne flinched and took a large swallow of her wine.

On a dreary afternoon, her father and his friends had burst into Liam's flat where she was still lying with him in his bed. They'd battered Liam senseless and dragged her to her home where her father delivered a message that had stayed with her to this day.

"I've been a Provo for fifteen years, and what I've done has been for our people. But things are changin', Annie. The future isn't bombin' and killin'—it's

gettin' an education and betterin' yourself."

She cried as he spoke, mostly from fear—she'd expected a beating—but he'd held her face in his hands and stared into her eyes.

"After what I've been through, and what I've endured, I'll not lose a daughter to the Cause. You listen to me, child; I'll say this only once. If you see 'im again, he'll be dead by the end of that day."

"I've missed you," Liam said.

His voice startled her out of her thoughts. He was staring at her and his boyish, hungry look made her push down the terror that was still in her heart. She'd really missed the way they'd made love, and separation from her father now emboldened her belief that she could indulge herself again without being caught.

She put her glass down on the table.

"You know, he made me stop seein' ya."

"I know." He placed his hand on her cheek. "But he's got no right to come between us. What we feel for each other concerns only us."

"Oh, Liam..."

He pulled her into his arms and kissed her on the lips.

Anne responded to the moment, lost in long buried feelings. He unbuttoned her dress and let it slide to her waist. His soft, slow touch unleashed a torrent of emotion, and she wrapped herself around him as he laid her on the bed.

When he finally entered her, they were both at a fever pitch. She reached behind her head and used the headboard as a brace while the rhythm of his movements took her over the edge.

****

Later that evening, she held him in her arms.

"You haven't told me why yer here."

"To be with you, of course." There was a twinkle of mischief in his eyes. She laughed out loud and halfheartedly pushed him away.

"Don't give me that. You didn't come here just to sleep with me. What are you really up to?"

He pulled her to him and nuzzled her neck.

"I'm here to do a job, Annie. Nothing special, just surveillance."

"A surveillance? Here?"

"A visiting Major from SAS."

"And you're supposed to follow him?"

"Wherever he goes. I'm to find out who he meets."

"Sounds boring."

She pulled away, rolled off the bed, and started to put on her clothes.

"And where do you think yer goin'?" he asked.

Anne looked at him over her shoulder. The hungry look in his eyes made her smile.

"I've got to take the car back." She reached for her dress and gave him a wink. "I borrowed it from a friend and I should've had it back an hour ago."

He shrugged and watched as she slid the dress over her head. "Will you go with me tomorrow?" he asked. "We can be together most of the day."

"I can't, Liam. I've got a paper to work on first thing in the mornin'."

"That's perfect." He eased off the sheet and rose to his feet. "I won't be goin' out 'till tomorrow afternoon."

She shook her head halfheartedly.

He smiled, walked over, and kissed her on the cheek.

"Tomorrow may be the last chance for a while, Annie. I won't be here much longer."

A pained look crept over her face.

"So, I'm just a one-night stand?"

He threw his head back and laughed.

"Not if you go with me tomorrow. Come on, darlin'."

She thought for a moment and considered her options. She wanted the sex —it was really exceptional—but what if her father found out?

"I don't know about doin' a surveillance."

"You won't have to do anythin', my love. You'll just be with me and we'll follow 'im around. Nothin' to it."

Anne looked for the truth, but his expression gave nothing away.

"If I do this, Liam, I don't want to spend all day ridin' around in a car."

He kissed her ear. "I'll make sure we have plenty of time for what you want."

She blushed.

He kissed her again and reached for his pants. He pulled out a pack of cigarettes, lit one up, and inhaled deeply.

"It's a very simple job. He'll be leavin' his hotel for a meetin', and we'll be followin' behind in my car." He smiled and gave her a wink. "Besides, it'll give you a chance to do somethin' for the Cause."

"I don't care about the Cause, Liam. Not like you do. If I do this, it's only to spend a little more time with you."

He flashed her a knowing smile.

Anne closed her eyes, then sighed.

"All right. I'll go, but my father better not find out."

"He won't," Liam assured her. "Can you stay a little longer?"

Her eyes locked with his and she felt her resistance beginning to melt.

"I don't suppose another half hour will hurt."

****

THREE

September 11, Saturday, Early Afternoon

By noon the temperature registered ninety-seven degrees on its way to a hundred. It was smoggy, windless, dry and miserable.

Sean Clarke gazed out the window of his room on the twenty-third floor of the *Westwood Hyatt Hotel*. At age fifty-two, he was losing what remained of the brown hair on top of his head, and his eyes showed the strain of his years in the Service. He was still in pretty good shape, but physical exhaustion had recently been a frequent companion; a condition he attributed to the stress of his years as a soldier doing battle with the IRA. Disgusted by the weather in Los Angeles, he thought with fondness of the temperate greenness of the hills near his residence in Dover. He missed his family and his homeland; he was tired of being on the road.

Paul Whitcomb, his adjutant, closed up the last of their bags. He was in his forties; a large man with an ever-present smile. He lifted weights to keep in shape, ran twenty miles a week when he had the time, and loved to hang out in his local, favorite pub whenever he was not on the road.

Clarke studied him briefly and wondered if he also hated the time they spent away from home. Probably not. Paul was recently divorced, still reasonably young, and likely still enamored with the excitement of world travel. Clarke sighed. Paul had yet to develop the cynicism that came from doing the job.

"Tell me somethin', Paul? Have you made plans for when you leave the Service?"

"Can't say I've given it much thought, sir. I've got seven more to go before I have my twenty in. I expect there's time once I rotate back into Royal Air."

Clarke smiled. "It's never too early to start plannin'. Retirement has a way of creepin' up."

"How close are you, sir?"

"I've got in twenty-six."

"That many?"

Whitcomb's eyes went wide as he lifted the bags off the luggage rack and placed them on the floor. "Will you be leavin' at thirty?"

"Actually, I've been thinkin' of goin' sooner than that."

Whitcomb frowned.

"If you'll forgive me for sayin' so, sir, I think that would be a mistake. Everyone says you're on the fast track, so why would you want to give it up?"

Clarke thought before answering. Although he'd never broached the subject with his colleagues in the Service, he'd recently experienced second thoughts about his country's struggle with the IRA. When the *Sandman* inquiry thrust him into the limelight, he was amazed to discover how quickly people branded him as an anathema to law and order. It had shaken him badly, as he was a man who'd never questioned his role as a modern-day soldier in a terrorist war. But when he'd been forced to examine the bigger picture, he didn't like what he saw, and it made him question whether he could continue to effectively do his job.

But doubts about the job was not the only reason. The truth was much closer to home.

"My wife and kids have fallen for that place we bought in Dover. I don't know, Paul, it seems so peaceful there. I don't think I could get them to give it up for another reassignment."

Whitcomb smiled.

"Peaceful's an understatement, sir. I've been to Dover and the people in your town are livin' in slow motion."

Clarke laughed.

"I suppose they do, and that's exactly why I like it. By the way, do you know that little pub near the center of town?"

"*The Quartermaster?* I stopped in there once, sir, when I had an hour to kill before the train back to London."

"What did you think of it?"

"It seemed like a nice place."

"Well, it's up for sale and I'm thinkin' of puttin' in a bid."

"You? A pub keeper?" Whitcomb couldn't control his laughter. "I'm sorry, sir, but you'd die of boredom within a month."

Clarke smiled.

"I don't think so, Paul. It's steady work and it would give me some time to do a little writin'."

"But the Service needs you, sir."

And that was the heart of his problem. His skills were needed, but the end was never in sight.

After Operation Sandman, and because he'd been publicly identified, Clarke had been transferred from his duties as squadron commander to a counter-terrorist teaching role at the training center in Hereford. But this assignment was only a facade. Because of his combat skills, acquired over nineteen years in the field, he was promoted to Major and assigned to the ultra-secret *SAS Planning Committee*. What free time he did get was taken up by his duties as an instructor. His cover required him to travel extensively, and in the last six months, he'd delivered more than a dozen briefings to police groups throughout the world. This trip to Los Angeles was more of the same; fly in, give a lecture, fly out. The kids were growing up without him; and his wife... well, she had the patience of a saint.

The alarm on his wristwatch went off. It was time to get down to business. He looked up at Whitcomb and smiled.

"We'd better shove off, Paul."

He walked across the room and picked up his bag.

Whitcomb adjusted his shoulder holster and put on his jacket.

"I'll get the car, sir, and I'll meet you out front."

****

They sat just across the street from the hotel in a dirty white Honda Civic. Cassidy was parked at the curb where he could see both the front of the hotel and the side entrance to the underground garage. Because of the heat, the windows were down and he fumbled with the radio dial, trying to find a station that played something of interest.

Anne pushed back the front passenger seat as far as it would go. Her door was open, and her sandaled feet rested on the dashboard. Even in shorts and a halter top, she was very uncomfortable. She fanned herself uselessly with a clothing catalog that had come from her purse. But it made no difference, the heat was appalling.

Liam was wearing jeans and a pale blue t-shirt, but he acted as though the heat was no problem.

"Aren't you dyin' in those jeans?" she asked him.

"It's all relative," he said. "Compared to Mexico, it's not so bad."

"Well, I don't know how much longer I can stand this," she said, wiping her brow with a handkerchief. "Can't we at least park somewhere in the shade. It's so hot it's makin' me sick."

"Relax, Annie, he'll be out soon." His eyes never left the hotel. "Besides, we have to park here because it's the only place where we can watch both exits."

Anne was not appeased by this explanation. For over an hour they'd been glued to this spot. It was boring, incredibly hot, and not what she'd had in mind when she agreed to this stupid idea in the first place.

"Liam, I really don't care if we see this guy or not." Her voice became more agitated. "I said I'd do this, but I didn't think we'd end up spendin' the whole day roastin' in this god-damn car."

He reached over and stroked her hair, but she pushed his hand away.

"You're bein' very patient," he said to soothe her. "We'll be movin' soon. He has an appointment at two-thirty, so he should be leavin' any time now. Once this business is done, I'll take you back to the hotel and we can use the pool. After that, we can drive up the coast and find a private beach and watch the sunset."

In spite of her anger, she laughed.

"You've a one-track mind, Liam Cassidy, but you won't find me so accommodatin' if we have to sit here much longer. Why don't you take me back to the dorm? You can pick me up later when you're finished. Then, if you're really nice, we might even fool around at my place before we go up the coast."

If he heard what she said, it did not register on his face.

A blue Plymouth pulled out of the underground garage and stopped in the driveway by the front door. Liam kept his eyes on the car and put on a pair of wrap-around sunglasses.

Anne turned her attention to the hotel.

"Is that him?" she asked.

The driver of the car walked back to the trunk and opened it with a key. He glanced around with a practiced eye, and within a few seconds, the front doors of the hotel parted and Sean Clarke walked out and placed his bag in the trunk.

"That's him!"

****

By the time they started following, she could just make out the Plymouth as it moved through traffic about half a block ahead. Glad to be moving, at last, she reached towards the dashboard to turn on the air conditioner.

"Leave it be," he ordered. His tone brooked no discussion.

She was taken aback by his abruptness.

"I don't understand. Why can't we--"

His stare stopped her cold.

She looked straight ahead. What the hell was going on? He said this guy had a two-thirty appointment?

Wait a minute? If he already knows the time of the meeting, then wouldn't he know where they were going as well?

A wave of cold fear gripped her heart.

At the corner of Wilshire and Comstock, the blue Plymouth, which was now in the right-hand lane, stopped for a red light behind another car. Cassidy was more than a dozen cars behind, but the parking lane was free, and if he moved up fast enough, he could trap them at the signal.

He quickly made up his mind. He swung into the parking lane and headed for the corner.

"Put yer head in your lap and don't look up," he told her.

She failed to react.

"*Just do it, Annie. Now.*"

Anne watched with horror as Liam pulled a handgun from the pouch on the driver's side door.

"*Noooo...*" she wailed as she buried her face in her hands.

He shifted the gun to his right hand and abruptly stopped the car.

****

Whitcomb had spotted the white car in his side view mirror. It moved up too quickly; something seemed terribly wrong.

"Car coming up on the right," he said to Clarke, who turned in his seat to get a look.

There was one car in front of them, so the right parking lane was their only avenue of escape. Without taking his eyes off the side view mirror, Whitcomb cranked the steering wheel hard and tried to pull into the parking lane, but the white car had already claimed the space, and Whitcomb was forced to brake the car hard to avoid a collision.

In that moment of hesitation, he lost any chance of escape.

Whitcomb fumbled in desperation for his gun.

****

Cassidy had stopped even with the back passenger window which gave him the line of fire advantage. He raised his handgun above the door frame and fired four quick rounds at the driver. The right rear passenger side window of the Plymouth exploded into pebble-like particles as the bullets entered the car.

The driver was hit three times, and the force from the bullets pitched him forward against the steering wheel.

As the Plymouth began to roll forward, Clarke tried to turn far enough around to get off a shot, but his seat belt was still fastened and he wasn't quick enough.

The next volley of shots came through the front side passenger window, and one of them caught Clarke just above the right ear.

Cassidy swung open the door, stood in the street, and emptied his remaining rounds into Clarke's lifeless body.

****

It happened so quickly and seemed so surreal that the people in the nearby cars who were stopped for the light initially thought they'd witnessed the making of a movie.

They watched in stunned silence as the man with the sunglasses jumped back into the white Civic and floored it. He gained speed through the intersection and disappeared down Wilshire Boulevard, headed towards Beverly Hills.

A few brave souls got out of their cars and tentatively approached the stalled Plymouth, but no one dared pursue the fleeing white car.

****

Anne's screams became wracking sobs as Cassidy gunned the car through traffic.

"You *bastard*!" she choked. "What have you done?"

He didn't speak. His concentration was fixed on where he was going, and whether or not they were now being followed.

"Let me out of this car." she demanded.

"Shut the fuck up," he yelled, drowning out her sobs.

He drove almost a mile but there was no one following. It was time to switch to his lay-off car, so he turned into a parking structure at the Beverly Hilton Hotel.

"We're goin' to park here and change cars. Do exactly what I say and we'll have no problems. Understand?"

Anne's crying turned to whimpering but she managed a nod.

He drove up several levels until he found an empty spot, but just before he stopped, Anne bolted from the car and ran towards the hotel. Cassidy jumped out and cut her off, then grabbed her arm and dragged her back.

"Take your hands off me!" She struggled to break his grip.

He was in no mood to argue in public.

"Come with me," he ordered. His voice was full of menace.

"Let me go, Liam. I don't want to be involved in this."

He shoved her forward and forced her back into the Honda.

"Here's a handkerchief," he said, placing it into her hand. "Wipe down everythin' you touched."

Anne was ready to throw up.

"I don't want to be part of this. I didn't do anythin'----"

Liam grabbed her by the neck and pulled her towards him.

"Don't you get it? You were with me. You're an accomplice. Now, do as I tell ya. Wipe the car down."

He shoved her back into her seat, and faced with no other choice, she worked furiously to get rid of her prints.

Liam did the same, and a few minutes later he pulled her from the car and walked her over to the nearest stairwell.

****

Forty yards away, Lou Berehens sat in his Dodge Caravan and watched them get out of the car. He'd seen the girl run, seen the man bring her back, and he'd almost intervened; but in the end, it looked just like a harmless domestic quarrel.

Or was it?

His curiosity was aroused. He'd been with the military police during a tour of duty with the U.S. Army and he prided himself on having a sixth sense when it came to spotting the unusual. He wasn't quite sure what was going on, but he was willing to watch them a few minutes longer.

When the man took a cloth and wiped down the door handles, Berehens knew instantly that something was wrong.

As they started to walk, he ducked down in the front seat to avoid being seen. He counted to ten, sat back up, and saw them enter the stairwell. The man held her by the arm, and it occurred to Berehens that she must be in some sort of trouble.

He got out of his car, hurried to the stairwell, and watched as they crossed the street below. They entered a nearby parking lot with the man still holding her firmly by the arm.

What should I do?

As he pondered his options, he was struck by the fact that the man used a key to open the door of a Ford Fiesta parked in the lot. He was switching cars.

He must have committed a crime.

Berehens ran down the stairwell and reached the street, sweating profusely and wheezing for breath. A heavy-set man, with a large beer belly, he wasn't used to running anywhere, and if it hadn't been for the adrenalin rush, he might have thought he was headed for a heart attack.

The Fiesta pulled out of the lot across the street, and as the car drove past, he studied the driver's face and committed the license to memory.

On the rear bumper, he could see a rental sticker from *Hertz*.

****

Cassidy stopped for a red light near Century City, a sprawling enclave of high-rise office buildings, condominiums, hotels, and a massive mall. He looked over at Anne who was slouched in her seat. Her crying had become insufferable.

What a spineless bitch!

He hated to admit it, but her father was right; she would never be IRA material. She'd fallen apart at the first taste of action. She was useless; and worse, unappreciative of his deed.

Anne was a liability who might go to the police, but for all they knew, she was in it as deep as him.

A smile crossed his lips. There was no way she'd *grass*---a Belfast girl knew the rules. If she talked, she'd die, and so would her loved ones. She'd keep her mouth shut. She had no choice.

But he had no illusions about winning her back; not now, not ever. In fact, he didn't really care. Because of what happened, and what she would face if she ever told a soul, he owned her body and soul. He could do whatever he wanted, she would never complain.

He smiled to himself.

Time to celebrate!

****

FOUR

September 11, Saturday, Late Afternoon

Renée Marin worked her black Mercedes sedan through traffic until she reached the police roadblock at Wilshire and Beverly Glen. A line of flares kept the streets closed for a block on either side of the shooting scene. She flashed her identification to an overweight officer who studied it casually before allowing her to pass through the flare line to a place where she was told to park her car.

She removed her high heels and donned a pair of tennis shoes, then walked down the hill on Wilshire Boulevard to a vehicle that was being used as the command post for the crime scene investigation. A police helicopter circled overhead to monitor the activities on the ground and to keep the news choppers at bay.

At thirty-six years of age, she was one of the youngest senior prosecutors in the District Attorney's office. Her fresh, good looks were the kind that always garnered second looks, and this was due, in small part, to the unusual color of her eyes. They were best described as hazel, but depending on the ambient light, they could appear to change color, the spectrum of which went from a sandy yellow to emerald green. Her hair was naturally blond, and in keeping with the style of the day, she wore it down to her mid back. She made time for a workout every other day, which kept her body toned and in excellent shape.

Arriving at the command post, she flashed her badge and waited while a uniformed officer logged her in.

"Who caught the case?" she asked him.

"Gibson and Donahue from Robbery-Homicide, Ms. Marin. Do you want me to have someone locate them for you?"

"That won't be necessary, Officer, but thanks. I know them both. I'm sure they're somewhere down by the scene. I'll head over there myself."

She walked farther down the hill past numerous high-rise apartments and hotels, finally arriving at the intersection where the shooting had taken place. She made her way towards a group of uniformed people who were huddled together outside several portable screens that were used to shield the scene from public view. She spotted Gibson right away.

At an even six feet tall, Ulysses S. "Gibby" Gibson appeared to tower over the others who were grouped around him. He was fifty-eight years of age with twenty-four years on the Los Angeles Police Department. Considered the elder statesman of the Robbery-Homicide Division, he'd spent years working alone until he was paired up with Jennifer Donahue, a feisty, long-legged blond who had the smarts and the temperament to compliment his approach towards the handling of homicide investigations.

Gibson was born in Louisiana but raised in Compton California. A man of color, an African-American, he went to work right out of high school as a claims adjuster for an insurance company. At the time, bored out of his mind, he joined the Army Reserve for the extra money it provided, and five years later, he married Claudette, his high school sweetheart and the love of his life.

In the buildup to the first Gulf War, he had trained as an Army Airborne Ranger; became a qualified sniper, and when the conflict began, he was detached from his reserve unit to work with a team that specialized in long range reconnaissance. He collected intelligence, disrupted enemy communications, and did hunter-killer missions in enemy-controlled areas. All in all, he'd been lucky, for he had survived three tours with nary a scratch.

When he returned to the States, he wanted to make more of his life, so he pulled down a business degree from the University of Southern California, welcomed two beautiful daughters into the world, and then went to work as a cop with the LAPD to support his growing family. After years of hard work to reach the rank of detective, he found his calling working homicide cases, and since that time, he'd never looked back.

Renée stopped several yards from the group of officers and watched as one disappeared behind the screens with a video camera on his shoulder. To her, it was evident that the investigation was just getting underway, as the scene would be filmed from every conceivable angle before anything would be disturbed.

Gibson spotted Marin and waved her over.

"Good afternoon, Counselor. Did we pull Cinderella away from the ball?" A quick smile passed between them. "Love the glass slippers."

Renée laughed. A blue print dress, jewelry, nylons and tennis shoes were not exactly *de rigueur* for a homicide scene.

"Are you making fun of my shoes, Gibby? Because if you expected me to show up in my glass slippers, you should have put your stinking command post a little closer to the scene. I had to hike all over hell and gone in this miserable heat just to check in, and I'll be damned if I'm going to do it in heels."

A chorus of laughter from the group broke the ice, and Gibson smiled broadly.

Marin smiled back.

"Actually, I was on my way to a terrorism seminar when my beeper went off. Are you the one who called me out?"

"I thought they were gonna send us one of your compatriots?"

Renée shook her head.

"Everyone else is tied up in court, so they pulled me away from the conference."

"Then I guess you're one step ahead of the game." Gibson shook his head and his voice took on a somber tone. "Funny how things work out. That conference you were going to? It's going to be cancelled."

"Canceled? Why? What's going on?"

"The featured speaker and his bodyguard were gunned down in their car."

"Oh my God!" Marin was dumbstruck. "You've got to be kidding, Gibby? Sean Clarke is a senior officer in the SAS. How the hell could this happen?"

"That's what we aim to find out." Gibson looked at his watch. "And I figure we've got about twenty more minutes before we start to see a parade of government big-shots who want to see what's happened for themselves."

Renée's shoulders sagged.

"That's all we need. Any chance I can get a quick walk-through before the circus begins?"

Gibson studied her carefully.

"Think you can you handle it?"

"Do I have a choice?"

"Yeah, you do. You can wait for the photos if you think this might be hitting a little too close to home."

Gibson was referring to the fact that Marin's husband had died six months before after a long battle with metastatic liver cancer. Only forty-one when he passed away, his death at such an early age had shattered her youthful feelings of immortality, and Gibson knew that she'd had a hard time coming to grips with what had happened.

She appreciated Gibson's compassion, but she also knew that the time had come for her to move forward. She was now a single mother with a daughter to raise and she could no longer avoid the specter of death which was such a big part of her chosen profession. She would have to suck it up and do what they paid her to do.

She reached out and placed a hand on his arm.

"I appreciate your concern, Gibby, but I have to do this. I need to start working again."

"Fair enough."

He gave her a friendly hug, then walked her over to the curtained scene.

They stayed on a defined path that had been checked and cleared of any physical evidence. Later, the rest of the area would be meticulously searched, grid by grid.

The car was still in the second lane from the curb where it had come to rest against the rear of the car that had been in front of it during the time of the shooting. It was completely concealed from public view behind a series of portable screens that were strategically placed around both cars to prevent the curious from staring at the bodies or taking unauthorized photographs of the victims.

Renée was escorted through an overlap in the panels to a spot about ten feet from the cars.

She'd been to homicide scenes more than half a dozen times during her career as a prosecutor, but she never got used to viewing the results of man's inhumanity towards man. She took several deep breaths, swallowed hard, and hoped that she could look at these killings objectively while keeping her natural revulsion in check.

As she approached the car, she was suddenly hit by a surge of adrenaline that immediately heightened her senses of sight and smell. For the first few moments, everything appeared surreal. She was acutely aware of the brightness of the colors, particularly the yellows and reds. In the unrelenting heat, the blood in the front seat had coagulated into dark, black pools, and there was human tissue spattered throughout the front compartment. The distinct smell of blood was overwhelming. She turned away, held her breath, and willed her nausea to subside.

"You all right?" Gibson asked.

Marin nodded but she struggled to frame an answer. "Just give me a moment, okay?"

Gibson waited while she caught her breath, then led her over to the driver's side door. He squatted down and pointed in through the open door.

"The guy behind the wheel is Whitcomb. Clarke is in the one in the passenger seat. Both men were apparently armed. We think Whitcomb managed to clear a gun from his shoulder holster, but we don't yet know if he got off any rounds." He pointed to a *Barretta* that was on the rear floorboard. "We believe that's Whitcomb's gun. He must have reached over the seat to fire just before he got hit."

He then pointed over towards Clarke.

"There's a second gun on the front floorboard next to Clarke's feet. I guess he dropped it when he was taken out."

Gibson looked back over his shoulder to see how she was doing and was pleased to note that her complexion no longer looked gray. He smiled to himself. She was one tough little lady.

He returned his attention to the car.

"As soon as the measurements and pictures are taken, the Coroner will remove the bodies, and then the lab folks will go through the car with a fine tooth comb. That's when we'll know if either of the victim's got off a shot."

"Any idea what type of weapon the killer used?" Her voice still sounded a little shaky.

He stood up and guided her away from the car, and although she would never say so, she was immensely grateful.

"The casings we found were nine millimeters, and the number of shots would indicate a semi-automatic or fully automatic machine pistol. If you look on the ground over by the passenger side of the car, you'll see a number of chalk mark circles. That's where we found the casings. I had the lab team take photos before someone stepped on them. Everything's already been bagged."

She looked around the area and tried to get a sense of the bigger picture.

"How do you think it went down?" she asked.

"Actually, if you look at the right rear and front side windows, you'll notice they were blown into the car. My guess is that the killer approached from the right rear and began firing from car to car before ending up at the front right side passenger window."

"Make that *killers*, Gibby," said Jennifer Donahue, who came up directly behind them.

"Compadre," Gibson said, by way of greeting. "Guess who rolled out to keep us in line?"

Donahue smiled.

"It's great to see you again, Renée. You doing okay?"

"I'm fine, Jen. Just trying to get back in the swing of things. But you were saying something about killers?"

Donahue nodded.

"I talked briefly with a couple of witnesses who stuck around. One of them was in the car that the victim's car rolled into. Anyway, the witnesses are saying that the shooter was a male, but there was a female in the car, too. A small white foreign compact, for whatever that's worth. Anyway, I put out a wanted on the car and I released a general description of our killers: two Caucasians, a male, and a female."

Gibson smiled.

"That's pretty general, Jen. We should end up with only a few hundred thousand sightings."

Donahue shrugged.

"We've got to start somewhere."

The photographer walked up and announced that he was finished, so Gibson signaled over to the Coroner's team, letting them know that they could now begin examining the bodies.

One at a time, they were lifted from the car and laid on plastic sheets. Renée watched as bags were placed over the victims' hands to preserve any gunshot residue. They would need to determine if either had managed to fire a gun. The bodies were checked for entrance and exit wounds, and a search was made of their clothing for any loose bullet fragments.

The Deputy Coroner produced a scalpel and raised the shirt of one of the victims. Renée turned away. They would estimate the time of death by determining the rate at which the bodies lost heat. The human body was known to cool after death at a constant rate so a liver temperature would be taken, and when compared to that of the air, a time of death could be estimated.

When the Coroner was finished, the victims were placed in body bags for removal to the morgue.

Gibson tracked down the latent print supervisor to get him started before the heat destroyed any chance to get evidence.

"When you're finished checking for lifts," Gibson told him, "have the car put on a flatbed and take it down to the lot below the Police Administration Building (PAB). I want it gone through with a fine-tooth comb."

The technician gave orders to several members of his team and they began to dust the outside of the car. The lifts that appeared were transferred to tape and stored on cards for future comparison with prints stored in computerized data-bases.

Gibson rejoined Donahue and Renée.

"What else did you find out, Jen?"

Donahue checked her notebook.

"At least two of about a dozen witnesses said they heard screams coming from the killer's car, and both of them insist that the screamer was a female."

"Could they make out what she was saying?"

"She wasn't saying words, Gibby. It was more like fear or pain."

Marin looked around. "Where are these witnesses now?"

"On their way to the West LA station. We're taking in everyone who knows anything. A team from RHD will do the initial interviews and we'll try to do a composite if any of them managed to get a good look at our suspects."

Gibson looked up the hill. Several undercover vehicles were now parked at the Command Post.

He turned to Donahue.

"Jen. Get over to the WLA station and oversee those interviews. I don't want any slip-ups on this." Donahue nodded as the three of them then walked away from the scene.

"Renée, you might want to go with Jen while I wrap things up over here. Once I get to the station, we can brief the Captain and set up a game plan." He motioned with his hand towards the command post. "You might want to become scarce. Look's like it's show time."

A large group of plainclothes and uniformed officials had gathered at the Command Post. Most were curious arrivals from the canceled seminar. It was a complication she knew that she'd rather avoid. Besides, considering how muggy it was, the idea of waiting in an air conditioned station was suddenly very appealing.

"Once again, Gibby, I'm guided by your superior judgment. I'll see you over there."

****

The West Los Angeles station, a modernized, two-story edifice that resembled a fortressed bunker, was grossly undersized for the population that it served. Built more for security than looks, it boasted dark glass doors to prevent drive-by shooters from sighting in on targets within the entrance foyer. Even the two officers assigned to the front desk answered their phones behind bullet-proof glass, and the parking lot was routinely scanned by a closed circuit camera to discourage any neighborhood vandals.

The acting watch commander, Sergeant Gregory Good, had twenty-five years on the job which gave him credibility with the station officers who assembled to listen to his plan of operation. Press cases were nothing but trouble. The brass would infiltrate his station to cultivate the media for a moment of recognition on the evening news. But that was not his chief concern; mixing the media with the rank and file was dangerous. Morale among the line troops had been bad for many years, and an errant remark by a disgruntled patrolman could find its way into the morning paper. If that happened, he knew he'd find himself downtown, defending his role as a supervisor, and he had no intention of becoming a victim of circumstances.

"Major Crimes from downtown will be needing a base of operations," he said to the assembled officers, "so we'll be clearing out of the detective squad room for a while. I've called the night watch in early, and when they arrive, I want them to provide traffic control and security around the station. We'll set up a press center in the basement assembly room, and I want sandwiches and coffee down there at all times to keep the wandering around by visiting personnel down to a minimum. Does everyone understand?"

There were nods of assent from the dozen or so uniformed officers who stood by at uneasy attention. Some of them had been injured on duty and were handling light assignments until they could return to their usual responsibilities. Others were there, having been reassigned from their duties in Patrol.

He called out the names of four of the officers, and there was a wave of smirking among those who were not chosen. He told the four, "Your job is to make sure that the visiting senior officers are kept in the press room and away from the people who are working on the investigation. Security in a case like this is paramount, so you'll give them briefings on the half hour, and you'll ply them with coffee. But above all, your job is to make sure that they don't bother the investigators."

Sgt. Good looked around at the dozen or so smiling faces.

"Most of you are short timers and don't remember what things were like during the O.J. Simpson investigation. The press will be here in full force, and all hell will break loose if we don't keep things under control. Now, I enjoy working days, and I suspect that the rest of you do too. So if you don't want to find yourselves working the morning watch, make sure that none of you becomes that mysterious person I'm always reading about in the *Times*---you all know who I mean---the infamous *confidential source close to the investigation*."

There was nervous laughter from the assembled group.

"All right then ladies and gentlemen, let's get to it. Dismissed."

Having done what he could to preserve his future, Good returned to his office to await the inevitable onslaught.

****

Reporters and their cameramen crowded around the front of the station, waiting to interview anyone with knowledge of the killings, while outside, various technicians worked furiously with telescoping antennas attached to their TV news vans to establish satellite hookups that would connect them with the rest of the world.

Renée cleared security at the front desk of the station and was guided to the squad room on the second floor. A vast, cavernous space, it was filled with rows of tables which were organized into various detective specialties. Along the walls were numerous desks and file cabinets that were strewn with paperwork and folders from other, numerous investigations.

In spite of its size, the crush of new arrivals made the room seem smaller. The underlying hum of overlapping conversations was punctuated by the incessant ringing of phones. Civilian witnesses were seated in chairs throughout the chamber while teams of detectives came and went in what appeared to be organized chaos.

Renée found Donahue standing alone in a nearby interview room. Donahue waved her in and handed her a stack of preliminary interview reports.

"Here you go, Renée. This is what we've got so far."

Marin scanned the first report, then looked up. "Anything of value?"

"I don't think so, but maybe you'll find something I've missed. You can use this room if you want. Just make yourself at home."

"Thanks, Jen."

Renée settled into a chair and Donahue drifted out. At least it was quiet.

She scanned the reports quickly then went back over them in detail. Donahue was right. There was nothing of substance.

She stood up to leave just as Gibson poked his head in the door. His face was expressionless.

"Have you got your laptop with you?"

"Yeah. Why? What's up?"

He put a finger to his lips. "Jen's getting the car. We'll talk when we're out of the station."

Once they were underway, Gibson turned around from the passenger seat to speak to Renée who was seated in the back. His stoic expression had melted and there was a twinkle in his eyes.

"Beverly Hills PD called. A citizen walked in and reported that he watched a male and female dump a white car in the parking lot of the Beverly Hilton Hotel. Apparently, he saw them drive off in a second car."

Marin's eyes widened.

"Where's the witness now?"

"Still at their station. Fortunately for us, the desk officer didn't kiss him off. He called their auto theft detective who had overheard our broadcast. He had the good sense to call us right away."

"What a break! Is the car still at the Hilton?"

"I've got an undercover unit on the way. If it's still there, they'll sit on it for a while and see if anyone shows up to claim it."

"Fat chance they'll come back," she said with a frown.

Ten minutes later, they arrived at the Beverly Hills station. The witness was seated in a conference room with an overweight detective named Colin Pierson. Once introductions were made, everyone took a seat.

Gibson took a moment to size up the witness.

Lou Berehens seemed nervous. The room was not hot, but there was a thin sheen of perspiration on his forehead just below a full head of dark, brown hair. He seemed to be in pretty good shape for a man in his fifties, and although his belly hung over his belt, his biceps and chest appeared to be sculpted. Gibson guessed that once upon a time the guy had lifted weights.

Gibson kicked off the questioning with, "If you don't mind my asking, sir, what type of work do you do?"

"I coach football over at *Crespi High*."

"No kidding?" Gibson smiled. "If I'm not mistaken, your boys took CIF last year."

"That's right. Best team I've had in fourteen years." He visibly relaxed when he talked about football, and Gibson could sense that he would make a good witness.

He spoke at length about the incident in the garage and Gibson took note when he described how the male had bullied the girl.

"Can you tell me about the car they got into?" Gibson asked.

"I can do better than that. I wrote down the license number, and the car had a rental car sticker on the back bumper." He pulled a crumpled piece of paper out of his pocket and handed it over.

Gibson looked at the number then passed the paper to Donahue.

"See if you can run this with the Department of Motor Vehicles?"

"I'll find you a terminal," Pierson said, and the two of them quickly left the room.

Gibson leaned forward in his chair.

"Can you identify them, Mr. Berehens?"

"I can ID the man," he said. "I thought he might be forcing that girl to go with him, so I paid pretty close attention to him. But I'm not too sure about the girl." He shifted in his seat and looked over at Renée.

"Can you tell me what these people have done?"

Before Marin could answer, Gibson spoke up.

"No way to tell just yet, but you did the right thing by reporting what you saw. I'd like you to work with one of our sketch artists to see if we can get a drawing of the man."

They left Berehens in the room and went in search of Donahue. They found her seated at a computer, waiting for a printout of the image on the screen. When it came out of the printer, she handed it to Gibson.

"He was right, Gibby. It's a rental car assigned to a Hertz lot out by the airport. A Ford Fiesta. I just spoke to the Captain and he's sending someone out there to see what they've got."

Renée's eyes met Gibson's.

"Don't you think we should tell Mr. Berehens what's going on?"

"Not yet, Renée. Not until he gives us a sketch. I don't want to spook him prematurely."

Marin felt sorry for Berehens. He had no idea what he was getting himself into.

"Are we taking him back to the station with us?" Donahue asked.

"Not with all the press hanging around there. I want you to stay here with him, Jen. See if these people have a sketch artist handy, then get him to give a full statement. Renée and I will head back over to the station. I've got a feeling we're gonna need a search warrant real soon."

Gibson's cell phone went off. He checked the number and quickly answered. When the call was over, he smiled broadly.

"They found a white car in the Beverly Hilton lot, right where Berehens said it was. It could be the one. It was reported stolen in Venice early this morning. We've got it under surveillance."

Donahue went back to finish up with the witness while Renée and Gibson made their way to Gibson's car.

"I'm troubled by the girl," Marin said. "I don't quite understand her role in all of this. Does it make any sense to you?"

"Not yet. From the way Berehens describes it, it sounds as if she might be a hostage. I guess we'll just have to ask her when we track her down."

****

Back at the WLA station, they were struck by the fact that things had gotten even worse. Members of the media had cornered old friends in their quest for a scoop while TV field reporters, anxious to meet deadlines, broadcast statements replete with innuendo and supposition.

In addition to the arrival of the Major Crimes Section, there were two Special Weapons teams gathered in the parking lot. Dressed in black fatigues, they lounged around on the hoods of their cars drinking coffee and killing time. The Metropolitan Division, made up of dozens of uniformed officers in unmarked cars, had assembled in an upstairs roll call room to await a possible assignment.

"No shortage of manpower tonight," Gibson told her. "It looks like we're going to war."

They climbed the stairs to the squad room where Gibson ran into his boss, Tom Elwood.

"I need to see you in private," the Captain said.

"I'll be right there, Tom." He turned to Renée. "I'll be back in a couple of minutes."

"I'll use the time to check in with my housekeeper," she told him over her shoulder. "It looks like this could go on for a while."

Gibson followed Elwood into a nearby office where he was directed to a well-worn chair.

Boyish in appearance, with neatly trimmed light brown hair, Elwood looked to be in his early thirties, but a hint of gray at the temples and a series of small wrinkles at the corners of his eyes were the only real clues to his forty-six years of age. The father of two boys, he was recently divorced, an occupational hazard when you worked long hours as a cop.

Gibson outlined what he knew about the killings, and when he finished, Elwood leaned forward in his chair.

"By now, I'm sure you've noticed this case has developed a camp following among our brass. I need to know exactly what's going on if you want me to keep 'em off your back."

"I appreciate that, Captain. When things start to break, you'll be the first to know."

"I'd better be," Elwood warned him. "I've ordered up SWAT and Metro. You should have the manpower to handle whatever comes up." His eyes narrowed and his voice dropped. "Now, I need to mention something else. There's pressure coming in from the State Department. They're pushing to get the FBI involved as soon as possible."

"You're kidding? We're perfectly capable of solving this one without their interference."

"For the present, Gibby, it's still our case. But if it turns out there are international implications, it may be out of my hands."

"Jesus, Tom! It's an assassination of two foreign military experts. It doesn't get more international than that. You might as well give them the case right now."

"Hold on. No one's taking the case from you yet. I just want you to know where things stand. The Chief will keep them out of our turf for as long as possible, but the longer the investigation drags on, the more pressure we're gonna get."

Gibson was simmering. They'd barely started the investigation and already there was a good chance that the Fed's would soon be taking it over.

"You're a big boy, Gibby. You know how the game's played."

Gibson shook his head. "Just once I'd like to be able to do my job without all the extraneous distractions."

"In your dreams," Elwood said with a tight smile.

Gibson found himself laughing in spite of his pique, so Elwood softened his tone.

"I've got Jack Ruchhoft screening the incoming tips, and unless you see any reason to change that, I'd like to keep him in the hot seat to free you up."

"Jack's a good choice. That will help a lot."

Elwood's eyes narrowed again.

"So, you ready for the bad news?"

"I thought I just heard it. There's more?"

"Afraid so. Mark Carlson has decided to handle the press."

Gibson's shoulders slumped. He shook his head in disbelief.

"We'll have to deal with him very carefully," Elwood said. "He's planning a press conference in about forty-five minutes. I won't tell him about your witness or the license plate—for the time being, that stays between us—but make sure you keep this lead close to the cuff. No telling who he's got his hooks into out in the squad room."

Gibson started for the door. "Just keep that asshole away from me, Tom."

"I'll do what I can, but I can't go over his head unless he crosses the line."

"Fine. Whatever you say. But he better steer clear of me and my case."

"Don't get into it with him, Gibby. That's an order."

Gibson raised his arms in a gesture of surrender, walked out, and made his way to the interview room where Renée Marin had just finished talking on the phone.

"The housekeeper will stay over, so I can hang in for as long as it takes," she told him.

But Gibson wasn't tuned in. He took a seat and slammed his notebook down on the table.

Renée flinched. "Jesus, Gibby!"

"Sorry, Renée." He took a deep breath. "I didn't mean to scare you."

She eyed him carefully. "Things go poorly with the Captain?"

"No, that went okay." He looked up. "We need to keep everything about our witness completely to ourselves. Apparently, Commander Carlson's going to handle the press."

She gave him a questioning look.

"You don't know about Mark Carlson?"

She shook her head.

"Well, if he sees you, I guarantee you'll get to know him. He's an incorrigible skirt chaser."

"So what does that have to do with his handling of the press?"

"He can't be trusted." Gibson leaned back in his chair. "On one of my gang murders, he tipped off a female reporter to the pending arrest of my suspect. By the time we got to the suspect's house, we found her knocking on the front door with a camera crew in tow. The morons wanted a statement from the suspect."

Marin rolled her eyes in disbelief.

"It could have cost us our lives," he added.

"Well, don't worry about me," she said, "I don't go for chasers."

Gibson smiled and stood up to leave.

"I've got to check on the phone tips. Have you got something to keep you busy?"

"I'm all set. I'm gonna work up a narrative for a search warrant, so go find me a location we can search."

"I'll do my best. Back in a few."

A knock on the door interrupted them, and Detective Dan Tippen stuck his head in and smiled.

"We hit pay dirt."

At thirty-three, Tippen was the youngest investigator assigned to Major Crimes. He'd earned his spot after nine years of experience working homicide cases at the divisional level.

Tippen noticed Renée and looked cautiously over at Gibson for guidance.

"Mrs. Marin's the DA handling this case," Gibson said. "So what have you got for us?"

Tippen nodded to Renée, then returned his gaze to Gibson. "The plate came back to a Ford Fiesta rented from the Hertz lot out on Imperial. They cater to airport customers. It was rented two days ago by one Michael Delaney; male Caucasian, age thirty-five. The car, a Ford Fiesta, was paid for with a Mastercard when he picked it up."

Gibson allowed himself a small smile.

"Can the rental agent make an ID?"

"The clerk who rented him the car is a twenty-two-year-old female who remembers him as being 'kind of cute.' He was alone when the car was rented, and he presented two sets of ID; an English drivers license and a British passport. She swears that the pictures on both of them were of him. More importantly, he gave her a local address; the *Radisson Hotel* over by LAX. The car is due back next week."

Gibson nodded.

"Okay. Let's think this through. He flies into town, rents a vehicle, and gives a local hotel for an address. He has to know we might find the car, so the address or the ID or both are phony; unless he's just plain stupid. Then again, he might not be staying there at all."

"My money's on the phony ID," Marin said.

"I agree," Gibson replied. "Did the clerk make a photocopy of his passport or his English drivers license?"

"She copied them both." He handed the two photocopies to Gibson. "I also brought in the rental contract so we could have it checked for prints." He held up the paperwork which he'd carefully encased in plastic.

Gibson studied the photos from the license and the passport. The pictures were clearly the same guy. But were they really the guy they were looking for, or just pictures of someone close enough in looks to enable their suspect to get by?

He slapped Tippen playfully on the arm.

"Great job, Dan."

He turned to Renée.

"Now you get a chance to go to work. I'll need a warrant for the car in the Beverly Hilton lot. I want to search it for prints, fibers, casings, a gun, and anything else you can think of. By the time you finish that, we'll know if he's actually got a room at the Radisson."

Marin opened her laptop.

"I'll have it ready in twenty minutes. Will you be the affiant on the warrant?"

"Yeah, that's fine. Can we do it telephonically?"

"No problem. I'll have the command post start working on lining up a judge."

"Sounds good. And while you're doing that, I'll print up extra copies of this guy's ID photos and I'll get someone to run him through Interpol."

Interpol, the International Criminal Police Organization, was a group based in Lyon, France that provided rapid access to controlled information. Names could be checked with Interpol to see if they were wanted or had criminal histories in any of 190 member countries.

He turned to Tippen.

"Can you check with the Beverly Hills PD? Jen Donahue's over there with a witness who's making a drawing. Have her fax it over here as soon as it's done. I want to compare it with the suspects ID photos. Oh, and tell her to get her butt back here ASAP."

Gibson located Elwood who was on the phone explaining to someone why he wouldn't be home for dinner. When Gibson entered, he hung up the phone and gave him his full attention.

"We've got a possible name and two photos based on ID presented for the car rental. It's Michael Delaney. He told the clerk he'd be staying at the Radisson out by the airport. I'm going to need two mobile crime labs right away."

Elwood reached for the telephone.

"I'll have SID send them over. Anything else?"

"I'd like two teams from RHD to help me with the leg work and I'll need the surveillance units to do a covert search for the rental car out at the Radisson."

"I'll have them ready in fifteen minutes. Is that it?"

"Not unless you've got a contact with Interpol?"

Elwood smiled. "I'll work on it."

****

FIVE

September 11, Saturday Evening

Forty minutes later, Gibson walked into the crowded basement roll call room that was filled with uniformed officers and plainclothes detectives. A short, overweight detective in a blue business suit was standing at a table near the front of the room. He introduced himself to Gibson as Sgt. James Cleymont from the LAPD's Organized Crime Division.

Cleymont, who was generally known to be a dour man, always carried a fresh cigar in his jacket breast pocket.

He locked eyes with Gibson.

"I hear you need a contact with Interpol?"

"I sure do, Sarge. But I need to deal with these other folks first. Can you take a seat? I'll get to you as soon as I can."

Cleymont located an empty chair just as Elwood walked up and tapped Gibson on the shoulder.

"Can I see you for a moment?"

They walked over to a quiet corner.

"Don't worry about Carlson overhearing the briefing. I've got Ruchhoft keeping him busy with our setup for handling tips."

Gibson smiled. He then made his way to the front of the room, and for the next fifteen minutes, he described in detail what was known about the shooting and the suspects.

"SIS is on their way over to the Radisson Hotel out by LAX to look for the Ford Fiesta. If they find it, nobody touches it. We plan to sit on it for a while, then we'll have it towed downtown and get a telephonic warrant before we search it." He looked around the room until he spotted a familiar face from the crime lab. "If we get the car, do the usual, but vacuum it for fibers in case that becomes important later. Also, I want the entire car printed, not just the knobs and mirrors."

"No problem," said the lab tech.

"How about the second lab team?" Elwood asked.

"We'll keep them here, in case something breaks," Gibson replied. "But in the meantime, they can spray the rental car agreement with ninhydrin. The car rental agent is downstairs, so we can get a set of her prints for elimination."

Another lab tech, obviously a supervisor, nodded to Elwood that Gibson's instructions would be followed.

Gibson walked over to Cleymont.

"Sarge, the rental agreement has the suspect's passport and British driver's license numbers, as well as his photos. Here are photocopies of what we have. I need them run through your contacts in the UK and at Interpol."

Cleymont accepted the photocopies and looked them over.

"That may take some time."

"Do what you can."

Gibson then passed out photocopies of the license and passport photo's of Delany to the entire group before giving them a warning.

"Don't leave these photocopies lying around. They're for your eyes only. No one outside of this room is to get a look at them. And I mean no one. If you're pressed about that by someone in your chain of command, you tell them to speak to Capt. Elwood directly. Everyone got that?"

There were heads nodding as many of the assembled began to commit the suspects face to memory.

Elwood stepped forward and added his own two cents.

"If the press gets ahold of this info or the photos, everyone in this room will be put on the poly and once we find out who leaked it, intentional or otherwise, there will be a work reassignment that will give new meaning to the concept of freeway therapy."

There was laughter throughout the room, but the message had had it's desired effect. No one wanted to have an hour or two each way added to their daily work commute.

Elwood continued. "I want a few RHD teams to work with the airport detail to see if Delaney boarded any international flights since the time of the killings. This has to be done right away, and if he doesn't turn up on the international lists, I want every domestic passenger manifest checked for all flights scheduled through tomorrow evening."

There was an audible groan from the detectives. A search of that type would take the rest of the night.

"Terry, you head it up," Elwood said, pointing to one of the detectives.

Detective Terry Alves gave him an acknowledging wave.

"Okay, have we overlooked anything?" Elwood asked.

Before anyone could respond, Dan Tippen came in with the composite artist sketch made from the description given by the eyewitness, Lou Berehens. Donahue tacked it on the board next to copies of Delany's license and passport. The drawing and the photos were a very close match.

"Looks like we're in business," Elwood said to the group. "You have your assignments. Let's get started."

****

Twenty minutes later, Renée finished the last sip of a now cold cup of coffee while Gibson read the affidavit for the search warrant over the phone, and when he was finished, the Judge on the other end of the line asked to speak directly to Renée Marin, and once she was on the line, he gave her his approval to sign the warrant on his behalf. It would allow them to search the white car used by the suspects in the shooting.

Gibson left the interview room in search of the crime lab team while Renée stood up to stretch her legs.

The chair she'd been using was hard, one usually reserved for suspects. Her back hurt and she craved a warm bath. She paced for a few moments, and then called her housekeeper to check up on her daughter. Her stomach began to growl, and she realized that she was starving.

Donahue opened the door and stepped into the room. "You ready to take a ride?"

"I am," Marin replied. She put the computer back in her carrying case and picked up her purse.

"Where're we headed?"

"Gibby's getting the car. SIS found the rental car in the garage at the Radisson Hotel. They're setting up on it now, so we're headed over there to see if our suspect has rented a room."

****

Thirty minutes later they arrived on the second level of a four-story parking garage half a block away from the Radisson Hotel. A field command post was already established, including a tactical communications van, a mobile field crime lab, a unit of special weapons personnel, and several supervisors from the SIS and the Metropolitan Divisions.

At the communications van, the supervisors made contact with their officers in the field by means of a communications array that filled the back of the unit. Watching them work, Renée was reminded of old photos she'd seen of World War II military commanders gathered around a radio while awaiting news from the front.

Elwood drove up a few moments later and joined them.

"Where's Carlson?" Gibson asked him.

"He's currently giving the press a briefing at the station. No one saw us leave, and he knows nothing about the hotel, so we should have no problems with the media while we try to get set up."

David Simmons, a square-jawed, uniformed Lieutenant from SIS, strode over to talk.

"About fifteen minutes ago we found the car four floors down in the lot directly beneath the hotel. We haven't approached it yet, but three of my people have it under surveillance. I've put six others inside the hotel and in various bars both in and around the lobby. They've got copies of your composite and photos, but so far, no one's seen your boy."

Elwood grabbed Gibson by the arm.

"Time to find out if he's got a room."

Gibson turned to Marin.

"See if you can put together another warrant for the car parked down in the basement. If it turns out he's registered as a guest, we'll need one for his room as well. You can set up your computer in the front seat of the van. That way, if you need a power source or a phone to reach a judge, it can be hooked up right away."

"It shouldn't take long, Gibby. Most of it's already written."

"What will you need for the warrant if he's registered?" Gibson asked.

"Just the room number, and whether or not anyone else is known to be staying in there with him."

"Okay. You get settled in, and we'll check back in a couple of minutes."

****

Donahue and Gibson entered the hotel and walked to the front desk. Gibson discreetly flashed his badge and requested to meet with the manager. The clerk announced their demand by phone, and shortly thereafter, they were led to an office adjacent to the lobby where they found the manager engrossed in a review of computer printouts.

She quickly stood up and extended her hand.

"Detectives, I'm Christina Cortez. What can I do for you?"

Gibson's first glance took in everything; short black hair, late forties, and glasses on a chain. Her severe blue business suit and a brightly colored scarf were a no-nonsense look that gave her an air of efficiency. She was pleasant, accommodating, and interested in helping.

Gibson told her what they were after and within a few moments, she was typing away at her terminal.

"Here it is," she said. "An M. Delaney; checked in two days ago, alone, room 4008 on the East side of the hotel. He's not scheduled to check out until tomorrow." Without being asked, she grabbed her phone and found the desk clerk who'd checked him in. The description provided by the clerk seemed to match their composite.

"Let me check with the housekeeping manager," she said, and once she had the fourth-floor janitorial supervisor on the phone, he reported that the room had been occupied since check in; the last entry for cleaning was at eleven a.m., this day.

"Has there been a complaint?" the housekeeping supervisor asked.

"No, Gilbert, but please keep your people away from the room until I call you back."

She hung up the phone and smiled at Gibson.

"If you want, I can have housekeeping go by to change the towels?"

"That won't be necessary."

Gibson used his cellular phone to reach Elwood at the command post.

"He's registered, Tom. Since the car's still in the lot, I think we have to assume that he might still be in the hotel."

"You may be right, Gibby. Dave Simmons just checked in. His people spotted a time stamped ticket stub on the dash of the Fiesta which shows he parked there about four hours ago."

Gibson rubbed the stubble on his chin.

"What do you think, Tom?"

"It's your call, Gibby."

He gave it some thought, and then made his decision.

"I think we have to go in."

"How about a warrant?" Elwood asked.

"We're in fresh pursuit of a murder suspect and we have reason to believe he's in the room. You can check with Renée, but I'm pretty sure that public safety is an exception, and if I'm right, then I think we need to go in right now."

Gibson could hear the muffled sounds of Elwood talking to Renée who was still working on the warrant. Within a moment, he was back on the line.

"She says to go on in to look for him, but don't search for physical evidence until she gets the warrant signed."

"Okay. Let's turn it over to SWAT."

****

It took thirty minutes to seal off the hotel grounds and to evacuate the wing where Delaney's room was located. When the entry team was in place, their leader used a telephone to attempt to flush him out. But after ten rings, when there was no answer, he gave his men the signal to go in.

The door went crashing down as the room was secured, but there was no one inside.

Gibson and Donahue walked up to the room and ordered everyone out. Donahue stayed by the door while Gibson took a look around. One of the beds appeared to have been slept in, and when he checked the bathroom, he found several damp towels thrown carelessly on the floor. The shower curtain bore no traces of moisture, so whoever had been bathing had been gone for quite a while.

"Jen," he yelled, and when Donahue joined him, he pointed out the towels. "Have the lab check the towels for hair, and while they're at it, they should check the sink and shower drains as well."

Donahue made an entry in her notebook.

"I checked the closet, Gibby. His clothes are gone."

"Yeah. I figure we missed him by a couple of hours." Gibson shook his head in disgust. "I doubt if he's still on the grounds, but we'll let SIS finish the search, just to be sure."

"Want me to put some guys on the Fiesta in case he comes back?"

"No. Lets take it downtown. Have them do a quick search first, in case he left the gun behind."

"I still think we should watch the garage in case he comes back."

Gibson thought about it.

"I guess it wouldn't hurt. Okay. Set it up."

They walked back into the hallway to await the arrival of the crime lab team.

Donahue shook her head in disgust.

"We were so damn close, Gibby."

Gibson's jaw tightened. "Well get him."

****

Angela Morrison, the senior lab technician, was a tiny, petite woman, barely five feet tall. She wore black rimmed glasses and looked as though she'd blow away in a good, stiff breeze. With a reputation for efficiency, she was often the first choice for complex crime scenes.

Her voice projected like a drill-sergeants, and Gibson heard her before the elevator at the Radisson had even reached the fourth floor. When the door popped open, he watched as she and her team stepped out into the hallway.

"Gibson," she bellowed when she spotted him, "are you in charge here?"

He smiled to himself. He'd worked with Morrison before, and time had proven that she was really the best. Her demeanor often sent the less experienced detectives running for cover, but he'd learned not to cower, and that had earned him her respect.

"I am, Morrison. Don't tell me you're gonna handle this scene?"

"They called for the best, Gibson. Needed someone who could make up for your shortcomings as an investigator."

There were gasps and there was laughter from several officers who were standing around. Morrison shot them a glare that silenced the group.

In spite of himself, Gibson laughed out loud.

"Welcome to my nightmare, Angela. Do you think you can find me something to work with?"

She walked right past him and directly into the hotel room. "Don't I always, Gibson?" She glanced around briefly, and then came back out. "Anything special you want me to look for?"

"Prints, hair, or anything else that can give us a DNA typing."

"What can you tell me about your suspect?"

Gibson thought for a moment. "Not much. Our boy is Caucasian, British passport, and maybe with a female."

"That's the best you hotshots can come up with?" She shook her head. "I'll do what I can, but just make sure no one comes into this room until my people are finished. I don't want my scene contaminated any further."

She grabbed the arm of one of her assistants.

"John, get a set of prints from every officer who entered the room." She turned back to Gibson. "I presume that you and your partner were also in there, so see John before you leave."

With that, she grabbed a photographer and reentered the room.

Gibson and Donahue each gave a set of prints to the tech and then left the hotel. Officers were still coming and going, but it appeared as though the search was winding down.

Renée and Elwood were waiting in front of the hotel, and Elwood gave Gibson a shrug.

"He's not on the grounds, Gibby. In another fifteen minutes we'll have to clear the scene."

"I don't think he spotted us coming, Tom. The room was used, but my guess is he's got about a two-hour lead. There were no personal belongings, so he's not coming back."

"What do you want to do?" Elwood asked.

"I'm going back to the station where I can pull together an overview and figure out where we're going. Everything's happened so quickly that I'm losing track of the bigger picture. I need to start writing stuff down for my reports."

"Anything you want me to do, Gibby?" Donahue asked.

"Yeah, Jen. See if you can get some guys to check with the cab companies in case he caught one here at the hotel within the past three hours. Oh! And go see Ms. Cortez, the manager. Tell her we want their security tapes. Take everything they've got. We can go through them later when we get some time." He sighed. "After that, join me back at the station. By then we may have some news from Interpol or the guys at the airport."

Renée grabbed Gibson's arm to get his attention.

"I don't see any need for me to keep hanging around. I'm going to head back to my house. But you call me if there's anything I can do."

"Thanks for your help, Counselor. You've been more than generous with your time. Let me get someone to drive you back to your car."

****

Mark Carlson pushed open the office door and strode in, interrupting Elwood's conversation mid-sentence. Tall and physically fit, he was an imposing figure, and the speed with which he moved was startling. Both Gibson and Donahue got to their feet, but Carlson ignored them, focusing instead on Elwood.

"I don't know who the fuck you think you are," he growled, "but I'll tell you this; don't mess with me again! When I say I want to know what's going on, then you damn well better tell me exactly what's happening." His broad, heavy face was flushed, and his heavy breathing was tight and controlled. "And I won't listen to any more excuses, either. I won't tolerate finding out what's happening from the press. You'll tell me first, or I'll have you taken off this case and reassigned to patrol."

Elwood's eyes narrowed. He looked momentarily at the others in disbelief before focusing his gaze back on Carlson.

"Who the hell do you think you are barging into my office in the middle of a meeting?"

Carlson's mouth fell open.

"What did you say?"

Elwood pointed to the door.

"Gibby, Jen... wait outside. I've got a few things to discuss with the Commander."

"Stay where you are," Carlson ordered. He was shaking with anger and so obviously out of control that Elwood glanced at his waistband to see if he was armed.

He was not.

Elwood looked back over at the detectives.

"Get out," he commanded. The firmness of his tone meant business, and they pulled the office door shut behind them.

Carlson raised his hand and pointed at Elwood's chest.

"I'll have your ass for this, Elwood."

"You son of a bitch! How dare you talk to me like that in front of my squad."

Carlson took a step forward, thrusting his chest out. He was used to using the advantage of his height for intimidation.

"I'll talk to you any way I want. You and your men disobeyed a direct order to keep me advised about the progress of the case. You interfered with my ability to do my job."

Elwood continued to stare at his face, watching for a sign that he was planning to take a swing.

"Now, that's truly ironic," Elwood said with a large dose of sarcasm. "We're interfering with your ability to do *your job*? I recall a time when you were briefed on one of our cases and you told a certain female reporter where she could go to watch us make the arrest."

"So what?" Carlson shot back.

"I'll tell you what, you pompous ass. You put a major homicide investigation of ours at risk because you were screwing that broad from Channel 7. I overlooked it then—not because I give a damn about you or your career—but for the sake of your wife and kids. I didn't want them to go through the humiliation of a public trial board based on your sordid little affair. But I promised myself then and there that it would never happen again. So, if you don't back off right now, I'll bring you up on charges and end your god-damn worthless career."

Carlson was stunned.

"You can't prove a thing." he stammered.

Elwood knew he had him.

"I certainly can. I put a little package together on you, and if I have to, you know I'll drop it on the man's desk myself."

Carlson stared at him for a long moment, then turned and walked to the door.

"Hold it," Elwood ordered.

Carlson turned around slowly to face him.

"I'll brief you on the investigation as it progresses, and I'll see to it that you get what you need to retain your credibility. But nothing gets released to the press until I review it, and if you say one word beyond what I authorize, I'll take you down."

He paused to let his words sink in.

"Do we have an understanding?"

Carlson stared back with hatred in his eyes.

"I won't forget this, Elwood."

He stormed from the office and slammed the door.

Within a few moments, Gibson opened the door and stuck his head back in.

"Everything okay, Tom?"

"It's settled," Elwood told him. In spite of being angry, he flashed a small grin. "Everything gets cleared through me."

Gibson nodded.

"Thanks, Boss."

****

Just after nine forty-five p.m., a call from Angela Morrison was transferred to Gibson's interview room.

"This is Gibson."

"Nice to see you're still working."

He laughed when he recognized her voice.

"I hope you're gonna tell me you got something good?"

"There's good news and bad news, Gibby. Which do you want first?"

"I'm getting too tired to care, Angela. Why don't you give me the bad news first, then we can end this conversation on a high note."

"We dusted all the surfaces in the room where we thought there might be prints. It looks as though someone thoroughly wiped it down. There were no lifts where we thought they should be."

Gibson rubbed his right temple. He felt the first dull throb of a headache coming on.

"However," she continued, "because *I am* the best, I did a UV light scan of the sheets, and I found traces of semen, so I had my people print the headboard of the bed..."

"And...?" he asked when her dramatic pause seemed never-ending.

"And *voila*, we got two lifts. They're digits rather than palms. It looks like someone grabbed on to the headboard during sex."

Gibson's mood picked up immediately. Leave it to Angela. She always came through.

"Did you get enough to run a make?" he asked.

"Both lifts are comparable, and I've already sent them off to CAL ID. They'll do a priority computer run against all the statewide prints on file. Hopefully, your suspect's been printed before."

"Great job, Angela. I owe you big time for this one."

"I'll remember that, Gibson. But in the meantime, the bedding and the vacuum collections are on their way downtown along with some hair we found in the shower drain. Before we leave the scene, I need to know if you want me to super glue the room?"

Gibson thought for a moment. The superglue fumes took hours to bring up prints that might otherwise have escaped the dusting process. The room would have to be sealed, and it would likely be damaged by the procedure. He also knew that other physical evidence could be destroyed by the fumes, and that might create problems if they had to go back later to recheck the room.

"No, let's hold off on that for now. Just seal off the room. We can go back later and do the glue if our other leads don't pan out."

"Okay by me, Gibson. I'll let you know when I hear back on the prints. In the meantime, we'll head downtown and take a thorough look at both of the cars you impounded."

"Thanks again, Angela."

****

By eleven-fifteen p.m., things had wound down significantly at the WLA station. The cadre of television reporters had drifted away when Carlson announced he was canceling his news conference. Elwood had forbidden him to discuss the hotel search to keep Delaney from knowing how close they were getting. The Metro, SWAT and SIS officers were all sent home, leaving only the Robbery-Homicide detectives to figure out what to do next.

Most of the detectives were gathered upstairs where Elwood surprised them with hamburgers and French fries from a local diner. The mood relaxed considerably while the tired officers took a few minutes to swap animated stories and laugh about things unrelated to the case.

Gibson and Donahue settled in at a table in the back of the room where they worked on updating their case chronology. Gibson stuffed several French fries into his mouth just as Sgt. James Cleymont came strolling in.

"You got a second?" Cleymont asked.

Gibson wiped his mouth with a napkin and rose to his feet.

"Sure do. Why don't we go down the hall and find a place where we can talk."

"No need for that," said Cleymont dryly. "What I got from London won't be of much value."

Gibson sat back down, brushing the trash on the table over to one side. "Join us," he said through a mouthful. He gestured to an empty chair.

Cleymont sat down.

"My contact in the State Department spoke to Scotland Yard. The real Delaney has been located. He claims he's been looking for his wallet and passport for almost a week. He assumed they were somewhere in his flat, but the thinking now is that they were probably taken in a burglary."

"No help there," Donahue said.

Cleymont eyed the fries.

"The Yard's confirmed that he hasn't been out of London for the past six months. I requested a copy of his passport photo and it just arrived by fax."

He handed the picture to Gibson who compared it to the composite and to the photos from the ID's used at the Hertz rental lot. He then passed everything over to Donahue.

"I don't think it matches, Jen. The real Delaney's photo is close, but it's not a match with the ID photos used to rent the Hertz car. See how thin the real Delaney's nose is, and his eyes seem closer together than the guy we're looking for."

Donahue agreed.

"So our boy stole the ID's or purchased 'em hot and made some alterations on the picture."

"Either that," said Gibson dejectedly, "or he looks close enough to the real Delaney to be able to get by without arousing suspicion."

Cleymont handed Gibson an email printout.

"Customs ran a computer check and discovered that one Michael Delaney arrived in New York from London three days ago. His whereabouts after that were untraceable."

Gibson shrugged.

"Okay, let's think about this for a moment. The killer gets Delaney's ID in London and then flies to New York. We lose him there, but he arrives in LA two days ago, uses the ID to rent a car, and then gets a room at the Radisson Hotel. He makes the hit, goes back to the room, and then disappears."

"That flies," Donahue said. "But when did he hook up with the girl?"

"There's no indication he was traveling with a female when he arrived in New York," Cleymont added. "He bought a single, one-way ticket in London."

"Still, he could have been on the same flight with her. Can we get a copy of the passenger manifest?"

"I don't see why not."

Cleymont continued to eye the French fries longingly.

"By the way, I've arranged with Customs to red flag anyone traveling on Delaney's passport. The alert is international. I faxed a copy of the composite to my contact at Customs on the Mexican border and I think we should send one to Canada as well."

"I appreciate the help, Sarge. Elwood said you were the right man for the job. Can you handle the Canadian officials for me?"

"Not a problem. Anything else you want checked out?"

"Yeah. See if we can locate anyone who was seated near him on the plane from London to New York. Maybe we can get a good ID or learn something about our boy that might have come out during idle conversation."

"That will be a lot tougher, but I'll see what I can do."

Cleymont got up to leave, then stopped.

"By the way, do you have any extra burgers or fries? I'm starved."

"Help yourself," said Donahue, pointing across the room. "There should be a few more in that box on the front table."

Gibson grabbed Cleymont's arm.

"If they're all gone, let me know and I'll get someone to go out and pick one up for you."

There was one hamburger left, and Cleymont waved his thanks. "Oh, by the way, Gibson," he said from across the room, "I almost forgot. London is sending someone out here. The guy's supposed to be a terrorist expert. I've been told he might be able to help you identify your suspects."

"When's he due to arrive?" asked Gibson.

"I'm not sure." He took a bite of the burger, chewed like crazy, then wolfed it down. "His arrival time's a secret. It wouldn't do to have him suffer the same fate as his predecessor."

He winked, nodded, and walked out of the squad room.

Donahue twisted in her seat.

"We should check the stolen list for any vehicles taken from around the hotel. If he's driving, he might try to make it to the Mexican border."

"I'll get Elwood to assign someone to it."

Gibson kept his eyes downcast, lost in thought.

"Something bothering you?" Donahue asked.

"Yeah, Jen, there is. I can't quite figure this guy out. He acts like an out of town pro, obviously planning this hit well in advance. But after the hit, instead of immediately going to a safe location, he goes back to the hotel, the one place we were able to locate, and then it looks like he even takes the time to get laid."

"If the killing was planned, then so was his escape," she told him. "He knew he'd have some time, and after the hit, he was probably excited. Maybe he needed some action to calm himself down."

Gibson shook his head.

"That's what I mean. You're forgetting what the witnesses told us. The female in the car was not a happy camper. Was he banging her or someone else? Did he arrive with the female, or did he pick her up here in the States? And if he was a pro, then where was his backup?"

Donahue shrugged.

"It doesn't feel right to me," Gibson said dejectedly. "There are just too many unanswered questions."

Donahue stood up and collected the wrappers and napkins from the table.

"We'll get it all sorted out eventually. He's been one jump ahead of us so far, but I don't think he figured that we'd get this close so quickly."

Gibson looked past her and spotted Terry Alves as he walked into the squad room.

"I hope you're right, Jen." He gestured to Alves to come over. "Maybe some good news has just walked in."

Alves continued to display a pained look on his face. Nearly fifty, he had twenty-nine years on the job and should have been thinking about retirement, but being a cop was the only thing he had going on in his life. He wore an ill-fitting suit—long out of style—that was rumpled from over-use. Intelligent enough when it came to his job, he was lumbering and disorganized when it came to everything else.

"Gibson, Donahue." He nodded to them both. "You guys ready for some bad news?"

"Why the hell not, Terry?" Gibson said without hesitation. "We might as well finish the evening off with a fizzle. Have a seat." He gestured to a chair. "What'd you find out?"

Alves flopped down, resting his elbow in a spot of grease on the table.

"I'm getting too old to put in this many hours. I should be at home now with my feet up."

Neither one took the bait. Any form of comment would send Alves off on a tangent, so when no one commiserated with his complaint, he chose to go ahead with his news.

"We contacted security for all of the international carriers. Since the time of the killing, no one has boarded an international flight using the name Delaney, and there are no reservations under that name for the next twenty-four hours. I've asked for a printout of all the names, and they'll be available to go over later if you find out he left town under a different name."

Gibson felt his energy waning.

"Do we have anyone showing photos to the passenger agents?"

"Everyone we can find is being shown the pictures. A lot of 'em went off duty before we got there, so it'll be sometime tomorrow before we get 'em all tracked down."

"Well, that just about does it for tonight," Donahue sighed. "We're fresh out of leads. What do you think, Gibby? Should we pack it in?"

"We might as well."

Gibson stood up and stretched.

"We won't accomplish much more by staying around here tonight. Go on home, Jen. I'll fill in the Captain before I leave."

"So you guys get to go home while I still have to work?" It came out as a whine. Alves held up both hands in a gesture of surrender. "Where's the justice?"

"There is none, Terry."

Donahue patted him on the shoulder as she and Gibson left the room.

****

SIX

September 13, Sunday Morning

By the time Gibson finished his briefing for Elwood, it was just after midnight. They had already released most of the squad and ordered them back for eight a.m. when it was hoped there would be more leads to run down.

As Gibson got up to leave, Tippen knocked on the door frame and stuck his head into the Captain's office.

"Gibby, it's Angela Morrison on line four for you."

Gibson grabbed the phone on Elwood's desk.

"I was afraid you might have gone home by now," she said when he picked up.

"I was just about to go out the door."

"Well, don't get your heart set on leaving. I have a feeling you're about to pull an *all-nighter*."

Gibson's pulse quickened. "I'm gonna put you on the speaker, Angela. Tom Elwood's here with me." He flipped the switch. "Is this working?"

"I can hear you just fine. Hi, Tom."

"Hello, Angela," Elwood replied. He leaned forward in his chair. "What have you got?"

"Okay. We ran the lifts from the headboard in your suspect's room through CAL ID. The computer made a preliminary match. They belong to a female Irish National named Anne Magruder. They were placed in the system when she applied for a student visa."

Gibson looked at Elwood, who was beaming. It was incredible how invigorating a little good news could be.

"Can you give us the info from CAL ID?" Elwood asked.

"I can. There's a full description on the print card, including her visa application number. I'll fax it over to you if you will tell me where to send it?"

Elwood gave her the number then walked down to the Watch Commander's office to await the arrival of the fax.

"You really came through for us, Angela," Gibson said. "I won't forget it."

"Promises, promises," she replied, hanging up.

Elwood returned with the fax of the print card, and Gibson looked it over.

"Too bad Berehens didn't see her well enough to give us a composite," he said.

"You can't blame him. He was concentrating on the guy, and in the long run, that will probably be a lot more important."

Gibson phoned Cleymont and caught him at home.

"Sarge, we just got a line on our female. I need you to wake somebody up at the State Department and get me a copy of her visa picture." He gave Cleymont her name and the visa application number. As he finished reading the number, he spotted a lightly written notation at the bottom.

He looked over at Elwood.

"Well, I'll be damned! She's a student at UCLA."

****

By three a.m., the WLA station was again alive with activity, but this time it seemed more controlled and purposeful. The press was absent—unaware of the development—and Elwood was the ranking senior officer, which suited Gibson just fine.

They'd decided to find her residence and put her under surveillance rather than arrest her right away. It was hoped she would lead them directly to the male shooter.

Elwood put down the phone.

"That was Cleymont. His contact at the State Department raised someone at Immigration, and they're faxing over her passport photo."

Gibson followed him to the fax machine to await the picture. When it arrived, both were struck by how young she appeared to be.

"Good looking girl," Elwood mused. "Too bad she'll lose her bloom so quickly in prison."

Donahue walked into the room, and Elwood handed her the fax photo. She studied it for a moment, then looked up and caught Gibson's eye.

"She's a student at UCLA?"

Gibson nodded.

"Anyone check Facebook to see if she's got a site?"

Gibson looked over at Elwood who rolled his eyes.

Donahue smiled.

"You guys need to keep up with the modern world. I'll check it out."

****

By the time the core group assigned to handle the investigation was re-assembled and settled in the roll call room, it was close to 4:30 a.m. Gibson looked around the table, noted the exhausted faces, and focused on the one that showed some promise of life.

Lieutenant David Simmons, the commanding officer of SIS, was wide awake and ready to go. A night person by choice, he was at his best when others could barely function. Average in size, he more than made up for it with a bigger than life personality, a keen intelligence, and a willingness to do whatever it took to enable his people to get the job done.

"Let me fill you in on what's been going on," Gibson said. "Dan Tippen called the UCLA campus police, and they advised us that Magruder has a dorm room in *Dykstra Hall*. Her roommate is a female named Tracy Prescott.

"Prescott has a car and a parking permit. Magruder does not. We managed to get ahold of a passport photo for Magruder and a California driver's license photo for Prescott."

He looked over at Donahue, who smiled. He then added, "My partner checked out the Facebook accounts for both women and got a few more photo's for us. She downloaded the best of them and printed them out."

"Thank God for social media," Simmons said. He looked back over at Donahue and gave her a wink.

Gibson passed out copies of the photos of both girls to everyone present. New life seemed to come to everyone in the room. There was nothing like a lead to wake people up.

"I guess my first question is rather obvious," Simmons said. "Do we have enough probable cause to get a warrant for her dorm room?"

Renée Marin, who was seated in the front row of the roll call room, turned in her seat to face the group.

"It's awfully circumstantial, Lieutenant. A car that may have been used for the crime is connected to a rental car, which in turn is connected to a room at the Radisson where her print is found. I can get you a warrant, but it's tenuous at best."

She glanced over at Gibson.

"Can we get Berehens to make an ID that puts her in the car?"

"We could show Berehens her picture in a six pack," offered Donahue.

Gibson thought for a moment.

"I'll tell you why I'm against that. Suppose he freezes up on us or can't make an ID; or even worse, suppose he tells us that the woman he saw is definitely not in the pictures. Wouldn't that prevent us from getting a warrant?"

Marin nodded. "Most likely."

"Then I think we should go with what we have. Why tempt fate?"

"You're ducking the main issue, Gibby. We don't have anything to connect her to the shooting. All we can prove is her connection to his room."

"That's true, Renée, but it's the best we're gonna do. Logic tells me that she's the one at the crime scene, but Berehens didn't think he could identify the girl, and if we show him the photos and he doesn't make an ID, he could really screw this up. At this point, he's more of a liability, and you said it yourself, we have enough circumstantial evidence to get a judge's signature, so let's just go with that. The most important thing now is to search her room. Who knows what we'll find in there."

He gave her a brief smile.

"We might even find our male suspect."

"Amazing," she said. "I must be exhausted because you're starting to make sense. I'll get you your warrant."

"Thank you, Counselor."

He turned to Simmons.

"We need to find out quickly if there's anyone in that dorm room. If she's there, I'll want your people to set up and follow her. Hopefully, she'll lead us to our boy."

"How long do we stay on her?"

"No more than twenty-four hours. If she doesn't lead us to him by then, we've got to take her in and see what we can get."

"How about the roommate?" Donahue asked.

"I think we should follow her too," Elwood replied. "We don't know for sure that she isn't involved."

Simmons shifted in his chair.

"I've got enough people to handle them both, and we can go to twelve-hour shifts if we have to, but if we start to have problems, do you want me to concentrate on Magruder?"

"She's the primary," Gibson assured him, "but as long as you mention it, under no circumstances can we afford to lose her. She may be our only link to the killer."

He let that thought hang with the group.

"Lieutenant," Elwood said to Simmons, "will you need Air Support?"

"As a matter of fact, Captain, once we find her, I'd like two helicopters committed to Magruder."

"Why two?" Elwood asked.

"One stays on her at all times, and the second goes up in replacement when the first is refueling."

"I'll see what I can do. Anything else?"

"If you have one, a picture of your male suspect, just in case my people run across him."

"I'll give you copies of our composite and the ID photos used to rent the car, but we don't have a true name or make on him yet."

Gibson walked over to a nearby table and handed a stack of the composites to Simmons.

"Your people need to know he's armed and dangerous. Once he's identified, he becomes the primary, and I'll want him taken down as quickly as we can."

"No problem," Simmons answered with a tight smile. "Takedowns are our specialty."

There was laughter from around the table. The Special Investigations Section was notorious for tailing armed robbers, watching them commit crimes, and then arresting them once they were clear of the scene. A surprisingly large number of the suspects were killed while resisting arrest, and although certain civil libertarians had launched a crusade to have the unit disbanded, the general public welcomed them with unabashed support.

"Tom, how do you want us to set up communications?" Gibson asked.

Elwood hesitated.

"I guess we should set up a Command Post here in the station. We can remain on standby and coordinate everything that comes up. SIS will use their scrambled frequency, which we can monitor here. We'll use Tac-Two frequency for any non-essential communications, and a land line for sensitive information. Anyone see any problems with that?"

No one did. As long as members of the press and the suspects could not monitor their surveillance, everything would probably work out.

"Sounds good," Gibson said. "Let's get started."

****

Thirty minutes later, Simmons held a briefing in the roll call room for the twenty-four officers assigned to the Special Investigations Section.

SIS operatives were experts at surveillance and counter surveillance, and they were also experts in blending in with their environment.

In teams of twelve, they were designated Red and Green, and each officer was given a number so that names would not be used over the air.

After discussing the facts of the case, Simmons allowed each team to choose a code name for their subjects. Red Team selected "Lover" as the name for Anne Magruder, while Green Team went with "Roomie" for the roommate, Tracy Prescott.

"I'm going to end this meeting by reminding everyone that the purpose of the surveillance is to follow the females until one of them leads us to our male subject who's using the name Delaney. His designation is 'Target.' As soon as we spot him, I want to know. We'll make the decision to take him down at the CP when we're sure we have enough backup. I don't want anyone hurt, so be careful out there."

While officers broke up into smaller groups to discuss their tactics and pairings, the leader of Red Team ordered two lead officers to scout the dorm and find out first hand if anyone was present in the dorm room.

****

Renée hung up the telephone, signed the judge's name to the warrant, then glanced at her watch. It was almost five thirty a.m.

She yawned, stretched, gathered up the paperwork, and left the room in search of Gibson. He was nowhere around, but she found David Simmons who was seated alone in the squad room with a cup of coffee and a map of West LA.

"Hello, Lieutenant," she said. "I see you're the only one still around. Do you have any idea where the others might be?"

"They're sleeping in the crash room. Can I help you, Counselor?"

"Maybe you can. But tell me first, what's the crash room?"

He smiled. "When the night watch gets off, some of the officers have to stick around for court, so we set up a room in the back where they can sleep till they're needed. It's nothing fancy, just cots and blankets, but it's dark and quiet. Do you want me to go back there and wake them up for you?"

"No, that's okay. They really need to get some sleep." She wandered over to his table. "I don't suppose you'd consider telling me where you got that coffee? It smells too good to have come from the machine."

He gestured for her to sit down. "This is homemade, freshly ground Colombian. But I need to warn you, although it smells great, it's about forty percent caffeine."

"If it tastes half as good as it smells..."

He smiled and poured her a cup from a thermos he'd stashed under the table. "I have to hide it from my men," he explained.

She laughed and accepted the cup with thanks.

"I can't decide whether I need to stick around here or not. My brain keeps saying *go home and get some sleep*, but I know if I leave, they'll probably call me back in before my head hits the pillow."

"That's always the case, Mrs. Marin, but if you drink about half that cup, the decision will be made for you."

She laughed again and tried a sip. Any hope of getting sleep was now out of the question. It was too close to dawn, and soon things would start anew; she just needed to get a second wind, and the desire to sleep would pass. She looked up at Simmons and smiled.

"Your coffee has made up my mind, Lieutenant."

She took another sip.

"Did you get the warrant?" he asked.

She nodded, too tired to talk.

He used his radio to inform the Red Team leader.

She talked with Simmons, and they swapped stories for a while as the members of Major Crimes began to drift back into the squad room. Most were dragging from lack of sleep, but someone brought in bagels and donuts, and soon they were talking and laughing in spite of the toll the long hours were taking.

But the mood in the room changed quickly when Simmons yelled for quiet. He listened to the message that was coming through his earpiece.

"Someone wake Gibson and the others," he snapped. "A light just went on in Magruder's dorm room."

****

Anne Magruder's head was pounding, and her stomach was queasy. She'd slept for a while, but it was fitful and disturbed.

How could she have been so stupid? She lay in her bed, paralyzed with fear. Between the police and her father, she didn't stand a chance. What was she going to do?

Her stomach knotted up with fear. What if Cassidy decided she might talk?

She quickly sat up and turned on the lamp at the head of her bed. As she reached for her robe, she noticed her roommate beginning to stir.

"What's wrong?" Tracy asked as she struggled to open her eyes.

"Nothin's wrong," Anne replied, a bit too quickly.

"You look terrible, Anne. Your face is all puffy. Are you crying?"

"I'm fine," she said, but her voice had cracked with emotion.

Tracy sat up and continued to stare, forcing Anne to reply.

"It's nothing," she said. She made an effort to sound convincing. "I had a fight with an old boyfriend, that's all. I just don't feel like talkin' about it."

"I'm sorry. I didn't mean to pry. I just wanted to help if I could."

Anne nodded to show that she understood.

"I've got an idea," Tracy said. "Since we're both up, why don't you join me for a run? After that, we can go to the Student Union for breakfast. If you decide you want to talk, I'm a good listener."

Anne hesitated. They were not really that close. Could she be trusted? She wanted to talk to someone, but it just might make things even worse.

"Thanks anyway, Trace, but I just want to be alone."

****

Gibson was awakened from a sound sleep. In the darkness of the crash room, it took a few moments to realize where he was, but he scrambled up when he learned about the light in the dorm room. He flipped on the wall switch, woke the others, and headed for the roll call room.

The command post was guarded by a uniformed officer to limit access to those assigned to the case. A blackboard set up near the front of the room contained the list of assignments for follow-up. Detectives, in turn, volunteered to complete each task and logged their names on the board after choosing an assignment. There was a sense of urgency as each man and woman resisted the impulse to drive straight over to the dorm.

Dan Tippen, bleary-eyed from a lack of sleep, made coffee in a large percolator that he found in a nearby storage room. Gibson poured himself a cup and joined Simmons and Renée. A scrambler was set up so they could monitor the surveillance units out in the field.

"Did you enjoy your nap, Gibby?" Renée asked.

Not fully awake, he just growled.

Simmons slid over the log sheet on which he maintained a chronology of the surveillance. As Gibson read the log, Simmons explained what was missing.

"We still don't know for sure if there is anyone inside. One of the teams was getting ready to approach when the light went on. They had to withdraw to avoid being seen."

"Are all the units in place?" Gibson asked.

"They are now, and I just heard from Air Support that they have a chopper fully fueled and parked on the roof of a high-rise building in Westwood. They're ready to go as soon as we need 'em."

Gibson gave him a smile. "Then all we can do now is wait."

****

A few minutes later, the scrambled radio came to life with a soft spoken female voice.

"*This is Red 7,*" she whispered. "*Roomie just came out. She's gone to the bathroom down the hall.*"

An extended period of unbroken silence from the surveillance teams kept everyone in the Command Post silent. They sat at the table, staring at the radio.

A male voice, who identified himself as Red 2, whispered, "*There's someone still in the room.*"

A muted cheer went up from Donahue and a few of the others. It was a very good bet that the other person was Anne.

Within a few minutes, surveillance advised them that Roomie went back to her room. Gibson paced the floor—the tension was unbearable—the radio remained silent for another five minutes.

"*Red 3 to Green 1,*" spoke a male voice. "*Roomie is on the move. She just entered the elevator heading for the lobby. She's wearing a white T-shirt, black leggings, and running shoes. No purse or bags. She's got a small radio with headphones in her right hand. Looks like she's gonna go jogging.*"

"*Green 1 to Green Teams,*" spoke a voice. "*Switch over to Tac Four.*"

In the Command Post, Simmons produced a second radio to allow him to monitor the Green Team frequency.

"How's this going to work?" Renée asked. "Won't this get horribly confusing with two surveillances going at once?"

"Jen's gonna run a log on the Green surveillance," replied Gibson. "She'll keep track of her position as reported by the watchers. Tippen will run one for the Reds—that way, we can keep 'em separate."

The radio sprang to life. *"Green 3. She's on foot and appears to be heading through the parking lot."*

"Green 5. I see her. She's crossing the greenbelt heading for Sunset Blvd. It looks like she's going to use the jogging trail that runs around the perimeter of the university."

"Green 2. I'm north of her position. I'm dressed to run. If she goes by, I'll fall in behind her."

"Green 5. She's definitely going for a run. She's on the trail now. Two, she's coming up on your position."

"Green 2. I see her... she's just gone by. I'll be running about fifty yards behind her. Hope she's not in training for a marathon..."

There was laughter around at the table. Donahue stood up and cajoled Simmons to let her have another cup of coffee from his thermos.

"Dave," Gibson asked, "do we still have some of your people watching the room?"

"I've got a team on the floor, and the others are stationed around the area."

Gibson signaled to Elwood and Marin, and the three of them huddled together in a far corner of the room to discuss their next move.

"When do you want to go in?" Elwood asked.

"That's what I wanted to discuss," Gibson replied. "Can we use the warrant to go inside more than one time?"

"Why would you want to do that?" Renée asked.

"If Magruder's inside and she leaves, we need to make sure that Delaney's not in there."

"You can't do it, Gibby," she said. "The warrant lets you enter only once."

"Okay, we'll hold off on serving the warrant until we see what happens during the surveillance."

He put his arm around her shoulder and walked her to the door.

"Renée, you go ahead and get some breakfast. It may be a while before we're ready to serve the warrant."

Marin knew what he was up to. They had every intention of going in twice, with or without the warrant. The need to determine if Delaney was inside was obvious, but she resented their lack of trust. She felt like a child being sent to her room.

"Damn it, Gibson. I'm not stupid." She stormed away to collect her computer and purse.

Gibson was right behind her.

"Wait a minute, Renée. You've got it all wrong." He was clearly embarrassed, and his face was flushed. "I'm only trying to protect you."

She tried to gauge his sincerity.

"I appreciate that, but I'm a member of this team. If I have a problem with something you propose, I'll tell you, but don't treat me like an outsider."

"I'm sorry." He seemed genuinely contrite. "I won't make that mistake again."

"Good." She put her computer back on the table. "By the way, under the emergency circumstances doctrine, you can make an entry without a warrant to see if he's in there, just as long as you don't search for physical evidence."

"Why didn't you say so in the first place?"

"You never asked."

****

Anne finished pulling on her jeans and sat back down on the bed to slip on her shoes. She was too antsy to sit around. She was worried about being arrested and the unpredictably of Liam Cassidy.

Instinctively, she knew she'd be safe in Ireland. Facing her father would be no easy task, but at least he wouldn't kill her. A plan of escape took form. She would go to the airport, use her credit card, and catch the first available flight to her homeland.

She searched for her purse. Where was it? She tore through her closet and belongings. It was gone. She slumped to the floor and sobbed. Her money and credit cards were in that purse. So was her passport. Everything she needed to get away.

She forced herself to think: *Where the hell was it?* She had it after the shooting when she was at his hotel. Did she have it after that?

Oh, dear God! I left it in his car!

Without the passport, she'd never get home. How was she going to get it back? Only one option came to mind, and that made her cringe. She would have to see Liam again.

But how would she find him? The hotel? He'd be long gone by now. What did he say last night? He had grabbed her wrist and pressed a piece of paper into her hand. "If you change your mind and want to see me again, here's a number you can reach me at tomorrow morning. But you'll have to call me by eight-thirty a.m. After that, I'll be long gone."

The piece of paper. Where the hell was it?

She finally remembered she'd thrown it in the bushes in front of the dorm when he let her get out of his car. She scrambled to her feet, opened the door, and ran down the hallway to the elevator.

From the corner of her eye, she became aware of another person in the corridor. A young woman with blond hair, but she quickly disappeared into the communal bathroom.

When the elevator arrived, Anne stepped inside and said a quick prayer that the paper would still be there.

****

"This is Red 7. Lover's moving, and she seems panicked."

Everything at the Command Post came to a halt. Within seconds more details came in.

"She's dressed in jeans, a white blouse, and tennis shoes. She has a key ring in her hand."

When Anne got off the elevator, she went to the street and began to poke around in the shrubbery.

"Red 4. Lover's looking for something in the bushes—she just picked up a piece of paper. It was crunched up—she's reading what's on it—I can't tell from this distance—she's going back up the front walkway to the dorm. Stand by,

Seven, she's back on the elevator."

A few moments later, the radio came to life:

"Red 7. Lover's now back in her room."

****

Anne searched for some money. She kept a glass with change on the book-shelf, and when she poured it out, there was just a little less than four dollars. She searched through her coats and jackets, and by the time the hunt was fin-ished, the total had risen to just over nine dollars.

It was only seven-thirty, and she had another hour to kill before he'd be on the phone. Her stomach growled. She wasn't really hungry, but she hadn't eaten since just before the shootings. She stood up and paced. The thought of staying in the room was unbearable. It made her feel trapped.

She'd take the money she had and walk to the Village. There she could find a safe pay phone, kill some time, and maybe get something in her stomach.

****

"Red 7. Lover's on the move."

Tippen logged in her movements as the ground units scurried about to im-prove their surveillance positions. When it was clear that she was headed on foot towards the Village, Simmons ordered the helicopter to go on station.

Air 16 climbed quickly to two thousand feet, where the spotter then watched her from a safe distance through very high-powered binoculars.

She walked to a McDonald's, went inside, ordered a coffee, then sat at a table in the back of the room.

****

Gibson fidgeted in his chair. "Now that she's out, we should find out if De-laney is in her room."

"I've got an entry team parked around the corner from the dorm," Simmons said with a nod. "They can be inside in less than five minutes."

"Let's do it, Dave, but tell them to go in quietly. I don't want anyone on the floor to know what's going on."

Simmons picked up his radio and gave the command.

****

Three casually dressed men stepped out of a dull, blue Plymouth and walked over to a locked exit at the side of the dorm. One easily picked the lock and all three climbed the stairs to the fourth floor. A female officer, dressed like a coed, stood alone in the hallway. When they arrived, she pointed out Lover's room then concealed herself in an alcove by the elevators.

The three men positioned themselves just outside the doorway. One of the officers placed a small briefcase on the floor from which he removed a fiber optic cable. He slid it under the door, turned on the television screen built into the case and slowly examined the interior of the room.

Using the light in the room that was still on for illumination, he could easily see that no one was inside. A bed was located on each side of the doorway, and there were twin desks at the head of both beds.

Using hand gestures, he signaled the other two that the room appeared clear. His partner pulled a master key from his pocket and inserted it into the lock. When they were ready, they pulled out their handguns and entered the room.

****

"Red 7," squawked the radio, "The entry team is in."

At the Command Post, everyone held their breath. It seemed like an eternity; but within two minutes, the voice came on again.

"Red 7. The room is clear...target's not there. Blue team is out and clear. We'll resume our watch on the room."

****

Used to the frequent disappointments that came with the job, most of the detectives left the Command Post and resumed their follow-up assignments. Simmons moved from desk to desk to monitor the two surveillances. Five minutes later, he took a call on line six. He turned to speak to Gibson but stopped when he noticed Renée.

"It's okay, Dave, we've got no secrets from Renée."

"You sure?"

"I'm sure."

"Okay. Blue Team left several bugs in the room, and one is in the phone. If she goes back and calls him, we'll know what's being said."

"Oh, *Jeez...*"

Renée Marin rolled her eyes and clapped a hand to her forehead. She looked over at Gibson. He was smiling from ear to ear.

"Don't *even* say it, Gibson." Her insistence on being told what was going on may have just made her an accomplice to a felony. "I'm going to the restroom," she said, and she quickly left the room.

Gibson burst into laughter.

"I don't know if that was such a good idea," Simmons said with a frown.

"Don't worry about it, Dave. She insisted on knowing everything."

"But you put her in a difficult spot?"

"When she comes back, I'll tell her we were just kidding. That will ease her conscience and keep her from getting too curious in the future."

****

Anne finished a cup of coffee, then left the McDonald's and wandered aimlessly through the Village. She stopped briefly at an outdoor newsstand, scanned the papers, then took a seat on a nearby bench.

"Red 3. She's just staring out at the street, checking her watch. I don't think she's waiting for a bus. She seems to be lost in thought."

And a minute later, from another vantage point.

"Red 5. Lover's crying."

Gibson smiled at Donahue. "It would seem she's under considerable emotional strain. I wouldn't be a bit surprised if she gives him up before the cuffs go on."

****

At eight twenty-nine, Anne got up from the bus bench and walked to a bank of two pay phones at the nearby corner. She was too smart to use her cell phone, and she was equally sure that the number that he'd given her was also a static land line.

She pulled out the crumpled piece of paper from her pocket and punched in the number.

After a short conversation, Anne hung up the telephone and quickly walked back towards the school.

****

"This is Red 3. She's just made contact."

He read off the digits of the number she had just dialed.

"She wants to talk to him about what happened---wants her purse back--- she listened for awhile---nodded---may have gotten directions."

****

Renée, who'd returned, leaned over to Simmons and whispered, "How the hell did he get close enough to get the number she dialed and to hear her side of the conversation?"

Simmons smiled.

"Red 3 is Matt Kirk. He likes to pose as a homeless drunk. He was probably pretending to go through a nearby trashcan or something like that."

Elwood put down his telephone and yelled to Simmons. "The number comes back to a pay phone in Marina Del Rey—13225 Mindanao Way—it's next to an ice cream store in a shopping center."

Simmons grabbed his rover radio and gave the address information to Air

16.

"Stay high," he added. *"I don't want him to spot you. We don't have any ground units in the area."*

"How long till the air unit gets there?" Gibson asked.

Simmons hit the transmit button again.

"16, what's your ETA?"

"ETA in ninety seconds."

Gibson thought out loud.

"For her to call a pay phone means they worked out a predetermined time for her call. Our suspect must be concerned about his security, but he doesn't seem too worried about her. I think she's going to lead us to him."

"Maybe so," Elwood said. "If it is him she's talking to."

Donahue groaned.

"Don't even think that."

"Dave," Gibson yelled out, "make sure Air 16 doesn't get in too close. If our target makes them, we'll lose him for sure. I'd rather take my chances following the girl."

Simmons cautioned Air 16 to stay out of view.

"Have we any ground units nearby?" Elwood asked.

"All of my people are on the surveillance," Simmons responded.

"We could send in a black and white?" Elwood countered.

"No." Gibson was adamant. "They wouldn't know what to look for."

He paused to consider his options. If I was this guy, what would I be doing? I'd put distance between myself and the pay phone, but I'd also want to know if I was being watched, so I'd wait to see if anyone checked out the phone.

"Dave, he might try a counter-surveillance. Can we pull some of your people off Roomie and send them down to the Marina? They can go into the shopping center and carefully look things over."

"Do you want us to pick up the roommate? If so, I can free up the whole squad."

"No, not yet. Keep a small crew on her. It's still too early to pull her in."

Elwood had been listening to their conversation.

"I can send a few detective teams into the area," he said. "They can drive around unnoticed, and if she makes another call to the Marina, we'll be right on top of him."

"Good idea, Tom, but keep them six blocks away from the shopping center. If I'm right about him watching the phone, I don't want anyone looking like a cop to be anywhere in the area."

"*16 to Base*," cracked the radio.

"*Base go*," Simmons replied.

"*We're eyes on. No one at the phone. There are some joggers moving around in the area. A lot of bike riders as well. The telephone is next to a heavily traveled throughway. No way to determine from this altitude if Target is among them.*"

 Simmons sighed.

"Okay, 16. Pull back and resume surveillance with Red Team."

"*16, Roger.*"

"Well, we're back to square one," Renée said to no one in particular.

"Not exactly," Gibson replied. "We know he's in town, somewhere near the Marina, and she's still in contact. All we need now is patience and a little luck."

****

SEVEN

September 13, Sunday, Late Morning

Peter Lee, a Detective of Chinese heritage assigned to the Major Crimes Unit, stuck his head in the doorway of the Command Post room.

"Hey, Skipper. You've got a visitor out here."

Elwood left the table and went out into the hallway.

"This is Captain Elwood," Lee said to the stranger, and to Elwood, he said, "This is Major Andrew Whitney from the Special Air Service."

The two men shook hands. Elwood noticed that he was carrying a both suitcase and a briefcase.

"You got here pretty fast, Major. Have you got a hotel yet?"

"Not yet, Captain. I wanted to check in here first."

"Well, come with me, and we'll bring you up to speed."

They walked into the squad room—Elwood made the introductions to Gibson and Donahue—and when he introduced Clarke to Renée Marin, Whitney reached out and took her hand.

"Pleased to meet you, Mrs. Marin," he said.

"Renée's the prosecutor assigned to assist us during the investigation," Elwood told him. "In fact, she—"

A soft laugh escaped from Whitney's lips.

"Excuse me, Major," Marin said with a touch of sarcasm. "Did the Captain say something funny?"

Whitney bowed his head slightly.

"Please forgive me, Mrs. Marin. I meant no disrespect."

"You could have fooled me," she replied.

"But I didn't mean it that way at all. On those few occasions when I've been to the Old Bailey, the only prosecutors I've seen have been much older chaps with wrinkled skin and prissy gray wigs. But you? Well, there's just no comparison. I can see that our system for selecting barristers is in dire need of revision."

Renée held his glance and decided for the moment that he meant what he'd said as a compliment. She gave him a half smile.

"Nice recovery, Major. No offense taken."

Elwood focused his smile on Renee.

"Okay. Now that we've got that settled, the Major is on loan to us from the British government. He works for the Special Air Service. He's a terrorist expert, and his area of specialty is the IRA."

Renée laughed.

Whitney cocked his head.

"Ma'am?"

"Forgive me, Major. The only foreign intelligence experts I've ever met have always been, well, somewhat older, stuffy, pompous, and far less attractive. I can see that I'll have to work on changing my preconceptions."

"*Touché*," he said with a smile. "I suppose I had that coming."

"You certainly did," she said with a laugh. "Now, would you like to see the photos we've got of our main suspects?"

"I certainly would. The only information I've received so far is that Sean Clarke and his adjutant were shot to death in their motorcar. I'm afraid I've been in transit since we first got the word."

Donahue handed him a photo.

"This is Anne Magruder. It's a photo we got off Facebook."

Whitney studied at it briefly.

"I may be able to get you some information on this young lady, but I'll need to make contact with London first."

"Fair enough, and while you're at it, do you have any idea who this guy might be?"

She handed him the photo's that they had of Delaney.

Whitney considered the passport photo.

"There's a certain familiarity, but to be honest, no one specifically comes to mind." He paused, then glanced over at Renée.

"If Mrs. Marin could spare a few moments to brief me on what's been going on, I might be able to to learn enough to make the right connections."

Renée smiled. Without missing a beat, Major Whitney had managed to manipulate the situation to enable him to speak to her alone.

This guy is smooth.

Very smooth, indeed.

****

They sat in the Captain's office, and for almost twenty minutes, Renée recounted the details of the assassinations and how they believed Anne Magruder was involved. When she was finished, Whitney opened his briefcase, set it down on the Captain's desk, and removed a portable telephone scrambler.

"Would you be so kind as to show me how to get an outside line?" he asked.

"Just punch in 9 and the number you want."

He thanked her and affixed the scrambler to the office's hardline telephone receiver.

Renée got to her feet. "I'll just wait outside while you make your call."

"That won't be necessary. The scrambler is simply to prevent anyone from interceptin' the overseas satellite signal."

Renée sat down again and watched while he finished attaching the scrambler. He then entered a series of numbers to make his connection. While he worked, she studied him intently.

His short dark hair, square jaw, and deep-set blue eyes gave him a rugged, outdoor attractiveness that fit with his military bearing. His smile was engaging and it appeared to come easily. He seemed quite self-assured and full of life.

He looked up, noticed she was watching him, shot her a smile, then returned to his work.

The call went through and he spoke to someone for a few moments before connecting the scrambler to a laptop computer with a self-contained telephone modem and fax. Once he was ready, he sent off a fax of Delaney's composite and the picture of Anne Magruder to *SAS HDQ, CHELTENHAM*.

While they waited for a reply, he engaged Renée in small talk about the weather and his flight, and a few minutes later, his screen came to life.

"I've requested everything available on Anne Magruder," he said. "For the most part, the information should arrive in narrative form. If there is anythin' available, it will be a compilation of declassified information taken from our raw intelligence files."

"Does that mean we won't get everything?" she asked.

"That's correct." His eyes narrowed. "Some of the information might tend to identify the source, and that could lead to rather serious consequences."

"How about Delaney? Will the photo help?"

"Possibly. They'll show it around at headquarters and someone might recognize him, but we'll have to wait until they run it through our facial recognition computerized system. But in the meantime, I think we've got a better chance of findin' out who he is if we concentrate on her associates."

"Why her associates?"

He looked up from the screen and noticed her puzzled expression.

"Don't women talk about their boyfriends, Mrs. Marin, or is it only men who like to discuss the members of the opposite sex?"

"I see your point, Major." She smiled. "We may have overlooked the obvious. And by the way, please call me Renée. The only people who call me Mrs. Marin are defense attorneys and their clients."

He winked.

"My friends call me Whit."

****

Thirty minutes later, Gibson watched them come back to the squad room, talking softly and smiling, and it struck him how relaxed they seemed to be for having just met.

Renée caught his stare and shot him a *mind-your-own-business* look.

"Have you got a moment, Detective?" Whitney asked him.

The radio background noise was constant from the teams reporting in, so Gibson suggested they go somewhere quieter. Elwood joined them and the four of them went to the far end of the room where they settled into chairs borrowed from several nearby desks.

Whitney spoke softly.

"I just heard back from London. Anne Magruder is the daughter of John Magruder, a member of the IRA's Ruling Council."

"What does that mean?" Elwood asked.

"How much do you know about the IRA?"

"Virtually nothing," Elwood admitted.

"Well then, let me give you a brief overview." He leaned forward. "The Provisional Irish Republican Army, called PIRA, is a group seekin' independence for Ireland from the UK. Assassinations and bombin's are their stock in trade. They're organized into small action cells, each one operatin' independently. However, all of the cells adhere to the mandates of an Army Council, and John Magruder is a leader in that group."

Gibson was surprised.

"What kind of a father sends his own daughter out to commit murder?"

"That may not be the case," Whitney replied. "Magruder's daughter was once recruited to be a runner for the Provos. Her job was to deliver messages in the Belfast area. Apparently, her father found out and sent her to school over here to keep her out of the war. That would seem to contradict any assumption that she's now a member of the Provos."

"You've lost me, Major," Gibson said. "If she's not a member, does that mean this isn't an IRA operation?"

Whitney shook his head.

"On the contrary, it has all the usual markings. But there's something about what happened that doesn't make any sense. Classically, there should have been a backup team at the site of the killings, but from what Renée's told me, there's no evidence that anyone else was there. And he rented the car and a room by himself, and that's just not very bright. It almost sounds as if he did this one on his own, and if that's the case, I can't imagine why Magruder's daughter would want to get herself involved."

"Maybe the killing was spur of the moment?" Renée said.

"Possible, but not likely. When a layoff car's been used, it's been planned. In any event, you may have a more immediate problem to deal with."

"What's that?"

"At some point, this killer may decide the girl's a liability. She's soft, and he has to realize if you pick her up, she's likely to grass."

"Grass?" said both Gibson and Renée in unison.

"Ah...I think the term you're familiar with is *inform*."

Donahue shrugged.

"Well, we can't let that happen. She may be the key to our getting a conviction, assuming we can arrest him and get him to trial."

"So, what do we do?" Elwood asked.

"The Major's theory makes sense," said Gibson, "but in the absence of proof that she's in any danger, I think we have to keep going. Hopefully, we can take him down before he has a chance to do anything to her." He turned back to Whitney. "Any clue as to the identity of our phantom Mr. Delaney?"

"Not yet. Maybe someone back home will recognize him, but it's goin' to take time. I've asked for personal data on all of Anne Magruder's associates, but so far, nothin's been located."

Gibson stood up and stretched.

"I don't know about the rest of you, but I'm getting hungry. Anyone volunteering to do a McDonald's run?"

All eyes shifted towards Donahue.

"Don't look at me," she mumbled.

They continued to stare.

"Oh, *all right!*" She threw up her hands in surrender. "I'll go this time, but don't think this means I'm gonna make the lunch run, too."

****

Anne walked over to the Catholic Youth Center, across the street from UCLA, spent an hour praying alone in a small chapel reserved for students, then meandered back to the dorm.

When watchers reported that she'd entered her room, Simmons opened a briefcase and produced a small receiver with earphones.

Marin watched with curiosity until she realized he was monitoring a bug in her room. When Gibson had told her that they'd only been kidding, she'd accepted his explanation, happy to be off the hook. He'd given her a way out, a plausible denial, and she'd be a fool to question him now.

Without saying a word, she stood up and walked out to stretch her legs, preferring to plead ignorance in the face of the truth.

As the minutes dragged on, those at the table grew increasingly somber. They needed a break and they needed it now.

Shortly after ten o'clock, the Green team reported that Roomie was headed back to the dorm.

****

Anne heard the key slide into the lock. Her stomach knotted with fear, but when Tracy stepped in, she groaned with relief.

"Anne? I thought you'd be long gone. Are you just getting up?"

"No. I've been out already."

"Are you okay?"

"I'm fine now, Trace. I'm sorry I was so rude this mornin'. I really do appreciate your concern."

"I could tell you were upset. Is there anything I can do to help you out?"

Anne took a deep breath. This was as good a time as any to ask.

"Maybe there is. I went out with an old boyfriend last night and I'm sure you can tell that things didn't work out too well. We ended up in a major fight, and when he dropped me off, I left my purse in his car."

She looked down at the floor and composed herself to go on.

"I called him this mornin', but the bastard won't bring it up here for me. I was wonderin'—if you didn't need your car this mornin'—could I use it for about an hour to go and get my stuff? He's got all my money and my credit cards."

Tracy interrupted her with a short laugh.

"Is that all? I thought you were going to say you were pregnant or something."

The absurdity of the misconception made them both laugh.

"It's no problem," Tracy said. "In fact, I'll drive you over myself. Maybe it will make things easier."

Anne smiled with relief.

"Thanks, Trace. I really owe you one for this."

****

"We've got him!" said Simmons. He grabbed a portable radio from the table.

"Did you copy the conversation, Green leader?"

"10-4. We'll be ready when they come down."

"Have you found Roomie's car?"

"It's in a student lot behind the dorm."

Simmons smiled again. He looked around and saw that he had a captive audience waiting to know what was going on.

"Well?" Gibson asked.

"She left her purse in Delaney's car, and the roommate is gonna drive her over there to get it."

A small cheer went up at the table.

"Do we know where they're going?" Gibson asked.

"They haven't said yet."

Simmons stopped talking to readjust the earphone.

"It sounds like they're changing their clothes," he said.

Gibson rose to his feet. His intuition told him they'd be heading back down to the Marina, and he had no intention of waiting around at the station. He wanted to be on scene when the arrests were made.

"Dave, we'll be heading over to the Marina."

He turned to Elwood.

"Captain, if it's okay with you, I'd like to set up an open car phone line on the scrambler. Tippen can stay here to let us know where they are."

Elwood nodded, and Gibson turned to Whitney.

"You can stay with me, Major. Let's find Renée and head for the car."

****

The Red Team was in position by the time the girls reached Tracy's car and the Green Team units withdrew with instructions to remain at least a mile behind the primary surveillance. Simmons called in Air 16 and positioned the helicopter downwind, at 3200 feet, to oversee coordination from above.

Once the girls pulled out, a small convoy of undercover vehicles quickly fell in behind them, regularly switching places to avoid detection. They drove to Wilshire Boulevard, turned west, and as the procession cleared the Village, they headed south down the freeway towards the Marina Del Rey.

"CP, this is Red 1. There are two undercover's pacing us about three hundred yards behind."

Elwood went ballistic and grabbed a portable radio.

"9 King 90 to 9 units on the San Diego South. Back off now—or else!"

In a few moments, Red 1 was back on the line.

"10-4 CP. They just pulled off the freeway."

"God-damn cowboys!" Elwood was actually livid. "You'd think I had a bunch of rookies out there instead of seasoned detectives. I'm gonna kick some ass when this is over."

****

The Marina Freeway turned into a surface street about a mile from the Pacific Ocean. If the girls were going to continue on that route, Gibson realized that they would have to pass this particular choke point in order to get to Delaney.

Donahue had stopped their car next to a restaurant and across the street from the spot where the girls and the surveillance units would have to leave the freeway. She parked between cars where they could watch the intersection without being noticed.

From the progress report provided by Tippen, Gibson calculated that the surveillance was still five miles away. Whitney took advantage of the delay, excused himself, ran into the restaurant, and returned a short time later with coffees for everyone in the car.

A bulletin from Tippen let them know the surveillance had closed to within two miles.

Renée took a sip and looked longingly at her coffee before opening the back door and dumping it out.

"Is there something wrong with it?" Whitney asked.

"Actually, it was pretty good, but I'd rather not have to find a bathroom in the middle of the action."

After a moment's thought, both Gibson and Whitney poured their cups out as well.

Donahue turned around in the driver's seat, took a sip of her coffee, then smiled.

"No TB here."

"TB?" asked Whitney.

"Tiny bladder," Gibson replied.

He looked back over the seat at Whitney and Marin.

"My partner has a hollow leg."

Their laughter was interrupted by Donahue.

"They should be here in less than a minute," she said, and without thinking, Renée slouched down lower to avoid being seen. When she realized what she'd done, she smiled to herself and promptly sat back up.

Whitney noticed her *faux pas* and started to laugh which caused her to blush.

"I'm sorry," he told her, "but that was charmin'."

"I don't get to do this sort of thing very often," she said by way of an excuse. "It just sorta happened."

He laughed again.

"Renée," Gibson said, "you might find this interesting." He gestured towards the freeway. "Watch the off ramp. Some of the undercover units will arrive before the girls do. They'll take up positions in front of them in order to make switches and avoid detection."

As he spoke, a light blue Mercedes convertible sped down the freeway off ramp and abruptly turned into a nursery across from their position. The driver did not park the car, choosing instead to let it idle just out of view behind a hedgerow. Gibson pointed out four others that quickly pulled over and vanished into the background of everyday activity.

Marin was impressed. The advance party was substantial and very well organized. With that many units involved, it was highly unlikely the girls would ever realize they were under surveillance.

"There's the chopper," said Donahue, pointing to the north. Renée could just make out a speck which seemed to move very slowly in their direction. It was up high enough that there was no discernible sound.

Within seconds, the girls' vehicle showed up and came down the off ramp. Five more surveillance vehicles were spread out in various lanes behind it. Tracy turned on her blinker and drifted to the left, and Renée watched with fascination as three of the five vehicles moved over behind her to make the same turn.

As the girls drove by, Marin caught a glimpse of Anne Magruder in the passenger seat. Struck by how ordinary-looking the girl seemed to be, she felt a twinge of sympathy that one so young could have thrown away her life in just a single afternoon.

Within a few moments, the surveillance moved past them and disappeared from view. Renée experienced a let-down, as though she'd just witnessed the end of a Fourth of July parade.

Donahue started the engine but remained in the lot. It was now in the hands of the experts, and once again, all they could do was wait.

****

Tracy drove slowly down Mindanao Way while they searched for the *Mainsheet Restaurant.* They soon found it; a gray structure that was obviously in the middle of a major reconstruction. The roof had been removed from the northernmost section and there was evidence of recent framing towards the back. The parking lot was partially fenced off to prevent the theft of construction equipment, and a large mound of dirt, used to encase an underground sewage line, was piled unceremoniously in the middle of the driveway. The site overlooked several hundred luxury boats that were moored in the state's most prestigious marina.

Tracy drove around the mound of dirt and stopped almost directly in front of the restaurant. She kept the engine running while Anne got out on the passenger side.

"Stay here, Trace. I'll find him and be back in just a few minutes."

"Are you sure you don't want me to come with you?"

"I'm sure." When she noticed the skepticism on Tracy's face, she quickly added, "Really, it'll be okay."

She started to walk away from the car before having serious second thoughts about what she was doing. Turning back, she spoke to Tracy through the open passenger window.

"If I'm not back in about ten minutes, get away from here and call the police."

Tracy was flabbergasted.

"What are you talking about?"

"Please don't ask me to explain. If he decides to do something stupid, I don't want you to become involved."

She spun around and walked away. Resolved to get this over with, she rounded the corner of the restaurant and headed down a flight of steps towards the Marina walkway; a cement path that wound around the entire perimeter of the development and provided access to the docks that expanded like spines into a dozen separate channels.

On the walkway, Anne stopped and carefully looked around. There were boats moored as far as the eye could see. The area was a beehive of activity, as joggers, strollers and bicyclists moved up and down the pathway.

She half expected Liam to be standing there, but he was nowhere to be seen. He'd instructed her to wait for his call at a pay phone which she spotted behind the restaurant.

She walked over to it, stood in silence, and momentarily allowed herself to hope that he might not show up.

****

Back at the WLA station house, Elwood and Simmons noted the location on a large street map which was carefully laid out on the table. Both had done this before and both knew what to do.

Simmons had to make sure there were enough surveillance units to follow everyone if the two women separated. He ordered the rest of the Red teams into the neighborhood to establish a perimeter if one became necessary.

Elwood was concerned about the safety of other officers. Afraid that they might stumble in and prematurely set things off, he designated a parking lot—at the rear of a supermarket a mile away—to be a staging area. All of his detective units were ordered to meet there, including Gibson and Donahue, and as a final precaution, he notified headquarters to place a nearby SWAT team on standby.

Having planned for every contingency, Elwood then left the Command Post and went to his car. He had a good feeling about the way things were going and he wanted to get to the Marina as quickly as possible. As a commanding officer, he seldom got a chance to be in on an arrest, and it was times like these that made the job worthwhile.

As he drove from the station lot, he was lost in his own thoughts, so much so that he overlooked the Channel 2 News van that pulled out of the lot behind him.

****

Three men, carrying closed duffel bags, walked out onto a dock behind the Mainsheet Restaurant. Eighty feet from the shore, they randomly selected a forty-six-foot sailboat and climbed aboard. Unoccupied, the boat was berthed between two other yachts that were not being used.

One of the men produced a lock pick and carefully opened the hatch door. His companions disappeared below to stow the duffels while he remained on deck. He slowly unlaced the canvas mast cover as a prelude to their heading out for a sail.

Within moments, they'd assumed the role of recreational sailors, indistinguishable from hundreds of others who came to the marina to use their own boats. But they had no intention of taking the boat out. One focused his attention exclusively on Anne while his companions watched the other nearby boats. Having brought aboard sniper rifles—which were immediately stowed below the deck—they were the close quarters contingent of Red Team, and they were there to provide cover for their people on the shore.

While Anne waited by the phone, a female approached on a ten-speed bicycle. Within her helmet was a microphone and earphone, and in her waist pack, she carried a badge and a small Beretta handgun.

She stopped twenty yards from Anne and popped the front wheel off her bike. Squatting down, she laid out a few small tools and began to make adjustments to the frame.

Although she regularly qualified for bonus pay based upon her marksmanship, her most valuable skill was her ability to read lips. Red 6 was there to intercept whatever she could and to transmit the details to other members of the team.

Red 7, a balding, stocky detective with twenty-six years on the job, was dressed in light blue Bermuda shorts and an oversized Madras shirt. He wore it pulled out of his pants to conceal his body armor. In a waistband holster, hidden above his groin, he kept a 9 mm handgun, and in his back pants pocket was a lead-filled sap, just in case it was needed for close-in fighting. His short yellow socks and black laced shoes were an embarrassment to anyone with any sense of fashion, but it allowed him to pass as a typical tourist, free to move about without unwarranted attention. An oversized straw hat, one favored by lifeguards, concealed his two-way radio, while his dark sunglasses concealed the movement of his eyes.

A camera was strapped around his neck, and as he meandered from the north towards Anne's position, he stopped along the way to take pictures of the harbor. He moved to within thirty feet of where she was standing to cover the approach behind Red 6.

****

The phone rang once and it made her jump. It rang a second time before she mustered up enough courage to grab the receiver.

Liam spoke softly, without any trace of rancor. The connection was fuzzy, and it gave her the impression he had called from a cell phone.

"Were you followed?" he asked.

"No."

His question was disturbing. She'd been so preoccupied with getting her purse back that she hadn't paid any attention to what was going on around her. She glanced around the marina, and for the first time, she noticed the woman who was working nearby on a bicycle.

"I'm alone," she said into the phone.

"So why'd you want to see me, Luv?" he asked.

She fought hard to keep the fear from her voice.

"I told you, Liam. I want my purse back."

"Is that the only reason?"

What did he mean?

She watched the cyclist work while she tried to determine what Liam was insinuating. Did he think she was setting him up?

"There's no other reason," she said evenly. "I just need my things."

His silence was unnerving.

"Are you still there?" she asked.

He laughed, and when he spoke, there was an edge to his tone.

"And here I was thinkin' you came back for another lay."

For a moment she thought she'd be sick.

"I don't have time for that right now," she stammered. "I had my roommate drive me down here and we have to get back right away."

The silence seemed interminable.

Was he still on the line?

"Maybe... a... maybe I should come back tomorrow evenin'?" she said, deciding she'd made a mistake.

"You know I'm leavin' this evenin', Annie. It's gonna be now or never."

This wasn't worth it. She knew what he wanted, and the thought of his touch was unbearable.

"Liam, Please! I'm runnin' out of time. I've got to get back to school."

He laughed again.

"Give us a smile, now, Annie. I'm watchin' you."

She shuddered, swallowed hard, looked frantically about.

"Where are you, Liam?"

She fought the urge to run.

"When I tell you to move, walk once around the buildin'. Come back to the phone and wait for my signal. Don't do anythin' stupid, or I won't be very forgivin'."

"I don't understand, Liam? Why should I walk around the buildin'?"

"I want to be sure you're alone, Annie. Now be a good lass and just do it."

He abruptly broke off the connection.

****

"Why... should... I... walk... around the building...," whispered Red 6 who was reading Anne's lips.

There was a pause while Anne continued listening to the phone, and when Red 6 spoke again, it was to advise the team leader that the connection had been broken.

"Copy, Six," replied Red Leader. He was seated in a car about half a block away and there were precious few moments to consider his options.

"All Red units, hold your positions. I think she's being watched. He's looking for surveillance."

The teams remained stationary while Anne disappeared around the corner.

"Keep your eyes open Six and Seven," said Red Leader. *"Target may show himself when she comes back around the building. Six, stay by the phone---he may call her back."*

Seven noticed a man step out from between two cars in a nearby parking lot. The man looked cautiously around before moving with purpose towards the Mainsheet Restaurant.

"This is Seven. I think I see Target on the walkway---just south of my 10-20 (position). He's wearing a white T-shirt and bluejeans---and he's carrying something in his right hand."

Red Leader thought quickly. If this guy was the wrong man, the investigation would be blown, but he couldn't let him get too close to the girl.

"Red Team," he whispered, *"wait until she comes back around the corner. If she recognizes him, we take the Target down. Six and Seven, you're closest. Seven will call it. Eight and Four, take down Roomie. Five and Two, take Lover. Seven has the call."*

At the staging area more than a mile away, the units all started their engines in unison. No one wanted to be far from the action. Donahue pulled out silently and headed towards the restaurant at high speed. The others fell in close behind.

The Target approached Red Six from behind. She sensed his nearness and carefully drew her weapon from the waist pack, concealing it from his view.

Red Seven approached the man inconspicuously from a flanking position.

"He's looking up towards Lover's location," he whispered into his microphone as he kept moving closer.

Anne appeared from around the corner. She spotted Liam and stopped in her tracks.

"It's our boy," said Seven. *"He's headed right to her—he's got a shirt covering something in his hand—Take him, Six..."*

Six stood up, spun around and extended her weapon.

"Police!" she yelled. "Don't move!"

Seven ran full speed and tried to pull his gun but somehow it got caught in his waistband. He cursed to himself and kept running towards the target.

Liam brought up his arm. His hand was still concealed under a shirt.

Six fired. The shot tore into Liams' arm. The gun, which he'd been carrying under the shirt which covered his hand, was sent skidding across the pavement.

Liam doubled over but remained on his feet. He grabbed his mangled arm and looked wildly around for his gun. Six was ready to fire again, but she had to hold up when Seven, who had reached him, used his sap on the side of Liam's head.

Liam crumpled to his knees and then pitched forward, face down.

"Shots fired! Suspect down," Six said into her transmitter. *"Roll paramedics to our 10-20."*

Anne began to scream.

Red Five grabbed her from behind and threw her violently to the ground. With a knee against her spine, he wrenched her arms behind her back and forced her hands into a set of cuffs.

She screamed again.

"Shut up," he snarled. He pushed her down harder. "You're under arrest."

****

At gunpoint, Red Eight pulled a shocked and frightened Tracy Prescott out of her car. She didn't resist, but she was clearly in shock and completely confused.

She was quickly cuffed, then frog-marched by Red Eight and Red Four to the back of their van where she was deposited unceremoniously into the back to await the stabilization of the situation.

As sirens approached from the ground, Air 16 swooped in and circled fifty feet above the scene, providing eyes in the sky for a fluid situation.

Red Team Leader, now short of breath from running from his car, sucked wind for a few moments before shouting out to be heard above the noise of the circling helicopter.

"Everyone okay?"

He received a "thumbs up" from Six while she snapped the handcuffs shut around the unconscious Target's wrists.

"*This is Team Leader,*" he yelled into the transmitter. "*Code 4--- all units. This location's secure. All three suspects are now in custody.*"

It wouldn't stop most of the units already en route, but at least they'd arrive without their guns drawn.

When Gibson and the others pulled up, they found Red Seven on his knees. He was using a towel to staunch the bleeding from Target's right arm. He looked up at Gibson and shrugged.

"He's still breathing, but I may have whacked him on the head just a bit too hard."

"Roll him over," Gibson ordered. "We need to have a look."

Seven rolled him over. He was a young Caucasian with short brown hair and a day's worth of stubble. His eyes fluttered briefly then closed.

"Does he look familiar, Major?" Gibson asked.

"As a matter of fact, he does." Whitney bent over to get a better look. "This might be a bloke named Liam Cassidy. I can't be sure, but get me a set of his prints and I'll know within the hour."

Gibson stepped back. "Jen, put Magruder in our car. We'll take her back to the station." He turned back to Whitney.

"Can you get us some info about his associates?"

Whitney nodded.

"He's got quite a past, so I'm sure there's a file on him. I'll put in a request as soon as we get back to your office."

"Do you want me to stay here?" Renée asked Gibson.

"If you don't mind? When the Captain gets here, he'll set up a grid search, and if they find anything, he may need you to get a search warrant."

Renée nodded.

"If she decides to roll on her partner, get what you can, but don't make any promises. We need to know a lot more about her involvement in this before we consider the possibility of cutting a deal."

"Don't worry," he chided. "I'll do everything by the book." He turned back to Whitney. "I'd like you to stay with me, Major. If she agrees to talk, I may need your help with the questioning."

"I wouldn't miss this for the world," Whitney said.

At that moment, Elwood walked up. He was fuming.

"I'm sorry, Gibby. A news van followed me from the station." His hands were shaking with anger. "I never even saw the bastards behind me until they tried to keep up when I flipped on the reds." He looked back over his shoulder. "I swear to God; I'll get their press passes pulled when we get back to the station."

"Where are they now?" Gibson asked.

"A patrol team has them isolated on the other side of the restaurant. No way they're gonna get any film."

Gibson smiled.

"It looks like we got our boy, Tom. He was carrying a gun when SIS took him down. Once the scene is secured, we need to determine if he has a crash pad down here. He's still unconscious, and I don't know if he's gonna pull through, but we should send someone good to the hospital in case he wants to talk."

"I'll send Rick Jackson with him. He can make a turnip spill its life history." He looked around. "How's Magruder doing?"

"Jen's having her moved to our car. We'll talk to her on the way in."

"And the roommate?"

"I'll get someone to bring her down to the station separately. For the time being, she's not a high priority, but we'll talk to her after things start to settle down."

Elwood nodded. He looked down at Cassidy's inert form and gave Gibson a slap on the back.

"Great job! I'll be writing commendations for a week."

****

EIGHT

16 Days Later

September 29, Tuesday, Late Morning

The line of cars and trucks waiting to cross the border from Tijuana into the United States was formidable. Traffic was backed up for almost two miles. It was hot and dry, and tempers were short.

A white moving van, emblazoned with the logo *Catholic Relief Charities*, had waited in the line for almost an hour, but the driver was not overly concerned. He made this run regularly to deliver food and medical supplies to a clinic just south of a cardboard shanty town in the hills above the city of Tijuana, and he knew from experience to expect long delays.

His truck was empty, and Aurelio Sanchez looked forward to a smooth drive on the 405 Freeway back to Los Angeles. When he finally reached the checkpoint, the uniformed Border Patrol agent looked him over, then typed the number of his license plate into the computer.

"Can I see some ID?" the agent asked.

Sanchez pulled out his green card and a California driver's license. He handed them over and waited while the man slowly looked them over.

The agent looked up.

"Anything in the truck?"

"No, man. It's empty. I just delivered a load of medical supplies to the St. Francis Clinic."

"Open it up," said the agent. He stepped out of the booth and followed Sanchez to the back of the truck. When the door was opened, and he could see that the truck was empty, he walked back into his booth and checked the computer screen.

"You're clear to enter the United States," he said matter-of-factly. "Have a nice day."

Sanchez nodded and put the truck in gear.

Across the street from the checkpoint, in a fast food restaurant parking lot, two men sat in a blue Chevy Nova and watched the truck as it finally cleared customs.

"Glad that's over," said Devon McGarry. He quickly lowered his binoculars.

Jimmy Cassidy turned the engine over then slowly pulled out into traffic. He settled back in his seat and savored the moment. The van contained just under ninety pounds of Semtex, a Czechoslovakian plastic explosive. Unbeknownst to the driver, it was secreted in a compartment beneath the floorboards, directly under the driver's front seat.

"Are we gonna follow him all the way up to LA?" McGarry asked.

He was an Irishman from Dublin with long, dark hair, almost down to his shoulders. His black eyes and bronze skin came from his mother's Spanish heritage, but he considered himself an Irish Catholic through and through.

"Not necessary," Cassidy replied. He checked his rearview mirror to see if anyone was following. "We'll go on ahead to LA and meet the others. We can get the stuff later tonight."

"Pullin' up those floor panels will make a bit of noise," McGarry pointed out.

"You worry too much, Devon. I've got the keys to the place. You'll be able to take your time."

He gave McGarry a good natured punch on the shoulder before switching lanes to drive past the truck.

****

"Marcia, get in here!" yelled Carlson.

Tim Marcia, his adjutant, got up from his desk and went quickly into the Commander's office; a sterile, interior, windowless room on the ninth floor of the Police Administration Building. Marcia was tall and filled out, maybe ten pounds overweight, but able to take care of himself. His brown hair was thinning, but parted and neat, and he sported a small, bushy mustache that was the focal point for his strong, well-tanned face. He'd given up smoking years ago, but had taken up the disgusting habit of chewing tobacco, and he could often be seen carrying around an empty plastic water bottle to use as a portable spittoon.

"What's up, boss?" he asked.

"I want you to call Tom Elwood for me at RHD. Confirm the time for Cassidy's arraignment tomorrow, and find out any details you can. Then put together a draft of a press release for me. I want to get it out by two p.m. this afternoon."

"I'll see to it right away."

Marcia turned to go back to his office, but after a moment's hesitation, he spun back around.

"By the way, sir, a reporter from an English newspaper just showed up with a request for a press pass. She says she's with *The Guardian*."

He paused momentarily.

"You might want to handle this one personally."

Carlson looked up from his paperwork to see Marcia smiling broadly while holding up ten fingers.

He took the hint.

"By all means, Tim, send her right in."

Moments later, an attractive, young female entered the Commander's office.

He stood up and came around his desk.

"Please come in, Ms...?"

"Collins, Lisa Collins," she said, extending her hand.

Carlson reached for her hand and gave her an appraising look. Her high cheekbones and creamy white skin contrasted dramatically with her dark black hair which was tied back in a thick French braid. There was a smattering of freckles across the bridge of her nose, and her blue-gray eyes locked on his while a broad, friendly smile spread over her face.

"It's a pleasure to meet you," he said. "Please have a seat."

He gestured to a nearby chair.

She sat down carefully and slowly crossed her long, slender legs. Carlson placed himself in a chair in front of his desk, one that directly faced hers.

"Well, Ms. Collins, do you have your request form filled out?"

"I do, Commander."

Her eyes twinkled when she handed him the form.

He glanced over the paperwork and located what he wanted to know; age twenty-seven, and single.

He looked up and caught her eye.

"It seems to be in order."

"I also have a letter of introduction from my employer."

She reached into her handbag and produced a letter which had been prepared on the official stationery of *The Guardian*.

Carlson looked it over and noticed it was signed by Llewlyn Crewe, her Editor-in-Chief.

He reached over to his intercom and summoned Tim Marcia back into the office.

When Marcia arrived, he said, "Sergeant, please contact the The Guardian and confirm Ms. Collins credentials."

He handed him the letter of introduction.

"Yes, sir," replied Marcia with a smile, and he quickly left the office.

Collins shifted in her chair.

"Tell me, Commander, are you this thorough with everyone who seeks a press pass?"

The question caught him by surprise.

"Actually, Ms. Collins, I am. It's nothing personal. It's just that in this day and age, it's important to double-check everything."

"It's Lisa, Commander."

She flashed him another bright smile.

He smiled back, unable to resist the urge to stare.

"Are you going to be in Los Angeles for any length of time?" he asked.

"I'm not sure. I've been assigned to cover the Cassidy case, but if it gets stretched out, I may have to go back to England during the intervals."

She re-crossed her legs, and Carlson's eyes followed the movement.

"Have you been to our city before, Miss Collins?"

"No, I haven't, Commander, but I'm lookin' forward to bein' here. There's so much to see and experience."

Carlson resisted a grin.

"In that case, perhaps you'll allow me to show you some of the sights."

"Perhaps," she responded, "but only after I get some of my background work done."

"I can help you with that, too," he offered.

"That would be very nice. Thank you. Can we start while we wait for your Sergeant to check me out?"

Carlson nodded.

"I don't see why not?"

She pulled a small notebook and pen from her purse.

"I need to know what's going on behind the scenes. It's so different here from what we're used to in London." Her eyes widened. "For example, when he goes to court tomorrow, will he be there all day or will it only take a few minutes?"

She paused and smiled.

"You see, Commander, I don't know your system, and I have to post a story every two days."

Carlson shifted in his seat and smiled. Her legs were driving him crazy.

"Perhaps the best way to get you up to speed, Lisa, would be for me to tell you about—"

****

Tim Marcia dialed the international operator, and after reading off the phone number from the letter of introduction, he waited patiently for the call to go through. The phone rang three times before it was answered by a very young sounding female whose perky voice sounded almost too cheerful.

"The Manchester," she said.

"Yes, hello. I'd like to speak to Mr. Llewlyn Crewe?"

"I'm sorry, sir. Mr. Crewe has left for the day. Is there anyone else who can help you?"

Marcia checked his watch.

Of course, he thought. *It's eight hours later in London. That would make it almost 7:00 p.m.*

He considered his options.

"Perhaps you can help me. I need to speak to someone who can confirm that you have a reporter on your staff named Lisa Collins."

"I'm sorry, sir," the woman replied, "Miss Collins is on a special assignment in Los Angeles. Is there anyone else I can ring for you?"

What a moron, he thought, but at least she confirmed that Collins was employed there.

"No, that won't be necessary. Thank you anyway."

****

He'd been talking for ten minutes and was now almost through.

"—and tomorrow morning, if the doctors say he's medically fit, he'll be driven from the jail in a small van." Carlson leaned forward in his chair. "We'll be keeping him separated from all of the other inmates in order to protect him."

Lisa raised her eyebrows and when Carlson noted her surprise, he said, "Since he's not connected with any of our prison gangs, he could end up being a target. The press attention will make him a celebrity, so some of the inmates might try to kill him just to make a name for themselves."

To him, Lisa appeared fascinated by his narrative.

"I had no idea," she told him. "This is really quite interesting."

"Anyway, we refer to his handling as 'special transportation.' He'll be driven to the basement of the courthouse directly from the county jail. From there, he'll be housed in a one-man holding cell in a specially designed unit on the floor below the courtroom. When it's time for him to be arraigned, he'll be taken from his cell and brought in to see the judge. It shouldn't take very long at all, maybe a couple of minutes. They'll set a date for a preliminary hearing, and after that, he'll be taken back to the jail."

"Doesn't sound like much of a story," she said. "Is there any chance to get a picture of him when they take him into court?"

"Not really. Cameras in the courtroom are within the discretion of the judge. You'd have to get the court's permission for something like that."

"I see. Will security be increased when you bring him to the courthouse? In England, it's customary to use special escorts when they transport the Provos."

"Oh, no," he said with a laugh. "We won't need anything like that. Our situation here is entirely different. He doesn't have a support group here in the

States."

"How about security within the courtroom?" she asked.

"There will be a number of deputies, due to the fact of press interest, and we'll set up a metal detector at the courtroom door, but I'm afraid there will be nothing more interesting than that."

His intercom buzzed and he picked up the phone. He listened briefly, then replaced the receiver in the cradle.

"Sergeant Marcia has confirmed your credentials. I'll be happy to issue your pass."

He signed her application form, hoping he hadn't given her too much information. What he really wanted most of all was to take her out to lunch. He pulled out a press pass from a sequentially numbered stack and handed it over to her.

"Thank you, Commander."

She flashed him a not-so-innocent smile.

"Can I buy you lunch?"

****

NINE

September 29, Tuesday, Early Afternoon

From her corner office on the seventeenth floor of the Criminal Courts building, Renée Marin enjoyed a panoramic view of the southeastern portion of the city of Los Angeles. In fact, on a clear day, she could see all the way to the Port of Long Beach, nearly twenty miles away.

Her office furnishings, euphemistically described as *governmental chic*, left a lot to be desired. She had a standard metal desk and a tilt-back leather chair. Having reached the level of Head Deputy, she was also provided with a long metal table, a credenza, and several straight-back, fabric-covered chairs. She'd added a few personal items to give the place a measure of warmth; plants, photographs, and a brown Turkish rug. It would never look elegant, but at least it was cozy.

She leaned back in her chair and closed her eyes for a moment to gather her thoughts. In the two weeks since the arrests of Cassidy and Magruder, she'd worked non-stop to get the case ready for the preliminary hearing. She'd talked to all the witnesses for untold hours, and now she finally felt confident that she had a handle on the case. There were going to be problems, there always were, but she had more than a couple of options. And as she mulled them over in her mind, her intercom buzzed and dragged her back to the present.

"Detective Gibson to see you, Ms. Marin," said the voice.

"Send him in," she replied.

Moments later, Gibson stuck his head in the door.

"Good afternoon, Counselor. How're you doing?"

"I'm fine, Gibby. Make yourself at home."

Gibson put down his briefcase, took off his coat, hung it on a nearby coat rack, and settled into a chair. He wore an old-fashioned pair of suspenders to hold up his pants, and a *Galco* shoulder holster that cradled his *Sig Sauer* handgun beneath his left arm.

He gave her a genuine smile.

"So, is your meeting with the DA still on?"

"So far as I know. He just got back from his vacation, so if nothing major comes along to bump me out, I'm scheduled to see him at two."

"You got everything ready?"

She pointed to the table behind her.

"Six notebooks full of statements, reports and case law. I even drafted a twenty-page summary."

She handed him a copy.

"I'll be giving an analysis to my boss later today," he said as he scanned the first few pages of her report. "You planning to read all of this to the DA?"

She laughed.

"Last I heard, the man could read just fine all by himself. This will give him something to work with later if he needs to talk to the press."

Gibson rolled his eyes.

"He's a politician, Gibby. He's gonna do what he can to catch the limelight."

"There's no better way to screw things up then saying anything to the press," he said, sagely.

"Don't worry about him. He won't say anything stupid. Our distinguished Chief Deputy won't let him."

"I hope you're right, Renée, but I just don't trust the guy. He might shoot off his mouth before we have all our ducks in order."

"You're too cynical, Gibby."

"Maybe so."

He cocked his head.

"So, have you decided what you're going to do with Anne Magruder?"

"I've given it a lot of thought. I'm going to recommend that we give her immunity in exchange for her testimony."

Gibson shook his head.

"Why do you guys always go that route?"

"*You guys*?" she said. "Is there something you want to tell me?"

Gibson recalled a case that he and Donahue had handled with the Office of the Attorney General. A senior prosecutor in the LA office had been charged with the murder of his girlfriend's husband, and a grant of immunity for the girlfriend had left a bad taste in his mouth.

"I just don't think you should be so quick to let her off the hook," he replied.

"There's no way to convict her on what we have, Gibby. I've got no proof that she knew what was going on."

"Things might get better. We've got a long way to go before trial."

"But the preliminary hearing is just around the corner. Our case against Cassidy is circumstantial and Magruder is the only one who can ID him from the crime scene."

Gibson leaned back in his chair.

"I know it's an uphill battle, but we've still got a little time. If you give her immunity now, and we find out later she was a willing participant, then it will be too late to make amends, not to mention how stupid we'll look."

Renée held his glance.

"You've been working the case for almost two weeks. Have you found a shred of evidence that implicates her in the crime?"

"She was in the car when it happened."

"And she was screaming like a banshee. *Remember?*" She took a deep breath and slowly let it out. "Does that sound like the actions of a willing accomplice to you?"

She knew she had him. Gibson was a common sense guy. He knew any case against her, at this point, would never get past any rational judge, but he had to press forward with the party line, the 'charge 'em all' mentality of the LAPD brass, and she respected him for doing his job.

She said, "I know I'm not going to convince you I'm right, but you need to trust my judgment on this."

Gibson shrugged. He didn't like it, but he wasn't a lawyer and therefore not equipped to protest with any authority.

"So, what if she refuses to cooperate?"

She smiled.

"She won't. Once I finish talking to her attorney, she'll testify. No one in their right mind would turn down a grant of immunity."

Gibson folded his arms.

"I hope you know what you're doing." Still thinking about the other case, he told her, "I've seen this backfire before."

"Thanks for the vote of confidence."

"It's just that immunity leaves us no options, Renée. If you're gonna cut her a deal, we should make her plead to something, even if it's just as an accessory. You can ask the court to put her on probation. That way, we have prison hanging over her head if she decides to piss backward on the stand."

"Won't work," she told him. "No defense attorney in his right mind would ever go for that. I'm afraid we've got no choice."

"You're the boss," he said, "but I just hope this doesn't come back to bite us on the ass."

She smiled.

"Well, if it does, it's gonna be my ass that gets nibbled, not yours."

****

She arrived at the District Attorney's outer office just before two. His executive secretary met her at the doorway and asked her to have a seat in the waiting room until District Attorney Aaron Rosen, was ready to meet.

Zane Savant, the former District Attorney for Los Angeles County, had lost the previous election as a result of the outcome of a murder case against one of his high-ranking prosecutors.

Gibson and Donahue had been part of that case, and Rosen—himself a senior administrator at that time—had taken advantage of the fallout from the way the case was handled, and it had paid off for him in spades. He won the election by a landslide, but he quickly proved to be cut from the very same mold as his predecessor.

Renée smiled to herself, as Rodger Daltry's memorable lyrics quickly came to mind.

Meet the new boss, same as the old boss.

Consequently, she had prepared for her meeting with him with the foreknowledge that his analysis of her case would be sifted by him through the court of public opinion.

Under Rosen, the current administration had one single saving grace. Glenn Kerin had been appointed by Rosen to be his Chief Deputy. It was the smartest decision that Rosen ever made, for Kerin turned out to be the voice of reason; a natural administrator with common sense, and on more than one occasion, his wise counsel had prevailed over Rosen's dimwitted approach to handling the offices' affairs.

Kerin entered the outer office from a locked side door that connected with his own luxurious suite. Tall and slim, with chiseled features and the physique of a long distance runner, his daily regimen usually included walking up the courthouse stairs each morning to his office on the eighteenth floor. The graying of his sandy blond hair was the only hint that he was now close to middle age. His deep blue eyes, intense and alert, quickly found Renée Marin seated on a couch.

She stood up to greet him and he gave her a gentlemanly hug.

"It's good to see you, Renée. How've you been?"

"I'm doing fine, Glenn. Thanks for asking."

"Good. Let's go in."

She followed Kerin into Aaron Rosen's office. It was far more extravagant than any of Rosen's predecessors. A decorator had chosen colonial pieces offset by artifacts from the American Southwest. It resembled a museum, and visitors, like Renée, were suitably impressed.

Once everyone was seated, Marin wasted no time as she launched into the details surrounding the case.

At first, Rosen took notes, but he soon put his pen down and listened. He was fully caught up in the story she told, and his piercing gray eyes never left her face.

When she was finished, Rosen leaned back in his chair.

"Quite fascinating, Renée, but let me ask you some questions."

Big boned and overweight, he concealed this human frailty with well-tailored clothing. Without a jacket on, his collar open and his shirt sleeves rolled up, he looked every bit the part of a hands-on administrator. His mane of silver hair, worn by preference straight back, lent an air of sophistication to his look. But his most arresting quality, a gravelly voice, was used to his advantage when he dealt with the press.

"Did this young woman, Anne Magruder, make a statement after her arrest?"

"No, she didn't, Aaron. She invoked her right to counsel."

"How about after she invoked? Did she say anything off the record?"

"No. The detectives told me she cried all the way to the station after her arrest, but she wouldn't say a word without a lawyer."

Rosen frowned.

"What about her roommate? Did she talk?"

"They couldn't shut her up, but she didn't know a thing."

She looked over at Kerin, then back again at Rosen.

"One other thing you should know, Aaron." She held up an intelligence report. "Anne Magruder is the daughter of an IRA leader named John Magruder."

Kerin frowned.

"That's an unusual complication."

Rosen rolled his eyes. "A classic understatement, Glenn." He stood up and began pacing. "Let's concentrate on the male for a moment. Did the gun they picked up at the time of his arrest match the bullets taken from the victims?"

"No," Renée told him. "Ballistics says the murders were done with a different gun."

Rosen shook his head in frustration.

"Did you find out where he was staying in the Marina?"

"No, and a search of Magruders' dorm room produced the clothing she wore at the time of the shooting, but nothing belonging to Cassidy."

Kerin leaned forward in his chair.

"Did anyone from the shooting scene identify the suspects?"

"So far, no one's been able to make an ID from the pictures, and we can't put Cassidy into a lineup until his wounds heal. We did get an ID from a citizen who saw the car switch, and there's a second one from the car rental clerk, but that's it."

The silence in the room was pronounced. Both Rosen and Kerin looked at Renée.

"I don't suppose this Cassidy fellow ever confessed?" Rosen asked.

"That's correct," she answered evenly.

"Then unless I'm missing something, this is a very fragile case against Cassidy and a virtually non-existent one against Magruder. Am I still on the right track?"

"Your assessment is accurate."

Renée was surprised. She hadn't considered him to be that astute. She added, "However, I think the case against Cassidy is still pretty good. We have motive, and we have an eyewitness who puts him at the car switch, and..."

"What motive?" Kerin asked.

"Major Whitney advised us that Cassidy's cousin was a young woman named Mairead Devenny. She was killed with three other Provos by the British SAS when they attempted to blow up the Prime Minister's residence. Our victim, Sean Clarke, was in charge of the unit that killed them."

Rosen digested that piece of information before turning to Kerin.

"What do you think, Glenn? Do we have enough to proceed against Cassidy?"

Kerin settled back and crossed his arms.

"I think we can make it, but I'd feel a lot better if the girl was going to testify against him."

Renée was relieved. Kerin had seen it the same way that she did. She suppressed the urge to smile.

"Any chance of that happening?" Rosen asked.

"She's retained Barrett McCrossen to handle her defense, and I'm meeting with him later today. Nothing's been said so far, but I can see if he's interested?"

"I'd rather we didn't give her immunity," Rosen said. "Let's see if we can get her to take a fall as an accessory."

"I can try, Aaron, but her attorney already knows we've got nothing. I doubt that he'll plead her to anything."

A pained look moved across Rosen's face. He glanced briefly over at Kerin and then back at Renée.

"When's your next court date?" he asked her.

"The arraignment for both of them is set for tomorrow. Up until now, Cassidy's been a medical no-show. The doctors are saying he'll be there tomorrow, so if we don't have any glitches, the preliminary hearing will go within the next ten days."

"Can we delay it?" Rosen asked.

"I can ask, but if they insist on proceeding, we have to go within the ten days or face a dismissal."

"I understand the law, Renée." His face showed his irritation. "What I want to ascertain is whether or not the defense will go along with a continuance while we complete our investigation?"

Renée was puzzled.

"For all intents and purposes, Aaron, the investigation is basically complete. We have a little follow up to do, but I doubt that the outcome is going to change."

"Try to buy us some time," he said, "I don't want to be pushed into giving her immunity prematurely."

She suddenly realized that the most recent office rumors were likely right. Rosen was not satisfied with being just the DA. He had higher political aspirations, perhaps Attorney General or even the Governorship, and if that were the case, it wouldn't help his political position to look as if he was soft on crime.

She pursed her lips as she realized that he'd learned a thing or two from his predecessor's political mistake, something she failed to anticipate before going into this meeting.

"And if I can't get them to put it over?" she asked.

"Do your best," he snapped.

Kerin leaned back in his chair.

"Aaron, it's in our best interests to put on the preliminary as soon as possible. We have a critical civilian witness who may get cold feet and decide to stop cooperating. We should do this fast and get his testimony under oath."

"Do you know how bad this looks if we give immunity to the daughter of an IRA leader?"

"But Aaron—" Renée began.

Kerin silenced her with a look and took the middle ground.

"I'll tell you what, Aaron. Let's see what happens during Renée's meeting with McCrossen. If he agrees to put it over, then we'll have a little time. If not, then we'll try to get her to plead out as an accessory."

He shifted his gaze to Renée. "You come to me if McCrossen demands immunity." He then looked back over at Rosen.

"I'm sure we can find a spin to put on it if we have to go that far."

Rosen seemed to acquiesce, more out of frustration than agreement. He waved his arm at Renée to signify the meeting was over.

She gathered up her files and headed for the door with Kerin right behind her.

"I'm sorry you were subjected to that," he said when they were alone in the outer hallway. "He often thinks out loud without using his brain."

"I hear he wants to run for Governor?" she asked.

Kerin's eyes narrowed.

"Where'd you hear that?

"Office gossip."

Kerin sighed.

"I don't know what his plans are, but once he thinks this through, I'm sure he'll see that you're doing the prudent thing."

Renée smiled without meaning it.

"I'm sure you're right, Glenn, but I feel very uncomfortable playing politics with a case."

"You won't have to. I promise."

She searched his eyes. Did he really see it her way?

"Okay," she finally said. "I'll let you know what's going on once I've spoken to McCrossen."

****

Gibson and Whitney looked up as Marin walked in. She moved over to her desk and slammed her files down.

"What a jerk!" she said.

Gibson studied her for a moment.

"What happened?"

"In a nutshell, he wants the preliminary hearing to be delayed to give you more time to investigate Anne Magruder's involvement." She shook her head.

"He wants her to plead to being an accessory."

Gibson started to open his mouth to speak, but Renée silenced him with a glare.

"Don't you dare say it, Gibson. This isn't a decision based on evidence. He's planning to run for higher office, so he doesn't want to appear to be soft on crime."

"I don't get it?" Whitney said. "Why put the hearing over?"

Gibson frowned. "Politics, Major. He doesn't want to look like a liberal to potential voters." He turned back to Renée. "Did you bring up the question of immunity?"

She nodded.

"Kerin left the door open, but it's obviously not Rosen's first choice."

She sat down unceremoniously in her chair; took a deep breath, and tried to relax. There was still a lot to do before her meeting with McCrossen.

"What's the plan for tomorrow, Gibby?" she asked. "Are you going to bring them over or will the Sheriffs do it?"

"I've ordered special handling for both of them. Cassidy will get here in a van about ten."

"What about Magruder?"

"She's in isolation over at the woman's jail. She'll come over about the same time in a different van."

"Make sure they don't run into each other downstairs. If she agrees to testify, I don't want her to see him on the way into court."

"That reminds me, Renée." Gibson leaned forward. "We've had dozens of inquiries from TV and the newspapers. We even have reporters from Britain and Japan. It's gonna be hectic around here."

"You think we need to beef up security?" she asked.

"It might not be a bad idea," Whitney told them. "I spoke with London this mornin'. There's no indication of a threat, but it's always better to play it safe. You never really know what these Provo splinter groups will try to do."

She made arrangements on the phone for additional deputies to be in the hallways and the courtroom, and after she had hung up the phone, a thought crossed her mind.

"Major, would you mind going downstairs and filling in the Sheriff's Watch Commander on what to look for? Their experience with terrorists is minimal."

"Of course. Do you want me to go now?"

"You might as well. Gibby and I can handle McCrossen. Just go to the third floor, Division 30, and ask for the Lieutenant-in-charge."

When Whitney left the room, Gibson said, "What time is McCrossen due to arrive?"

"In about twenty minutes."

"Do you know much about the guy? I've never heard of him."

Renée played with a pencil on the desk.

"It would surprise me if you had. He handles mostly civil cases, but he's been known to do criminal if the publicity's right."

"Oh, one of those?"

"He's not so bad. He used education and sports to escape from the projects. In fact, if I'm not mistaken, I think he played football at Notre Dame."

"I'm impressed," Gibson said.

"He married into money, made all the right connections, and set up his own private practice. He's a heavyweight in the field of entertainment law."

"But is he any good at defense work?"

"What difference does that make? With you by my side, we'll kick his ass."

Their laughter was interrupted by the buzz of the intercom.

"Mr. McCrossen is here to see you, Mrs. Marin. He's waiting outside at the front desk. Should I have someone bring him in?"

"Please do, Myrna," Renée said.

She removed the case summary from the top of her desk and slid it into a drawer. No reason to let the opposition see her personal notes.

"By the way, Gibby. Be careful what you say. Don't volunteer any information."

Gibson smiled.

"On advice of counsel, I refuse to say a word."

****

Liam Cassidy sat on the steel cot in his isolation cell and reflected on his current situation.

After his arrest, he was confined to the Jail Ward at the County General Hospital. Although chained to his bed, he was at least afforded the luxury of a television while he recuperated from his wounds. But this morning, he'd been moved to the Los Angeles County Jail in preparation for his arraignment, and his current cell setup, which was devoid of even the slightest of amenities, meant there was nothing to do but sit and stare and count the minutes as they slowly dragged by.

He was housed in a section reserved exclusively for inmates who bore the designation "high power." Somewhat of a misnomer, for the inmates in this section were completely without power. It was a place to put those whose personal notoriety could get them killed in the general population.

The housing did not please Cassidy, for it made any chance to escape more difficult, and escape was now his foremost thought.

His arm and right shoulder were in constant pain, and both were encased in a cast. He refused his pain pills, preferring instead to be mentally alert to be able to probe for any weakness in the system. He was going to need the help of other inmates to plan an escape, but in his current situation, how would he ever make contact?

He shivered as he lay on his back in the bunk. Cold air pumped in through a vent in the ceiling, and the single thin blanket they gave him just wasn't enough to keep him warm. He stared without seeing, thinking that he would have one hell of a time just trying to make it through the day.

In hindsight, he'd been a fool to involve Anne Magruder in his plans. It was a miscalculation of enormous proportions. She'd led them right to him, and he hadn't seen it coming. How could he have been so stupid?

It was impossible to sleep; and *damn,* it was cold!

He stood up slowly and used his good hand to brace himself as he rolled off the bed. His cell was eight feet in length and not much to work with, but he'd have to start somewhere if he wanted to get back in shape.

He began to pace, slowly at first, then faster.

Suddenly, there was a loud snap as the lock slid back on his solid metal door. He spun around just as two large deputies appeared in the doorway.

"Turn around and place your good hand behind your back."

He did as he was told. The deputies entered his cell and slipped a chain around his waist. His good hand was then inserted into a cuff which, in turn, was attached to the chain. When he was secured, they spun him around.

"Where am I goin'?" he asked.

"Visitor," one of the deputies replied.

"Do you think you could loosen the cuff, mate? It's awfully tight."

One of the deputies pulled him close.

"Here's how it works, *mate*. When we leave this cell, you walk on the blue line that's painted on the floor. It leads directly to where you're going. We'll be right behind you. Don't talk on the way and don't stop unless I say to. Do you understand the drill?"

"What if I step off the line," he said smugly.

"Don't be a smartass," the deputy warned. "You like that pretty pink jump-suit you're wearing?"

"It's not me best color."

In spite of himself, the deputy laughed.

"That's too bad," he said, "because that color is used to designate an informant. You step off the line or get too close to the others, and *pow!* You're liable to find yourself dead."

"*Comprende mate*?" said the second deputy.

"You *fuckers!*" Cassidy said through clenched teeth.

"Yeah? Well, fuck you, too, Cassidy, and welcome to County Jail."

The first deputy shot him a menacing glare.

"You'll get no special privileges here. Just stay on the line and do as you're told."

Cassidy refused to break off his stare.

"You're a real hard case, aren't you, asshole?"

The deputy gave him a shove.

"Move out...*now*."

Cassidy walked out of his cell, followed the blue line, and moved through the corridor while he studied his surroundings. Only nine cells and each appeared soundproof. He'd get no assistance from anyone inside.

In the main corridor, the inmates moved freely, but they stepped to the side and faced the wall in silence as he walked on by. The looks they were able to give him were pure hatred, and all because of the fuckin' pink jumpsuit.

He arrived at a room for attorneys and their clients, and they placed him in a booth with a stool that was bolted to the floor. The room was divided in the middle by plexiglass, and a single round hole, two inches in diameter, allowed him to speak to the visitor. Because he was the only inmate in the room, they removed the cuff from his good hand as soon as he was seated.

"Just sit there and don't get up," the deputy told him. "If you get out of line, the visit is over."

The deputies walked away, and he sat in silence as a female came into the room. She took a seat across from him and gave him a nod.

"Mr. Cassidy," she said through the plexiglass hole. "I'm Allison Cooper, your Public Defender. How are you doing today?"

She was a reasonably attractive woman, well dressed, and wearing the kind of jewelry that indicated money. Her blond hair was permed with spiral curls—a bit too full to suit his taste—but her green eyes were bright and curious.

He smiled thinly. She might not be bad if he wanted a lay, but she was not what he wanted for the courtroom.

She studied his face and recognized all the signs.

"Something bothering you?" she asked.

He smiled at her brashness.

"When do I get a real lawyer?"

"You wouldn't know a real lawyer if one bit you on the ass." She leaned closer to the screen and let out a short, sharp laugh. "I'm all you're gonna get for the time being, Cassidy, so wipe that attitude off your face."

He shook his head, but maintained his grin. She seemed tough enough. Perhaps she knew what she was doing.

She stared at him over the top of her reading glasses.

"Love the pink jumpsuit. The bastards do like their fun."

She leaned forward and gave him a cursory once over. "I'd say you're okay —no signs of a beating. Does the arm hurt much?"

"We're not here to talk about me arm," he answered. "What's goin' to happen with me case?"

"You'll be going into court tomorrow. They'll read off the charges and you'll enter a plea." She leaned back in her chair. "I assume it will be not guilty?"

"Very perceptive, " he said coarsely. "What happens after that?"

"You'll get a preliminary hearing within ten days—or later if we choose to drag it out—and if the judge feels there's enough evidence to go to trial, you'll be told to appear in superior court for another arraignment."

Cassidy thought for a moment to consider what she said. "And if there's not enough evidence?"

She smiled thinly. "Don't concern yourself with that, Mr. Cassidy. They'll be more than enough evidence to hold you for trial."

Was she mocking him?

"Whose side are you on?" he demanded.

She stared at him briefly in silence.

"Let's talk realistically, okay? I'm not on your side. I'm just your attorney, and while I represent you, I'll do my job well. You're facing two counts of pre-meditated, first-degree murder, and in this state, that means lethal injection or life without parole. Now, you can face the reality of your situation, or we can sit here and play games and waste the twenty minutes I have to spend with you."

He shrugged. The bickering was getting him nowhere, so he decided to soften his stance.

"Whatever you say, Miss..?"

She flashed him a genuine smile.

"Cooper. Allison Cooper. Okay, Mr. Cassidy, let me start by telling you what I'm sure you'll feel is good news. I'm only representing you for the ar-raignment. The attorney assigned to handle your case, a Mr. Hugh King, is cur-rently on vacation, so until he gets back, you're stuck with me."

Cassidy nodded.

"First and foremost," she cautioned, "don't talk about your case with anyone. There are snitches everywhere, and they'll sell you out in a heartbeat. And don't say anything on the jail telephones; the Sheriffs listen in on a regular basis."

Cassidy smiled. She was full of surprises.

"I'll keep that in mind."

"Good! Now here's the routine. The Sheriffs will bring you to the courthouse tomorrow morning and—"

"How will they get me there?" he interrupted.

"What do you mean?"

"By bus? By car?"

She thought for a moment. "By bus. Actually, by van. You'll probably be driven alone for your own safety. Why do you ask?"

"What time will they take me?"

She studied him carefully.

"You're set for arraignment at ten and they'll get you to the courtroom sometime before that. Anything else you need to know?"

"What happens when I get there?"

"I thought you'd never ask," she said with a smile. "Once you arrive at the courthouse, they'll put you in a holding cell, and when the court is ready, you'll be brought in. The judge will read the charges, you'll say you're not guilty, and that will be that."

"How about bail?"

"Bail?" She almost laughed. "Are you naive? You're not entitled to bail in a capital case."

Her sarcasm was getting under his skin.

"Nevertheless, I want you to try for the bloody bail just the same."

"Fine, Mr. Cassidy. You can continue to ignore reality, but you can no longer waste my time. I'll ask for bail tomorrow, but you'll have about as much chance of getting it as you do of winning the lottery."

She started to get up, and strangely enough, he realized that he wanted her to stay. Not that he liked her—he didn't—but talking to anyone was better than facing the hours of isolation in his cell.

"Don't you want to discuss the case?" he asked.

"Not really," she said from over her shoulder. "You can do that with Mr. King. I know what I need for tomorrow."

She stepped behind her chair and prepared to leave.

"Wait, please," he said. "What about Annie? Will she be there?"

"Anne Magruder? Your codefendant? Yeah, she'll be there, but if I were you, I wouldn't get too attached to her. Based on what I saw in the police reports, I think it's a safe bet they'll cut her a deal to testify against you."

"She'll never talk," he blurted.

"Aren't we smug. Well, don't bet on it. Ever hear of immunity? Lots of true believers spill their guts when they get immunity."

He could feel his blood rising as he contemplated the unthinkable—he'd been so sure that she wouldn't—but what if she did? She could keep him in here forever.

"Ah, ha," said Cooper, "I can tell by your face that reality has finally sunk in."

"Fuck off!" he told her.

If he could've gotten through the glass, he would have killed her.

She knew what he was thinking, but she didn't really care. She simply gave him a smile and walked away.

****

Barrett McCrossen stepped through the threshold of Renée Marin's office and extended his hand.

Tall, with broad shoulders, and dressed in a well-tailored suit, his very presence in the room was bigger than life. His grip was firm and confident and his smile was engaging. Sophistication was the first word that came to mind.

His mustache and goatee, black with flecks of gray, was well trimmed and showcased his deep blue eyes that were the color of a mountain lake. His mouth seemed frozen in a permanent smile, one which only disappeared when he was pleading on behalf of a client.

"Ms. Marin, it's a pleasure to meet you."

"Mr. McCrossen."

His eyes twinkled.

"Call me Barrett, please."

She introduced him to Gibson.

"Please, have a seat, Barrett, and let's discuss your client."

"Ah, yes, my client."

He pulled up a chair and sat down.

"Do you have an offer in mind, Mr. McCrossen?" Gibson asked.

Renée flashed him a withering look.

McCrossen looked from one to the other, then smiled.

"You're very direct, Detective Gibson. The truth is, I've had a chance to review the discovery materials, and I'm here to inquire if the charges will be dismissed?"

Renée shifted uncomfortably in her chair. "There's no justification for a dismissal, Barrett. She was with him during the killings, and quite probably a willing accomplice."

His smile disappeared.

"I must respectfully disagree, Ms. Marin. Unless you have some information that I've not yet received, we both know you haven't got a case. Oh, you might be able to hold her to answer at a preliminary hearing, but you'll never get past a dismissal at trial. You've got no direct evidence of her involvement in the crimes."

She knew he was right on track; it was time to run a small bluff.

"I don't need direct evidence, Barrett. I can make her circumstantially. A dismissal at this point is out of the question."

McCrossen shrugged.

"I was afraid you'd take this stance." He looked from one to the other. "I must confess that I'm not surprised by your position. Given the political history of this office, I'm certain an outright dismissal would not be in the best interests of your boss."

"Now wait a minute—"

McCrossen raised his hands in a gesture of conciliation. His smile quickly returned.

"Forgive me, Ms. Marin. I didn't mean to imply that any decision of yours would be politically motivated. But I do know how business is conducted in this office, and disposal of high-profile cases like this one generally requires the concurrence of the District Attorney. It's Aaron Rosen's motivation that I'm finding to be suspect."

She tried to conceal her surprise. He was on the money again.

"Let's be frank with each other," he continued. "You can drag this out for a year or more, but we both know there won't be a conviction, so something else must be going on." He smiled at her thinly. "Are you holding out to get my client to testify against Mr. Cassidy?"

She tried to sound casual.

"Is that an offer?"

McCrossen frowned.

"I'm sorry to say it's completely out of the question. Her life would be over the moment she hit the stand."

"That doesn't leave us much room for discussion."

"I'm afraid it doesn't." He shrugged. "Do the right thing, Ms. Marin. Dismiss the charges now. There's nothing to be gained by having her stay in custody. It won't soften her up. She's never going to testify against him."

"Even for immunity?" she asked.

McCrossen rolled his eyes. "Not a chance."

Renée was at a crossroads. To comply with the mandate from Aaron Rosen, she had to buy some time. She tried to sound nonchalant.

"Will you be requesting a delayed start for the preliminary hearing?"

Her hope was that he would, but McCrossen quickly put the issue to rest.

"I see no reason for a delay. The sooner the clock starts running, the sooner she's out."

"Well, I'm sorry, Mr. McCrossen. I just can't dismiss the case."

"Since you're so intent on going to trial, Mrs. Marin, could you see your way to agreeing to bail for my client?"

She shook her head.

"That's would be impossible. It's a capital case."

"Well, then, I guess there's nothing more to be said. Thank you so much for your time."

McCrossen stood up, shook their hands, wished them a pleasant day, then started for the door. And then, almost as an afterthought, he turned around to face her.

"There's one more thing I'd like you to consider, Mrs. Marin. Anne Magruder's father is waiting outside by the elevators, and he has asked for an opportunity to speak with you directly. Would you consider meeting with him as a courtesy to me?"

Renée was stunned. *Was he kidding?* The chance to speak with a leader in the IRA was an opportunity she couldn't pass up.

She looked over to Gibson who also seemed surprised, and she could sense his unquestioned approval.

"Sure. Why not? As a favor to you, I'll speak with him."

"I appreciate that, Ms. Marin. If you'll excuse me for a moment, I'll go to the front hallway and bring him right back."

When he was gone, Gibson smiled.

"If I keep my big mouth shut, can I sit in on this?"

"Can you?" she asked, but she was smiling.

He gave her a wink, then asked, "How about Whitney? Should we get him up here?"

She reached for her phone.

"You're reading my mind."

*****

He was not what she expected.

For some unknown reason, she'd pictured John Magruder as being tall and thin with a full head of hair; an intellectual who'd be more comfortable with words than people; a man supremely confident with his own self-identity. But what stood before her now was a man she would describe as purely working class; with big hands and arms, thinning black hair, a full, meaty face, and an inherent sadness that was deeply etched into his flat, green eyes. Crammed into an out-of-style, poorly fitting suit, he was a man in distress and plainly ill at ease.

He extended his hand, and when she took it, she discovered that his palm was moist.

"Thank you for agreein' to see me," he said softly. He turned to greet Gibson, but when he learned he was a detective, he looked back to McCrossen for guidance.

"It's all right, John," McCrossen said. "He's the investigating officer on the case."

Renée gestured to Magruder to take a seat, and once he was settled, an uncomfortable silence fell over the room.

Magruder nervously cleared his throat before beginning to speak.

"Ms. Marin, me lawyer said you won't drop the charges unless me daughter testifies. I hoped I could tell you a bit about her so you'll be understandin' as to why she can't do what you ask."

"I'll hear you out, Mr. Magruder," she told him, knowing full well that she was about to listen to a father's plea for mercy, "but you must understand, it's unlikely to change my decision to prosecute."

Magruder seemed crushed, but he nodded his understanding as he tried to muster his thoughts and convert them into words.

"Anne's the first member of me family to ever get a chance for a university education." He smiled with pride. "She's a bright child, Ms. Marin, and because she's such a good student, she was given a chance to leave the violence in Belfast to go to school over here." A look of pain crossed his face. "I know you know all about me, but I pray you won't hold that against me daughter."

Not waiting for a response, he quickly went on.

"She met Liam Cassidy in Belfast. He was in the PIRA's, and he started usin' me daughter as a runner. Not only that, he seduced her." He clenched his fists, and a vein began to throb near his temple. "I found out about it," he said evenly, "and I paid him a visit. He had no right to bring her into the war, and no right to use her like he did. I... I had him beaten, and as a warnin', I told him I'd kill him if he ever saw her again."

Renée found herself caught up in his story. He was clearly a man who was about to share the blame for his daughter's situation, and as a parent herself, she could identify, to some extent, with what he was going through.

She began to feel a sense of sorrow for his plight.

He cleared his throat.

"Yesterday, I talked with her about him. Apparently, he came to your city on his own. He told her he was just goin' to follow Colonel Clarke, not kill him. She went along with him, not because of what he was doin', but just to be with him." Magruder shook his head, and his voice softened. "She was with him when he did the killins. She said she tried to stop him, and after that, she tried to get away, but the bloody bastard wouldn't let go." His voice choked up, and he looked down at the floor. "He raped her afterward to celebrate what he'd done."

Marin offered to get him a drink of water, but he held up his hand. It took him awhile to regain his composure.

"I think he brought her into this to get even with me, and I know you want her to testify against him, but you don't understand what that means. The IRA will kill her. It's how they ensure their security. And even I can't protect her if she ever takes the stand."

But Renée was not convinced.

"Perhaps we can protect her, Mr. Magruder. We can put her in the federal witness protection program, and as long as she refrains from contact with any-one from her past, they'll never be able to find her. She would get a new identi-ty and a new start on her life."

"They'll find her," he said emphatically. "Our intelligence gathering is far more extensive than you know. Cassidy has family and friends, Ms. Marin, and he's not without his supporters. Make no mistake. She would be found."

Again, there was an uncomfortable pause. Renée had to admit she'd been moved by his story, and most of what he said was confirmed by the facts. His daughter's defense would be ignorance and, very likely, it was true. Cassidy's motive was probably his hatred for the father.

How easy it was to forget that these were ordinary people with ex-traordinary problems.

What a mess!

McCrossen broke the silence that shook her from her thoughts.

"Ms. Marin, we appreciate the time you've taken to speak with us. I would simply hope that you'll consider what Mr. Magruder has said, and if you can see your way to doing what is right, we would be most grateful."

McCrossen stood up, but Magruder did not rise. Renée noticed he was watching her intently as if he were making up his mind about something.

Quite suddenly, he spoke up.

"Ms. Marin, I wonder if I could talk to you in private? Perhaps Mr. Mc-Crossen and Detective Gibson could wait outside?"

"John, this is not a good idea," said McCrossen.

Magruder turned to Renée and ignored McCrossen's warning.

"Please, Ms. Marin? Just a moment more? I have something to say that I think you might want to hear."

Up to this point, it had all been quite predictable; part of a courtship before a deal was struck. But now, in speaking to him alone, there would be no witness to what he would say; and that could turn out to be fraught with danger. But she did not sense that she was in any physical danger, and her instincts were telling her to hear him out, and just that quickly, she made up her mind.

"I'll speak with you, Mr. Magruder." She looked from McCrossen to Gibson. "Gentlemen, if you can give us a few moments?"

Gibson rose to his feet and left the office while McCrossen remained seated. He started to speak, but then thought better of it when Magruder took him by the arm, raised him out of his chair, then walked him to the door and closed it behind him.

Renée waited for him to settle back into his chair.

"Me daughter can never testify."

His voice seemed to her to grow stronger.

"If you put her in the witness program, the Provos' will find her, and if they need to flush her out, they'll kill off her family members one by one." The look in his eyes was intense. "I must make you understand, they will succeed."

"Correct me if I'm wrong, Mr. Magruder, but didn't the British and the IRA sign a peace accord?"

He nodded. "That's true, but old grudges remain, and there are those who do not accept the terms of the agreement." He studied her intently. "Most of us are tryin' to adhere to the accord, but there are some who continue to stir up the troubles, and Cassidy is but one of many."

She started to speak, but he held up his hand.

"Please, don't get me wrong. I'm not worried about myself. If they decide

147

to go after our family, it's her mother and cousins I fear for. Even though they're not involved in the movement, these fanatics will kill 'em all just the same."

"But—" she started, but he would not be interrupted.

"Barrett tells me you have no case against her, and if she has to go to trial, she'll be in your jails for more than a year before the court sets her free." He shook his head in disbelief. "A whole year, Ms. Marin. She wasn't even involved."

"We've been over this already," she finally interjected. "There's just no way I can dismiss this case."

He stared at her with a coldness that made her afraid. She started to get up, but his look began to soften.

"Please, wait. I've an offer to make you, Ms. Marin; one to take the place of me daughter's testimony. But before I speak it, you must agree to never repeat it to anyone else."

Renée hesitated. Her initial fear was replaced by curiosity. She eased back into her chair.

"I would need to discuss any offer with the District Attorney," she told him.

"No." He was adamant. "You must tell no one."

"But I have to. He's my boss." She did not like being bullied. "Besides, if I did say yes, what makes you think I would keep my word?"

"From all I've been told, you're a woman of principle. If you give me your word, you'll keep it."

His answer surprised her. The man was far more perceptive and well informed than he looked. She decided to hear him out.

"All right, Mr. Magruder, I will hear you out."

Magruder lowered his voice.

"I will only say this once. If you free me daughter without makin' her testify, I'll give you advance warnin' of a bombin' in London that could kill many civilians. Set her free, Ms. Marin, and when a bomb is planted, I'll tell you where you can find it."

Renée was on her feet.

"How dare you try to bribe me like that. This conversation is over. Get out of my office!"

"No! Wait. Please. You've misunderstood. Let me explain. I would never sanction a bombin' against civilians, but others in my country have no such scruples. Even with a cease-fire, there are those who plan to stir things up. And when it happens—and it will—I'm willin' to grass in time to save innocent lives."

Marin was stunned. The ramifications of his offer overwhelmed her.

"I don't know what to say," she told him. "If I do go along with this offer, how do I know I can trust you to keep your word?"

"Me daughter is innocent, Mrs. Marin. I love her very much. I will keep my promise to you."

"I can't agree to this without bringing it up with the District Attorney."

"No. You must not tell anyone. Our intelligence is very good—the Provos would know within a few days—and I'd be dead within a week." He gave her a small smile. "If that happens, Mrs. Marin, they'll be no one around to sound the warnin'. So if you really want this to happen, no one else must ever know."

Renée was in a difficult spot. It seemed fairly certain that the girl would never testify. More importantly, based upon what she now knew, she'd be ethically bound to consider a dismissal, irrespective of Magruders' unusual offer. If she were to decide to dismiss the case without an agreement from Anne to testify then perhaps his offer was the best she'd ever get.

"If I'm going to consider this, Mr. Magruder—and that's a big 'if'—I've got a condition or two of my own. I want to interview your daughter tomorrow morning, and I want her to tell me the truth. I won't use it against her, but maybe she'll say something that will help to improve my case against Cassidy."

Magruder reached for her hand. "You're an understanding person, Ms. Marin. She'll speak to you tomorrow, but your conversation with her must be done in secrecy. McCrossen must never know."

"I can't speak to her without her attorney. It would jeopardize my case."

Magruder leaned forward in his chair and lowered his voice. "Barrett Mc-Crossen serves two masters. Is me meanin' clear?"

That got her attention.

McCrossen linked to the IRA?

"Your meaning is clear, Mr. Magruder. However, you must understand that I have to follow the law. This is getting very complicated, and I'll have to think this through. I'll give you my decision tomorrow."

Magruder stood up, nodded, and opened the door.

"Thank you for your time, Mrs. Marin."

****

Once Magruder and McCrossen were gone, Gibson came back into her office. With him was Whitney who had just arrived.

"Did you see him, Whit?" she asked.

"I did, and in anticipation of your next question, that was John Magruder." She nodded.

"Sit down and let me fill you in."

She recapped for Whitney and Gibson what McCrossen had said about his daughter giving them an interview, but she intentionally left out his offer to turn informant, as she wanted to think about it further.

Gibson was skeptical. "So? Do you plan to talk to her?"

"I will, but since I don't have a case and she won't take the stand, ethically, I don't have a choice. I'll have to dismiss her case. At least by talking to her, we may get something we've overlooked that will help us nail Cassidy to the wall."

Gibson scratched at his chin.

"I'm still confused. If Magruder had nothing of importance to say, then how come he wanted us out of the room while he talked to you?"

"Magruder doesn't trust McCrossen. He doesn't want him to know that the girl will talk to us."

"Whoa! Aren't you prohibited from talking to her without him knowing?" Gibson asked.

"I am, but here's the nature of the problem. I suspect McCrossen has been hired by the IRA to make sure that Anne doesn't talk."

"Do you know that for a fact?" Whitney asked.

"Magruder suggested as much."

Gibson thought this over for a moment.

"Even if that's true, how do you get around talking to her while the guy represents her?"

Renée leaned forward.

"I read about an organized crime case once where the attorney involved reported directly to the mob. The prosecutor went to a judge, told him that the defendant wanted to be interviewed, but that his lawyer couldn't be trusted. The court-appointed a private attorney who spoke with the defendant, then reported back to the court. The court then ruled that the defendant could talk with the prosecutor in the presence of the court appointed attorney. All parties were sworn to secrecy, and the results of that interview were later upheld by the Appellate Court."

"Sounds complicated," Gibson told her. "I hope you know what you're doing,"

"Look, Gibby, I'm not going to put my career on the line by doing something unethical. I'll spend some time with the law books, and I'll see if we can pull this off. If we can't, then we'll forget the interview. Will that make you happy?"

"This is not about my happiness, Renée. What you're talking about doing is something that could impact the case against Cassidy. If you're positive that we have nothing to risk, then I'm all for it. But if you're not, then let's just let it pass."

"Fair enough. We're both on the same page."

"Good. So how do we set this up?"

"I'll petition the court for the confidential appointment of a second attorney for Anne Magruder. If the court agrees, I'll put together a court order to release her to your custody so that you and Donahue can bring her over here. We'll do the interview before the arraignment, and if she tells us the truth, we'll go ahead and dismiss her case."

"What time do you want her in here?" he asked.

"If I get the court order, you get her here by eight. That should give us enough time."

Gibson stood up stiffly.

"You're the boss, Renée. But do me a favor. No more private meetings. It sets us all up for some pretty heavy criticism."

Renée nodded and watched him go.

Whitney, who had remained, watched her for a moment before breaking his silence.

"You want to tell me what's really goin' on?"

She had trouble holding his glance.

"There's nothing going on, Whit. But if you want to be of some help, can you check out Barrett McCrossen for me? It might help if we had some documented information that would independently connect him with the IRA."

****

TEN

September 29, Tuesday, Evening

"I'm glad you could make it on such short notice," Whitney said, "I was tired of eating alone."

"Thanks for inviting me."

The waiter pulled out her chair, and Renée sat down at the table. *Lulu's* was a restaurant of moderate size; cozy, pricey, and renowned for its' food.

"Trendy little place you've selected, Whit. I had no idea you were so hip to the LA food scene."

"The truth is the concierge at my hotel recommended this place. I'll have to thank him again when I get back."

The waiter interrupted her response.

"Can I bring you a cocktail before dinner?" he asked.

"Yes, please. A white wine. Chablis."

"And a scotch and soda for me," Whitney added.

Their drinks were delivered a few minutes later, and they raised their glasses in a toast.

"To a successful prosecution," Whitney told her.

Renée took a sip.

"You said on the phone that you've got some information on McCrossen?"

"He sits as a board member on a number of Catholic charities. One of them, on the East Coast, raises funds for the IRA."

"Mmm... well that could explain why he's on the case. Did you find out anything else?"

"There's nothin' more in our files, but my people will be doin' a full workup. The fact that he represents Magruder in a criminal case means it's likely they trust him completely."

"Have them check out all his local contacts," she added.

"I will. Oh, and by the way, somethin' else arrived today." He pulled a piece of paper from his pocket. "You might find this interestin'."

He passed her a copy of a fax, and her eyes grew wide as she scanned it.

She looked at him and held his glance.

"He's wanted for a bombing?"

"That's right. London's placed a detainer on Liam Cassidy with your State Department, and when you're finished with him, we want to collect our pound of flesh."

"You can have him with my blessing." She raised her glass and took another sip.

Whitney smiled.

"So, now that we've finished talking business tell me a little about yourself?"

"What would you like to know?"

He buttered a small piece of bread.

"Everythin'."

"That's a pretty tall order, Major. Do you have all night?"

Whitney looked up in surprise and grinned broadly.

"I didn't mean it *that* way!" She could feel herself blushing.

He winked. Then asked, "So how'd you end up doin' terrorist cases?"

"Actually, it's not much of a story. When I got out of law school, I came straight to the DA's office. I volunteered for every trial that came along, and pretty soon I had a decent reputation. I did some high profile cases, the ones that get media attention, and after a few quick promotions, I was appointed to run the Organized Crime/Anti-Terrorist Division."

"That's no small accomplishment. I'm impressed."

She leaned forward and smiled.

"In truth, I was lucky. It so happens that I was the right woman, in the right place, at the right time.

"Two years ago, Rosen came in as the new DA and decided it was important to showcase a few females in top management positions. There are those who claim that I owe my appointment to his quota system; but damn it, I worked really hard to get where I am."

"I'm sure you deserved it, Renée. Just remember, in the end, you'll be judged on your performance and not on how you got there."

"So philosophical." There was laughter in her voice. "You surprise me,

Major. I had no idea you were so deep."

"I'll take that as a compliment."

He took a piece of bread, buttered it, and popped it into his mouth. "So how's your husband handling your success?"

Her smile vanished.

"He passed away, Whit. Almost six months ago."

Whitney stopped mid-bite, looked away for a moment, then reached out and put his hand over hers.

"I'm terribly sorry, Renée. I had no idea. I saw the wedding band, and... well, I just figured—?"

"I haven't gotten around to taking it off yet."

"I feel awful—"

She was touched by his embarrassment.

"It's okay, Whit. Really it is. I don't mind talking about it."

He eyed her carefully.

"You sure?"

"Michael was an architect. We met while we were undergraduates at USC. It was one of those whirlwind romances. We got married right after graduation. He was my best friend."

She paused, looked off into the distance for a moment, then returned her gaze to his.

"When Julie came along, the three of us were just like peas in a pod."

"Julie's your daughter?"

She nodded and her eyes lit up.

"She's the light of my life. I'm sure you'd find her charming."

"I'd like to meet her sometime. I have a suspicion she's a miniature version of you."

Renée laughed.

"I suppose you could say so. She's got my stubborn streak, that's for sure, but in spite of that quality, my daughter really is amazing."

"If she's anything like you, then I'm sure she is."

Renée blushed again. Not quite sure how to respond to his compliment, she chose instead to redirect the conversation.

"Enough about me. Let's talk about you?"

"Well, I'm thirty-eight, and I like to swim."

She couldn't suppress a laugh.

"Rather shallow, Whitney. You'll have to do better than that."

He lowered his voice to a whisper.

"Okay. After I finished at the university, I joined the Royal Navy, trans-ferred into Special Air, then spent two tours in Northern Ireland. I caught a few promotions along the way, landed in London, and now, well... here I am."

She leaned forward in her chair and lowered her voice.

"Why are you being so secretive? And why are we whispering?"

He threw back his head and laughed.

"Good question. Force of habit, I guess." He toyed with his glass for a mo-ment and then looked up. "I guess I'm not used to talkin' about myself."

"Well, give it a try."

"Honestly, there's really not a lot to tell. I'm single. I love to cook. I hate doin' laundry, and I'm not the least bit interested in redheads."

He reached for his glass and took another sip of his scotch.

"That's it? That's Andrew Whitney in a nutshell?"

"I told you there wasn't much to tell."

"You don't give me much to work with, Whit. But I'll bite. Why the aver-sion to redheads?"

He smiled wanly.

"An old love who found solace with someone else while I was doin' my thing in the North."

In the glow of the light from a lone candle that burned on their table, she studied his face.

"You're like an onion, Andrew Whitney, and I can see you're going to force me to peel you back, layer by layer."

He leaned forward and smiled.

"I'll look forward to it, Renée."

His comment caught her off guard. He was very attractive, and she was flat-tered by his interest, but this was absolutely crazy. Not only did they have to work together on the case, but once it was over, he'd be headed back to London, and she'd be picking up the pieces of her life once again.

No way. This was doomed from the start, and she'd have to make sure that it ended right here.

She leaned forward and tried to smile.

"Look, Whit, I'm a bit embarrassed to be saying this, but I'm worried that I might have given you the wrong impression. I'm flattered by your interest, but I'm just not ready to start anything right now. The timing's all wrong and..."

Her voice trailed off and she looked down at her hands. They were shaking.

"Listen to me," she said, "I sound like a babbling idiot."

Whitney studied her face.

"I understand."

She looked up. "You do?"

He reached for her hand, brought it to his lips, and kissed it softly.

"You know where you can find me if you change your mind."

****

ELEVEN

September 30, Wednesday, Morning

Renée arrived at her office shortly after seven a.m. This would be a busy day, and she wanted to be sure that everything went smoothly. If she finished the interview with Magruder by nine, she would have to hustle to see Kerin to get his approval to dismiss the case. After that, they'd have to race Anne down to Division 30, get the court to cut her loose, and get her out of there before Cassidy arrived at ten. And of course, no matter what else happened, she'd have to spend time with the press.

She took a sip of coffee from a styrofoam cup that she'd purchased at the snack bar, then plunged into her legal research.

She found the case she was looking for, and by prearrangement, she made her way down to Department 121 where Judge Robert Schuit was waiting to consider her situation. A reporter took down what was said at the meeting, and after Schuit learned about McCrossen's connection to the IRA, and about Anne Magruder's desire to speak in secret to the prosecution, he appointed a private attorney to represent Anne. He made an order that the transcript of his meeting in-chambers with Renée Marin was to be sealed and not disclosed to the defense. However, he cautioned her that if the charges against Anne were not dismissed, he would revisit the decision not to disclose the details of the in-chambers meeting to McCrossen, who would still remain Anne's counsel of record.

She made her way back upstairs to her office at just before eight, and a short time later, Gibson appeared at the doorway in a well-tailored blue suit that he always wore to court.

"Where's Anne?" she asked.

"Outside in the hallway with Jen. Are we ready to start?"

"Not quite. Whitney hasn't arrived."

"He's outside with Jen and Magruder. By the way, how do we stand in the eyes of the law with this interview?"

"We're on solid ground. Judge Schuit is a legal scholar, and he's given us the go-ahead. We'll need to wait for the private attorney he appointed to arrive, but she should show up in a couple of minutes. She'll sit in on the interview, which will be recorded, but they'll be no problems if we end up dismissing the case against Anne."

"And if we don't dismiss?"

"That's another can of worms that I'd rather not even contemplate right now."

Gibson didn't react. He still wasn't happy that Anne was going to walk free without being forced to testify against Liam Cassidy, but Renée was a solid prosecutor, and it wasn't his call to make, so he understood that he would just have to live with the decision.

"By the way," he said, "she didn't say anything on the drive over here." He motioned towards the door. "Want me to bring her in?"

"Let's wait until the new attorney arrives."

He got up and stepped outside to fill in Donahue and Whitney just as Attorney Cathryn Carradine walked up.

She was short in stature but big in attitude. She didn't give a hoot about fashion, and her naturally curly head of blond hair was so out of date that behind her back, she'd earned the nickname of *Little Orphan Annie.* She was a walking ball of energy, known for her attention to detail, and she did not suffer fools for clients, nor incompetence on behalf of prosecutors who were not completely prepared.

She walked right past Magruder and the others and made her way directly into Marin's office.

"Is my client here?" she asked without preamble.

"Nice to see you, too, Cat."

But Carradine was unfazed.

"Schuit told me you'd fill me in on what's going on?"

Renée offered her a seat, and spent the next five minutes bringing Carradine up to speed.

"And you're going to dismiss all of the charges against her?"

"That's the plan," Marin said. She looked at her watch. "And we're under the gun. I need to wrap this up by nine."

"Let me talk to her alone for a few moments, and we'll see where we're at."

After consulting with Gibson, who refused to unshackle his prisoner or let her out of his sight, a compromise was reached. Carradine was allowed to talk to Magruder down the hallway where their conversation, though witnessed by Gibson and Whitney, could not be overheard.

Ten minutes later, Carradine walked Anne back over to the group. She was then escorted into Renée's office for the formal interview.

Magruder was dressed in a jail-issued pale green outfit. The clothes could have passed for hospital garb except for the fact that *Sybil Brand Institute* was stenciled evenly across the back of each piece. Her face was devoid of makeup, her hair was tied back in a loose ponytail, and her hands remained cuffed securely behind her back.

Most noticeable to Marin were the deep, dark circles around Anne's eyes. Jail didn't agree with her, and she'd aged noticeably during her two weeks of confinement.

Anne yawned several times and appeared on the verge of falling asleep. High power inmates, confined alone to their cells, often slept long hours out of boredom and depression.

Gibson removed the cuffs and had her take a seat in front of the desk.

When everyone was settled, Renée turned on a digital recorder.

"Miss Magruder, I'm Renée Marin, the Head Deputy District Attorney assigned to prosecute you. I'm putting the first part of this conversation on tape for my own protection. I understand that you've requested an opportunity to talk with me?"

Anne nodded and spoke matter-of-factly.

"I talked with my father last night, and he said I should."

"Did you also speak about this with your attorney, Mr. McCrossen?"

"No. My father said to leave him out of this."

Renée knew she was walking a very thin line. If Anne didn't claim the decision was hers because of McCrossen's involvement with the IRA and his possible conflict of interest as it related to Liam Cassidy, then the State Bar would be looking at her for interfering with the attorney/client relationship.

She decided to confront the issue directly.

"Anne, we were advised of your desire not to involve Mr. McCrossen in this interview because of his possible connection to the IRA, and Mr. Liam Cassidy's involvement with that organization. I have consulted Judge Robert Schuit, and he has appointed Ms. Carradine to interview you to confirm that speaking to us is your decision and that you are doing so freely and without hesitation or pressure of any kind. Is that correct?"

Anne looked over at Carradine who nodded.

"That's correct."

"And would you tell us please the reason that you don't want Mr. Mc-Crossen involved with your decision to be interviewed?"

Anne looked around the room before returning her glance to Marin.

"Because I can't trust 'im. He was sent by the PIRA."

"By the PIRA, do you mean the Provos? The Provisional Irish Republican Army?" Renée asked.

"That's right. He warned me not to say anythin' to anyone."

"That's generally considered good advice," Marin told her.

Anne shook her head. "You don't understand. He meant I couldn't talk about it with anyone, or *else...*"

"You mean he threatened you?" Renée asked.

"Not directly, but I knew what he was sayin'."

They were going around in circles, so Renée decided to try a new approach.

"Miss Magruder, it appears as though Mr. McCrossen hasn't said anything to you that isn't good advice, given your current situation. I don't think I can really talk to you without notifying him unless you can provide me with a specific reason why you don't feel you can trust him."

Anne looked up, and for the first time, she seemed to come alive. Her eyes grew bright and her temper flared.

"Are you daft? This whole thing is a nightmare! First, Liam drags me into this—he knows I'm innocent, but he'll never say so—and now I've got an attorney who tells me that I'm goin' to die if I ever tell anyone the truth. He expects me to sit in jail and keep my mouth shut. I swear he's more interested in helpin' Liam than he is in helpin' me."

The anguish in her voice was pronounced.

"McCrossen's not interested in me, Miss Marin. Nobody fuckin' cares about me!"

She began to sob and the tears streamed down her face.

"I just want to talk to someone who can make this go away!"

Renée let her cry; the record would have to speak for itself.

When Anne spoke again, it was more like a little girl's voice. "Please, Miss Marin. My father says I can trust you. Please, help me."

"It's okay, Anne." Renée handed her a tissue from a box in the desk. "I think you've articulated a belief that your attorney has a conflict of interest. If Ms. Carradine, your new court-appointed attorney, agrees with this assessment, I'll allow you to talk to us without Mr. McCrossen being notified."

Carradine leaned forward in her chair.

"Miss Magruder is agreeable to speaking with you on condition that she will not be called to testify against Liam Cassidy; that what she says to you about her case is not recorded; that no one outside this room or senior management in your office ever learns that she has spoken with you; and that all charges in her current case will be dismissed this morning once this interview is over." She locked eyes with Marin. "Is that correct, Ms. Marin?"

"Not quite. I still have to get approval from my office to dismiss the charges, but in the unlikely event that my recommendation is turned down, nothing said in this interview would ever be used against Miss Magruder in any forthcoming prosecution."

"*I don't know*—" Carradine began, but Magruder cut her off.

"I want to tell them what happened," she said, and based upon that, Carradine had no choice but to completely acquiesce.

Renée turned off the recorder and Gibson led Anne Magruder through the details of her early relationship with Liam Cassidy. He covered Cassidy's arrival in LA and the events that led up to the shootings.

Anne had to stop several times to compose herself, and each time she did, Gibson let her cry it out until she was ready to resume.

"You okay now?" he asked.

She nodded that she was.

"Okay, Anne. Where did the two of you go after you switched cars?"

"He drove me to a hotel by the airport and he made me go up to his room."

"Did you stop anywhere along the way?"

"No."

"What happened when you reached the hotel?"

"He parked the car in the garage and wiped off the fingerprints. Then he walked me to the elevator and we went directly up to his room."

"What happened then?"

Anne looked away.

"He raped me. He kept sayin' I deserved it, that I never stood up to my father. He said I had it comin', and he called me names."

Her voice trailed off, and Marin couldn't help but feel a great deal of sadness for what this girl had gone through. Cassidy had used her to get even with her father, and in the process, he'd saddled her with overwhelming guilt and shame.

"Where did you go when you left the room?" Gibson asked.

"He drove me back to the dorm and dropped me off. He acted like it never happened. The bastard even said he loved me."

"Did he tell you where he was going to stay?"

"No. He gave me a number and said to call him in the mornin', at eight, when I came to my senses. He warned me not to talk. He said if I did, he'd tell the authorities that I was involved in the killin's."

She looked from face to face, seeking a sign that she was believed, but no one gave a hint of what they were thinking.

"What did you do with the phone number that he gave you?" Whitney asked.

"I threw it away, but I got it back when I remembered my purse was still in his car."

Renée asked, "Do we know where that piece of paper is, Gibby?"

"I don't recall seeing it," he replied. He looked over at Anne. "Did you have it on you when you were arrested?"

"I think so. I don't remember."

"I'll make a note to go through the booked property again," Gibson said. "Maybe it was overlooked."

Renée watched her eyes, trying to discern the truth.

"Why did you call him again, Anne?"

"My passport and money were in that purse. I wanted to go back home, but I couldn't leave without my documents. I was afraid he might kill me, but I didn't know what else to do?"

Whitney jumped in.

"Anne, at any time while you were with him, did Cassidy say he was workin' with anyone else?"

"The only time he mentioned someone was when we were at the hotel. He said he was movin' to a place that belonged to a friend."

Renée's attention picked up.

"Did he say anything else about this friend?"

"No, nothin'."

"Did he call anyone while he was with you?"

"No."

Renée glanced from face to face, but there were no further questions.

"All right, Anne," she said, "we're finished for now. Do you have anything you want to add?"

"I just want to know what's goin' to happen?"

Renée thought for a moment.

"I'll be honest with you. I believe your case will be dismissed, but before I can do that, I've got to get permission from my boss. If he agrees, and I see no reason why he shouldn't, then we'll try to get it done this morning. If not, then we may have to set a date for the preliminary hearing to buy a little more time to get the details of the dismissal worked out. Do you understand what I'm saying?"

"I think so," she said, but she started to cry again.

Renée handed her a tissue, then looked over at Donahue.

"Jen, can you walk her down to Division 30. Use the freight elevator, and make sure they put her in an isolation cell."

Donahue nodded and rose from her chair. When Anne stood up, Donahue cuffed her hands behind her back.

"I'll go with you," Whitney said, and he followed them out the door.

Carradine slowly got to her feet.

"Did you get what you want?"

Renée shrugged.

"Not sure there's anything new, but I believe her."

"Then get her a dismissal. I'd rather not have to litigate the ethics of what we've done here today."

"You and me both."

When Carradine was gone, Renée turned to Gibson.

"So? What do you think?"

"For what it's worth, I think she's telling the truth. She never had a clue what he was going to do. I hate to admit it, but you were right. A dismissal is in order." He shrugged. "I just wish that we could find a way to make her testify."

"I wish we could too, but we can't. Now, all I can do is hope that my boss is in an understanding mood."

****

Kerin smiled as she entered his office and took a chair.

"So, bring me up to speed."

Marin began by telling him about McCrossen's refusal to cut a deal and his insistence on a dismissal for Anne; how she spoke with John Magruder, and his warning that if Anne were required to testify, the IRA would go after her innocent family members. She intentionally chose not to mention his offer to grass about a future bombing operation in London, and she concluded with Anne's desire to tell her version of the events without McCrossen knowing what she was doing. She told him how she presented the situation to Judge Schuit, and his appointment of Carradine for the interview with Anne.

"Schuit approved going behind McCrossen's back?"

"Yes, sir. He called McCrossen's loyalty to the IRA a conflict of interest."

Kerin gave that some thought.

"Well, McCrossen's going to find out what she did when Schuit takes him off the case."

Renée took a deep breath. This was the moment she'd dreaded. She swallowed hard.

"Actually, Schuit is under the impression that we're going to dismiss against Anne Magruder later this morning. McCrossen will still represent her, and that will eliminate any ethical issues that could arise if McCrossen were taken off the case."

"*What!* How did Schuit get the impression that we were going to dismiss?"

"I guess he got it from me." She steeled herself for an outburst, but it didn't come, so she quickly continued.

"I've gone over our evidence a dozen times, Glenn, and my IO and I are both convinced that the girl is completely innocent. By her own statement, she was in the car with him because she loved him, and the shooting of our victims was a complete surprise. The few eyewitness we located at the scene have corroborated her story. They heard her screaming at him before the shooting began."

"Then let her testify to that effect," Kerin said.

"We can't. Her father insists that if she does, the PIRA's won't stop until she's dead."

Kerin looked off for a moment to marshal his thoughts.

"The mafia uses the same fear tactics, Renée, and that's why we have the witness protection program. The girl is unmarried, no strong community ties, a perfect candidate for a new identity."

Marin shook her head. "There's another problem, Glenn. Magruder hinted that the IRA has penetrated the witness protection program. Apparently, their intelligence gathering is far more extensive than we imagined. That alone would be reason enough to keep her off the stand, and Major Whitney agrees that if they can't find her, they'll go after her family to force her to show herself, and we both know there's no way to protect them in Ireland."

"Her extended family is not our problem, Renée."

She stared at him in disbelief.

"I think it is, Glenn, and I'm not aware of a policy that says that a case should take priority over innocent lives."

"Come off it, Renée. We force people to testify every day of the week in gang cases."

"But those are run-of-the-mill cases and local in nature. We can move those people fifteen blocks and the gangs will never find them. In this case, we're talking about real terrorists. Guys with money, power and extensive connections. These people put bombs on passenger trains and blow up military barracks. For God's sake, they assassinate public officials. They're entirely different from the teenage thugs who blow a kid away for flashing the wrong gang sign."

Kerin frowned, then leaned back in his chair.

"To a ghetto family, gang intimidation is just as severe as anything being done by the IRA."

Renée bristled. Moving a witness and making them forego any connection with their past was onerous, to say the least, but to expect their every living relative to voluntarily give up their lives and go into hiding just to help the prosecution make an admittedly serious case seemed to her to border on the unconscionable.

"So what's your point, Glenn? Are you suggesting this is somehow a racial issue?"

"Not on your part, certainly, but from where I'm sitting, I think the community might conclude that we've got a double standard."

"You know that's not true." Renée was growing angrier by the second. "Color has never been a factor for any lawyer I've ever worked with in this office. In fact, the rule around here has always been that if we can't protect our witnesses, we don't use them."

She shot him a blistering look.

Kerin twisted in his chair. "I respect what you're saying, Renée, and I believe you're correct. Perhaps I misspoke when I said her family was not our problem. But I need a solution that enables us to cut her loose without creating any problems for Aaron?"

It felt like someone had punched her in the stomach. Why did it come back to politics and the DA's ability to keep his political career alive?

Her shoulders slumped. "Fine, Glenn. I give up." She got to her feet.

"Wait a minute..." he said.

"No, you wait a minute! Politics are not my concern. I'm just an ordinary prosecutor, and the only reason I know for dismissing this case is the fact that the girl is innocent. To withhold a dismissal that she's already entitled to as an inducement to get her testify is probably unethical and it certainly isn't justice, and I won't be a part of it. So unless you want to pull me off the case, I plan to cut her loose later this morning."

She suddenly wondered if she'd gone too far.

Kerin frowned, but he kept his temper in check. He studied her face and seemed to consider her words.

"I've no intention of removing you from the case. You're absolutely right. You must do what you believe is ethically correct, and I believe your decision is totally justified. Aaron will just have to deal with the fallout by stressing the propriety of what we've done. You have my approval to dismiss the case against her with no prerequisite that she agrees to testify."

Renée tucked her file under her arm, and realizing that she'd been holding her breath, she exhaled slowly.

"Thanks, Glenn. We're doing the right thing."

"I'll speak to Aaron," he told her. "I'll give you time to get down to the courtroom and dismiss her out of the case before I let him know. That should prevent him from overreacting and doing something stupid. Once you're finished, call my secretary and we'll release a press statement from up here. Just refer any inquiries directly to me."

"I'll call as soon as we're finished. Thanks again."

Kerin smiled. "I should be thanking you for reminding me what this job is all about."

She smiled back and headed for the door.

****

With Gibson in tow, Marin stepped off the elevator on the third floor of the Criminal Courts Building where they encountered a large crowd of curious people who were milling about near the two metal detectors that were set up in front of the doorway leading into Division 30. Rope guides channeled the spectators into a single file line, while a cortege of Sheriffs stood about and surveyed the gathering crowd.

They made their way down the hallway, bypassing the press, and quickly entered the courtroom.

Division 30 was an oversized room built specifically to process large numbers of defendants. Most of the courtroom was for public use, while the working area contained several large tables to accommodate the hundreds of case files that passed through the system each day.

They paused for a moment at the back of the courtroom. Most of the seats were already taken and Renée spotted Whitney standing off to the side.

"Anyone unusual show up?" she asked.

He shook his head.

"Nobody fittin' the profile."

"Good. Come with us and we'll wait up front."

They walked up to the railing, passed through the swinging gate, and took seats in a section reserved for attorneys. The judge was busy talking to one of the inmates seated along the opposite wall.

"I've watched for half an hour this mornin'," Whitney whispered. "I can't believe how many people go through here."

Marin leaned over and whispered back: "They bring the custody cases out first in groups of thirty. The defendants sit on benches behind the bullet-proof glass. The judge reads them their rights then arraigns them one by one."

"He spends less than a minute on each case," Whitney said. "How does he keep things straight?"

"Most of the work goes on behind the scenes. Before they bring them out, the attorneys talk to their clients in back, then they see the judge in his chambers. The judge puts notes in the case file if anything's decided. It really speeds things up when they get out here."

"Will you be seein' him in chambers about our case?"

"Of course."

"Assembly-line justice." Whitney shook his head. "What will you Americans think of next?"

She met his gaze with a smile.

"You Brits are just jealous 'cause we thought of it first."

On the bench, Judge James Brandlin was engaged in a vigorous colloquy with a very talkative robber. When Renée looked up, he nodded a dignified greeting in her direction, and as the robber was led away, Judge Brandlin got to his feet.

"Ladies and gentlemen, we'll take a ten-minute recess. I'll see all counsel on the Magruder case in my chambers."

****

They had parked the stolen car in the back of a lot that was just to the side of the *Zimmerman Brothers* bail bond office, across the street from the access road that led directly to the county jail. From this vantage point, they had an unobstructed view of the driveway used by the inmate transport system.

"This won't be easy, Jimmy, there are too many bleedin' buses. We might never spot 'im."

"You worry too much. He'll be in a small van. That narrows it down quite a bit."

Michael Kelly, who was seated behind the steering wheel, raised his field glasses and scanned a bus that was pulling out of the driveway. The bus was too large to be transporting a single, keep-away inmate. He lowered the glasses and passed them over to Cassidy.

"They certainly do move a lot of blokes."

Jimmy Cassidy took the glasses and raised them to his eyes. He scanned the front of the jail, but saw no sign of counter surveillance, either mechanical or human, so he resumed the watch on the driveway.

"You'd think they'd vary their pattern, but they don't. Every bus goes out the same way." He smiled without taking his eyes off the road. "They won't be expectin' us, mate."

Kelly glanced down at his watch which was partially covered by a black leather glove, It was almost nine thirty-five a.m.

"He should be comin' out soon," he said as he started the engine and let it idle.

A small prisoner van soon appeared at the end of the driveway and turned west onto Vignes Street. Two deputies were seated in front and one inmate was sitting in the back. They could see the cast on the prisoners' shoulder through the metal bars that covered most of the windows.

"That's him," Cassidy whispered. "Stay with 'em, Michael, but not too close. We don't want to give ourselves away."

He then picked up a hand-held radio.

"They're comin' your way, Devon."

****

Renée entered the judge's chambers with Barrett McCrossen close behind.

Judge James Brandlin stood behind his desk with a cup of coffee in his hand. His robe was off, and she could see that he'd gained some weight since his appointment to the bench. She also noted, with a smile, that his hair had gone from a shade of dark brown to almost completely gray. It gave him a very distinguished and scholarly look.

He had started his career in law enforcement as a California Highway Patrol officer, went to law school at night, then became a D.A. When appointed to the bench, he started hearing criminal cases right away, and soon he enjoyed a reputation for fairness from both sides of the counsel table.

"Renée, come on in," he said with a smile. "Can I get you a cup of coffee?"

"Thanks anyway, Your Honor, but I've already had more than my usual limit."

He put his cup down on the desk and greeted her with a hug, then reached out and took her hand.

"I haven't seen you since the funeral. You look terrific. How are you and your daughter doing?"

"We're both fine, Judge. We seem to be getting back to normal."

"Time has a way of making things easier to handle, Renée. Barbara and I think about you often."

"I know." She smiled. "Barb calls me once a month to invite me over for dinner."

"You should take her up on the offer."

"Until now I haven't really felt like going out, but I promise we'll make it soon."

Learning to deal with the death of her husband had not been easy for Renée. The grieving process was overwhelming at first, a generalized lethargy that rendered her unable to make even the most basic of decisions, including what to wear or what to eat. The loss of ambition and drive was particularly devastating, as she had always had a natural energy that carried her through in times of high stress. But not this time. The recovery had been a slow process, one foot in front of the other, thinking only of the present and how to get through it. Eventually, she made her way into counseling, and with the help of her daughter who had counseling, too, the two of them had slowly reached a balance between the longing for the past and an appreciation for the gift of a future.

He squeezed her hand. "Good. I'll have her call you this week."

He turned his attention to McCrossen.

"Counselor, I hope you understand. Mrs. Marin and I came up together in the DA's office. We haven't seen each other for quite some time and we have a lot of catching up to do."

"I understand completely, Your Honor."

"Good. Help yourself to some coffee."

McCrossen shook his head.

"That's quite all right, Your Honor. Thanks anyway."

Brandlin flopped down in the chair behind his desk and gestured towards the couch where both of the attorneys quickly sat down.

"I looked over the file and found a message from my clerk that you wanted to talk to me out of the presence of counsel for Mr. Cassidy?"

"That's right, Your Honor." Renée leaned forward. "I haven't had a chance to speak to Mr. McCrossen yet this morning, but I'm planning on asking for a dismissal for his client."

McCrossen raised his eyebrows in surprise, then smiled broadly.

"Thank you, Ms. Marin. You're doing the right thing."

Brandlin looked puzzled.

"Are you going to dismiss on Cassidy as well?"

"No, Your Honor. We'll be proceeding against Cassidy as planned. He'll be getting here shortly, so I want to take care of this dismissal before he arrives."

Brandlin reached over and picked up his cup of coffee. He then leaned back in his chair.

"This is a high profile case, Renée. Mind telling me what's going on?"

"Actually, all the evidence we have indicates that she was present for the murders, but she had no knowledge they were going to occur. She wasn't part of any conspiracy, so plain and simple, we've got no case."

Brandlin looked thoughtful.

"In that case, I expect she'll be testifying for the people. Do you want her ordered back for his preliminary hearing?"

"No, Your Honor. That won't be necessary. She won't be called to testify."

Brandlin raised his eyebrows again, but before Renée could speak, Mc-Crossen jumped in.

"She'd be killed if she ever testified, Judge. There's just no way she can take the stand."

Brandlin glanced back and forth between them.

"Have you considered the witness protection program?"

"We have, Your Honor," Marin said, "but that won't work either."

Brandlin stood up and reached for his robe.

"Okay, Renée. It sounds like you've given this some thought. Let's get it done."

****

Anne shuffled slowly out of the lockup, escorted by two female deputies. She kept her head down, aware that the room was full of reporters.

After walking into the now empty bulletproof cage, she was guided to the far end where she could speak to her attorney through an opening in the glass. Her hands were cuffed to a waist chain, and she stood with stooped shoulders as she watched McCrossen come out of the judge's chambers and over to the glass that separated her from everyone else.

When he told her the charges were going to be dismissed, she became light headed and shaky; her knees buckled once and she started to fall. A nearby deputy grabbed her arm and helped her take a seat on the bench.

With tears in her eyes, she looked over at Renée Marin who was talking to

Gibson on the other side of the room.

When they made eye contact, she mouthed the words...*Thank you.*

****

The actual dismissal of the case came without fanfare. In fact, it occurred so quickly that many in the audience never even realized that it had happened. At McCrossen's request, Brandlin issued an order for the Sheriff to release her from the courthouse, thus eliminating the need to transport her back to the jail.

Anne was ushered from the courtroom and into the lockup where McCrossen was allowed to rejoin her. Once she'd changed her clothes, he whisked her down a back elevator to a limousine that he had hired which was waiting in the basement parking lot, directly under the courthouse.

He placed a call from his cell to John Magruder, and in an excited voice he told him that his daughter had been released. But he was in for a bit of a shock when he discovered that Magruder did not seem at all surprised.

McCrossen ran his hand through his hair while he thought about all that had happened. He supposed he'd have to give the old man all the credit. Whatever he'd said to Marin when they met together in private had likely been the impetus for her to change her mind.

He allowed himself a smile. It seemed that the old man had the juice when it counted the most.

****

When the Sheriff's van carrying Cassidy pulled into the underground parking lot below the courthouse, the two vehicles that had been following it continued past the building for several blocks before doubling back around and coming to a stop within a rarely used public parking lot.

Having surveilled Liam Cassidy's trip to the courthouse, the men met together in the back seat of one of the cars where they finalized their plans for

Cassidy's return to the county jail.

****

TWELVE

September 30, Wednesday, Mid-morning

Marin forestalled having to deal with the press by pretending to immerse herself in paperwork at the counsel table while she waited for Cassidy's attorney to show up.

Allison Cooper came out of the lockup and made her way over.

"Are you the DA handling the Cassidy case?" she asked.

Renée nodded. "I'm Renée Marin. Are you representing Cassidy?"

"Unfortunately, I am," she said dryly. They shook hands. "Can we go into chambers and speak to the Judge? I need to talk about his status at the jail."

"No problem. Let's see if Brandlin can see us now?"

They walked over to the clerk and soon they were standing with Brandlin in his chambers. He greeted them warmly and gestured for them to take seats.

"You wanted to see me, Allison?" he asked.

"Yes, Judge." She settled in on the couch. "My client wants to delay entering his plea until he can get his own attorney."

Renée was surprised. This would cause a delay that she hadn't considered.

"How much time does he need?" Brandlin asked.

"He says he needs about a month; but if you ask me, Judge, something else is going on."

"Oh?" Brandlin's face registered his concern.

Cooper smiled.

"He wants me to get you to set bail for him at one hundred thousand dollars. He says he can make it."

"I'm sure you explained to your client that in a capital case I can hold him without bail."

"I most certainly did, Judge, but he wants me to ask you anyway. I told him I would, but for what it's worth if he were to make bail, I suspect he'd be long gone."

Renée was shocked by such candor. Allison Cooper apparently had a well-developed sense of ethical responsibility.

Brandlin smiled.

"I don't think we're going to have to worry about that, but bring it up in the courtroom and we'll put it on the record."

"One more thing," Cooper said. "He's also asked me to discuss with you the matter of his classification. He's on the hospital side of the jail at the moment, in a one-man cell, and they've got him classified as a K10. He gets out of his cell to exercise for fifteen minutes a day, and apparently he feels that's not quite enough. Would you consider changing his classification and putting him in with the mainline population?"

"I can't so that, Allison. The Sheriff's Department classifies all inmates based on their safety concerns. They obviously know what they're doing. Make your request, but it will have to be denied."

"Would you consider issuing an order to allow him out of his cell for at least an hour a day? That's not unreasonable, Judge. It's awfully hard to mark time with little or no chance to get out of your cell."

Brandlin was not swayed.

"He should've thought of that before he chose his current line of work. Confinement's an occupational hazard."

Cooper smiled.

"He also feels he should be accorded political prisoner status, whatever the hell that means?"

Brandlin threw back his head and laughed.

"Your client sounds like a dreamer."

"I think I'll let you tell him that, Judge." Cooper flashed him a smile. "He's got an attitude and a temper to go with it."

Brandlin stood up.

"Well, bring him out and let's see what happens." He looked over at Renée. "Did you have anything to add or are we ready to get started?"

Marin leaned forward.

"Only that we have several witnesses to protect, Your Honor, so the longer this goes over, the more difficult it is to guarantee their safety and cooperation. I'd ask the court to give him two weeks to get counsel, not a month. We're anxious to move this along as quickly as possible."

"I'll keep that in mind. Is he upstairs yet?"

"He's in the back, Judge," Cooper told him. "I just spoke with him."

"Very well. I've got a call to make first, but I'll be right out."

Renée and Cooper stood up and walked into the hallway which led them back to the courtroom. Cooper was in the lead, but she stopped abruptly and turned around.

"I forgot to ask you, Ms. Marin, what's happening with the codefendant?"

"We dismissed on her about twenty minutes ago."

"Will she be testifying against my client?"

"No, I don't plan to call her. She wouldn't give us a statement and we didn't have enough evidence to take her to prelim."

"Well, that should please Cassidy," Cooper said. "Nothing else today is gonna make him happy."

"Tell him she's not cooperating with us," Renée said.

"I'll tell him, but he'll never believe it. He's a real shit-head. Just be glad you don't have to deal with him personally."

*****

The door leading from the lockup swung open and a deputy stuck his head out and briefly looked around. Upon a signal from his Sergeant that everyone was ready, he returned to the lockup and ordered Cassidy out.

When he walked into view, a hush fell over the courtroom. The lone television camera, which supplied a feed to all of the other stations, followed him closely as he moved down the row. He looked at the audience, seemingly curious about the setup, but he showed no surprise at the attention he received. He stood by the glass, next to Allison Cooper, and they spoke in whispers while she briefed him on her meeting with Renée Marin and the judge.

A buzzer went off which signaled to the staff that the judge was coming out. The deputy assigned to the courtroom issued a call for silence as Brandlin took his seat on the bench.

"In the matter of Liam Cassidy," Brandlin began, "let the record reflect that the defendant is present in the courtroom. Will counsel state their appearances for the record?"

"Allison Cooper for the Public Defender's Office, representing Mr. Cassidy, Your Honor."

"Renée Marin for the People."

Brandlin leaned forward to address Cassidy.

"Is Liam Cassidy your true name?"

"It is," he replied.

"Mr. Cassidy, your attorney advises me that you wish to delay entering a plea at this time in order to obtain counsel of your own choice. Is that correct?"

"Yes," he said firmly.

"How long do you need, Mr. Cassidy?"

Cassidy paused for a moment.

"I need four weeks."

"Do the people have any objection?" Brandlin asked.

"Yes, Your Honor. We would ask the court to put this over for a maximum of two weeks. That's sufficient time for Mr. Cassidy to obtain the services of private counsel, and if he can't, the Public Defender will still be available to handle the preliminary hearing. We have witnesses to protect in this case, Your Honor, so we're anxious to see that it proceeds expeditiously."

Brandlin looked over the top of his black frame reading glasses.

"I agree that two weeks is sufficient time," he said. "If you don't have counsel by then, Mr. Cassidy, the Public Defender will step in to represent you."

Brandlin leaned forward to speak directly to Renée.

"Ms. Marin, would you arraign the defendant and take a time waiver, please?"

Renée picked up the Complaint and began reading out loud.

"Mr. Cassidy, you're charged in Complaint No. LA 9743707 with two counts of willful, deliberate, and premeditated murder in violation of Penal Code Section 187. We are also alleging two special circumstance allegations of multiple murder, and lying-in-wait. A finding of true to either of those allegations could subject you to the death penalty. Additionally, it is further alleged that you personally used a firearm in the commission of these offenses."

She looked over at Cassidy and at Allison Cooper.

"Do you waive further reading of the Complaint and a statement of your rights?"

"We do, Your Honor," Cooper responded.

"Mr. Cassidy, do you also understand that you have the right to a preliminary hearing within ten days of your arraignment? By requesting that this matter be continued for two weeks, do you understand that you will be giving up that right?"

Cooper whispered to Cassidy.

"Yes," he replied.

"In addition to that, do you further understand that we will have ten days from the date you have requested for your preliminary hearing in order to find a courtroom to hear it?"

Cassidy nodded affirmatively.

"You'll have to speak up, Mr. Cassidy," Renée said. "The reporter has to take down your words."

Cassidy's look was contemptuous.

"Yeah."

"Very well," Brandlin said, "this matter will go over for two weeks from today. Now, are there any other matters that either counsel wish to take up at this time?"

"Yes, Your Honor." Cooper smiled. "We'd ask the court to consider entertaining a request that bail be set in this case."

"You may be heard on that matter at this time, Miss Cooper," Brandlin told her.

"Your Honor," she began halfheartedly, "we would ask that bail be set in the amount of one hundred thousand dollars. That amount will be sufficient to ensure that Mr. Cassidy will make all of his court appearances."

"Has he filled out a background form, Miss Cooper?"

"Not yet, Your Honor. There was no time this morning before coming into the courtroom."

The judge returned his attention to Renée.

"What is the position of the people, Ms. Marin?"

"We'll resist the setting of bail under any circumstances, Your Honor. This was a politically motivated crime and the defendant is nothing more than a criminal assassin. He has no ties to this community or even to this country, and the death penalty is a very strong likelihood given the strength of our evidence. He used a false passport to enter the United States, and he's undoubtedly a flight risk. He's a very dangerous person and he presents a grave risk to society at large."

Renée stopped speaking, confident that the record would be sufficient to deny him bail. Brandlin looked over at Cooper.

"I'm afraid Miss Cooper that I can't even consider setting bail without a background report. Except for what the prosecutor has presented, I don't know anything about your client." He leaned forward in his chair. "And besides, Miss Cooper, this is a capital case. I would not be inclined to set bail until a magistrate could review the evidence presented at the preliminary hearing. I'm afraid that your motion to consider setting bail will have to be denied."

Brandlin paused for a moment.

"Is there anything further, Miss Cooper?"

"Yes, Your Honor. Would the court consider ordering the Sheriff's department to change the custodial status of my client? He is currently designated a K10—that's high power status and it keeps him away from other inmates—and he only gets fifteen minutes outside of his cell each day." Her voice trailed off as she could think of nothing further to say.

"I'll hear from the people," Brandlin said.

Renée knew from experience that she could use this opportunity to bring up information about the defendant's background. It was a good chance to swing public opinion against the defendant by letting the press know what a bad guy he really was.

"The defendant is a known member of the Provisional Irish Republican Army which is classified by our government as a terrorist organization. I've been advised by the LAPD that it is very likely that the charged offenses were financed by funds allocated for international terrorism. Additionally, I learned several days ago that the government of the United Kingdom has filed a detainer on Mr. Cassidy with our State Department. It appears there is an outstanding warrant in England for Mr. Cassidy which alleges that he took part in a bombing in the London financial district. His current status in the jail is designed to protect other inmates from his level of sophistication as much as it is to protect him from violence at the hands of other prisoners. It is believed his political affiliations and notoriety could easily make him a target within the jail."

Brandlin raised his hand.

"Let me interrupt you right there, Ms. Marin. His status is a question of security, and that is solely a matter left to the sound discretion of the Sheriff's Department. I won't order a change in his designation as a K10."

Cassidy muttered to himself under his breath. Visibly angry---seemingly at Renée for muddying him up in front of the press---he sensed that the refusal of his request for change of status made his chance for escape now all but impossible.

"I want to be heard?" he yelled out.

Brandlin looked him over.

"Speak through your attorney, Mr. Cassidy, and not directly to the court."

"I want to represent myself!" he yelled again, and this elicited a murmur from the audience.

Brandlin scanned the courtroom and spoke into the microphone on his bench.

"There's to be no talking by members of the audience. If there are any further comments, I will have the Sheriffs Department clear the courtroom."

The noise immediately ceased and Brandlin returned his attention to Cassidy.

"Mr. Cassidy, do I understand you to be requesting this court to relieve the Public Defender's office so that you can represent yourself?"

"That's correct. I want to be me own lawyer. It's obvious that the one I've got is unable to protect me rights."

Brandlin smiled.

"On the contrary, Mr. Cassidy, Miss Cooper has done an excellent job of presenting your requests and demands. Unfortunately for you, most of what you seek would not be granted to you or to anyone else who was in your situation."

Cassidy was not swayed.

"The fact remains that I'm not bein' treated in accordance with me rights.

I'm a political prisoner. I demand the right to be treated accordingly, and Miss Cooper doesn't see it that way. I want to represent meself until such time as I have a good lawyer."

Brandlin leaned forward.

"Well, let's talk first about your demand to be treated as a political prisoner."

It was obvious to everyone in the courtroom that Brandlin was losing his patience.

"The last I heard, the United States was not directly involved in the Irish conflict with the United Kingdom. Now, since you are accused of committing these crimes in the United States, I fail to see how politics becomes a factor at all. I mean, it's not as though you're accused of killing a Democrat or a Republican."

There was laughter from the audience.

"And even if you did commit a crime for political reasons, in this country we make no distinction concerning the way we handle individuals who are charged with committing crimes of violence. Everyone is treated the same, rich or poor, citizen or immigrant."

"That's a fuckin' lie," Cassidy said.

Brandlin stared in disbelief.

"If there's another outburst like that, Mr. Cassidy, I'll have the Bailiff's return you to the lockup and we'll continue without you."

He looked over at the prosecutor, then back at Cassidy.

"Your request to represent yourself means that I must make a determination that you are competent to handle your defense. If I allow you to represent yourself as a pro per, you must realize that you will be given no breaks because of your inexperience. You will be expected to conform to the rules of court at all times, and you will have to know and understand the rules of evidence and procedure. You will be held accountable for any breach of those rules. Do you understand what I am saying, Mr. Cassidy?"

"I hear ya. I harbor no illusions about the kind of trial I'll get and the way I'll be treated. I can represent meself as well as any of these paid lackeys of yers."

Brandlin shot forward in his seat, but again, he managed to hold himself in check.

"I will make a finding that you have been adequately warned of the dangers and that you appear competent to represent yourself. I'm going to relieve the Public Defender on your case. You are now your own attorney."

Cassidy smiled.

"I want an investigator be appointed to assist me in the preparation of me case."

Brandlin sighed.

"Let's hear your reasons for wanting an investigator, Mr. Cassidy."

While Cassidy tried to convince the judge, Renée leaned over and whispered to Whitney, "He's doing this to get special privileges. He gets unlimited use of the phone, runners to help in his investigation, and use of the law library on a daily basis. That will give him more freedom of movement and keep him out of his cell for a large part of the day."

"It makes him an escape risk," whispered Gibson, who slid over in his chair to be heard.

Renée frowned.

"It also means this case will take forever to get to trial."

After listening patiently to Cassidy for almost ten minutes, Brandlin concluded with remarks of his own.

"Your request for an investigator will be denied at this time, Mr. Cassidy. I will reconsider it when you provide me with a list of the things you wish the investigator to do. Is there anything else at this time?"

"I want to speak to the prosecutor for a moment," he said.

Brandlin looked at Marin and she nodded affirmatively.

"Come with me, Gibby. I want you to witness this conversation."

She motioned to Whitney to stay where he was while she and Gibson walked over to the glass.

"What can I do for you, Mr. Cassidy?" she asked.

"Who's he?"

"Surely you remember Detective Gibson. He's the investigator assigned to this case and he'll be a witness to our conversation."

"No," said Cassidy. "I'm not talking about Gibson. I mean him." He pointed directly at Whitney.

But Renée was not ready to tell him.

"I have no intention of answering that question, so get to the point. What do you want?"

"Wait a minute." Cassidy kept his eyes glued on Whitney. "He's a Brit. I know I've seen him somewhere." He thought for a moment before the light went on.

"I know. He's the one who came over to me when I was shot. That's him, isn't it?"

"You're wasting my time," said Renée, not taking the bait.

He shifted his eyes from Whitney to Renée and she noted they were cold and full of undisguised hate.

"I want a copy of all the reports and a list of all yer witnesses," he said.

"You'll get a copy of the reports delivered to you at the jail in the next few days. They'll have to be sanitized first."

"What's that mean?" he asked.

"It means that all of the addresses and telephone numbers of the witnesses will be removed from your copies, Mr. Cassidy. I'm sure you realize that we can't have you attempting to contact our witnesses directly. If interviews are necessary, we will make our witnesses available to be questioned by a court-appointed investigator on an occasion that is mutually agreeable."

Cassidy smiled.

"I hear you've let Annie go. Would that be in exchange for her testimony?"

"No, Mr. Cassidy. She's refused to make a statement and her attorney says she won't be a witness."

Cassidy laughed and shook his head.

"Don't hand me that *shite*. I know ya don't have a case against me unless ya use that lyin' bitch. Tell me, Marin, is she one of the witnesses ya have to pro-tect?"

Renée glared at him.

"From now on, Mr. Cassidy, if you want to communicate with me, you can put it in writing. We'll do everything on the record after this."

She abruptly walked away.

"Ya *whore!*" he yelled at her back. "Yer in bed with the Brits, aren't ya?" His voice got louder and it carried across the courtroom. "They're the ones pullin' the strings and they've got ya in their pocket."

He was yelling through the hole in the glass, now directing his remarks towards the members of the press who were writing quite furiously as he spoke.

"Ya said all those things to make me look bad and keep me in solitary, didn't ya?"

Brandlin interrupted him with a yell.

"Sit down, Mr. Cassidy, and be quiet."

"Now I know him," Cassidy said out loud. He stared at the audience and gestured towards Whitney. "He's the reason they put me in isolation."

He looked back and pointed at Marin.

"You're no better'n they are bitch. You're lettin' 'em frame me for somethin' I didn't do!"

A deputy grabbed him from behind, but Cassidy struggled and kept on his feet.

"What goes around comes around!" he yelled at Renée.

"Get him out of here," Brandlin yelled to the deputies.

Three husky deputies moved into the docket and wrestled Cassidy down to the floor. He screamed in pain when pressure was applied to his injured right arm. When the struggle was over, they pulled him to his feet and dragged him back into the lockup.

Renée and Gibson joined Whitney at the counsel table.

"Wow!" She whispered. "He really went off."

"Don't worry about it," Gibson told her. "He's just an asshole blowing off steam. Anyway, you've got far more pressing problems than Cassidy."

He gestured at the reporters who were crowded at the door.

"I think the sharks are ready for lunch."

****

Inside the lockup, Cassidy stood facing a concrete wall while two deputies waited nearby. His left hand was cuffed to a chain around his waist, his feet were tightly cuffed to a walking chain, and his right shoulder and arm were throbbing.

The door from an inner hallway swung open and in walked Deputies Richard Mutter and J. D. Parker, the Sheriff Department's transport team. Both men were dressed in suits, but only J.D. wore a Kevlar vest under his dress shirt. It made him look larger and more intimidating than he already was.

"How's our boy doing?" asked Mutter.

He rubbed his bald head as he looked from Cassidy to the deputies who were watching him.

"Not too good," said one them. He then filled the transport team in on Cassidy's courtroom antics.

"He said that to the prosecutor?" Mutter asked in disbelief.

Both he and Parker took a long, hard look at Cassidy.

"A real ball buster," Parker said, "but not a very bright one, is he?"

Parker grew up in the projects in South Central Los Angeles. No stranger to gang life and the streets, he'd developed a hardness that didn't take to intimidation of any kind, and at six-foot-five, two-forty, he had the wherewithal to easily back up his play.

"You shouldn't have acted up like that," he said. "These fine people have shown you nothing but respect, and look how you've behaved."

"*Fuck off!*" said Cassidy, holding Parker's glare.

"A real tough guy," said Parker. "I like tough guys."

He and Mutter moved towards Cassidy with speed, and Parker got to him first. He grabbed Cassidy by the back of the neck, spun him around, and pressed his face up against the wall.

"Hold him there, J.D.," Mutter said. He slipped a velcro belt around Cassidy's waist, and when the belt was securely fastened, Parker spun Cassidy back around.

Mutter entered Cassidy's personal space, standing eye to eye, only inches apart.

"Listen up, tough guy. I'm gonna explain a few things to you about this belt. You might not be able to feel it yet, but there's a special little package now resting against your right kidney. That's what we like to refer to as *an immobilization unit.*"

He took a step back, and Parker snickered, "Show him the best part."

Mutter held up a small black object that looked suspiciously like a pager. He waved it around for Cassidy to see.

"This little item in my hand is called an *electronic transmitter.*"

Cassidy's eyes grew wide.

"*Ahhh...*" said Mutter. He looked over at the bailiffs. "It appears that Mr. Potty Mouth is beginning to grasp the bigger picture."

The two bailiffs laughed.

"Let's go over the rules, shall we?" Mutter found himself smiling. "If you behave yourself, the belt will come off when we get you back to the jail. But if you step out of line, cause a disturbance, use foul language, anything like that, then I get to push the button, and all you're gonna hear is one loud beep."

Parker smiled like a Cheshire Cat.

"Pay attention to this part, tough guy. This is the really good stuff."

Mutter continued, "If the belt goes beep, it means that I have exactly five seconds to push the abort code. If I don't do it in time, then...*zap!* You'll be the proud recipient of our grand prize for the day, an eight-second jolt of two hundred and fifty thousand volts."

Everyone but Cassidy laughed, and Mutter acknowledged their platitudes with a slight bow.

"One eight second jolt is all you'll need," he continued, "You'll be a drooling, pissing, defecating mess." He paused for a moment to let his point sink in. "Do we understand each other, tough guy?"

Cassidy lowered his eyes and grunted his assent. His defiance in the courtroom had cost him dearly, and he cursed himself for making his situation worse.

"You guys ready to take him now?" asked one of the courtroom deputies.

"I believe we are," Parker responded.

With that, Mutter opened the inner door that led to the prisoner's elevator. "This way, Cassidy."

****

Outside the courtroom, in the main corridor, Renée Marin was confronted by a sea of reporters. They clamored for a statement and yelled out questions about Cassidy, most of which were focused on his role as a bomber who was wanted in London.

She tried to pacify them all with a broad, general statement about courtroom proceedings and his representing himself. But when they pressed her to comment on Cassidy's threats, she broke off the questioning and retreated to the safety of her office.

****

Jimmy Cassidy received a call on his cell phone. He listened for a moment, then hung up.

"He's headin' for the bus," he told the others. "Let's go."

****

Mutter led the way out of the building and into a caged transport zone. The van was parked next to a loading dock, well under the building and away from public scrutiny. The van was an oversized Ford Econoline, with three rows of seats and tinted windows all around. There was a sliding rear door on the passenger side and double doors with tiny barred windows at the rear of the chassis.

Parker slid back the side door, ordered Cassidy onto one of the bench seats, then cuffed his waist chain and leg irons into a bracket that was fused to the frame of the truck. He slid the door shut, locked the exterior sliding door with a key, climbed into the front seat, then placed the keys on a chain that was suspended from his belt.

The rear portion of the van was separated from the driving compartment by a heavy-gauge, steel mesh screen, and once the door was shut, the van became an impregnable moving cell.

As they pulled out of the parking lot, Parker took the activator for the immobilization unit from Mutter's hand and slipped it into a leather pouch on his own waistband.

"Why do you get it?" Mutter asked.

"'Cause you're driving," Parker said with a smile.

The jail was more than a mile from the courthouse, and for more than six months, Mutter had driven back and forth as often as four times a day. Traffic conditions were usually bad on the nearby Hollywood Freeway, so he'd learned to stay on city streets to bypass the worst of the congestion.

The repetition of this daily routine had worked against his sense of awareness. Today was no different than any other day, so he stayed on the route most commonly taken by most of the transport vans.

****

Devon McGarry had stationed his car in a small parking lot near *Olvera Street*, the historical center of the city. A van appeared in traffic, and as it passed by him, he could just make out Liam Cassidy through the tinted side windows.

He moved his radio to his lips.

"They just went past me, Jimmy. Two guys in the front seat. I'm movin' up behind 'em right now."

McGarry was in his late forties, average in height, with a head of thick, black, unkempt hair. He had a nervous tic, a twitching eyelid, that often showed up when he was under stress. The lid was twitching now.

He pulled his Escort from the lot and pushed it hard to close in on the van. When he got within two car lengths, he flipped off the safety on his handgun and placed it beside him on the seat.

Two blocks ahead, Kelly and Jimmy idled their car in a warehouse parking lot. Parked close to the sidewalk, they craned their necks to watch for the van that was coming right towards them from the South. When it pulled into sight, Jimmy jumped out of the car and walked down the sidewalk away from the corner.

Jimmy wore a dirty watch cap which was perfect with his stubble beard. It made him look like a derelict. As he staggered down the sidewalk, eyes on the street, he fingered a machine pistol suspended on a rope that he wore just under his grease stained coat.

Kelly was a dour man with dark black hair and a pockmarked face. He drove the car down the driveway but stopped on the sidewalk instead of entering the street. He idled there while he watched intently as the van drew closer, and just before it reached the driveway, he lurched his car forward and into the street, which forced the van to skid to a stop.

McGarry pulled up behind the van, trapping it between the two cars. He then jumped out and scanned the streets for any sign of trouble.

Jimmy flipped back his coat, brought up his weapon, and fired it into the van.

At first, Mutter believed they were dealing with a drunk driver. Who else would pull out into oncoming traffic like that? But that was his very last thought. Mutter wasn't wearing his bulletproof vest, so when the rounds started coming through the window, one entered his chest where it severed an artery and lodged in his spine.

From the corner of his eye, D. J. Parker, who was seated up front in the passenger seat, caught the image of a man on the sidewalk coming up with what looked like a gun. It was happening fast, too fast, and as he turned his head to face him, he caught a single round in his bulletproof vest.

It slammed him forward, head to his knees, a position which saved his life because s a second volley of rounds streamed in through the blown out window, passing over his head.

But unfortunately for Parker, one clipped the door frame and caught him in the side.

He lay there, slouched over in the front seat, panicked and gasping for breath. His brain was telling him to go for his gun, but instinct took over and he calmed himself down. His survival depended on playing dead.

****

Jimmy ran up to the van. He tried the side sliding door but it was solidly locked.

"The one in the passenger's seat has the key," yelled Liam from inside the back of the van.

Jimmy opened the front door and searched Parker's slumped body. He found the ring full of keys on his belt. He grabbed it, tried several different ones, then found the right one.

The sliding door finally sprung open.

"I knew you'd come," said Liam to his brother. "I'm cuffed to a chain that's hooked to the floor. There's another set of cuffs on me feet."

Jimmy had brought along his own handcuff key which he kept on a cord around his neck. He pulled it out, grabbed his brother's wrists, slipped in the key, and undid the lock.

****

Det. Rodrigo Amador was on his way back to the Criminal Courts Building from the county jail. A tall man with big arms and a barrel chest, he'd been a detective with the LAPD for more than a dozen years. He'd spent the morning at the jail with an untested informant; a man with promising information on a homicide case, and if the DA was inclined to agree, the man would give up his homeboy for a grant of straight probation on a run-of-the-mill commercial bur-glary case. Amador smiled to himself. It was the kind of a deal he was willing to do anytime he could get it.

He turned onto Vignes Street and was jolted from his thoughts by the sounds of automatic weapons fire. He scanned the road ahead but saw nothing unusual. Accelerating quickly, he reached for his Rover.

"4 King 87," he said excitedly. He waited for Communications to give him a response.

As he came closer to the intersection at Bauchet Street, he noticed three vehicles seemingly locked together at the corner.

His first thought was that he was looking at was a traffic accident, but then it registered in his brain that one of the vans was a prisoner transport, and from where he was seated, he could see that there was movement near the passenger side sliding door.

Someone's trying to escape!

He slammed to a stop and brought the Rover to his lips.

"4 King 87. Shots fired! Prisoner escape in progress! Bauchet at Vignes. Officer needs help!"

****

"Behind you Mic," McGarry yelled. "In the blue car!"
Kelly spun around and saw Amador's car as it slid to a stop at the corner.
Without hesitation, Kelly raised his gun and began to fire.

****

Amador saw the gun coming up. Acting more on instinct than calculated thought, he threw his car in reverse, punched the accelerator, dropped flat on the seat, and held on to the wheel. He prayed there was nothing in the lane behind him.

Over the radio, he could hear his call for help going out.

His car roared backward, jumped a curb, and crashed into a masonry wall. Bullets shattered the windshield just above his head and bounced around the inside of the car. Time came to a stop while he held his breath. He was sure that any moment he was going to be hit.

And then, just as suddenly as it had started, the firing came to a stop.

In the eerie quiet that followed, Amador opened his eyes, and to his absolute astonishment, he realized that somehow he'd been spared from an untimely death.

Flushed with his good fortune, he crawled across the seat and slid out through the passenger side door. His only thought was to keep the car as a buffer between himself and the shooter.

On his knees by the side of the car, he gulped in air and tried to regain his composure. His hands were shaking uncontrollably from the excess adrenaline, and blood trickled down into his eyes. He knew he hadn't been shot, so he quickly concluded that he probably struck his head when the car ran into the wall.

He pulled out his gun and crawled on all fours towards the front of his

Plymouth.

****

"Hurry, Jimmy!" Devon yelled. "We haven't got much time."

A lone siren could be heard in the distance. Then others…

Precious seconds were lost when Jimmy hit the ground behind the van, the result of confusion brought on by Kelly's first volley of shots. But when no one fired back from the Plymouth, Jimmy scrambled to his knees and tried to get the key into his brother's ankle lock.

His hands were shaking and he almost dropped the key.

"Give it to me!" Liam screamed.

Jimmy reached up and handed him the key. There were more sirens now and they were getting closer.

"Hurry up, Liam!" Jimmy said.

D.J. Parker, who still lay motionless in the front seat, hardly daring to breathe, was well aware that his life was still in danger. Although he couldn't see them working in the back, his attention was focused on their words.

The air was punctuated with the sound of sirens approaching from everywhere, and as they came closer, he assessed his chances for survival. They were markedly better as the seconds ticked by, and once he began to believe that he might make it, he returned his focus to what was going on behind him in the back of the van.

In that instant, a long-buried sense of duty came to the surface and a plan began to take shape.

Cassidy would soon be free and there was no better moment to act. Inching his left hand to the transmitter hanging on his belt, he placed his finger over the button.

Liam got the key in and turned it.

"Got it!" he yelled.

And at that very moment, J.D. Parker depressed the activator button which, in turn, set off the immobilization unit.

A loud beeping went off in the back of the van which startled both of the brothers.

"What the hell?" Jimmy cried. He looked over at Liam for an answer.

Oh, Jesus..!

Liam knew right away what it was. He tried to get out of the van while clawing at his waist.

Too late!

His back arched violently as the voltage entered his body and poured through his kidney. He dropped like a stone to a spot between the seats.

Jimmy stood outside the van in frozen disbelief as Liam's body twisted around violently on the floor of the van.

"Get up!" he screamed.

Liam stopped twitching but did not move.

McGarry came running up to the van from behind.

"Leave 'im Jimmy! They're on us!"

Jimmy looked around frantically. Numerous flashing police lights were on top of them. They only had seconds to get away.

"C'mon, Jimmy!" McGarry tugged violently at his arm.

The two men locked eyes.

"We can't leave him," Jimmy screamed.

"We have to," McGarry yelled. "He's dead, Jimmy. He's dead."

Kelly pulled up in McGarry's car and flung open the passenger door.

"Get in," he ordered. *"We go now!"*

****

As the attackers made their getaway, J.D. Parker exhaled heavily. He started to experience the kind of relief known only to those who've faced certain death, yet somehow managed to survive. But this was not the time to celebrate. His partner was dead, and he still had no idea as to whether or not he had managed to stop Liam Cassidy before he could get away.

So in spite of his pain, Parker slid out of the damaged transport van and into the street where he could look through the now open sliding door and into the back of the van.

He was astounded to discover the body of Liam Cassidy. It was still lying on the floor, wedged between the seat and the security screen.

"I'll be damned!" he said to himself. *"The fucking thing worked."*

He struggled for a moment to retrieve the transmitter from the pouch that he kept on his belt. Then moving partway into the van, he crouched over Cassidy's inert body and pressed the triggering button again and again.

He watched with satisfaction as Cassidy's body twitched violently, much like an epileptic seizure.

"That's for my partner, you asshole!"

****

Amador's first sweeping look caught the image of the Escort as it pulled away from the van. He raised his gun, but his hand was shaking so violently that he never got off a shot.

He got to his feet and ran over to the van just as a unit pulled up and stopped about twenty feet away. He waved it off in pursuit of the Escort while he hooked his badge to the outside of his jacket to make sure that he wouldn't get shot by one of the units that were now pulling up in significant numbers.

He checked on Mutter first--no pulse, fixed pupils--it was obvious to Amador that he was dead. On the passenger side, he found Parker who was now sitting in the street, slumped up against the side of the van. His eyes were open, but it looked as though he was starting to go into shock.

"Help's almost here," he told him. "Are you hit?"

"My side," Parker moaned. He closed his eyes.

Amador saw a blood stain on the deputy's shirt.

"Just hang on, partner. You're gonna make it. The paramedics are on their way."

He heard running footsteps getting closer by the second.

"I'm LAPD... LAPD!" he screamed. "Get the paramedics here, Code Three. We've got two officers down!"

Amador tore off his shirt, balled it up, and held it against Parker's side. It was then that he spotted Liam Cassidy still on the floor in the van.

"There's a prisoner in the back," Parker managed to tell him.

Amador stood up, pulled out his gun, and pointed his weapon at Cassidy.

"We've got a prisoner down in the van," he yelled to officers who were now running towards their position. "Somebody check him out."

He knelt down again next to Parker who suddenly reopened his eyes.

"Don't worry about him," Parker whispered. A smile crept over his face. "I just put him through training for the electric chair."

****

THIRTEEN

September 30, Wednesday, Late Morning

Renée was seated in her office, waiting for a call from Glenn Kerin, the Chief Deputy District Attorney. She wanted to tell him about the dismissal, but he was still in a management meeting, so she was killing time and wishing that she was headed out for lunch.

When the phone rang, she answered it immediately, not waiting for her secretary to pick it up.

"Renée? It's Glenn. I just got a call from LAPD. There's been a shooting over near Chinatown. Someone opened fire on the transport bus taking Liam Cassidy back to the jail. Two deputies have been shot."

Marin's eyes went wide.

"Oh my God!"

That explained all the sirens she'd been hearing for the last ten minutes.

"Did Cassidy get away?" she asked.

"Apparently not, but he's down, too. I want you to get over there right away. Is Detective Gibson with you?"

"He and Whitney just stepped out to get a cup of coffee," she replied.

"Find him and have him call his office. His cell must be turned off."

"I'll take care of it right now."

"Good, but before you go, what happened on your case?"

She filled him in, the Reader's Digest version, then hung up to search for the others.

****

Kerin used a a door marked private that led to Rosen's office. He knocked once, waited, then used his key get in. Rosen was seated at his desk.

"Have you heard about the breakout attempt?"

Rosen nodded.

"I just got off the phone with the Sheriff."

Kerin cleared his throat.

"We dismissed on the girl, Aaron, and Cassidy has gone pro per, so it looks like this is gonna go on for a while."

Rosen looked up.

"Is the girl going to testify?"

"That's not part of the deal."

Rosen put his pen down and glared at Kerin.

"Do you want to tell me why?"

"We had no choice. Magruder's lawyer won't cut a deal, and we have no case against the girl. We've done the right thing, and I'm sure we can sell it that way to the press."

"I don't like the position you've placed me in, Glenn. The public will be incensed about this breakout attempt, and they'll question our decision to let the girl off the hook."

"The trial's a long way off, Aaron." He took a chair across from Rosen. "Besides, I've thought of a way you can handle this."

"Oh?" Rosen's interest piqued. "What did you have in mind?"

"We don't have to say she's cooperating, but we can create the inference that she is."

Rosen smiled.

"You mean a half-assed denial and a wink?"

"Even more subtle. It's all in how you say it."

Rosen thought for a moment.

"Not bad, Glenn, Not bad."

****

Gibson, Whitney, Donahue and Renée arrived at the scene of the shooting ten minutes later. The area was cordoned off with yellow crime scene tape and the command post, set up across the street from the van, was a beehive of activity as units checked in for their assignments.

Gibson signed them into the log book, then the three of them went hunting for the deputy-in-charge. They found him draped over the hood of a nearby car, consulting a map of the Chinatown area.

"Are you in charge of this case, Lieutenant?" Gibson asked.

Sheriff's Lieutenant Barry Lipman looked up. A tall man, with short gray hair, a prominent nose, and deep-set eyes, he perfectly fit the Hollywood perception of the no-nonsense law enforcement official. Lipman worked at LASO's Homicide Unit. They had insisted on taking over the search for the suspects because the deceased Deputy Mutter had been one of their own.

Because the shooting had taken place in the city of Los Angeles, LAPD units had been the first to respond. By mutual agreement, Lipman was running a joint agency investigation.

When a cop went down, everyone in law enforcement got involved.

"Hold on for a moment, Detective."

Lipman consulted his map one more time, then initiated a broadcast over his Rover. Once he was finished assigning his units to a search grid, he returned his attention to Gibson and the others.

"Now, what can I do for you?"

Gibson filled him in on his connection with Cassidy, and when he was finished, Lipman told him, "Our two deputies were taking your boy back to the jail. Best we can determine, three male Caucasians boxed them in by the intersection and opened fire without warning. One of our guys is dead; the other caught a round in the side." Lipman gestured towards the van. "If you want a look, the body's over there, still in the front seat. The wounded deputy has been transported to County General Hospital."

"How's he doing?" Donahue asked.

"He's critical, but he was talking when they wheeled him away." Lipman sighed. "Your prisoner was wearing a stun belt, and apparently, he never made it out of the van."

"Is he dead?" Renée asked.

Lipman shook his head.

"Not dead, but he was zapped pretty good. His brain's a little fuzzy, but I understand he's coming around."

"Have you moved him from the scene?" Gibson asked.

Lipman pointed over his shoulder.

"We've got him in an unmarked unit, just around the corner. The paramedics are there now checking him out."

Lipman's radio suddenly crackled to life.

"7 Mary 21 to CP. We've located the vehicle in an underground parking lot on Spring. No sign of the suspects. They may have made a switch."

"Damn it!" Lipman turned towards Gibson. "They got past our perimeter."

He picked up his Rover.

"Don't let anyone near the car until the lab team arrives."

He looked back at Gibson.

"Anything else, Detective? I'm a little pressed at the moment."

"No, I've got what I need, Lieutenant. Thanks for your time."

They turned and walked away from the command post.

"What now?" Whitney asked.

"You and Renee can wait for me at the car. I want to take a quick look at our boy."

He left them standing in the street while he headed for the unit where Cassidy was now being held. Several uniformed officers stood guard nearby with shotguns at the ready.

Cassidy was seated in the back seat, his good hand securely cuffed again to a waist chain, while a Fire-Paramedic team checked him out.

When they were finished, Gibson walked up and flashed his ID.

"How's he doing?" he asked.

"He's okay," said one of the paramedics. "Can't talk yet, but he knows what happened and where he is. We're gonna take him down to County General for observation."

"I need to speak with him for a moment. *Alone.*"

The paramedics looked at each other, and with some reluctance, they stepped back and walked out of earshot.

Gibson squatted down next to the open door and put his face in next to Cassidy's.

With a meaty hand he grabbed him by the jaw and squeezed.

"I know you can't speak, so listen up, *asshole.* Your friends just killed a Sheriff's deputy. If you want to help yourself, you'll tell me who's responsible, and if you do, I'll see what can be done on your case."

Cassidy struggled to pull his jaw free from Gibson's grip. The look in his eyes was a mixture of terror and hate, but Gibson squeezed Liam's jaw even tighter.

"If you don't cooperate, I'll see to it that you spend what days you have left on this earth in a hellhole called Pelican Bay. It's a prison so shitty that even a tough guy like you will be begging to die within a few weeks."

He let go of Cassidy's face.

"Think about it, asshole. If you want to talk to me, do it soon. Otherwise, you're going down for the count."

Gibson stood up to leave, then had second thoughts. He leaned back into the car.

"By the way, Cassidy, the DA on your case is a personal friend of mine. The next time you mouth off to her, I'll see to it that someone takes a piss in your jail food."

He stood up slowly and walked away from the car.

****

Aaron Rosen entered the DA's private conference room and noted, with satisfaction, that the chamber was filled to capacity. There were more than a dozen cameras lined up in two distinct rows, representing all of the networks and the cable stations. What space was left over was standing room only. There were journalists from several dozen newspapers, including four from Great Britain and two from Japan.

For the past two months, Rosen had been putting out feelers with leaders within the Republican party about his chances in a run for Governor. He wanted to be perceived as a leader, and as the point man on the Cassidy case, he knew he would be furthering his chances for a future campaign.

When he reached the podium, camera lights were turned on, and technicians made adjustments with their meters. He laid out his written statement and waited for his cue.

"All set, Mr. Rosen," said his press secretary.

"Good afternoon, ladies and gentlemen." He paused long enough to make sure that he had their full attention. "This morning we announced the dismissal of murder charges against Anne Magruder in the deaths of the two British Special Air Service Officers, Sean Clarke and Paul Whitcomb." He stared directly into the cameras with his most sincere look. "Although Miss Magruder was present with her codefendant at the time of the killings, we believe that the evidence against her is insufficient to prove that she had knowledge of his criminal intent. Her co-defendant, Liam Cassidy, was advised of the charges against him this morning, and he has deferred entering his plea for another two weeks. He is currently representing himself, but he has advised the court that he will retain his own counsel in time for his pending arraignment."

He looked up from his prepared statement. "Are there any questions I can answer for any of you?"

The room exploded as a dozen different voices yelled questions all at once.

Rosen smiled, looked around, and tried to decide who to call on first. He settled on the blond from Channel 7.

"Yes, ma'am," he said, pointing expansively in her direction.

"Mr. Rosen. Will Miss Magruder be testifying for the prosecution?"

He smiled inwardly. He was ready for this one.

"Naturally, we are studying all of our options in this case, but at this moment in time, we have no agreement from her that she will be testifying."

"Does that mean you expect to have one in the future?" asked someone from CNN.

"It's one of our options."

"Is immunity an option?" asked a journalist from the Washington Post.

He smiled. "Yes, it's an option."

"Will she be getting immunity to testify?" The question came from FOX News.

"As I said, we are considering all of our options."

He sounded like a broken record, and worse, like a man without a plan. He had to guide things back to a topic that would allow him to pontificate on general information.

He sought out the attractive brunette from the *Daily News*. He could always count on her to steer things back his way.

"Miss Bergstrom," he called out, looking in her direction. She was leaning against the wall.

"Mr. Rosen. Can you prove your case against Cassidy without the testimony of Anne Magruder?"

He began to squirm. He had no intention of being dragged into a discussion of the merits of the case. That would mean trouble if he made a mistake. It was time to go to the fall-back position.

"Ms. Renée Marin, the head of our Organized Crime and Terrorism Division, will be handling this case personally. She has advised me that the case can be proven without the testimony of Miss Magruder. I have high confidence in her judgment, and I'm sure that if she decides at some point that the testimony of Miss Magruder is necessary to enhance the case, then we will undoubtedly proceed accordingly."

He gestured to an attractive female from Channel 2 News.

"Is the case against Mr. Cassidy a strong one?" she asked.

Rosen smiled to himself. Finally, a milquetoast question that would allow him to sound authoritative.

"Yes, ma'am," he replied. "We don't file any charges unless we believe we have proof beyond a reasonable doubt."

Channel 7 smiled broadly.

"Then why did you file the case against Miss Magruder if you didn't have proof beyond a reasonable doubt?"

There was a general snickering throughout the room and he knew he'd walked into a trap. He cleared his throat and stalled for a moment to compose his answer.

"Well, in Miss Magruder's case, we had to file within forty-eight hours of her arrest. At the time we filed, we believed we had enough evidence to prove our case beyond a reasonable doubt, but a subsequent investigation has convinced us that the evidence really wasn't there, so a dismissal of the charges was in order."

"Then how do we know that a follow-up investigation won't also clear Mr. Cassidy?" The question had been posed by a man from NBC.

Rosen felt himself starting to get hot under the collar. They were coming at him like sharks.

"It would be improper for me to discuss the merits of our case against Mr. Cassidy at this time. I can only say that I'm satisfied that our evidence is sufficient."

"Is Ms. Marin available for comment?" asked the reporter from the *Times*.

"At the moment I'm afraid she's out in the field handling a follow-up situation related to this case."

Several of the network television crews killed their lights, sensing that the conference was over. A few of the print reporters started for the door. Realizing that he'd lost them, Rosen tried to end things with a modicum of decorum.

"Are there any further questions before we call it a day?"

When no one responded or paid him any attention, a dejected Aaron Rosen folded up his written statement and went back to his office.

****

Gibson caught up with Whitney, Donahue and Renée back at his car.

"Learn anything?" Renée asked him.

"No. He's still not able to talk, but I don't think you'll have to worry about his insults anymore. I told him his behavior was completely inappropriate."

She looked at Gibson and tried to fathom his meaning.

"Should I ask what you said?"

"Better you don't."

"Then thanks. I guess?"

He started the engine and looked over at Whitney.

"We've underestimated these people. We've got to do a better job of anticipating their plans."

"So how do we prevent another breakout attempt?" Renée asked.

"That will never happen again," Gibson told her. "The Sheriffs will see to it that he'll get a well-armed escort everywhere he goes. But if his pals can't get him out, then their next logical move would be to get rid of the witness."

Gibson turned down his police radio to make conversation easier.

"The rental car clerk should be no problem," he said. "She's single and we can relocate her without a big hassle."

"What about Lou Berehens?" Whitney asked.

"That's a much bigger problem, but for the time being, I can arrange for Metro Division to set up on his house and stay with him around the clock. But if push comes to shove, we may temporarily have to move him to a safe house."

"Who's gonna pay for all of this?" Renée asked.

Gibson smiled.

"This case has the attention of the world press. All the publicity will force the government to spend whatever it takes to keep our witnesses safe."

"You're terribly pragmatic," Renée said.

"It's how the game works."

He looked over at Whitney.

"Can you get us any photographs of Cassidy's known associates? We've got a couple of police officers who survived that shootout. Maybe one of them can make an ID."

"I'll see what I can do. In the meantime, why don't you drop me off at my car? It's over by the courthouse. I'll need to get over to the consulate to put in my request."

Gibson started up the car and headed to the courthouse.

"Renée? How about you?"

"Drop me off at the office, Gibby. I need to check in with Kerin."

Whitney reached over the front seat and tapped her on the shoulder.

"I was wonderin' if you'd care to join me for dinner again tonight?"

She laughed.

"You're desperate for companionship, aren't you?"

"Does that mean you will?"

"I can't, Whit. I've got to spend some time with my daughter. Can I get a raincheck?"

He was silent for a moment, then, "What's a raincheck?"

She laughed.

"You know, a coupon that says when it rains you can come back and... *never mind*. What I meant was, can we do it some other night?"

"I'm still confused. Does that mean I have to wait until it rains?"

His smile made her laugh. She turned back to Gibson.

"Where are you headed?"

"I'll go back to the station and get our witness security situation under control. After that, I'll probably help out on the shootings. Will you be on your cell phone this evening?"

"No way. Once I get home, I'm in for the night."

"Okay, if anything breaks I'll call you at home."

He stopped at a lot near the courthouse and let Whitney out before driving up to the building. As Renée got out of the car, she turned back and gave him a smile.

"Can I ask a favor?" she asked.

"Sure."

"Could you quietly check into Whitney's background for me?"

Gibson winked.

"Do we need to know if the Major is married?"

She smiled sheepishly.

"He's been giving me the rush, but it's more than that. I just realized that we've accepted him on face value. He shows up out of nowhere and we've made him one of the team. What do we actually know about this guy?"

Gibson's eye's widened. She was absolutely right.

"I'll get on it right away."

****

FOURTEEN

September 30, Wednesday, Evening

Whitney spent the better part of his afternoon on the telephone with London. Although it was the middle of the night in the United Kingdom, he'd managed to track down the duty clerk at the SAS Intelligence Headquarters at *Cheltenham,* England.

To reduce the risk of a terrorist attack, the facility was concealed on a nondescript military base with a small and infrequently used airfield. Deterred by double rows of barbed wire fencing, the uninvited never ventured past the sign that proclaimed it a *Noxious Waste Disposal Research Station.*

They were housed in a hanger with accompanying support offices. A small sign above the door bore the inscription "Liaison Unit."

Inside the facility, a full array of IBM mainframe computers was interfaced with the very latest in telecommunications equipment. The operation was staffed by intelligence specialists who processed and evaluated everything they could concerning terrorist groups and their related activities.

The raw data came in from around the world. Cross referenced into all conceivable subcategories, it enabled the analysts to determine patterns and weaknesses among the groups being monitored. Once shortcomings were discovered, the data was forwarded to operations personnel for future exploitation. Quite naturally, the IRA received a high priority regarding analysis and resources.

The duty officer located Lieutenant Robert Martin, the principal analyst at the IRA desk. Whitney filled him in on the escape attempt and asked him to pull up whatever he could about Liam Cassidy's known associates.

"I sent through my first request almost two weeks ago," Whitney added, "but I never heard anythin' back."

"That's strange, Major. I don't remember seeing your request?"

Whitney was puzzled. What had they done...*lost it?*

"How long will a new request take, Lieutenant?"

"Three hours or so. I'll have to eliminate identifying factors, like the names of sources from the raw data, but it shouldn't take too long."

"Okay. Send it as a priority encoded transmission over a diplomatic line to the consulate in Los Angeles."

Whitney drove to his hotel in Brentwood; a twenty-story circular hotel with a view of the San Diego Freeway. There were no messages to be answered, so he showered, watched the early news, then dressed in casual slacks and a sports coat. With nothing else to do, he drove back to the consulate to await the promised report.

The Consulate was located in a sturdy old house set in the foothills above Hollywood. Built in the style of a colonial mansion, it was surrounded by an eight-foot wall topped with wrought iron spikes. The gardens were expansive and trees abounded within the three-acre compound.

He pulled up to the gate and flashed his identification into the lens of a small security camera. A short time later, the gate slid open and he drove to an entrance in the back.

He was escorted to a basement room adjacent to the communications center where he showed his ID at a window, then advised the duty officer that he was there to receive a transmission. With nothing to do and time to kill, he settled into an overstuffed chair to catch a well-deserved nap.

Two hours later, when the transmission finally arrived, he was shocked to discover how little had been sent—only three pages of text, and *no photographs.*

He pored through the material, personal family history and suspected criminal activities, most of which was decidedly low-level data. All in all, he found the report to be very disappointing.

He reviewed the section which purported to be a history of Liam Cassidy's involvement with the Provos. He'd started as a runner in Belfast and worked his way into an action group by the time of his twentieth birthday. Through innuendo and supposition—most of it unconfirmed—he was suspected of involvement in three separate sniping's: two against the Protestant police force in Derry, the third against the British in Belfast. At age twenty-two, he went underground, his whereabouts and activities unknown.

Whitney smiled. That was probably when he'd gotten himself into trouble with John Magruder. He would have to remember to pass that story on to his mates. He could only surmise what Cassidy did while in hiding—training somewhere, perhaps in the *Beqaa Valley* in Lebanon—someplace where he'd managed to learn about bombs.

A confidential informant had fingered Cassidy for the bombing in London. The details of the blast were all too familiar—anonymous warning, chaotic evacuation—two dead and twenty-one injured. He'd disappeared again after that, and according to a notation from Lieutenant Martin, he hadn't surfaced in the last three years. Whitney scanned the report again. There was nothing about his associates.

What the hell was going on?

He rubbed his temples and tried to fathom the reason for this oversight. Did they think the information was going to be released to an unsecured agency? That would be nonsense. He was cleared to review everything, even raw material, so why was his access being restricted?

There had to be more data on file. Once he was fingered in the bombing, there should have been an all-out effort made to determine the names of his associates. So where was that information? And why didn't he get it? The more he thought it over, the angrier he became.

He read the report again, carefully this time, just in case he'd missed something of importance. He discovered a reference to *James*, an older brother of Liam.

And he couldn't help but wonder if James was a Provo, and if so, then why wasn't that addressed in the report?

Whitney threw it down on the table in disgust. He had to learn more and he had to learn it fast. Calling Lieutenant Martin back would be a waste of time. He was too low in rank to provide him with any answers. He would have to go to the top.

He walked out of the study and down the hall until he came to the door of the security center where he pushed a buzzer, identified himself, and waited while they opened the steel security door.

Whitney took a seat at the computer console and composed a confidential memorandum to Col. Nigel Ward, the Director of MI-5.

To Command One. Request made this date for all raw intelligence of non-

compromising nature on Liam Cassidy and Associates from SAS INT HDQ
CHELTENHAM. Information received was filtered and devoid of value. Mention
made of brother James with no accompanying profile. Request Priority One.
Need information on associates of Liam and James Cassidy from MI-5 files.
Time of the essence. Attempt made today to free Primary. Casualties encoun-
tered by locals. Regards, Tracker 1.

Whitney coded the message and sent it over a secure satellite line directly to
MI-5 headquarters in London. And then, almost as an afterthought, he took a
few moments to flash a quick inquiry about Cassidy to an old friend from the
Regiment at SAS Belfast in Northern Ireland.

He left the consulate and went back to his hotel, unable to shake the feeling
that something was very wrong.

****

Devon McGarry entered the driveway of the duplex and drove to the back
of the property. He pulled the silver Buick sedan into a detached two-car garage
and shut off the punched ignition. The three men removed their equipment from
the trunk of the car and climbed the stairs to their second-floor unit.

Claire Harris, a petite brunette with shoulder-length brown hair, was waiting
at the top of the stairs.

"How'd it go?" she asked.

Jimmy Cassidy brushed past her, saying nothing. He swung his duffel bag
onto the kitchen table, opened it up, and removed an armor-plated vest, a machine pistol, and several spare clips of ammunition. He then headed for the bedroom without answering her question.

McGarry entered the kitchen and took a seat at the table.

"Where's Liam?" she asked him with concern in her voice.

He looked up and shook his head.

"We had to leave 'im behind. He collapsed before we could get his cuffs
off."

Kelly walked in and took a pistol from the duffle bag and began to break it down for cleaning.

"I don't understand what happened?" he said. He looked over at McGarry. "No one was shootin' when it happened."

"Maybe he had a heart attack," McGarry suggested.

Jimmy Cassidy reentered the room and walked over to the sink. He turned on the water and drank directly from the tap. He stood up, shut his eyes, and hoped an idea would take shape. What were they going to do?

He slowly opened his eyes and discovered that everyone there was watching him. No time for recriminations about what happened. It was time to start thinking operationally again.

"Claire," he said, "turn on the telly and see what you can find out." He watched her leave the kitchen before turning back to the others.

"Do you think he's still alive?" McGarry asked.

"How the fuck would I know," Cassidy snapped. "We should never 'ave left 'im."

"Do we pack it in?" Kelly asked. He unconsciously rubbed at the stubble on his chin. "I mean, if he is alive, I don't think they'll be givin' us another chance to spring 'im?"

Cassidy answered his question with a glare. He turned to McGarry.

"I want you to start makin' a bomb."

"But we don't even know if he's alive, Jimmy?" McGarry said. "What good would it do to build one now?"

Cassidy's eyes narrowed.

"Just make the fuckin' thing."

He knew he was losing it; he could see it in their faces.

"Look, Devon, we'll know soon enough if he's alive, and if he is, we'll be needin' to change our approach."

McGarry thought about it for a moment, then acquiesced.

"So what do we blow?"

"I'm not sure yet. We'll have to hit 'em with somethin' that scares the *shite* out of 'em."

Cassidy glanced over at Kelly.

"Go over to the courthouse tomorrow and see if you can get us a layout.

Find out what you can about Liam's prosecutor. Maybe that will give us an edge?"

"Do we know who the prosecutor is?" McGarry asked.

"Not yet, but we'll find out more when I check in with our friend."

Kelly placed the freshly oiled gun on the table.

"Would you mind me askin' a question, Jimmy?"

"That depends on the question?"

"I'm just wonderin' what we're gettin' ourselves into?"

"We're already in it, Mic. Nothin's changed but the scenery."

"But he may be dead, Jimmy?"

"And he may be alive." Cassidy clenched and unclenched his fists. "Do you have a problem with that?"

Kelly held his gaze.

"I've got no problem with that, but Liam got into this all on his own. We're runnin' blind in this country, and we may be in over our heads."

Cassidy looked at them both. He could see that McGarry was also concerned, but not quite as much as Kelly.

"This is no different than any other mission. We'll not be takin' any more serious risks. They'll be puttin' all their energy into guardin' Liam, and we'll have to come at 'em now from where they least expect it. Fear is our weapon. It'll work here. They're soft and unprepared."

"If you say so, Jimmy." Kelly looked down. "But we're all alone here."

Cassidy walked over and placed his hand on Kelly's shoulder.

"You're a good soldier, Mic, and you're right. We need to take new precautions. I'll call our friend tonight and arrange for a safe house; then tomorrow, I'll have Claire find us a place to use as a backup."

****

The motel she'd selected was just off Sunset Boulevard in Brentwood. It was small and off the beaten path, but its Tudor appearance gave it the feeling of class, despite the fact that it was commonly used by wealthy west-siders for discreet, illicit trysts.

Lisa Collins waited with patience for Commander Mark Carlson to appear. Seated on the bed, she wore a sleeveless summer dress that accentuated her body and stopped just above her knees. The TV was on, mostly for the company, but the light it emitted would also set the mood.

When he knocked on the door, she lay back on the bed and adjusted her skirt.

"Come in," she cooed.

Carlson opened the door and stepped into the room. He said, "You really should keep your door locked. You never know who might try to get in here."

"I knew it was you," she said with a smile. She noticed that his gaze was riveted to her legs, so she crossed them slowly to get his full attention.

"Why don't you fix yourself a drink?" she said.

She'd placed a bottle of bourbon, a bucket of ice, and a liter of club soda on the dresser. He walked over to the dresser and put ice in a glass.

"I'm touched that you went to all this trouble," he said. "Would you like one too?"

"Yes, please." She watched him mix the drinks. "Are you goin' to tell me what happened today?"

He walked over to the bed and handed her a drink.

"Is this on or off the record?"

"Whatever you want," she said with a smile.

He removed his suit jacket, placed it on a chair, and sat next to her on the bed.

"It's a fucking mess," he said as he took a pull from his drink. He reached over and placed his hand on the skin of her bare leg.

"Off the record, it looks like a group of terrorists tried to break him out. They killed one deputy and wounded a second."

"What about Liam Cassidy? On the telly they said he's in the hospital. Was he shot?"

Carlson shook his head. He couldn't repress a smile.

"The deputies had him fitted with a stun belt, and they set it off before he could run. He'll get out of the hospital sometime tomorrow." He took another swallow of his bourbon. "I really needed this."

"Any leads on the terrorists?" she asked.

"Not yet, but we may get something soon. A Liaison with the SAS is doing a background check on Cassidy's associates, and maybe that will give us a lead."

She reached up with both hands and massaged his upper shoulders.

"What's goin' to happen with Cassidy?"

"What do you mean?"

"I mean, what kind of security will they have to prevent this from happenin' again?"

"He'll be brought to the courthouse with an armed escort." He finished his drink and put the glass on the bed stand. "There's no way it'll happen again."

"Can any of this be on the record?" she asked.

"Not yet. Wait till things settle down a bit, and I'll see to it that you get a chance to beat the competition."

"Fair enough." She took a small sip of her drink. "I'd like to do a background piece on the prosecutor. Can you help me with that?"

"It shouldn't be a problem. I might be able to get something to you by tomorrow."

"You're sweet, Mark, and I really do appreciate the help." She reached over, took his hand, and slid it up her thigh. "And so does my editor."

His eyes grew wide.

"I've heard it called a lot of things before, Lisa, but calling it an editor? Baby, you're just too funny."

****

FIFTEEN

October 1, Thursday, Morning

Michael Kelly arrived at the Criminal Courthouse in downtown Los Angeles a little after eight in the morning. He parked in a public parking lot, commented negatively to the attendant about the exorbitant rate he was being charged, then made his way into the building. He was wearing a suit, carried a briefcase, and his face was neatly shaven. He looked like an attorney, and because he did, he blended in nicely with the hundreds of others who all had business in the courthouse.

He did what he had to do in less than an hour, and then he walked two blocks to a different public parking lot where Devon McGarry was sitting behind the wheel of a different car, listening to the radio.

Kelly opened the passenger door, climbed in without fanfare, and even though the sun was not shining in through the windshield, he pulled down the visor to minimize the risk of being seen by people walking by.

McGarry turned off the radio and pulled out a notepad.

"Tell me about the prosecutor?"

"I set up on the address I got online from her voter's registration," Kelly said. "It's good. She came out about seven thirty and drove straight down here. I watched her park her car in a government lot up the street, on Broadway. There's only one bloke on duty there, and gettin' into her car would be a snap."

McGarry was writing furiously.

"What about the buildin'?" He gestured towards the courthouse. "What happened when she got here?"

"They've got metal detectors set up, but she flashed a badge and they let her walk around it." He smiled. "I got lucky. There were no lines, so I got through right away and we caught the same elevator. She got off on the seventeenth floor. They have security locks on the doors up there, combination type, you punch in a code."

"Did you get the code?"

"No. She got inside before I could get close enough to see what she was punchin' in."

McGarry frowned. It would have been so much easier if he'd gotten the numbers. "Any sign of dogs in the lobby?" he asked.

"Are you kiddin'?" Kelly laughed out loud. "Mate, this is nothin' like home."

McGarry relaxed. This would be a piece of cake. He glanced up at the building. It was huge. There had to be a hundred offices on her floor alone.

"Do you know which office is hers?" he asked.

"No. There's nothin' by the elevators that have her name or office number, and you can't get into the back hallways without knowin' the code."

McGarry glanced out the windshield. There were people walking through the lot who were headed towards the building, but no one paid them any attention. He looked back at the building.

"Which way did she go in?" he asked.

"When you get off the elevator, it's the door to the east. By the way, there were restrooms on her floor, out by the elevator, and anyone can use 'em."

McGarry looked over and smiled.

"Good job, Mic. That's what I needed to know. I'll take over from here."

He climbed from the car and walked slowly up the street and back to the front of the building.

****

Whitney, Gibson and Donahue were waiting for Renée to arrive, and their presence in her office this early in the morning had caused her some concern.

"Has something happened?" she asked, putting her briefcase down next to her desk. She looked from one to the other.

Whitney opened his briefcase.

"I asked Gibby and Jen to meet me here because I've got somethin' to show all of you."

She slid her briefcase behind her desk and sat down.

"Who brought the donuts?" she asked as she took a glazed one from the box on her desk.

"Guilty as charged," Gibson replied. "Help yourself."

"Try and stop me."

She took a quick bite, then leaned back in her chair.

Whitney consulted a piece of paper from his briefcase.

"When Cassidy was first arrested, I went through channels and asked for his file and info on his associates, but I never got it. So I checked again last night, and headquarters claimed they never received my inquiry."

"Sounds like your bureaucracy is as bad as ours?" Renée mused.

"That's what I thought, so I made my request again. This time they sent me a report in a matter of hours, but the whole thing was garbage." He looked over at Gibson. "I thought maybe there was a screw-up on my clearance code, so I sent a special message to my Director."

"Did you get something back?" Renée asked.

"Not from him, but I also sent an inquiry to a former mate of mine who's still assigned to our units in the North. He got back to me early this mornin'."

He passed the piece of paper to Gibson who looked it over, showed it to Donahue, who then gave it to Marin.

At the request of the Director of MI-5, London, the complete file on Liam Cassidy and his associates was forwarded to London 21 June.

"What does this mean?" Gibson asked.

"MI-5's had the file since well before the assassination here in LA," Whitney said. "Yet when I asked for it, they sent me data that was filtered to the point that it was useless. Not only that, but I'd certainly like to know why someone asked for the file three months before the killin's?"

"Their request for the file could be routine," Gibson said. "The important thing now is to clear up your clearance problems so that we can get what we need."

"When do you think you'll get something of value?" Renée asked.

"Officially? Maybe sometime later today; that is, once the Director gets back to me. However, *unofficially,* my friend in the North kept a copy of the raw file, includin' photographs, and he downloaded the lot to me early this mornin'."

He reached back into his briefcase. "Unfortunately, the quality of the photographs leaves somethin' to be desired, but at least it's a start."

Renée briefly studied the photo's then passed them on.

"They look like booking photographs," Donahue said.

"I'm sure they are," Whitney replied. "The first picture near the top is Jimmy Cassidy. Notice the resemblance to Liam? He's the older brother. The second photo is a thug named Devon McGarry, and at the bottom of the page is a Provo named Michael Kelly."

"Where are they now, Whit?" Renée asked.

"Whereabouts unknown on Cassidy and McGarry, but the report says Kelly was detained in Ireland six months ago under the *War Powers Act*. From there he was transferred to *Hearthstone Prison*, just outside of London."

"Is he still in custody?"

"So far as I know. My source seemed to think he was a candidate for grassin', and if he was, there ought to be some fairly good intelligence on Cassidy's group. I'm thinkin' it might be a good idea to interview him, that is, if we ever get the chance?"

"I'd love a trip to London," Renée said with a smile. "How about it, Jen? Think you can get your department to spring for a couple of tickets?"

Donahue smiled. "It would take a lot of selling."

Whitney opened his briefcase again.

"While your figurin' out how to get a free vacation, I've got the raw data from Ireland with me."

"Can you give us an overview?" Gibson asked.

Whitney opened his folder and shuffled through several pages.

"The Cassidy boys are Catholics from an enclave in central Belfast. Older brother James has been runnin' an action team for the last four years." He paused, "Oh, and that reminds me. Did the deputy who survived get a look at any of them?"

"The deputy didn't," Gibson replied, "but the LAPD officer who stumbled on the scene got a quick look at two of them. I saw him last night, but he's not sure he can make an ID."

"Even so," Whitney said, "show him the photos of Jimmy Cassidy and

McGarry. Maybe we'll get lucky.

Renée looked at the photos again.

"Tell me about his brother, Whit?"

"Jimmy was on the fringe of the IRA throughout his early years. As a teenager, he was arrested in possession of an automatic weapon. He spent three years in prison under the Internment Act, and while he was there, he hooked up with the Provos, including Devon McGarry, who was doing three years for possession of explosives."

"Oh, brother." Renée leaned up in her chair. "Let me guess. Jimmy's had training with explosives?"

Whitney nodded.

"McGarry's the real expert. Once he joined up with Cassidy, bombin's been one of their specialties."

"Just what we needed to hear," Donahue said. She scribbled furiously in her notebook.

"They planted a bomb at a military base in Essex; seven died and thirty-six were injured. Six months later, they brought their war to the streets of London when they detonated a bomb in the London financial district. That killed two and wounded twenty-one."

Renée shook her head.

"These are very serious people."

"That they are," Whitney said with a nod. "Shortly after that, they went underground. Our sources think they've become involved in an internal dispute with the leadership of the IRA."

"Over what?" Donahue asked.

"The usual. Targets, funding, the course of the war. Most likely the peace process figures into it as well."

Renée looked over at Gibson.

"Do you think brother Jimmy might be involved in the shoot-out?"

"Looks like it," Gibson said. "The wounded deputy heard someone yell the name 'Jimmy' when they were trying to free Cassidy." He turned to Whitney. "Can you can free up those pictures? I'd like to turn them over to the team from the Sheriff's that's handling the shootout?"

"No problem," Whitney replied.

"Great. I'll get someone to run a bunch of copies off."

Renée came out from behind the desk.

"I can do it now," she said. She collected the photocopies from Gibson and left the room.

When she returned, she handed Gibson and Whitney several sets.

"Thanks, Renee." Gibson put the copies in his briefcase. "Before I take off, let me tell you all about the shootout."

For the next three minutes, he told them what he'd learned from the detectives who were handling the case.

"What kind of guns did they use?" Whitney asked.

"Casings from the scene were nine millimeters, probably from a Mac 10 or 11. The rounds were soft-nosed, a type of ammunition not generally sold in this country."

"Where are the vehicles they used?" Whitney asked.

"We had them towed over to Parker Center. DHQ's getting a warrant for them this morning. The lab will go through them, but I was told they look pretty clean. We'll be lucky if we get some trace evidence."

Renée shook her head. "So far we've grossly underestimated these people, Whit. Any thoughts on what they'll do next?"

"This may sound alarmist, but you'd better start thinkin' about explosives. If this group is involved in this, then this courthouse could end up a pile of rubble. We should make a few notifications; and while we're at it, Renée, you had better arrange for some security for yourself."

"Not a chance," she said. "I'm not at risk."

Gibson cleared his throat.

"I think the Major has a good point, Renée. These people are extremely dangerous, and you just never know."

"I don't agree. Prosecutors are rarely ever targets. There's no percentage in it. If anything ever happened to me, there would be a dozen other volunteers ready to take my place."

"Nevertheless, it could happen." Gibson was adamant. "Look, if you're embarrassed to bring it up with your boss, then Whitney and I can make the call."

Whitney took her silence for assent.

"Good. I'll take care of it."

Gibson stood up and stretched.

"Okay. I'm heading back to the station." He closed up his briefcase.

"Gibby," Renée asked, "what's being done for our witnesses?"

"I called Magruder's' attorney last night. He said the family will put her in hiding for awhile, and Metro's gonna babysit the others."

"Good. That's a relief."

Gibson nodded, then he and Donahue left the office.

When he was gone, Renée gave Whitney an embarrassed smile.

"You're not really going to insist I get security, are you?"

"I certainly am. We've badly miscalculated their determination, and that's a mistake we can't afford to repeat. Think about yourself for a moment, and if you won't think about yourself, then think about your daughter. What if something happened to you? Why take a chance?"

"Okay. You've managed to scare me into it. Go ahead and call Kerin. In the meantime, I'll just hide here under my desk for a while."

He looked up and caught her smiling.

"You've got a wicked sense of humor, Renée. I'll call him today."

****

Devon McGarry stood in the courtyard just outside the entrance to the Criminal Courts Building, the actual name of which is the *Clara Shortridge Foltz Criminal Justice Center*. She was California's first woman attorney, a pioneer who opened the profession to future generations of California women, including Renée Marin.

But the irony of this was lost on Deavon McGarry who lounged against a stone wall and smoked a cigarette while he watched the comings and goings at the doors. Jurors and others lined up to go through the metal detectors, while officers and employees with identification cards were allowed to bypass the lines.

The system was flawed. Only two deputies worked each machine, and the numbers of people waiting in line forced them to rush through the process. The whole thing seemed a little sloppy.

He carried the Semtex around his waist and beneath his shirt. It was wrapped in a plastic sheath and fashioned into small blocks. He could get it through security because they were not equipped to detect any non-metallic substances.

He planned to use the timeless method of an electrical timer fashioned from a watch that he wore on his wrist. The power unit for the detonator was encased in plastic—small just under an inch—and getting it through the checkpoint was going to be his most difficult challenge.

He studied the movement of the line. As people approached the machines, they emptied their pockets into small plastic baskets which bypassed the detector while they walked on through.

He couldn't believe it! This was the weakness he'd been looking for. Except for a visual inspection, what went into the basket was never even scanned. Could it be as easy as that?

He stubbed out his cigarette and found a quiet spot away from prying eyes. When no one was watching, he removed the power unit from his jacket pocket and fastened the timing wire to his key ring. The finished product resembled a car alarm activator. He smiled to himself and headed for the doors.

The line had increased in size and he spent almost six minutes waiting for his turn to enter the building. At the front of the line, he removed the key ring, and along with some loose coins. He nonchalantly dropped them into the basket.

He had to wait a few moments to go through the machine, and when he did, he stepped forward with confidence. Once he was cleared, he turned to retrieve his keys, but as he did so, he noticed a deputy staring into the basket and at his device.

Just then the alarm behind him went off. It was triggered by a woman who'd neglected to remove a metal bracelet from her wrist. Startled, the deputy he'd been concerned about moved toward the woman and away from the basket.

McGarry reached in, picked up the keyring with his device, and quickly placed it into his pocket.

He moved through the lobby and onto an elevator that took him to the upper floors. When it reached seventeen, he got off behind three other people who quickly disappeared behind one of the security doors. He stayed by himself in the hallway, and within a few moments, he was alone.

He tried to get his bearings. He was in a large lobby which was fed by twelve elevators. There was no furniture to sit on and no place to stand without drawing unwanted attention. He had no choice. He'd have to keep moving.

He inspected the security door, but no surprise, it was locked. He walked back through the lobby and over to the other side of the building where he found another security door and the door to a men's public restroom.

He walked into the restroom through a set of double doors. It was small, with only three urinals and two toilet stalls, but no one was inside. He entered the stall farthest from the door and closed it behind him. Mounted on the partition wall, next to the rolls of toilet paper, was a good sized metal holder that was full of paper covers for the toilet seat.

He sat down on the commode and reviewed his options. He could try to get inside the security door—and maybe get closer to the prosecutor's office—or he could plant it right here and avoid the risk of detection. Jimmy had given him the leeway to put it where he wanted; where the blast would send a message that would further their plan.

Trying to get it closer to the prosecutor's office was completely unnecessary, and as far as he was concerned, it was not worth the risk.

The container proved smaller than it looked. There was no way he could use all the Semtex he had, but what he could use would surely be enough to make their point.

He pulled out his shirt, removed the package of Semtex, and placed it on his lap. Taking the paper seat covers from the metal holder, he molded the Semtex to fit inside the bottom of the container. Taking off his watch, he wired it to the detonator, set the alarm, and attached it to a probe that he placed into the explosives. He then covered his work with the paper seat covers before hanging the holder back up on the wall.

He pulled out a paper cover and was pleased to note that it came out without a hitch.

A slow smile spread over his face. The chance that his handiwork might fall prey to an inadvertent discovery was now very small indeed.

The excess Semtex went back into the wrapper which he secured to the belt around his waist. With everything in place, he walked out of the restroom and into the lobby.

As he came around the corner, he noticed two people who were waiting for an elevator to arrive. The man had the look of a cop, so McGarry hung back, just around the corner, and just out of their sight, to wait until they were gone.

When one of the elevators arrived at the floor, Gibson and Donahue got on, and when the doors were finally closed, McGarry came around the corner and waited for the next elevator to take him down to the street.

****

Kerin picked up his phone.

"Glenn, this is Edgar. Can you join Aaron and me in the conference room? We need to talk about security."

"I'll be right over."

He hung up the phone and wondered what the two of them had in mind?

It galled Kerin to treat Edgar White as an equal, and he suspected the feeling was mutual. Known by his detractors as *The Mule*---a nickname derived from his bouts of tunnel vision---White was a drinking buddy of Rosen's who'd been elevated to the rank of *Chief of the Bureau of Investigation*, a position of some power and influence.

Kerin dreaded these infrequent meetings, for when Rosen and White got together, they often hatched plans that were ill-conceived.

"Pull up a chair, Glenn," Rosen said when he walked into the room.

Kerin chose a spot several seats away from the two of them while Rosen cleared his throat.

"Given what happened yesterday, I've asked the Chief here to put together a security plan to deal with the terrorists, and he was just starting to tell me about it." He turned to the Chief.

"Why don't you start over again, Edgar, and tell us what you've come up with."

White leaned forward and reviewed his notes. Not known as a stylish dresser, his gray flannel suit was ill-fitting and tight. Overweight and bloated, his florid skin and the spider web veins that laced his bulbous nose pegged him as a very heavy drinker.

White rested his beefy arms on the cherry wood table.

"I think we have two issues to deal with, Aaron. The first is your security, and the second deals with our facilities."

Rosen smiled and nodded for him to continue.

"As to your security, I'm going to add three more deputies to assist your driver. From now on, they'll be a chase car that will go wherever you go. When you do personal appearances, we will double that number, giving you eight."

"What about my wife and our house?"

"We'll keep your house under twenty-four-hour surveillance. A minimum of two investigators when no one is home, and two more when you and the Misses are in for the evening." White looked up and smiled. "Naturally, I'll see to it that two of our best investigators are assigned to protect your wife. You'll have nothing to worry about there."

Kerin could feel his anger rising. Rosen was playing politics with a crisis. A security detail would draw media attention, and he'd parade them around for maximum exposure. The public was impressionable, if not very bright. They'd likely conclude, if incorrectly, that his importance was measured by the size of his entourage.

But Kerin grudgingly admitted to himself that he admired the overall strategy. Rosen was nobody's fool. Strong impressions meant votes, and if he wanted to run for Governor, it was certainly a clever move.

He allowed himself a tight, little smile. To him, the whole thing was transparent and the press would certainly see through it, too.

He looked up and noticed that Rosen was staring at him with a curious look. *Yes, Aaron. I've figured out what you're up to.*

White rubbed his nose to ward off a sneeze, and with a brief swipe of a linen handkerchief, he was once again ready to continue.

"Now, about the security of the office. I'd say we better take these people very seriously. They have the ability to place explosives, so we have to assume it can happen right here."

Rosen leaned back in his chair.

"What do you suggest, Edgar?"

"I've talked to the Sheriff's, and they'll control the entrances with extra deputies."

"Will that be enough to do the job?" Rosen wondered.

"No matter what we do, Aaron, if they want to blow this place up, they can always get their stuff in."

Kerin shook his head.

"That's totally unacceptable, Edgar. We have to do better than that. What will it take to guarantee security on all of our working floors?"

White did nothing to conceal his frown.

"I'll tell you what, Mr. Kerin. We could shut the building down, but short of that, there's no way to protect all the floors. And let me remind you, this is the first time we've dealt with a major terrorist threat. For the last three years, I've presented budget requests to upgrade the security of our offices and you've kicked them back every time. As a result of your short-sightedness, we're extremely vulnerable to an attack by explosives, and frankly, there's not a hell of a lot we can do about it.

He looked over at Rosen for a moment, then back at Kerin.

"Now, if you want me to roll out a foolproof plan for building security, the time might be right to submit it to the Board of Supervisors. Who knows? Perhaps we can get some emergency funds to ensure the safety of everyone. And, if not, well ..."

He let his words trail off while he shrugged his shoulders. Having made his point, he was convinced that his argument was unassailable. Building an empire was a bureaucratic preoccupation, and those who excelled were the ones who knew how to manipulate a fear driven situation.

In this situation, a real or imagined risk of a bombing was an opportunity that Edgar White was not about to pass up.

"You're absolutely right, Edgar," Rosen said after some reflection. "We need to put pressure on the Board of Supervisors."

He looked over at Kerin.

"Glenn, get with our Budget Section and make sure that Edgar's figures are up to date. Then get the paperwork over to the Board."

Kerin nodded. He would get nowhere if he argued with these fools. He would need to take a different approach.

"All that will take time, Aaron," he said. "In the meantime, what if we used the Bureau personnel already assigned to each of our facilities?"

He turned to White.

"Do we have the equipment and manpower necessary to protect our own people?"

"In a nutshell, the answer is *no*," White shook his head sharply. "We have thirty-three offices spread throughout the county. We'd be stretched very thin if we tried to secure every one of them. We have two portable metal detectors of our own, but we have no x-ray equipment. I'm sorry to say this, Kerin, but unless we get an immediate infusion of funds, there just isn't any way to protect everyone."

Kerin was tired of listening to what they couldn't do. They needed to move forward right now.

"All right, Chief. Assuming there is no 'immediate infusion of funds', what do you suggest we do?"

"In that case, I'd recommend we concentrate on protecting this facility since this is where the trial will be. It's the most logical target. We can put our people on each of our floors and restrict all entry beyond the lobby. Also, the stairwells can be locked so that employees can use them to get out of the building, but once they enter the stairwell, they can't get out on any of the working floors."

"That sounds fine, Chief." Rosen smiled, glad that the discussion now seemed to be concluded.

"Does it meet with your approval, Glenn?"

"With all due respect, Aaron, I think it stinks. Major Whitney came to see me a short time ago and he believes that the IRA would seek the most available target. If we don't protect all of our buildings, they'll find what's unprotected, and that's where they'll strike. As it is, most of our offices have adjacent parking lots, so God forbid, if they decided to use a car bomb, it could really wipe us out."

"Then what do you suggest, Glenn?"

Rosen was starting to fidget and he seemed to be losing his patience.

"If you have some ideas, let's hear them now."

"The only thing I can think of is to bring the Sheriff's into this."

Rosen scoffed.

"Be realistic, Glenn. Without a specific threat, they won't provide the man-power. We'll just have to see this through ourselves." He glanced over at White and smiled. "I think the Chief has given this a lot of thought, so we'll follow his recommendation. We'll concentrate on this building while we pressure the Board to give us more funds."

He turned to White.

"Edgar, how long will it take to set things up?"

White smiled.

"Well, we'll have to shift some of our personnel to make sure we can handle multiple shifts; cancel days off, things like that. But I would imagine that we can be set up and ready to go by noon tomorrow."

"Excellent, Chief. I'm sure that will be soon enough. Thanks for coming by."

White started to rise, but Kerin wasn't finished.

"Hold on a second, Chief. We haven't yet discussed what arrangements you plan to make for the security of Renée Marin and her daughter." He locked eyes with Rosen. "At the very least, she should have a Bureau team assigned to her around the clock."

"By God, I almost forgot about that." Rosen looked over at White. "What about it, Chief? Can we spare the resources?"

"We'll be spread pretty thin, Sir, but I can arrange for a couple of investigators who live in her area to drive by her place on their way into work. That way, she can get an escort into the office, and I'm sure we can work something out when it's time for her to go home. But there's no way to put a team on her residence; that is, unless I use some of our people assigned to the Child Support operation."

Kerin could no longer contain his frustration.

"*Jesus*, Aaron. Those guys don't have any training for work like this. They're paper pushers who'd be about as useful as security guards."

"They're peace officers, Glenn. They'll do the job. Besides, their presence alone will serve as a deterrent." Rosen folded his arms across his chest, a sure sign that he'd made up his mind.

He locked eyes with White and said, "Chief, pull three teams from child support, one for Renée, one for her child, and the third for her house at night." Having made the decision, he quickly got to his feet.

"Well, gentlemen, I think that does it for now. Chief, you go ahead and set it up. Glenn, you talk to Marin."

"I think you should reconsider, Aaron."

"Reconsider what, Glenn?"

"The level of protection for Renée. She's the logical target, if, in fact, there is one."

Rosen shook his head and smiled.

"Nothing will happen, Glenn. This is all a precaution. That's all."

****

SIXTEEN

October 2, Thursday, Late Morning

A block from the courthouse, Devon McGarry caught a public city bus and rode it into Hollywood. When he arrived at the corner of Sunset and Gower, he sauntered into a nearby shopping center called the Gower Gulch.

Located reasonably close to the Gower Studios, the facade of the building was constructed in true Hollywood style. It resembled a western movie set with each structure labeled with old west designations such as Livery, Chemist and Feed Store. These euphemisms dovetailed nicely with their modern day counterparts, the actual tenants of the center, which included an auto parts outlet, a drug store, and a donut shop.

McGarry walked through the parking lot to a public telephone that was mounted on a wall near the drug store.

"It's me," he said when the phone was answered. "Bring the car to the parkin' lot at Sunset and Gower."

"Twenty minutes," Cassidy replied.

"Drive it carefully, Jimmy."

McGarry chose to wait at a bus bench on Sunset Boulevard where he could have an unobstructed view of the lot. From the corner of his eye, he saw Cassidy drive up in a black Olds Cutlass that Kelly had stolen from an apartment complex in Glendale. They'd given it a cold rear plate which they'd taken from a Cutlass in a mall in West LA.

McGarry had spent the better part of the night packing Semtex into the trunk. The bomb was relatively small—a mere fifty pounds—with a timing device activated by a battery-powered clock. Although primitive by modern standards, he was leery of using a remote-controlled activator. After all, this was America, the land of gadgetry, where garage door openers, toy cars, cell phones and hand-held radios were the rule rather than the exception. Errant signals were everywhere, and since they had to drive the car across town, he had no intention of becoming the inadvertent victim of his own handiwork.

He watched as Cassidy selected a parking spot several rows from the donut shop. Jimmy killed the ignition, climbed out of the car, and quickly removed his gloves. He walked across the street where he waited by the curb, and a few moments later, Claire Harris drove up in a gray Toyota and quickly drove them both away.

McGarry walked over to the Olds. He pulled on a pair of surgical gloves then slid behind the wheel. Using the wires which hung from the already punched ignition, he quickly started it up.

A little after eleven o'clock, he arrived at the Mid-City Center.

It was Jimmy's idea to target this complex, a shopping mall that was world renowned for its modern design and upscale stores. Ten stories in height, with the bottom six floors dedicated to parking, the top floors were filled with many dozens of small stores. There were restaurants, markets, theaters, tourist attractions, and across the street, just to the North, was a major, four-star hotel.

All in all, the bomb would wreak havoc wherever it was placed.

McGarry pulled down the driver's sun visor and put on dark glasses to conceal his face from the video cameras set up at the entryway to the parking lot. He grabbed a ticket from the automated dispenser, placed it in his shirt pocket, and drove the car up to the top of the garage.

His reconnaissance conducted the evening before had disclosed that the electrical generators for the shopping center floors were behind a cement wall, almost directly under a department store to the North and west of the building. He drove around, biding his time until he found an open space nearly adjacent to the wall.

He parked the Cutlass, concealed the dangling ignition wires, climbed into the back seat, and checked the timing mechanism one last time. When he walked away from the car, he was confident that he had left nothing behind that could connect him with the coming explosion.

 He quickly made his way down to the street.

Claire Harris and Cassidy had circled the building while they waited for McGarry to emerge. Once he was in the car, the three of them drove away and headed straight for the San Fernando Valley.

****

Once he knew that the others had completed their task, Michael Kelly drove south on the San Diego Freeway through the city of West Los Angeles. It was the height of the lunch hour traffic, and although the traffic was moving at a snail's pace, he was in no great hurry to get where he was going. He loved the sights in LA.

To be sure, the sky was a little hazy, but the sun was out, and it was getting warm. He hated the cold back home, and wistfully wished he could live in this city somewhere close to the beach. He was willing to endure the overcrowding and the traffic in exchange for the sunshine all year round.

He got off the freeway on Jefferson Boulevard, headed east, and scanned the buildings for a pay phone, one with access to the freeway and a measure of privacy. He was just about to turn back and try a different street when he spotted a phone on the wall of a closed liquor store.

He parked on the street, about forty feet away, and waited in his car. At one-fifteen, he slipped on his gloves and walked to the phone. A piece of paper in his pocket contained a number provided by Cassidy's source. He called it once, but the line was busy.

Kelly laughed to himself. This was something he hadn't considered. If the call didn't get through, things were going to get very messy.

He took a deep breath, tried the number again, and this time it was answered on the second ring. He checked his watch when the connection was made.

"DA's Command Post. Rust speaking."

"I know you're recordin' this, so I'll only say it only once—"

Rust activated the recorder.

"—Listen carefully. There's a bomb in the downtown criminal courthouse. It will go off today at one thirty-two, so ya better start clearin' the buildin' right now. This is just a sample a what we're able to do. We want Liam Cassidy released, and after it goes off, we'll call ya back with more instructions. If ya don't turn 'im loose, the next one will take lives. And to be sure that ya know that yer speakin' with us, we'll identify ourselves with the phrase '*Free Derry.*' Ya got that?"

Rust tried to stall for time while he punched in a number on a separate phone for the Sheriff's Building Security Office.

"I'm sorry," Rust said to the caller. "I didn't get what time you said it was set to go off?"

"Too bad."

The caller hung up the phone.

Kelly looked at his watch. He'd been on the line for less than twenty- five seconds. Not bad. Not bad at all. They'd never have time to trace the call.

He walked back to his car and drove to the freeway. He had another call to make from somewhere farther up the road.

****

"This is Rust in the DA's Command Post. Who am I speaking to?"

"Deputy Washington. What can I do for you, Rust?"

"I just got a call from a male stating there's a bomb in this building and it's set to go off at one thirty-two. Claims he's IRA. I'll call LAPD, but I need you to evacuate the building right away!"

"You think it's the real thing?"

Rust was flabbergasted. *Was this guy kidding?*

"Get started, Deputy! We're running out of time!"

As he hung up the telephone, the building security alarm went off. Rust knew there would be problems. The alarm was frequently used for a variety of purposes including fire, inmate fights, and deputy requests for assistance. It rang too often to be taken seriously. Evacuation would need to be by word of mouth.

He jumped up from his desk. There was not enough time to go through the chain of command, so he yelled to the investigators seated nearby in the outer office.

"Listen up, everyone. We've just received a bomb threat. It's gonna go off at one thirty-two. I called building security, and they're going to try to evacuate the building, but I need you people to divide up our floors and order everyone out through the stairwells." He looked out at a sea of blank faces. "Get moving!" he shouted. "This is not a joke!"

As they ran from the room, Rust returned to his desk and called 911.

When he hung up the phone, he looked at his watch; it was one-twenty. He punched in the number for the District Attorney's office, and Jake Braden, Rosen's beefy personal bodyguard, answered the phone.

"This is Rust. Is he in the building?"

"He sure is Randy. What can I do for you?"

"Get everyone out, Jake. We've got a bomb threat from the IRA. It's somewhere in the building. It's set to go off at one thirty-two. Everyone's been notified; we're evacuating right now."

"We'll use the East stairwell," Braden said.

Rust hung up the phone and grabbed the cassette he'd made of the threat. He wanted to have it handy to justify his actions in case the call turned out to be a phony. He started for the door but stopped mid-stride. He'd forgotten to warn Renée Marin.

"Marin speaking," she said when she answered the phone. Her voice sounded tired.

"This is Randy Rust at the Command Post." He filled her in on the threat. "You're office would be the logical target, Mrs. Marin. I suggest you get out right now."

"We're on our way."

"Use the stairs," he said as an afterthought, "and be careful when you hit the streets. If it's you they're after, there might be a sniper."

"What a lovely thought, Randy. See you downstairs."

****

By one thirty, people were streaming from the courthouse through all of the stairwell exits. The Fire Department had dispatched five engine companies and three paramedic units, many of which were still in the process of arriving. The ranking Sergeant from LAPD Central Division took control of the scene and issued instructions to the arriving units. The streets were cordoned off while they waited for the bomb squad. There was nothing else that anyone could do.

By one thirty-two, only a few stragglers still remained in the building. With traffic around the courthouse now nonexistent, an eerie stillness fell over the crowd that milled about in the parking lot just south of the Criminal Courts Building.

Renée spotted Rust standing next to a bus bench. He was clutching a cassette in his hand.

"Is that a tape of the call?" she asked.

"It sure is."

"Can you get me a copy?"

"Sure." He was focused on the building as the time for the explosion came and passed.

"Well," he sighed, "looks like it was a false alarm."

Glass suddenly rained down from several windows on the seventeenth floor. A second later, the sound of the explosion became audible to the crowd. A dust cloud appeared where the windows had been, and it was followed by smoke, which meant there was a fire.

They watched in shock for a couple of moments before Renée turned to Rust and reached out to touch his shoulder.

"You're a hero, Randy. You probably saved our lives."

****

Michael Kelly found a pay phone at a Union Oil station in Westwood. He dialed the overseas operator and used a stolen calling card to reach a number in London that was answered by a machine. As soon as he heard the beep, he spoke.

"This is Shamrock. Two packages have been wrapped. The first one's been opened, and the second will be opened later today."

He hung up the telephone, got back in his car, and headed over the hill to the San Fernando Valley.

****

SEVENTEEN

October 2, Thursday, Afternoon

Within the first hour, the fire was completely extinguished and the building was searched for secondary devices. When nothing else was found, an "all clear" was given, and with the exception of the seventeenth floor, which now was designated a crime scene, employees on other floors were allowed to reenter the building.

But most of the public and many of the employees refused to go back, and out of an abundance of caution, the Presiding Judge gave the order to close the building for the rest of the day. After that, only key personnel were permitted back inside, and most of those were restricted to the lower floors.

Renée and Whitney took a freight elevator up and met Gibson and Donahue at the Command Post on the seventeenth floor.

"How bad is it, Gibby?" she asked. The Command Post was at the opposite end of the building from where the explosion had taken place.

"Not too bad. ATF and the bomb squad are sifting through the wreckage now hoping to figure out what was used. The blast leveled two walls and four windows. No one was injured, but a fire got started in the crawl space between floors. It burned out some wiring, but they got it knocked down before it spread too far."

"I'm amazed," Whitney said. "I thought the damage would be much worse."

"The blown walls and the fire are only part of the problem," Gibson said. "There's asbestos in the ceiling, and they had to tear it up to knock down the fire. It'll take weeks to get the fibers collected, so no one can go back in there without wearing a moon suit."

"You mean I can't get into my office?" Renée asked.

"As of now, your wing's been sealed."

"But how will I get to my files?"

"You won't," Gibson said. "The danger of fibers in your stuff is too great. But I can get you another set of reports from my office."

"My God!" Renée shook her head in disgust. "I spent weeks getting everything organized. The thought of doing it again just makes me sick."

"It'll go a lot faster the second time," he said to console her. "Can you find a place to work?"

She looked around "I guess I'll have to."

"Good! I'll get a set of reports for you later today."

Rust walked into the Command Post waiving a copy of the tape. The investigators seated in the squad room gathered around to hear what was said.

Kerin walked in just as it ended.

"Hey, Glenn," Renée said. "Have you heard the tape yet?"

Kerin nodded.

"Aaron's got a copy upstairs. Are we set up in case they call back?"

"LAPD's gonna handle it," Rust said.

Kerin turned to Renée.

"When you're finished down here, Aaron wants you to handle the press on the bombing."

"Why me? I don't want to talk to those people."

"It's simple, Renée. If Aaron makes a statement, then it elevates the importance of their demands. He wants to downplay their threats to deny them recognition."

Renée rolled her eyes. What a crock! Rosen would never pass up a chance to talk to the press. Something else was going on.

"That doesn't sound like Aaron," she said.

Kerin laughed.

"Just between us, they gave him a pretty bad time at the last press conference. He's still licking his wounds."

"Do I have any say in this, Glenn?"

Kerin's eyes narrowed.

"I'm afraid not."

"In that case, when does he want me to do it?"

"Right away. He's called in the media for four o'clock."

"What am I supposed to tell them?"

"Just give them the facts and stress that we won't negotiate with terrorists." Kerin smiled thinly. "After you work up a rough draft, bring it up to my office and we'll go over it together."

Kerin nodded to the others then left the command post.

Gibson gave Donahue the high sign and both prepared to leave.

"I'll call you later, Renée," he said. "We're gonna head back to the office and catch up on the paperwork. We'll get a complete set over to you once you get a new place to work."

Renée nodded.

"How about you, Whit?"

"I was goin' to go by the consulate to see if anythin's come in. Why?"

"I don't know. Things are happening so fast around here. I feel very unsettled."

"I'll stay close," he said. A small smile crept over his face. "Any chance you want to give me that rain check tonight?"

"I can't," she muttered, "but why don't you come to my house for dinner on Sunday? You must be tired of restaurant food, and---"

"Say no more. I'd love nothin' better."

****

At four o'clock sharp, after meeting with Kerin, Renée faced the press in a makeshift conference room that was hastily set up in a Sheriff's assembly hall down on the first floor of the courthouse.

"Good afternoon, ladies and gentlemen. I'm Renée Marin, Head Deputy of the Organized Crime and Terrorism Division. As you are no doubt aware, a bomb was detonated today on the seventeenth floor of this building. The center of the blast was a men's room accessible to the general public in an unsecured area of the building. The explosion caused moderate damage to portions of the seventeenth floor, and, happily, there were no causalities.

"Just before the explosion, we received a warning from a person we believe to be associated with the Irish Republican Army.

"Let me take a moment to thank that person publicly for giving us time to evacuate the building to avoid any injuries to our employees and visitors.

"The caller demanded the release of Liam Cassidy, a demand which cannot be complied with under any circumstances. We will not negotiate with terrorists, and for the protection of all innocent parties now and in the future, this is a policy that will be maintained."

She put down the prepared statement and signaled that she was ready to answer questions.

"Ms. Marin," said a reporter from Newsweek. "Has the IRA threatened to blow up any other facilities?"

"We've had no further communication with the caller since the first warning, and nothing was said about any other facilities. But I can tell you that we plan to do everything possible to see that there's no reoccurrence of what we experienced today."

"Who makes the final decision on releasing Cassidy if that were to be an option?"

"It's not an option," she replied firmly.

"Where's Mr. Rosen?" asked a voice from the middle of the room. "Why isn't he here?"

There was some snickering from the group.

Renée had to bite her cheek to keep a straight face.

"The District Attorney is currently meeting with our Bureau personnel to finalize plans to secure all of our facilities. He regrets that he is unable to address you personally."

"Yeah, I'll bet," said another voice in the front of the room, and there was more laughter.

For the next ten minutes, the press managed to ask the same questions over and over; and, in kind, they received the same answers. Renée threaded her way through the minefield by sticking to the company line.

When she wrapped it up, there was one point on which everyone in the room was clear. Liam Cassidy's release was not subject to negotiation.

****

Jimmy Cassidy and the others watched Renée's press conference live on the four o'clock news. They listened intently as she repeated over and over that

Liam Cassidy would not be released.

A smile crossed Jimmy's face.

"She'll soon change her tune." He turned off the television.

"Do we give them a warnin' this time?" Devon asked.

Cassidy flashed a stern look.

"Of course we will. We're not interested in killin' innocent people."

"Will you be wantin' me to make the call?" Kelly asked him.

Cassidy thought it over for a moment.

"No, they already know your voice. Claire can give 'em the bad news this time."

****

By late afternoon, the Command Post was quiet, so when the phone began to ring, it startled the two investigators who remained there on duty.

A lieutenant from LAPD grabbed an open line to the phone company.

"Incoming." he stated. "Start a trace."

He then picked up a second line connected directly to the Emergency Command Center in the basement of City Hall.

"Begin monitoring," he ordered.

He nodded to his associate, a DA Investigator, who started the tape and picked up the ringing line.

"DA Command Post. Eaton speaking."

"Free Derry!" She spoke with a thick Irish accent. "You'd better let 'im go. We're prepared to push this as far as necessary, so the longer ya delay, the more troubles you'll get."

She paused for a moment to let her words sink in.

"Put Liam on a plane and fly 'im to Tripoli. You have until Sunday night at six. If you don't let 'im go, ya gonna pay the price."

Eaton tried to interject to stall for time.

"Please, Miss. We'll do--"

"In the meantime," she said, cutting him off. "Just to show that we mean business, at five forty-five tonight, a bomb will go off in the Mid-City Mall."

The line suddenly went dead.

"Damn it!" Eaton exclaimed.

"Did you get it?" asked the Lieutenant into the open line. Seconds counted now; she'd be getting away. He looked at his watch. She'd been on the line for twenty-eight seconds.

Would that be long enough?

"Got it!" said the man from the phone company. "A pay phone at 51506 Ventura Boulevard., in Van Nuys."

The Lieutenant repeated the address to the ECC where a dispatcher was waiting on the line.

"All units in the vicinity and 9 Robert 24—"

As she put out the call, she typed out the message for a simultaneous broadcast on the in-car computer screens of every police vehicle in the city.

"Special Occurrence threat from a pay phone at 51506 Ventura Boulevard, Van Nuys. Female, young, with an Irish accent. 24 Handle Code 3."

"Twenty-four," came the first response. *"We're two blocks away. ETA thirty seconds."*

At 51506 Ventura, the two pay phones were at a gas station on a wall to the east of the pumps. Officer Colin Freeport and his partner Lois Good could see both of the phones as they entered the lot, but there was no one standing nearby. Whoever had made the call was already gone.

Freeport screeched to a halt in front of the cashier's booth. He jumped from the car and ran over to the window.

"Did you see someone on the pay phone over there?" He pointed to the two empty phones.

A young Hispanic female clerk, polishing her nails, momentarily stopped what she was doing.

"When you talking about?" she asked.

"Just now! A young female, probably white?"

"Oh, yeah. I saw her."

He waited for more, but it was not forthcoming.

"Where the hell did she go?" he yelled through the space where credit cards and cash get passed on through to the cashier.

The girl looked confused and hurt. He tried to size her up. Young, probably a recent immigrant; she wore heavy eye shadow and meticulously painted lips. He'd need to show some patience or she'd start to play it dumb. He quickly changed his approach.

"Nice nails," he said.

"Huh?"

"I said your nails look nice."

She smiled shyly.

"Did you see where the white woman went?"

The girl pointed towards the freeway.

"Did she get into a car?"

She shook her head.

"How was she dressed?"

She thought for a moment. "She was wearing jeans, I think, and a white blouse."

"Thanks. I'll be back to talk to you later."

As a large number of other units poured into the area. Officer Good put out a broadcast and a physical description, and within minutes, a systematic search of the neighborhood was underway.

While Good secured the phones to wait for the crime lab to thoroughly dust for prints, Freeport and several of the other responding officers walked the boulevard all the way to the freeway searching for anyone who might have seen their suspect. They spoke to more than a dozen people, but no one saw her get into a car. It was clear that she had slipped their containment area, which meant that she had probably hit the freeway before they'd even arrived.

The cashier was now their only witness and Freeport made a mental note to tell the responding detectives to be sure to begin by complimenting the girl on her nails.

****

The Mid-City Mall, a shopping complex built on land that was once a part of La Cienega's sleepy restaurant row, was a mecca for tourists from all over the world. Many were attracted to the celebrity-owned restaurants, while others simply came to watch the beautiful people stroll the corridors past trendy stores.

After the underground bombing at the World Trade Center in New York, a conference had been held between the landlords and the tenants to investigate ways to minimize the risks of a similar incident occurring at their mall. Although little could be done for prevention, a mobilization plan emerged to maximize resources, just in case of a terrorist threat.

At five twenty-five p.m., the LAPD went on tactical alert. Units from throughout the city were pressed into action to facilitate the evacuation of more than seven thousand people believed to be in the mall complex.

The private security officers assigned to the mall began evacuations floor by floor. They sealed off the garages and forced the shoppers to leave on foot. As people reached the street, they were herded like cattle to a parking lot that was located one block north.

Adding to the confusion outside the building was the quitting time exodus from nearby office buildings. Cars and people poured into the streets, and within a short time, the area around the mall was completely gridlocked.

At five fifty-two, the bomb went off.

The mall visibly shook as though riding on a wave and then shuddered convulsively with a loud cracking sound. The noise of the explosion roared from the building while the shock wave smacked the adjoining high rise structures. Power stopped abruptly, windows cracked and shattered, and panels of splintered glass showered down into the street.

Panic set in, and people ran for their lives, abandoning cars and belongings in a thoughtless dash for safety. A fire broke out in the electrical vault which sent clouds of dark smoke through the air conditioning vents. Hundreds of people still stuck in the stairwells suffered smoke inhalation and irritated eyes.

By seven o'clock, the news on Channel 4 was the first to report that there were six known deaths attributable to the explosion. Buried in the drama of the loss of human life was the estimated damage of thirty million dollars.

****

EIGHTEEN

October 2, Thursday, Evening

Jimmy Cassidy watched the eleven o'clock news with grim satisfaction. The networks blended some of the footage from Renée Marin's press conference with coverage of the aftermath of the explosion, and in hindsight, it made the "no negotiation" stance seem rather short sighted.

"I'll bet she's regrettin' her words," Cassidy said. "The arrogant bitch."

McGarry was more pragmatic.

"She's not in charge, Jimmy. Some other bloke's runnin' the show. She's just the window dressin'."

"You may be right, but she'll be the one we deal with. You mark my words."

Cassidy then left the apartment to make some telephone calls.

****

Within hours of the explosion, more than a dozen callers had already tried to take credit for the bombing, but it was the use of the code phrase "Free Derry" that gave the current caller instant credibility.

"Tonight's explosion was a sample of what we're capable of doin'. If you don't release Liam by Sunday night, more people are goin' to die."

"We need a little more time, sir," said Capt. Don Carroll in a slow, measured tone. As the DA-Bureau hostage negotiator, he wanted to build rapport and keep the caller talking. "The government of Libya does not cooperate with our State Department, so—"

"No extensions," the caller said in a firm tone of voice. "Ya have until Sunday night at six."

The line went dead.

"*Jesus!*" said Carroll as he placed the phone back on the receiver. "That guy's a real hard-ass. This won't be easy."

****

Cassidy drove to the city of Pacoima in the San Fernando Valley. Fear was his best weapon, and if he used it correctly, he believed he'd achieve his demands without another bomb.

He placed a call to the *Los Angeles Times* and delivered the same message to make sure that the public was aware of his statements. Community fear would pressure those in charge to accede to the demand for his brother's release.

****

After watching the early news reports with the others at their duplex, Devon McGarry left the building in a mood to celebrate. He walked five blocks to a neighborhood bar, consumed two beers, and studied a blond who was seated nearby. He pegged her as being late thirties, a pretty good figure, too, but her makeup was way too heavy. He smiled to himself. She'd dressed to accentuate her breasts—one of his many weaknesses—but best of all, she appeared to be alone.

He got off his stool, approached her, and offered to pay for her drink. They spoke for twenty minutes, and when he made his proposition, she responded with a smile and a hand on his thigh.

They walked to a nearby motel. It was nothing fancy, just a place where rooms were rented by the hour or the day. Within a few moments of entering their room, they coupled like teenagers out on a date.

When they were finished and she'd fallen asleep, he seized upon the moment and quietly slipped from the room.

It was so much simpler that way.

****

NINETEEN

October 3, Friday

The Friday morning edition of the LA Times ran page one photographs of Jimmy Cassidy and Devon McGarry, courtesy of Donahue and the LAPD. Because of the second bombing, the Chief had elected to go public with their best lead. Since Whitney believed that Kelly was still in custody in England, his photograph was withheld from circulation to the press.

Detective Rodrigo Amador had been shown the two photographs, but it turned out he was not able to make a positive identification of either man. Considering the stress he'd been under during the shootout, the inability to recognize either one of the two men had not come as a surprise to Gibson. Different people react differently to overwhelming stress, and Amador's mind had been exclusively focused on the only thing important, his survival.

Under the photos, the articles stated that they were wanted for questioning as members of the IRA.

****

"Counselor? This is Gibson. You busy?"

"Hey, Gibby."

Renée shifted the phone to her other ear and leaned back in her chair.

"I was just sitting here in my new office trying to get motivated to redo my files." She yawned. "Sorry about that. I didn't get enough sleep last night. I looked for you out at the scene, but I guess I missed you?"

"It was pretty hectic. I've been told the FBI and ATF are going to handle the investigation of both bombings."

"That's what I heard, too. At least this will give us time to concentrate on building our case. By the way, I saw the photos in the Times. Did we get any leads yet?"

"Not so far, but the day is young."

"Forever the optimist."

She tilted her chair back and put her feet up on the desk. She was feeling drained, both emotionally and physically. The loss of life because of the explosion was incomprehensible, and while she knew she wasn't directly responsible for what had happened, she couldn't help but feel that she'd played a role as a member of an organization whose proclamation of a policy of non-negotiation had forced the bombers to set the second one off in order to make their point.

The stress and guilt were exhausting, and they were taking a toll.

"Not to change the subject," Gibson said, "but how's your new office?"

"It stinks. I'm in an unused interior office over by the mail room. Until today, it was used for storage. No windows, no carpet, no plants, and it's dusty. The only silver lining is there's no one else around."

"Well, if you've got a few moments, I've got some info for you on Major Andrew Whitney."

She perked up right away.

"What'd you find out?"

"Is he with you now?"

"No, I've no idea where he is. When I saw him last night, he was talking with the Feds, but I haven't seen him today."

"Well, he's quite a piece of goods," Gibson said. "For starters, he's career military and unmarried—"

She smiled. Gibson was playing at being big brother.

"—and he's the son of a British diplomat who's held posts throughout Eastern Europe. His mother was a teacher. She traveled with his father and taught at the embassy schools. The Major studied abroad until college. He went to Cambridge, got a degree in engineering, and put in for a posting with the Royal Air Force."

"You're right," she said. "That's quite a background."

"It gets better. He served three years as a helicopter pilot before being accepted into the Special Air Service."

Renée toyed with a pencil in her hand. She was taking notes as Gibson spoke.

"Did he fly choppers for the SAS?" she asked.

"Actually, he didn't. My source says he completed the mountain tactics and small boat assault schools. They were gearing up for the Falklands invasion, but just before his unit shipped out, he was pulled from his Regiment and sent to Northern Ireland instead."

"Now why do you suppose they did that?"

"My source says Whitney's father is a friend of Nigel Ward, the head of MI-5, and the father wanted to keep his son out of harm's way, so Ward used his influence to see that Whitney got sent to the North instead."

"I can imagine that didn't sit too well with Whit?"

"You're probably right, but he did as he was told. He got six months of language training, during which time he perfected his regional accent. By the way, he's fluent in *five* languages."

"You're kidding?" She was genuinely surprised. "He's never mentioned that?"

"He's pretty tight-mouthed about a lot of things, Renée. He spent the next three years in Belfast, where he ran a clandestine intelligence team whose sole responsibility was to identify members and sympathizers of the IRA." Gibson laughed. "That may have been his way of telling his father not to mess with his career."

"I suspect you're right. Anything else?"

"The next two years are a blank. There's nothing in his file. After that, he pops up in London to work as a liaison with foreign governments."

She thought about the two-year gap.

"I wonder what he was doing?" she mused.

"My source doesn't know. The only thing he could verify was that Whitney was still on active duty during that time."

"Covert operations?"

"That's his best guess, too."

Renée shuddered. Whitney's past was a lot more interesting than she'd suspected. Make that interesting and scary. They really didn't know him at all.

"What do you think, Gibby? Can we trust him?"

"According to my source, he's fine."

"Can I ask who's your source?"

"I don't see why not," he replied. "I've got a contact in the U.S. Secret

Service. Don Flynn. You know him?"

"No," she said.

"He used to work criminal investigations here in L.A. We worked a few cases together. Anyway, he got on the fast track and he's now the number two guy in Washington, D.C. His title is Assistant Director, and I'm sure I don't need to tell you, he's got access to sources all over the world."

"Well, on that note, I'd say your source is gold. But I still would like to know more about Whitney's two missing years?"

Gibson chuckled.

"Good luck with that."

She smiled into the phone.

"I'm up to the challenge. He can't resist my charms."

"Now, if I had even suggested anything like that, someone I know would be screaming sexual harassment."

"Well, you didn't, and it would be." She smiled. "Is there anything else I should know about?"

"Not at the moment, but I'll let you know if something else turns up."

She could hear him yawn into the phone.

"When was the last time you got some sleep?" she asked.

"I'm not sure, but I get this weekend off."

"Well, get some rest. I'll talk to you on Monday."

"Only if I'm awake by then."

****

"Gibson, line six," yelled a detective.

Having just finished his call with Renée, he reached again for the receiver.

"Gibson speaking?"

"Detective Gibson? My name's Joel Price. I work Homicide in North Hollywood and I've got an informant I think you should talk to."

"Give me the short version, Price. I'm pressed for time at the moment."

"She's a married woman. Her husband works nights, so she was out at a bar last night, a joint called the *'Throwback'* on Ventura Boulevard. She was waiting for her old man to get off work when she was picked up by one of the guys in the paper today, the one named McGarry. He banged her at a motel a few blocks away, then left her when she fell asleep."

Gibson felt his adrenalin surge. "Does she know where he is or did she get us a car?"

"No such luck," Price replied, "but she thinks he lives nearby because they walked from the bar to the motel. He never offered to drive."

Gibson waved frantically to Elwood.

"Listen to me, Price. I want you to get someone over to that motel. Find out which room they were in and seal it off. I don't care if someone's in there now. Kick 'em out, stash 'em somewhere so we can get their prints, but don't let anyone in the room until the crime lab shows up. And keep this low key. I don't want a bunch of black and whites in the area. Are you with me?"

"I'll take care of it."

"Good. Where's your informant now?"

"I've got her here in the station, but she doesn't want to get involved. She's afraid her old man will find out she's been sleeping around."

"I don't care what she wants; she's not free to leave. As of this moment, she's in protective custody. Don't let her out of your sight, and don't tell anyone what's going on. We'll be out there as soon as possible."

Gibson hung up the phone, took his gun and shoulder rig from his desk and put them on. When Elwood walked up he explained what he'd learned from the call.

"I'll need about a dozen undercover teams, Tom. Their vehicles need to be nondescript. I want to run a canvass of the neighborhood, radiating out from the bar. They'll need photos of McGarry, and they should work all the motels first. If they come up dry, have them try the managers of all the apartment buildings for six square blocks."

Elwood reached for the phone. "I'll have to get the okay from the Deputy Chief, but I'm sure there'll be no problems. I'll send them over to North Hollywood station, and you can roll call the men over there."

"Thanks, Tom."

"Where you gonna be?" Elwood asked.

"Once I track down Donahue, we'll go out to North Hollywood to talk to the informant. Maybe she knows more than she's saying? By the way, where is she today?"

"She's off for a few days, burning up some overtime."

"Damn. Okay. Would you see if we can get some of the guys to start calling real estate offices in the area? We should determine what's been rented in the last two months."

"Consider it done."

****

Lisa Collins sat on her bed reading a copy of *The Los Angeles Times*. She glanced at her watch, annoyed that Carlson was more than an hour late. He'd never missed an afternoon rendezvous, and his failure to show up had her gravely concerned. Something was happening, and she was willing to bet it had to do with the photos in the Times.

She reached for the telephone next to the bed and dialed his number at work. It was answered by his adjutant who put her call through right away.

"Lisa," Carlson said in a muffled voice, "Sorry I didn't get a chance to call you. I'm not going to make it this afternoon."

"Why? Is something going on?"

He was silent for a moment.

"I can't talk about it now."

She was not used to being put off, and it made her angry.

"Then maybe you can tell me how the Times got the exclusive on the suspects?"

"I can explain—"

"Pictures and everything. You should've let me know."

"It's not like that," he said defensively. "The info came in from the British government. Major Crimes let it go to the Times to flush the suspects out. I had no say in the matter."

"Well, my editor was hopping mad. He thinks I'm out here having a vacation and ignoring my job."

"I'm sorry, Lisa. It's not my fault."

"Then tell me what's going on, Mark? I can't afford to find out about it from the Times."

There was a long pause, and she knew he was weighing his options.

"Okay," he said softly, "but you have to keep it to yourself. Hold on for a moment."

She heard him put down the phone and walk away. The sound of a door shutting in the background was followed by his return.

"We've got a lead on where they might be staying," he whispered.

She sat straight up.

"What kind of lead?"

"One of the two suspects picked up a woman in a bar last night. He was on foot, so we know their general residential area. We've got teams out there now, and with any luck, we should be able to determine where they're staying within the next few hours."

She could think of nothing to say.

"Are you still there?" he asked.

"I'm here." Her mind was racing. "How about if I come down to the press room at the station. I'll need to get all the background I can."

"Wait a minute, Lisa. You can't say anything about this until they're in custody." His voice had an edge to it. He sounded nervous as well.

"I know, but I can start working on it so that I'm ready to go when you give it to the others."

There was a long pause as Carlson seemed once again to be weighing his options.

"Okay. Meet me down here. I'll see what I can dig up."

"Thanks, Mark. You're really sweet."

"I've got to go, Lisa," he whispered. "I've got some calls to make. Try to get here right away. Things may start to break pretty quickly."

She was already off the bed.

"I'll be there in twenty minutes."

****

"Hello?"

Kelly listened for a moment, then put down the receiver and signaled to Jimmy who reached for the phone.

"Yeah?" said Jimmy into the phone.

He listened for a moment, then slowly turned towards the others who were now quietly going about their business while they eavesdropped on his conversation.

Cassidy's eyes went wide.

"*What?*" The tone of his voice stopped the others in their tracks, and as Cassidy's eyes went from face to face, he realized that they were watching him expectantly.

"How the fuck did they find us?" he said into the phone.

As he listened to the explanation, his gaze quickly settled on McGarry's face.

Bloody stupid bastard!

He slammed down the receiver, then said to the group, "They got photo's of McGarry an me plastered all over today's papers."

"*What?* How'd they get our pictures?" McGarry asked.

Kelly, who's eyes never left McGarry's face, said, "A gift from the SAS."

"*Bloody hell!*"

****

Gibson, Donahue, and Elwood stood quietly with several other officers in the darkness of a carport across the street from a duplex on Warner Avenue in North Hollywood. Although she was required to use up some of the massive amount of overtime she was carrying on the books, Gibson knew she'd skin him alive if he didn't call her in for a possible arrest.

By calling all of the real estate offices in the area, detectives from Major Crimes had managed to locate a broker who remembered the recent rental of a furnished duplex apartment to a female who'd claimed to be from England. She told him she wanted the unit for about three months, and she'd paid the rent in advance for all three months *in cash.*

Surrounded by elm trees, the two-story building had thick Spanish walls and red roof tiles. A narrow driveway ran the length of the oversized lot to a detached garage at the back of the property. There were large apartment buildings on both sides, but the neighborhood itself was quiet.

It had taken the better part of several hours to get the operation underway, so by the time they'd established a perimeter around the property, it was quickly approaching eight p.m.

They'd called out SWAT, and a detail had quietly surrounded the location. During the evacuation of nearby neighbors, one of them—a woman whose apartment overlooked the duplex—mentioned that she had seen one of the male tenants working on a car the night before the explosion. When she was shown a photograph of Devon McGarry, she said that she thought that it looked like him.

"Are we all set?" Elwood asked.

The Lieutenant from SWAT gave him a nod. "My people are ready," he said.

"Fine. Send 'em in."

The Lieutenant mumbled into his radio, and a team of officers, dressed in battle fatigues, closed in on the building from all four sides. Those who approached from the back broke out windows and tossed in several flash grenades. This was done to confuse the occupants while entry was made from the front.

Two minutes later, the SWAT Lieutenant, who had monitored the entry on his earphone, turned to Gibson and tapped him on the arm. "The place is clear, Gibson. No suspects inside."

The Lieutenant escorted them into the building.

"Other than the broken windows, the place is just as we found it," he said. "Be careful what you touch."

"Thanks, Lieutenant."

Elwood's eyes swept over the room.

Donahue shook her head in disgust.

"Looks like someone might have tipped 'em off."

Elwood placed a finger to his lips, then gestured with his head that they were not alone.

Donahue acknowledged the warning with a nod then pointed at the plates on the table. There were remnants of a half-eaten meal—ground beef, potatoes, and corn—as well as several pans and pots still on the stove that contained what little remained of the food that was out on the plates.

"Looks like there were four of 'em," Gibson said. He pointed to the four place settings.

Gibson carefully surveyed the room, then wandered over to a phone on the kitchen counter. He copied the number to a page in his notebook.

"I'll get someone to run a their phone records. Maybe they made a few calls."

Elwood poked through the kitchen cupboards, then checked the refrigerator.

"Looks like there was only enough food for a couple of days. They must go shopping quite often."

The Lieutenant from SWAT finally wandered into another room, so Elwood walked over to Donahue.

"What makes you think we've got a leak?" he asked her.

'The photos were printed by the Times in this morning's edition, but from what they were serving, it looks like they didn't get the word until lunch or more likely during their dinner. And even if they learned about the photo's, there's no way they could know that we had a lead on where they were staying. Either someone tipped 'em off or they're exceptionally cautious, and my gut is telling me that we've got a leak."

Elwood turned to Gibson.

"What do you think?"

"For now, we don't say anything to anyone. I need some time to think. When we get back to the station, I'll probably start by making a list of everyone who knew about what we were going to do."

The Lieutenant came back into the room.

"Captain? I need you gentlemen to leave now. The bomb squad wants to go through here and check for booby traps and explosives. My Captain's outside and he's leaning on us to clear the scene so that the neighbors can get back into their homes."

Elwood's eyes widened.

"You mean they didn't do a search for booby traps before you brought us in to look around?"

"Sorry, Captain." The Lieutenants face was impassive. "I just assumed you wanted to get in here as soon as possible."

Elwood shuddered. "I did, but not before the place was secure? Damn it, man, I'm too old for this."

Gibson worked to suppress a grin.

"We'll wait up the street until you're finished, Lieutenant. Just give us a call when it's safe."

****

TWENTY

October 3, Friday Late Evening

Jimmy Cassidy and the others had gathered around the television to watch the eleven o'clock news.

Although his contact in Los Angeles had offered to provide them with a safe house in the northwestern San Fernando Valley, Cassidy had turned the man down. Their contact was a guy who liked to play it safe. He would put up his money, even make a phone call if he had to, but that was it. He couldn't be trusted in a pinch. He'd give 'em all up if he had to.

People like him always did.

Instead, Cassidy chose to rely on his instincts. They'd gotten him through some difficult times, and instinct told him to keep their location a secret, so he had Claire Harris find them a place that no one else knew about.

The city of Lancaster, once a sleepy desert town, had gone through a rapid expansion in recent years. When big business moved in, lured to the high desert by inexpensive land, people had quickly followed—drawn primarily by the jobs —and subdivisions had flourished east of the city center as far as the eye could see.

By freeway, Lancaster was only a thirty-minute drive through the mountains from the San Fernando Valley, but in terms of the lifestyle of its residents, it might as well have been several hundred miles away. It retained its small town feeling, due in large part to its isolation from the big city, and despite the substantial new growth to the east, the land to the west remained rural.

The house they'd rented was west of the city, on three rolling acres of low, barren hillside. Isolated and quiet, it was more than ideal as a place where they'd be able to hide in plain sight.

But their choice of location would not be problem-free. In all small towns, people got curious, and the release of the pictures might give them away. To forestall any possible detection, Cassidy had decided that only Claire Harris would venture into the city while the rest of them stayed in the house. No one knew about Harris, not even the Brits, and with any luck, their connection to her would remain a secret, thus ensuring that their location would continue to be safe.

When the evening news ended at eleven thirty p.m., he got up from the couch, turned off the TV, and demanded everyone's attention.

Claire Harris came out of the kitchen and took a seat on a straight-back, wooden chair.

"What we've done to free Liam may not be good enough," he said. "When I made the last call, they gave me some rubbish about needin' an extension. I don't need to tell you that an extension will work against us. The more time they have, the greater the risk to us."

There were nods of agreement. He looked sternly at McGarry who averted his eyes.

"Now that they've gotten so close, they might just try to play this out." He paused to let his words sink in. "I've been thinkin' it over, and if we're goin' to succeed, we'll be needin' to stay ahead of 'em. We'll have to keep 'em off balance so's they can't get close again."

McGarry looked up.

"I can't make another bomb, Jimmy. I don't have enough stuff left to make anythin' worth while."

Cassidy shook his head.

"I was thinkin' of somethin' more personal, mates. We're gonna do a snatch."

"You're kiddin', right?" Kelly's eyes widened. "We just blew the bloody hell out of 'em, Jimmy. There's no way they'll cave in on a snatch."

"He's right," McGarry echoed. "A hostage is nothin' but problems. It's too risky; they'd never go for a trade."

Cassidy remained impassive.

"It depends on who we snatch."

McGarry got to his feet.

"I don't like it, Jimmy. This whole thing's gettin' out of control." He looked to Kelly for support. "We came here to get Liam out of the slam and now we're blowin' up buildin's and takin' hostages. For God's sake, Jimmy! They've got our fuckin' photos!"

"Devon's right." Kelly said. He didn't particularly want to go up against Jimmy, but he wasn't happy with the way things had escalated so quickly. More cautious than the others, if he was going to take a stand to end this downward spiral, it had to be now or never.

"When's it gonna end?" Kelly asked.

"It ends when I say so," Cassidy said sternly. "I'm still callin' the shots."

"But Liam's a big boy," blurted McGarry. "He's the one that got himself into this mess—"

Cassidy's glare cut him off. He wasn't used to being challenged in this way, but if he lost his temper now, it would all be over. His men were clearly on the edge of revolt, and any mistake, any show of weakness at this moment, and his brother Liam would be on his own.

But he was not about to cut them any quarter, particularly McGarry, whose stupidity had compromised the entire operation. It was time to end this discussion once and for all, and if they didn't acknowledge his unquestioned authority, then perhaps an example would have to be made.

He put his hand behind his back and felt the rough, patterned surface of the handgrip on his hidden weapon.

His eyes locked with those of McGarry, and his voice took on a firmness that sent them all a clear message.

"We won't be leavin' without him, Devon."

McGarry rolled his eyes. His frustration had reached the boiling point.

"But it's his own fuckin' fault he got caught."

At that moment, you could have heard a pin drop. It was as if the very air had been sucked out of the room. The unspeakable had been uttered, and beneath that complaint was the sentiment felt by the rest of them; one that the others lacked the courage to say.

He'd acted on his own, without formal sanction. So why risk our lives to save Liam?

Claire Harris looked down at her lap. The first to distance herself from the remark, she was not about to stand up to Jimmy.

Kelly looked nervously from one to the other. Like two male alphas in the midst of a challenge for leadership of the pack, one wrong word, one demeaning gesture, and the room would explode with a level of violence that was sure to consume them all.

Cassidy's eyes glazed over. His voice dropped to barely a whisper, but there was no mistaking the menace in his tone.

"We'll not be leavin' him behind."

It was a statement that brooked no dissension, and while it was aimed directly at McGarry, the challenge was meant for the others as well.

In the next few seconds, Kelly made up his mind, for as far as he could tell, the point was moot. This whole dispute now boiled down to a risk assessment, and as he assessed the situation, he realized that he stood a greater chance of dying if Cassidy got pissed off then he did if they carried out his ill-conceived rescue mission. Neither option was good, but at least the latter would postpone for a while what might turn out to be inevitable.

Always the pragmatist, he shifted his feet and turned ever so subtly away from Cassidy and towards McGarry. A clear sign whose meaning was crystal clear. He was casting his lot with Cassidy, and in doing so, he would back his play.

He stared at McGarry. The next few moments would decide it all.

For his part, McGarry was not a fool. There'd been a sea change in attitude in the room, and as things now stood, he was completely alone. The lines were drawn, and the odds were against him. He could take his chances and push things forward, but to do so would be tantamount to suicide.

McGarry was no stranger to violence, but when it came to taking action, he lacked the cold-blooded ruthlessness of an angered Jimmy Cassidy, a man whose reckless disregard for the consequence of his actions meant there was no such thing as a measured response. With Cassidy, it was always all or nothing, and while there were certainly better ways to handle a volatile situation, Jimmy's way of doing things made him a truly terrifying threat.

McGarry assessed his chances and wisely concluded he was not yet ready to die.

He broke off from Jimmy's stare.

"Fine. Okay. I'm in."

Kelly sighed silently with relief. He turned to Jimmy.

"If we do this snatch, who'd you have in mind?"

Cassidy exhaled. The adrenaline was still coursing through his veins, but it was time to ratchet things back. He turned to face Kelly, his breathing now measured.

"We'll snatch the prosecutor's daughter."

McGarry shuddered. "They'll hunt us down like dogs." It was delivered as a warning and not a challenge.

"You're wrong, Devon. When we take her child, they'll have no choice but to let Liam go."

McGarry bit his lip. He dared not say what he knew to be true. Not now. Not after what had just happened. The prosecutor would have no say in the matter. A decision like that was not hers to make. The politicians would be calling the tune, and like politicians, they would all be following their own agendas.

Kelly was thinking the same thing, but he, too, was not about to risk a challenge.

"So, how do we do this?" he finally asked.

Cassidy flashed a self-confident smile.

"I'm glad you asked. For the past several days, I've had Claire watchin' the child. An old woman takes her to school, and a two man escort follows in a chase car. But once the girl goes inside, her watchers stay in the car which they park on the playground. The school is small, so we can walk in and take her anytime that we want."

They worked out the details for another forty minutes, and by the time they were finished, they had a solid plan that looked for the most part like it would succeed.

"When do we do it?" Kelly asked.

"There's no reason to wait too long." Cassidy glanced at the calendar on his watch. "If they don't meet the deadline on Sunday, we'll do it on Monday mornin'."

As the meeting broke up, Claire Harris cornered Cassidy in private.

"If we're goin' to have a child around here, Jimmy, I'll need to get a few things from the store."

"When do you want to do it?"

"I'd like to go now. There's a small grocer in the city that's open all night. I can get in and out without havin' to stand around."

He pulled a set of keys from his pocket.

"Take the blue van."

She nodded and quickly left the house, but on the way to the store, she stopped at a payphone to make a call.

****

TWENTY-ONE

October 5, Sunday, Evening

At six o'clock sharp, there was a knock at Renée's front door. She paused in front of her hallway mirror, smoothed an errant lock of hair—gave herself a quick nod of approval—then opened the door.

Whitney smiled and produced a bouquet of flowers from behind his back.

"They're lovely, Whit," she said. "C'mon in. Let me get them into some water."

"They're not for you," he said without missing a beat. "They're for the little lady of the house."

Renée smiled. It was very thoughtful of him to think of her daughter.

"I'm sure she'll be charmed."

She stepped back and allowed him in.

His glance swept over the entryway, then settled on her.

"Your home is lovely, Renée, and you look absolutely beautiful."

"Well, thanks."

He smiled, then gestured with his thumb towards the front of the house.

"I see your security's in place," he said, referring to the team of District Attorney's Investigators who were sitting in their car which was parked in her driveway.

"It's so oppressive," she said with a sigh. "On the one hand, I guess it's a relief to know they're out there, but just having them around is a constant reminder of what's been going on. I wasn't going to let it interfere with my activities, but I end up staying in just because it seems so difficult for everyone involved whenever I want to go out."

"You'll get used to it," he told her, "and this might help you forget they're outside." He produced a bottle of Chablis from behind his back. "This is for the grownup lady of the house."

Her laughter was interrupted by a series of thumps as her eleven-year-old daughter came flying down the stairs. In her hand was a leash, attached to a black and white blur that strained to get free by jumping up and down.

"This is Julie," she said to Whitney while she helped her daughter get the puppy under control.

"I'm pleased to meet you, Julie. Who's this little ball of fire?"

"That's Cinder." Julie beamed. "She's a Dalmatian."

"She's so well behaved," he said, and as if on cue, the dog began to climb his leg. He smiled, reached down and patted the puppy until she rolled over on her back.

He scratched the dog's belly, straightened up, then handed Julie the bouquet.

"These are for you."

Her eyes grew wide.

"Cool! Thank you."

"I'm glad you like them," he told her.

Renée put her arm around Julie's shoulder and directed her towards the kitchen.

"Sweetheart, ask Mrs. Jeffreys to find you a vase so you can put them in water."

Julie and the puppy scampered off, and Renée took Whitney's arm.

"I think you've made a friend."

When dinner was finally served, the three of them ate together by candle-light in the dining room. Chicken, pasta, and a tossed green salad—comple-mented handsomely by the Chablis—were followed by strawberry pie and dark Columbian coffee.

Renée and Whitney talked softly, almost oblivious to Julie's presence at the table until Whitney noticed that Julie was blowing ever so slightly on the candles to make them flicker, no doubt thoroughly bored by the evening's events. He blew one out, then pretended to play innocent. It grabbed her attention and made them both laugh.

"Tell me somethin', Julie," he said. "Are you goin' to be a lawyer like your mum when you grow up?"

"I want to be a teacher," she replied.

"That's a wonderful profession."

"Or an actress."

"That sounds fine, too."

"Or maybe a lawyer."

"I see." He laughed. "Anythin' else?"

"I guess I'm not exactly sure, but I've got lots of time to make up my mind."

"Well, take your time. I didn't decide to become a flier until I finished up at the University."

"Do you fight in wars and stuff?" she asked.

"I've done a little of that, but mostly I fly helicopters."

"You do? That's neat! Could you take me for a ride someday? I've never been in a helicopter."

He looked over at Renée. "Sure. But your mom will have to come with us."

"Cool! Can we, Mom?"

Renée smiled. "We'll see. Maybe someday."

"Maybe someday? C'mon, Mom. It would really be fun! *Please?*"

"We'll just have to wait and see."

She then turned to Whitney and whispered, "Thanks a heap. I'll never hear the end of this."

"Please, Mom. Can we do it?"

"Finish your desert."

"Does that mean yes?"

"It means finish your desert."

Renée looked over at Whitney and gave him a *"see I told you so"* look.

Later that evening, and after a protracted game of Monopoly, Renée walked Julie to her room.

"G'night, sweetie." She kissed her on the cheek. "I hope you had a good time tonight."

"I did, Mom. Whitney's really neat. I mean, he's not the same as Dad, but he is pretty cool."

Renée shut off the light to prevent her daughter from seeing her tears.

Whitney was at the bar fixing her a nightcap when she returned.

"Thanks again for having me over," he said. He handed her a drink.

She smiled. "The pleasure was all ours."

"Cheers," he said.

They clinked their glasses together and each took a sip. He put his arm around her and gave her a hug.

"Your daughter's very charmin'."

"You made quite an impression on her. The flowers were very sweet."

There was an awkward moment of silence, and Whitney could sense that something was wrong.

"I've got a small confession to make," she said.

"Let me guess. You find me irresistible?"

"No, Whit. I'm serious." She averted his gaze. "I had Gibson check you out."

He stared at her for a moment before speaking.

"Why?"

She swallowed hard.

"We had to be sure about you. After all, you've had complete access to our investigation."

He studied her face. She seemed genuinely upset.

"And what did you find out?"

"That you're who you said you were."

"Well, that's reassurin'."

"I also learned a few things about your work in Northern Ireland."

Whitney's smiled tightened. "Someday you'll have to tell me who your sources are?"

She didn't return his smile.

"Do you want to talk about my time in the service?" he asked.

"I don't want to pry, Whit, but I don't really feel that I know you."

"You know me, Renée, but if my past concerns you, then by all means, let's talk."

She moved to the couch, and he followed her lead.

"I ran an undercover unit in Belfast. My men moved into the Catholic enclaves, went on the dole, and kept their eyes open. Once they were accepted by the locals, information would come our way, and we'd use it to prevent violent attacks on our people."

He took a swallow from his drink and finished it off. She was watching him intently.

"It was strictly long term. Most of the men didn't have any families—we couldn't afford to have people wonderin' where they were—and if they were killed, well, we didn't need any questions about what they were up to."

"*Jesus, Whit!*"

"They were all volunteers, Renée."

"How long did they have to live like that?"

On average, most were down for five years. I got lucky and promoted out after three."

"You actually worked undercover?"

"You seem surprised?"

"It's just that I heard you were sent to the North—"

"I know, to keep me out of the action in the Falklands."

He shook his head, stood up, walked to the bar, and poured himself another drink.

"I'll let you in on a little secret, Renée. I was always scheduled for service in the North. My true mission has always been classified, so there's never been a chance to openly challenge that vicious slander."

He stared at her, hoping she'd accept his explanation without further elucidation. He walked back to the couch and sat down.

"Your official file is blank for a two-year period, Whit. Is that the classified mission you're talking about?"

This was the moment he'd dreaded. How would she feel if he told her what he'd done? Hell, with her connections, she might already know.

"That's correct. I was assigned to a group that did counter-terrorist missions." He watched her eyes to gauge her reaction. "We went after people who did the killin's and bombin's, and it was my job to take 'em out."

Her eyes grew wide.

"You mean you assassinated people?"

"I guess you could say that."

"You didn't bring them to trial? You just killed them?"

He sighed. "A trial would have been counter-productive."

"But... how could you, Whit? Doesn't the right to a trial mean anything to you?"

"Much like the situation you find your country in right now, mine was also at war with an enemy that had no constraints. To save innocent lives, we had to take the offensive."

"But couldn't you take the offensive by putting them into prisons?"

"They were killers, Renée, not soldiers. They were nothin' more than common thugs who cloaked themselves in a mantle of religious righteousness. We hunted down the ones who detonated bombs— bombs that killed innocent non-combatants—and murderers who chose to gun down their neighbors because of their religious beliefs." He shook his head. "If we didn't take 'em out, many more people would have died, and we just couldn't let that happen."

Her cheeks became flushed and her eyes narrowed.

"But they would have been neutralized in prison. When society suspends the rules, it becomes its' own worst enemy."

He grimaced openly. This was not going well.

"It doesn't work that way. If you put one of them in jail, it creates a whole new set of problems. What's going on here in your city is a perfect example. The bastards are just like a cancer. First Cassidy shows up, and people get killed, then his friends come to rescue him, and even more people get killed. It's a vicious cycle, Renée, and it never stops."

"But the law—?"

"Laws work fine in peacetime, but not very well in war. There's only one way to deal with terrorists, and believe me, it's the only way that works. An eye for an eye, there's truth to that sayin'. It may not stop the violence, but it does keep it down."

Renée was clearly disillusioned.

"That's the same approach the Israelis have used for years against the PLO and Hamas, and it doesn't work."

How was he going to get through to her? She seemed to be oblivious to his words.

"But it does work, Renée." He smiled ever so slightly. "It's all in how you measure success. The Israelis still have their country, and the losses they sustain are the price they're willin' to pay for their existence."

"But that's comparing apples and oranges."

Whitney shook his head.

"Even with a ceasefire, the war in the North is not goin' to end any time soon. It's been ragin' for too many years, and it will keep on goin' because it's fueled by religious hatreds and not by reasonable grievances. By doin' what we did, we kept the lid down tight on wholesale anarchy."

Renée stood up. Her hand was shaking as she pointed at his chest. "You're wrong. What you've described is murder, and what you're defending is a form of state-sanctioned killing. Society's founded on the principle of law. Civilized people surrender to the government the right to redress their grievances in exchange for the promise that justice will be sought by a fixed set of rules. When you circumvent the law for the sake of expediency, then you sell out the principles that make our countries great."

"It's not murder," he responded.

"It certainly is, and since Nuremberg, soldiers have an obligation to disobey any order to commit murder. And that tired old refrain, '*I was just following orders*' is not a legally accepted defense."

She glared at him in silence, but he could think of nothing that he could say that was going to change her opinion. He'd wanted the evening to advance their relationship, not destroy it, but as things stood now, everything seemed to be teetering on the edge.

"I guess you feel pretty strongly about this, don't you?" he said softly.

"Of course I do." The anger faded from her voice as she appeared to sense a softening of his position. "My belief in the system is at the very core of my work."

"But the system doesn't always work, Renée."

"But it does, Whitney. On a case by case basis, the results themselves don't matter. The only thing important is the process."

She was doing it again—getting under his skin—why couldn't she just leave it alone?

"C'mon, Renée. Laws are subject to interpretation; they change every day."

"But the law is the law, Major, and whatever the outcome—whether we like it or not—it's justice."

"Try tellin' that to the innocent people in the Mid-City Mall, the ones who lost their lives."

From the look on her face he knew the evening was totally ruined. They had reached an impasse, and he wished with all his might that he'd never told her what he'd done.

"I can see that we don't share the same views on this topic," he said. "And I'm sorry that you're so upset. Maybe we should call for a truce?"

She took a deep breath.

"That's probably a good idea. Perhaps we should call it a night, too."

He finished his drink and placed his glass on the bar before she walked him to the door.

"Thanks for the dinner," he said again. "I really did appreciate the invitation."

She gave him a forced smile.

"I guess I'm still glad you could make it."

He started out the door then turned back.

"Look. I feel really bad about the way this turned out. I might be out of line at this point, but just because we don't agree on everythin' doesn't mean that we shouldn't see each other again."

A small smile crept over her face.

"I'll give that some thought. "

She moved in and brushed his cheek with her lips.

"I'll see you tomorrow at the office."

****

TWENTY-TWO

October 6, Monday

At seven-thirty in the morning, the Marin's Scottish housekeeper, Madeleine Jeffreys, an old-fashioned woman in her early fifties, led Julie out of the house and into a black GMC SUV. Their escort unit was waiting across the street.

The two District Attorney Investigators assigned to protect Renée Marin's daughter were sharing coffee and donuts with members of the night crew who were there to watch the house. As Mrs. Jeffreys pulled away, the chase car fell in line behind her and shadowed her progress to the *Crawford Academy*, a small private school that catered to children from the third grade through the eighth.

Mrs. Jeffreys drove between the tall brick buildings and into the playground that served as a parking lot before the start of classes. After making sure that Julie had her book bag and her lunch, she led her by the hand through the schoolyard and into the building that housed the classrooms. Julie stopped on the steps, turned, and waved to her escorts before she vanished into the hallway.

The officers watched her go into the building before parking their vehicle in the corner of the schoolyard. To enhance their security, they backed their car up under a tree next to a high brick wall that separated the school from an alley. From this position, fifty yards from the classrooms, they could monitor the schoolyard and the rear of the building.

Claire Harris stood in the corner of the hallway where she appeared to be reading the student compositions that were pinned to a bulletin board on a wall outside one of the classrooms. Numerous parents milled about, so she blended right in, her presence not that unusual.

From the corner of her eye, she watched as the woman led Julie to a classroom near the front of the building. A short time later, the old woman came out and went back out to the playground to get to her car, Claire casually walked down the hallway and out the front door where she headed for the street.

Forty minutes later, Claire returned to the playground from behind the corner of the main building. Classes were in session, so the playground was empty except for the two bodyguards.

She wore a short, revealing dress and a cable knit sweater, and with a shopping bag of groceries held against her chest, she strolled purposefully towards the two officers. She hoped that they'd be so distracted by her appearance that they wouldn't wonder what a woman was doing crossing the playground with a bag of groceries.

Thirty feet from their car, several items fell from her bag. She stopped, turned her back to them, and bent over at the waist to pick the items up.

"Check it out," said the Investigator in the drivers' seat who pointed in Claire's direction. He'd been watching her since she'd appeared on the grounds.

The other man lowered his crossword puzzle and gave her the once over. "She knows we're watching her, too."

Cassidy came over the wall directly behind their vehicle. The two men were completely oblivious to his arrival.

Wearing gloves, he crept up on the vehicle and pointed a silenced twenty-two caliber revolver into the driver's side window and fired six muffled shots.

Both men were struck in the head, and both died instantly. Cassidy reached into the front seat and dropped the gun on the floorboard.

He stood frozen for a moment, looked around, waiting to determine if there was a reaction from the school. When no one came out, he leaned back into the car, removed the driver's ID badge from inside his right breast pocket, then casually walked away and out to the street.

McGarry and Kelly waited in silence in a stolen blue Plymouth that they'd parked in front of the school. Both wore slacks and dark blue sports coats, and each had trimmed their hair to give the impression that they were detectives. Both men carried handguns in holsters which hung noticeably from their waists.

When Cassidy walked up to their car, he handed McGarry the badge that he'd taken from the dead officer before continuing on foot up the street. McGarry and Kelly got out of the car and moved quickly into the building.

Claire Harris was waiting just inside the hallway door. She pointed out Julie's classroom and whispered, "She's in there."

McGarry walked up to the classroom door and looked through a small glass window. Some of the students were working on computers while others read quietly at their desks. A middle-aged woman, probably the teacher, moved from desk to desk, while a second woman, who appeared much younger, spoke to a child near the back of the room.

McGarry checked the door; it wasn't locked. He opened it up and stepped inside.

Everything came to a halt as the students and teachers looked up. "Good mornin'," he said, addressing the older woman. "I'm Dave Taylor with the DA's office. Can I speak to ya in private for a moment?"

He watched as the older woman looked over at the younger one, who then stepped forward. He'd made a mistake. The younger one was the teacher in charge.

"I'm Mrs. Carley Baker," the teacher said. "Can I help you?"

He studied her face. She was cautious but not yet suspicious.

"Yes, ma'am. I need to talk to you outside for a moment about Julie Marin."

She followed him out of the classroom.

"I'm Dave Taylor." He flashed the stolen badge. "We're handlin' security for Julie, and we've just received a call from downtown that there's been another threat. We've been ordered to pick up Julie and take her to her mother."

Baker was speechless, apparently in shock.

He added, "If you can give us her homework, I'm sure her mother will be very grateful."

Baker came to life.

"Of course, detective. This whole situation is so horrible. I'll get Julie right away, and please, tell Mrs. Marin to let us know if there's anything we can do to help out."

The request for homework had been a nice touch; that, and the badge had deflected her suspicions.

"I'm sure she'll appreciate your offer," he said.

She started to go back into the classroom, then noticed that McGarry was close on her heels.

"Please remain out here so we don't disturb the rest of the class. I'll bring Julie out in a moment."

She entered the classroom, walked over to Julie who was seated at one of the computers and asked her to join her near the front of the room.

"Julie," she whispered, "there are several policemen in the hallway. They want to take you downtown to be with your mother."

"Has something happened to my mom?" she asked nervously.

"No, dear, your mother is just fine. She just wants to see you. That's all."

Julie smiled with relief while Mrs. Baker tousled her hair.

"By the way, dear, what's the name of your puppy? Your mother said we should use the puppy's name as a code word to make sure we don't release you to the wrong people. Just whisper the name in my ear."

"It's Cinder," she said softly.

"Okay. Get your math and spelling books and meet me out in the hallway."

Mrs. Baker stepped into the hallway, letting the door swing shut behind her.

"She'll be out in a second, detective. She's getting her books. If you can tell me the code word, I'll be happy to release her to you."

Code word?

McGarry had no idea what she was talking about.

"I'm sorry, Mrs. Baker." He tried to think quickly. "I wasn't provided with a code word. This is an emergency situation, and I guess someone forgot to give it to us."

Mrs. Baker's eyes narrowed.

"I don't know, detective. Can't you call Mrs. Marin?"

"That's impossible," he told her. "Mrs. Marin's very busy at the moment, and we're in a hurry."

Mrs. Baker stepped back.

"Then I'm afraid I'm going to have to see your identification again."

"Certainly."

He pulled out his handgun, and in one sweeping motion, he struck her on the side of the head.

Mrs. Baker's knees buckled and she dropped like a stone to the floor.

The door to the classroom swung open and Julie Marin came out. She stared at her teacher who was lying on the ground and that's when she started to scream.

Kelly ran over and clamped his hand over her mouth.

"Keep quiet," he ordered, "or I'll break your bloody neck."

He tightened his grip, and when she stopped struggling, he lifted her up and carried her down the hallway with McGarry close behind.

When they got to the Plymouth, Kelly put her in the back and placed a pillowcase over her head. Duct tape was used to secure her hands and feet.

McGarry drove them north for almost a quarter of a mile before he turned to the west. In the middle of the block, he abruptly stopped behind a green Suburban van.

Cassidy waited in the front of the van while the girl was transferred by Harris and McGarry from the Plymouth to the back of the van.

****

By early Monday morning, enhanced security measures were firmly in place at most of the city's governmental buildings. The LAPD placed barricades throughout the civic center, creating vehicle-free zones around the courthouse and other governmental facilities. Everyone was searched, even government employees who might otherwise have resented the intrusion. The explosion made believers of them all, and everyone seemed grateful that something positive was being done.

In her temporary office, Renée spent time with the lawyers of her division, discussing their cases and giving advice. When time permitted, she began returning the hundreds of calls that had come in since the bombings began.

Whitney waltzed through the doorway with two cups of tea and a bag of freshly baked croissants. He put them down on the desk and waved a white handkerchief.

"Is our truce still on?" he asked.

She smiled and nodded, and he pulled up a chair.

"Can we talk about last night?" she asked.

"Absolutely, but it will have to wait for a few moments." He uncovered a cup of tea and handed it to her. "There's some packets of jelly for the croissants in the bottom of the bag."

She laughed, then took a sip of tea and placed her cup on the desk. "I just wanted to tell you how sorry I am that I unloaded on you last night. I had no right to criticize—"

"Stop it," he said. "You don't owe me an apology. I thought a lot about what you said last night, and it made a lot of sense. The problem is my government has interpreted the rules of law to permit the killing of terrorists for the public good. It may not be right, and I'm not particularly proud of what I've done, but there is a moral justification for what we do. Anyway, I wanted you to know that I think you were right. Maybe we do go a bit too far. And, well, I'm sorry that things got out of hand."

She laughed.

"Wow! I finally meet a man who's not afraid to admit he's wrong, and..."

"And what?" he asked.

"And this time you're right. You were wrong."

He smiled. "Very funny, Renée."

She smiled back.

"Actually, I also did a lot of thinking last night, and I realized that I was the one who was out of line. I made things personal—"

"It's okay--"

"No, it's not. I think I was looking for a reason to push you away so that I didn't have to deal with *us*, and that wasn't fair to you. The fact that we disagree about some things shouldn't stand as a barrier between us. I mean, what you did was all in the past---"

"Can we go back to what you said a moment ago?" he asked. "The part about us?"

She smiled at the way he abruptly changed direction.

"The truth is, Whit, I still don't know what I want. I enjoy being with you, but, I just don't know. Everything seems to be so complicated."

"I don't think it's complicated," he told her. He flashed her a smile. "If we enjoy being together, we should give it a try."

"It's not that easy. For one thing, we have to work together; and for another, one of these days you'll be going home. Our lives are different, Whit; our worlds are *so different*. I just don't think it could ever work out."

"Maybe it won't." He put down his tea. "But if you don't take a chance, then how will you ever know?"

"I guess I just don't want to get hurt."

The silence was palpable.

"I think you're being too cautious. And not to change the subject, but I'm goin' back to London tonight."

"Tonight?"

"I've been summoned to see the Old Man, my Director."

"How long will you be gone?"

"A few days, maybe longer."

She concentrated on putting some jelly on a croissant.

"Well, that's a bit of a reality check."

"I suppose you're right." He moved slowly around the desk. "But you know what? I think you need to loosen up a bit. You're puttin' the cart before the horse. We should be spendin' time together to see if our attraction develops into somethin' more."

Before she could reply, the intercom buzzed and startled them both. Her secretary was on the line.

"Mr. Kerin just called. He wanted to know if you were in yet. I told him that I'd put him through, but he said he was coming right down."

"Thanks, Myrna."

She turned to Whitney. "I wonder what's up?"

"Maybe Rosen wants you to handle another press conference?"

"I doubt that."

They could hear footsteps approaching in the hallway.

"I guess we'll find out soon enough," Whitney said.

Kerin walked in without pausing to knock, followed closely by Gibson and Donahue. Their faces were ashen and drawn.

"I'm glad you're here Major," Kerin said as he closed the door behind them.

Gibson cleared his throat.

"Renée, I won't drag this out. We just got a call from WLA. Your daughter's been taken from her school."

"What do you mean taken?"

"She's been kidnapped, Renée." Gibson said it almost as a whisper.

"Kidnapped! What the hell are you talking about Gibby?"

"All we know at the moment is that the two investigators who were watching over her have been shot and a teacher was injured when she tried to intervene. We're doing everything we can—"

But those were the last words she heard. Everything went intensely bright just before she collapsed in a heap and fell to the floor.

****

She could sense movement around her, but she couldn't quite focus her eyes.

"Lie still, Renée," Whitney said, his face close in next to hers. "You're okay. You've just fainted."

It wasn't a dream.

My baby is gone! Oh, Jesus!

"I've got to find her," she said as she tried to sit up. "Help me, Whitney. *Please...*"

"Lie still, Renée. There's nothin' you can do at the moment. Just wait 'till you feel a little better."

Her eyes finally focused and her gaze swept over the room. Gibson was on the phone and Donahue and Kerin were standing by the door. She struggled herself up into a sitting position.

"Gibby," she pleaded, "please take me out of here. I've got to get to her school."

Gibson put down the phone.

"You can't do any good over there, Renée. We've got the school covered. I just spoke to Elwood. He wants you back at your house in case they try to call you at home."

"Gibson's right," Whitney said. "I'll take you home." He helped her up into her chair.

"We'll provide you with an escort," Kerin volunteered.

Whitney glared. "Do your people know what they're doin'?"

"Look, Major, the use of our Child Support investigators was an obvious mistake. From now on we'll be using people from the criminal side. There'll be six of them on duty at all times, and I guarantee—"

"Wait a minute..."

Whitney took a step forward.

"Are you tellin' me her people weren't trained for security? *Christ, man!* You made her take the lead in this case with the press. You set her up!"

Renée struggled weakly but managed to get to her feet. She looked over at Kerin with an angry stare.

"If I don't get my baby back..."

"We'll do everything we can, Renée," Kerin said. "I promise."

****

At one forty-seven that afternoon, the phone rang in the DA's Command Post. Captain Don Carroll flipped on the recorder, picked up the receiver, and identified himself.

"Free Derry," the voice said dryly.

Carroll recognized the caller as the man he'd spoken to after the bombing of the mall. He had clipped out the head shots from the newspaper and he reviewed them now, hoping to get an impression of the man on the line.

"We've got the little girl," said the voice, "and she won't be hurt if you let 'im go."

"You have to give us time," Carroll said evenly. "We want to work with you. We're doing everything we can. In fact, let me tell you what we've done so far."

There was a pause on the line. Would he take the bait? Carroll wondered if he could keep him talking long enough.

"Are you there?" he asked.

"I'm here," Cassidy said. "How soon until he's free?"

All right! He'd gotten him talking.

"It's going to take a little more time," Carroll said. "The government of Libya won't cooperate. They don't want responsibility for him. Is there any other place we can send him?"

Carroll was lying. The Libyan government had never been contacted.

"There's no other location," said the man in an angry tone. "Just put him on the plane. We'll deal with it at the other end."

"But they won't let the plane land. We want to do what you're asking, but there are other problems we have to deal with. There are no direct flights to Libya. We have to get permission from several other governments to fly him on one of our planes over their territory. It all takes time."

"Time you haven't got," the man snapped. "Look, I'm tired of the delays. Don't stall on this. If you want the girl back, turn him loose."

"Just give us a deadline we can work with?" Carroll pleaded. He could sense that the man was about to hang up. "I promise we'll do everything we can to do whatever you ask."

"All right," the man conceded, "You have until Wednesday at noon. If he's not on a plane by then, we'll start sendin' you little pieces."

"Please, you don't have to hurt her---"

But the phone went dead.

"*Shit!*"

Carroll looked hopefully over at the detective who was still on the line with the phone company.

"No dice, Captain," the detective told him. "They traced it as far as a switching unit in the western end of the San Fernando Valley, but he broke the connection too soon."

Carroll slammed down his receiver.

"Someone better decide if we're gonna do a trade. That bastard means business, and if we don't do something soon, that little girl is gonna be done for."

****

Rosen had been in meetings throughout the morning and part of the afternoon. Things were happening too quickly and everyone around him was in a state of shock. His political advisors were counseling him to carve out a leadership role, to become highly visible as a man with a plan. It wouldn't take much doing; just call a few meetings, get a consensus, and be the first one to step forward while the others held back. This tactic was risky; things could always backfire, but staying in the shadows could be far worse. In the midst of a crisis, the public wanted leaders, and those who failed to act would soon be unemployed. He stood in his private bathroom and looked at himself in the mirror. He was starting to look exhausted.

The national press was gathered outside and they were waiting *for him*. If all went well, he'd soon emerge as a leader and that would go a long way in his bid to get elected as Governor.

He put on his coat, smoothed his tie, glanced at his watch, and walked out of his private bathroom. His advisors, who were waiting in his outer office, fell in step as he led them into the conference room.

The mood of those waiting was somber and dark. The city was in crisis, the press wanted answers, and for once they afforded him the respect he felt he deserved.

He walked up to the podium, and a hush fell over the room.

"Ladies and gentlemen. It's my sad duty to advise you that shortly after eight this morning, Julie Marin, the young daughter of Renée Marin, the prosecutor in charge of my Organized Crime and Terrorism Division, was kidnapped by members of the Irish Republican Army. During the commission of that crime, two of our finest investigators were killed while they tried to prevent this abduction from happening."

He paused for emphasis and let the continued silence work to his advantage.

"We've been in contact with the kidnappers, and they've demanded the release of Liam Cassidy, who is currently charged in this jurisdiction with the murder of two military officers from Great Britain. In exchange for Cassidy's release, they've offered to release Ms. Marin's child."

He removed his reading glasses, a gesture meant strictly for the cameras.

"This cowardly act is but the latest in a series of incidents perpetrated by these terrorists and which are designed to undermine the principles of our judicial system. They are trying to erode the very core of our nation's democracy, and I, for one, will not allow this type of extortion to succeed."

He had their undivided attention and he savored the moment as he slowly put his glasses back on.

"This morning I presided over a series of emergency meetings held with the Mayor, the Chief of Police, the Sheriff, and other concerned city and county officials. This afternoon we conferred extensively with our counterparts in the Federal Government, and I have just concluded a frank and serious discussion with the Governor of our great state. We have developed a plan to deal with this emergency, and I am authorized to release some of the details to you now.

"First and foremost, this series of attacks and the cowardly kidnapping of a child will not result in the release of the prisoner. On this point, all concerned are in total agreement. We will not establish a precedent that would force law enforcement officials everywhere to fear acts of personal terrorism while engaged in the performance of their duties.

"So if any of the terrorists are listening to me now, let me tell you that there is nothing to be gained by injuring the child. You will only bring shame and ridicule to your cause if she is not returned to her mother. You'll accomplish nothing by keeping her as a hostage, so do the right thing and release her without harm.

"Secondly, an interagency group has been formed and is meeting at this very moment. This task force will pull together the resources of a dozen separate agencies and they will do whatever it takes to track down the terrorists and bring them to justice."

He paused to catch his breath.

"And lastly, the Governor has agreed to deploy the National Guard by noon tomorrow to provide security at all government buildings and all facilities deemed critical to our community.

"Make no mistake about it, this will be a battle, and I believe our adversaries will find us well suited to the task."

He took off his glasses once again and slowly looked around the room.

"Now, are there any questions?"

****

Whitney grabbed the phone on the first ring. He was seated in Renée's living room in case the kidnappers decided to call.

"Yes?" he said expectantly.

"Major Whitney? This is Glenn Kerin. How's she doing?"

Whitney visibly relaxed.

"She's holding her own."

"Good." He cleared his throat. "We've heard nothing since the first call. Have you been watching the TV?"

"No," he said cautiously, "It's off. Gibson calls here every hour or so to let us know what's goin' on. Why? What's happenin'?"

"Aaron's been meeting all day with various state and federal officials, and he's just concluded talking with the Governor. I'm afraid they've decided that they won't negotiate for Julie's release."

Whitney shut his eyes in disbelief and struggled to remain calm. "You do realize you're signin' her death warrant, don't you?"

"I pray we aren't, Major, but we really have no choice." Kerin swallowed hard. "If we were to agree to negotiate, then every prosecutor's family would end up fair game for those who would try the same thing. We can't afford to let that happen."

"That's a fine policy in the abstract, Kerin, but it won't work with these people. They've got nothin' to lose by killin' the girl if they don't get what they want."

"For what it's worth, I had no say in the matter."

"Well, make sure they keep this decision to themselves," Whitney demanded. His mind was racing ahead. "At least we've got until Wednesday to try and track 'em down."

Kerin spoke again when he found his voice.

"Actually, I'm afraid that the terrorists will soon know that we won't be negotiating. Aaron's just held a press conference. It was agreed to by everyone concerned that we should make our position known as soon as possible. When they realize we won't negotiate, perhaps they'll turn her loose."

"Agreed to by everyone?" Whitney was livid. "Who in the bloody hell is everyone, Kerin? You didn't ask the child's mother about this. I can't believe you people are this stupid. You pathetic bastards!"

He slammed down the phone.

"Whit? What's the matter?" Renée stood at the doorway; eyes puffy from crying.

He walked over to her.

"That was Kerin. I'm afraid your government has decided they won't negotiate with the terrorists."

Her head snapped back.

"No, they can't do that. That's my baby, Whit! They have to do something to get her back!"

The look in her eyes went from desperate to vacant. She began to cry again, wracking sobs, devoid of the tears that would no longer flow.

He held her tightly, consoling her until he got an idea. He grabbed the phone and called a secondary line at the DA's command post.

"Carroll speaking," said the voice."

"Investigator Carroll? This is Andrew Whitney. Has anyone advised you we won't be negotiatin' for Julie Marin?"

"You're kidding? What moron made that decision?"

"Apparently the DA and others have decided to announce a no-negotiation policy. Rosen just held a press conference, and I suspect you'll be gettin' a nasty call from the IRA once they hear the news."

"Oh, man. This is not good."

"I've got an idea. If they do call, tell 'em that Rosen's message was just for public consumption and you're still workin' out the details for the release. String 'em along. We need all the time we can get to find the girl. Can you do that for me?"

"Hell, yes, I'll do it! Just find the bastards in time."

****

When the intercom on his desk in the Oval Office buzzed sharply, he reached over and flipped it on.

"Yes?"

"Mr. President? The call from London has come through. It's on line two."

"Thank you, Maureen."

He reached over, pushed the button and picked up the phone.

"Mr. President?" said a voice.

"Yes, Prime Minister. How are you?"

"I'm fine Mr. President, and how are you?"

"I've had better days. What can we do for you today, sir?"

"I wonder if you'd mind if I put you on the speaker phone, Sir? I have Lord Carrington, my Defense Secretary with me and I'd like him to take part in our conversation."

"Certainly, that's no problem," replied the President. "I'd like to do the same at my end. I have my Chief of Staff here and my Secretary of Defense."

"That will be fine, Mr. President. Now... if I can just figure out how to do this without disconnecting you... Ah, there. Are you still on the line?"

"Yes, Prime Minister. We can hear you just fine. Good afternoon, Lord Carrington."

"Good morning, Mr. President," Carrington replied.

The Prime Minister cleared his throat.

"Mister President, gentlemen. I'm calling today to offer my greatest sympathies to your countrymen for the pain and damage they have suffered at the hands of the IRA. We are all very shocked that they've decided to perpetrate these horrible crimes against innocent American citizens. We want to extend our condolences to the families of the victims of that terrible explosion, and to tell you that our prayers go out to the family of that poor child they've taken as a hostage."

"Thank you, Prime Minister. The American people will be pleased to know of your concern, and I'm sure that the child and her family can use the prayers."

There was a momentary awkward silence on the phone. Now that the formalities were over, both men knew that it was time to discuss the real purpose of the call.

"Uh... Mr. President? Lord Carrington has presented me with a proposal this afternoon, and I'm inclined to think that it has some merit. I'd like to run it by you, if I may?"

"Certainly, Sir. This line's secure."

"Well, Mr. President, much the same as your Justice Department has approved worldwide jurisdiction for apprehending terrorists who commit acts against the United States, our Internment Act provides the same jurisdiction for crimes perpetrated against British citizens or in furtherance of a conspiracy against the British government. It is our belief that the unfortunate murder of Colonel Clarke and his adjutant on American soil was part of a broader conspiracy against our sovereign government, and these continuing acts of violence are a furtherance of that conspiracy. We would, therefore, like to request the permission of your government to launch an operation within your United States which will be designed to apprehend these vicious criminals and bring them back to face trial under our War Powers Act."

The President was caught flat-footed.

"I must say, your request has caught me by surprise. I know the FBI and the local authorities haven't made a lot of progress so far, but I'm confident they'll track these people down in the very near future."

The Prime Minister's voice was grave.

"I'm sure they will, eventually, but I must tell you, their attack in your country has caused us a great deal of embarrassment. In fact, it's threatened the cease-fire with Northern Ireland that we've worked so hard to obtain. We see this as a new phase of intimidation by dissidents within the IRA, and we believe that a decisive move at this time is absolutely necessary to prevent future episodes like this from happening in other places around the world."

The President leaned back in his chair and looked longingly out the window at the tranquility of the rose garden.

"I can understand your concern, Prime Minister, but allowing foreign troops on our soil is a rather a big step."

"I understand your concerns, but you need to understand that these people are like a cancer. Unless they're stopped right away, they'll multiply, and so will their victims. By allowing us to remove these predators from your soil, we believe you will be free of any future acts of terrorism designed to force you to release these same terrorists once you have them in custody. We want to stop the cycle before it gets a foothold in your country, so to that end, we propose to send over a Special Air Service hostage rescue team to handle the capture once they are located. By letting us handle the situation, we will, of course, shoulder the blame if anything goes wrong."

"Assuming we agreed to allow this, I would like to stress that this is not like an airline hijack situation. We have no idea where these people are hiding, and time is of the essence."

"I am assured by Lord Carrington that our SAS Intelligence people believe that they will be able to obtain an address from a confidential source within a matter of days."

The President was suddenly intrigued. He sensed another level being played out in this crisis, but he knew from experience there'd be nothing more forthcoming over the phone.

He looked over to his men for advice. The Secretary of Defense held up a thumb in concurrence, but his Chief of Staff wanted to speak with him in private.

"Prime Minister, I'm going to need a brief moment to discuss this request with my staff."

"Of course, Mr. President."

The President placed the call on hold and turned to his Chief of Staff. "What do you think, Kevin?"

"Sir, there may be some merit to this proposal. By letting the British take the initiative, you can pacify your allies, protect American law enforcement officials who might be at risk if there is an assault, and we can avoid the enormous expenses associated with bringing a case to trial; not to mention the expense of confining these people to prison both during and after the proceedings."

"Any downside?" he asked.

"The only negative I can see would be the flack you're gonna catch from the other side of the aisle. They'll find a way to accuse you of abrogating our territorial integrity. But, hell, if it all goes well, you'll end up looking as wise as King Solomon."

That was all he needed to hear.

"Fine. Then let's do it."

"One moment more Mr. President," said his Chief of Staff. "We should bargain for a quid pro quo. Our commercial airline carriers have been trying to secure additional landing rights at Heathrow for the past three years. The talks have bogged down, and we seem to be getting nowhere. Perhaps we can obtain a guarantee of a speedy resolution to these talks—"

The President cut him off mid-sentence with a smile. He took the call off hold.

"Mr. Prime Minister? We do see the merit in your request, and I'm sure that we can work out something that will accommodate your needs."

"Thank you, Mr. President."

"And while I have you on the line, I wonder if you'd be so kind as to make some inquiries for me into the stalled negotiations over our request for additional landing rights at Heathrow?"

****

Renée Marin sat in a rocker in her bedroom and looked past her backyard to the canyon beyond. It seemed so tranquil. The pine trees gently blowing in the breeze, the buttery-yellow wildflowers playing host to honey bees. But this little bit of paradise might as well have been on another planet, for its beauty was completely lost on Renée who couldn't think beyond her missing daughter and how her people had let her down.

It was difficult to comprehend that her government had refused her plea to negotiate. She'd done her job; everything they'd asked. Weren't they supposed to take care of her? But that's not how it was shaking out. Her daughter, her baby, was an innocent victim, and for the sake of a principle, she would be a victim again.

She'd cried until the tears would no longer come, until her sorrow had turned to anger. And when that happened, she was hit with a resolve that was born of inner strength. She wasn't going to let this happen. Not now, not ever! If her people wouldn't help to get her daughter back, then she was going to have to do it herself.

Raised as a Catholic, but not a church going kind of girl, she found herself rummaging through her dresser drawers in search of a printed prayer to Saint Jude, the Patron Saint of Lost Causes. She had come across this prayer many years before when a friend of hers was suffering from cancer. She'd held on to it then without ever really knowing why, but today, for the first time, she needed it more than anything else.

When she found it, she read it over, and in a moment of solemn reflection, she got down on her knees and prayed to a higher power.

A few minutes later, having found a new sense of inner strength, she walked downstairs to her kitchen where she found Andrew Whitney seated quietly at the table.

"Is there anything new?" she asked.

"Actually, there is. I spoke to Gibson about ten minutes ago. The kidnappers heard Rosen's remarks about no negotiations, so they called the DA's Command Post and spoke with Captain Don Carroll. He's convinced them that the negotiations are still on and that Rosen was just posturing for public consumption. They weren't happy, but it looks like they bought it, so we still have until Wednesday to track them down."

"Thank God for small miracles."

She walked over to the table and sat down beside him.

Whitney reached for her hand.

"How're you feelin'?"

"Like I've been run over by a truck."

He reached up and caressed her cheek.

"I know how difficult this must be, Renée, but you have to hold on and see it through. We'll get her back," he said convincingly. "In the meantime, do you feel like talkin' a little business?"

She nodded.

Whitney leaned forward.

"I've been on the phone all afternoon and I found out somethin' that's very disturbin'. Do you remember when I told you I was havin' my contact in Ireland forward Cassidy's file to London so that I could get it through channels? Well, I got a confirmation from London this afternoon tellin' me they've already sent me everythin' they have."

"What does that mean?" she asked.

"It means that someone in London has intentionally withheld a portion of the file, includin' the pictures. All along I thought there was somethin' wrong with my security classification, but apparently, that's not the problem. Someone seems intent on holdin' somethin' back."

"But you've already received a copy of the backup file from your friend in Ireland, so what difference does it make?"

"The difference is that London doesn't know that I've seen the complete file, and that may work to our advantage."

She was still having trouble understanding where this was going.

"What advantage, Whit? There was nothing in that file of any real value. Why would they want to hold it back?"

"I think I may know why."

He pulled out the picture of Michael Kelly and placed it on the table.

"I never gave Gibson this picture of Kelly because I was led to believe that he was still in *Whitmoor Prison*. I just checked with a friend who's stationed there, and Kelly's not there. In fact, no one seems to know where he is."

"Are you telling me he's here?" she asked with concern.

"I don't know, but if he is, I'm startin' to wonder who he's workin' for?"

"You've lost me again." She rubbed at her temples. A headache had taken hold. "Maybe I'm just tired, but I don't understand what you're saying?"

"Kelly was moved to London because they thought he might end up being an informant. After that, he disappeared from sight. I'd say that's a pretty good indication that he's workin' for my government, and if that's the case, and if he's here, then someone in London must know where they're hidin' out."

She finally grasped the import of what he was saying and it left her speechless.

He walked over to the kitchen counter, picked up a coffee pot, poured them each a cup, then brought both cups back to the table.

"I'm still goin' to London tonight, Renée. I can't just sit around and do nothing. I'm like a fish out of water in this city. Maybe I can find some answers back home that will somehow help us track your daughter down."

She leaned over and gave him a hug. His concern had touched her deeply.

"What time are you leaving?" she asked.

"I'm booked on a flight at nine p.m."

Renée sighed. She was going to have to see this through by herself.

"I've also left messages with my sources in Ireland," he continued. "Perhaps someone over there has an informant who might be able to help us out."

She had a sudden flash of insight.

Of course!

She stood up abruptly and headed for the door.

"Where your goin'?" he called out after her.

She waved him off, her mind still churning. She hurried from the kitchen and ran upstairs where she rummaged through a desk in a bedroom she'd converted to an office.

Where was the number? Where was the god-damn number?

She finally found it filed in her desk caddy, and after punching in the numbers for Belfast, she held her breath and said a quick prayer that he would be the one to pick up the phone.

"*Iron Gate Pub*," said a deep male voice with a thick Irish accent.

A pub? There must be some mistake.

"I'd like to speak to John Magruder, please?"

There was silence at the other end, so she repeated her request.

"Who's this?" said the voice.

"Marin, Renée Marin." She spelled it out for him.

He put down the telephone, and in the background, she heard the sounds of raucous laughter.

"Hello," said a voice.

"Is this John Magruder?" she asked.

"Yes, Mrs. Marin. It's me."

"They've taken my daughter---"

"I know. I heard."

She took a deep breath.

"I need your help, John. My government won't negotiate for her release, so I'm begging you. I know we have an understanding---"

"Stop," he said firmly. "Not on the telephone."

She suppressed an involuntary sob.

"But I need your help. She's all I have!"

There was a long, uncomfortable silence before he spoke in a very hushed tone.

"I can't talk with you on the telephone, Mrs. Marin. It's not safe. Do you understand what I'm sayin'?"

"Yes," she said, although she really didn't.

"How soon can you get yourself to London?" he asked.

"London? But I can't go to London. They've got my baby! What if I'm gone and they call?"

"You'll have time," he told her, and he said it with such authority that she wondered for a moment if he was somehow involved.

"Can't we just talk on the phone?" she asked. "I'm sure I can get us a line that's secure."

"Out of the question. Face to face and alone. That's the only way."

"I don't suppose you'd consider coming over here?"

"I've me own security to think about now, Mrs. Marin. I can meet you in London. That's the only way."

She sighed in exasperation.

"Very well, there's a plane leaving here tonight at nine. I think I can still make it."

"You do that, and be sure to come alone. When you get to Heathrow, I'll have someone meet you. Are we clear on that?"

"Yes," she said.

"Oh, and by the way, travel light. Just an overnight case. And wear pants. It's cold in London this time of year."

It seemed a little bit gratuitous, his telling her what to wear, but she let it go. She needed to find out what he knew, and if it meant wearing a bikini in the middle of a snow storm, she was going to do it, come hell or high water.

Magruder continued. "I don't suppose I need to warn you not to tell anyone about this call or that we're gonna be meetin'."

He hung up and left her staring at the receiver.

****

She telephoned Gibson to let him know that she was planning on leaving the country.

"Where are you headed?" he asked.

"To London, but please don't ask me who I'm going to see. I can't tell you that right now."

Gibson was silent and confused by her plans. "I think you should be here in case something happens."

"I know what I'm doing, Gibby. You need to trust me on this."

"Are you going there with Whitney?"

His question surprised her.

"I think we're going over on the same flight, but once we get there, we'll be going our separate ways."

Gibson took a moment to think before responding.

"Look, Renée. Keep an open mind about what I'm going to say. Elwood and I suspect that someone close to the investigation here in LA has been providing information to the terrorists."

"What?"

"Someone on the inside tipped them off just before we hit that duplex. We're making a short list of everyone who knew what we were doing in North Hollywood. The list is small, Renée, and Whitney's name is on it."

She almost laughed. "Don't be ridiculous, Gibby. That's crazy."

"I know how you feel about him, but Whitney's our big unknown. He's the only one on the list with any prior connection to the IRA."

"C'mon, Gibby." She was indignant. "This is nonsense. What possible motive would Whitney have to provide those bastards with any information? This is too crazy to even consider. I know this guy. He's not working with the enemy."

"The truth is we don't know all that much about him." Gibson was not in the mood to brook a discussion. "The guy worked with an intelligence gathering unit in Northern Ireland. That means he worked with informants, and one of the occupational hazards of that kind of work is that friendships develop that can blur the line. Information gets traded. It becomes a form of currency. Maybe he gives a little to get something else back—"

"That's not Whitney. He'd never do anything like that."

"I'm not saying he did. What I'm trying to stress here is that we need to take a hard look at him before we make any judgment concerning how much he needs to know." He softened his tone. "For what it's worth, I like the guy and you're probably right. But we can't be sure of anything at this point. Okay?"

She stared at the floor and tried to come to grips with his warning.

"Point taken," she said. "I'll call you when I can."

She hung up the receiver and walked over to the window to collect her thoughts. One thing was becoming painfully clear. If there was an informant inside law enforcement, she'd have to keep her plans to herself.

God in heaven! Too much was happening too fast.

****

In the rolling hills of Prince George County in Maryland, satellite dishes continuously monitored the signals being sent by ground stations to an array of satellites leased by the nation's phone companies. The transmissions they captured were those that carried the international code, and once intercepted, the digitalized signals were routed by land line to a nondescript facility in Virginia. There they were stored on tapes and scanned by supercomputers for key phrases and terminology.

More than ten thousand words from many different languages were considered so significant that they triggered a signal for further action. Included on that list were phrases that referred to narcotics, explosives, weapons and nuclear materials. Also flagged were the names of various terrorist groups and the names of their known individual members.

Renée's subsequent call to Belfast was scanned, and when she mentioned the name John Magruder, a signal was triggered, and the call was automatically categorized and stored with other similar references.

Once every hour, the tape containing the stored calls was taken to a lab where the digitalized signals were converted to words. Once the conversations were printed, a transcript was sent to the CIA's *Irish Intelligence* Desk.

The analyst assigned to process the data was a former professor at Harvard. He paid attention to current events and had a working knowledge of the bombings in LA. He read the transcript, made the connection between Marin *the pros-*

ecutor and Magruder *the terrorist*, he knew right away he was on to something important.

He picked up his red phone and passed on his findings to the Deputy Director of the CIA.

****

Renée and Whitney boarded the British Airways Flight and settled into adjoining business-class seats, courtesy of a call by Whitney to the Head of Security for BA. A steward took their coats, gave them pillows and blankets, and offered them champagne which both declined.

Before heading to the airport, she told Whitney she was meeting a contact at *Interpol*, a statement he seemed to accept at face value. But as the flight got underway, it soon became apparent to her that the secrecy surrounding her Interpol meeting appeared to have him concerned.

"Is there anythin' I can do to help you when we get to London?" he asked.

"Thanks anyway, Whit, but I've got it all worked out."

He gave her a questioning look, one that let her know he wasn't buying into her story.

"Look, Renée, I don't know what you're plannin' to do. It's your business, and I won't interfere. But I'm pretty sure you're gettin' into somethin' that's over your head. I've got a lot of friends over here and some very good connections. Maybe I can be of some help?"

She had no doubts about his sincerity, but Gibson was right. She didn't really know him that well.

"I'll be all right, Whit. Don't worry."

"You sure?" he asked.

"I'm sure."

****

Mark Carlson sat frozen at his desk. The door was closed, and in spite of the air conditioning, he could feel himself sweating profusely. His stomach was in knots; he felt a weakness in his bones.

Had he made a terrible mistake?

There was a rumor spreading through the PAB that the terrorists were tipped off before the raid, and speculation had it that Internal Affairs had started to snoop around.

He wasn't worried about having given Lisa a jump on the competition. He'd owed her that much. And besides, what he'd told her about the search had never gone any farther than her notes. No, Lisa was not his concern. What he had to fear was the polygraph exam.

If Internal Affairs was involved, the poly was inevitable. And if they put him on the box and asked about Lisa, he knew he was screwed. Sleeping with a reporter was a major taboo, so if he told the truth and admitted the affair, he'd get fired just as quickly as if they caught him in a lie. So either way, it looked to him like the poly was going to end his career. He would lose his pension if they gave him the ax, and if that happened, how the hell would he ever survive?

And what about his wife? How would he explain this mess to her?

He took a deep breath and tried to calm his heart rate. It was time to review things in the light of the day.

No one knew that he'd learned in advance about the search in North Holly-wood. He'd been upstairs on another case when he'd overheard the Chief and his adjutant. There was no way they'd ever connect the dots. For God's sake, he wasn't even in the information loop.

The more he thought about it, the more he believed that he had nothing to worry about. He began to feel better. Since Lisa could never be forced to take a poly, and since there was no way he'd end up on their short list of suspects—people who'd had knowledge of the raid before it happened—he was in the clear. The connection would never be made.

Finally, his stomach began to settle down. He would get through it this time, but this scare had been a wake-up call, too close for comfort to suit his taste.

So he came to a decision, one that he believed was in his best interest. He would give Lisa a call in the morning. They were gonna have to cool it...at least for a while.

****

TWENTY-THREE

October 7,

3:00 p.m. GMT, Tuesday, Afternoon

After an uneventful flight that seemed to last forever, the plane landed at Heathrow Airport, Terminal 3, a little after three in the afternoon. As it taxied down the runway towards the terminal, Whitney reached over and handed Renée a slip of paper.

"Here's my office and cell phone numbers. Call me if you need anythin'."

"I will."

She reached over and squeezed his hand.

They'd both packed for one day, so their gear was stored in the overhead. When the plane pulled up at the gate, they gathered their carry-on bags and de-planed. Renée made Whitney agree to make it appear that she had been traveling alone.

It took thirty minutes for her to clear Immigration and then Customs, while Whitney was able to by-pass the line with the help of an adjutant who escorted him out through a private doorway. When no one was waiting to meet Renée at the gate, she hurried out through the front terminal door.

As she left the warmth of the building, she was struck by a blast of cold air. Magruder was right. London was cold. It nearly took her breath away.

She shivered, then stopped to pull out a lightweight parka from her bag. It wouldn't do much, but it was better than nothing. She put it on, zipped it up, and scanned the front of the terminal.

A few feet away, a motorcycle pulled up, and the driver gave her a wave.

Black leather jacket, collar up against the cold, black jeans, scuffed boots, and a helmet with a darkened face mask? It was not exactly a reassuring sight.

Renée took a single step backward, intent on returning to the terminal when the biker suddenly reached up and pulled her helmet off her face.

"Anne? *Anne Magruder?* Is that you?"

"Hello, Mrs. Marin."

Renée shook her head.

"We're gonna ride on this? You've got to be kidding? No wonder your father said to wear pants."

Anne handed her a helmet.

Renée took it but still wasn't convinced she wanted to do this.

"Are you sure you know how to drive this thing?"

Anne laughed.

"Just hang on tight. I have to make sure we're not bein' followed."

Renée put on the helmet, draped her carry-on bag over her shoulder, and climbed aboard.

Anne wasted no time getting started. She moved quickly through the steady stream of traffic that jammed the highway leading off towards London.

For the first five minutes of the ride, Renée had her eyes shut tight.

****

As the motorcycle sped through traffic, a black Citroen pulled out and tried to follow. It soon became mired behind a steady line of cars. The driver cursed once and grabbed his phone.

"Six to One. She's on the back of a motorcycle, and I'm losin' them in traffic. They just made the turn to London. She's wearin' a black parka, a helmet, and dark pants. The driver has on a black leather jacket, dark pants, and a helmet with a face shield. They're really movin'. Get someone on a bike to the first roundabout or, I think we're gonna lose 'em."

"One to Six. We'll do what we can."

****

As she drove through the streets of London, Anne made use of a series of rounds—streets that fed into a center-divided circle—to double back and check for pursuers. On two occasions, she drove into high-rise parking structures, only to exit immediately on adjacent streets.

It took twenty minutes, but when Anne was finally satisfied that she wasn't being followed, she guided the motorcycle through a number of small streets before stopping at the rear of a neighborhood pub.

She pulled up at the back door and removed her helmet. Renée climbed off and removed hers as well.

"You're a pretty good driver," Renée told her as she let out a short, nervous laugh. She'd actually been scared to death.

"I've had a lot of practice since I got here," Anne said. "My father bought me this motorbike to help me get around."

"Are you living here now?"

Anne nodded.

"My father felt that London was the safest place to be. I'll go back to my schoolin' next quarter, and best of all, no one here knows anythin' about my past."

"I'm glad you're happy, Anne."

Renée looked over at the back door to the pub.

"Is your father inside?"

Anne nodded.

Renée handed her the helmet and walked up several steps and into the back of the pub.

****

The Lieutenant guided Whitney to an Opel sedan that was driven by a trooper with a handlebar mustache. There was very little talk on the way to Blackmore Road, the site of his meeting with Nigel Ward. Whitney stared blankly out the window. He was slightly apprehensive, but also hopeful that the Old Man could tell him what was really going on.

Blackmore Road was a quiet, expensive residential street near central London. Off the beaten path and fairly discreet, the four-story, stone row house's stately grandeur closely resembled all the others on the street. Cement porches and iron railings graced the facades, while an assortment of gargoyles kept watch from the corners of the slab, slate roofs.

Whitney was shown to a second-floor parlor with a view of the street. He was offered a drink which he refused. He ambled over to the fireplace and settled into an overstuffed armchair to await the arrival of his host.

The room was warm, and Whitney soon recovered from the biting cold. He leaned back, closed his eyes, and besieged by jet lag, he soon nodded off, only to be awakened a short time later by the Lieutenant's strong hand on his arm.

"He's just arrived, sir."

Whitney opened his eyes and yawned.

"Thank you, Lieutenant."

He stood up, rubbed his eyes and yawned again. Within a few moments, he heard footsteps on the landing beyond the closed door.

Colonel Nigel Ward trooped into the parlor and studied Whitney's face while the Lieutenant took his coat. He glanced into a mirror, adjusted his tie, and asked the Lieutenant to retire from the room.

When they were alone, he turned back to Whitney.

"You've had a long flight and I'm sure you must be tired. Will you join me for a Sherry?"

"Yes, thank you, sir."

Ward ambled over to a dry sink near the fireplace and poured three fingers worth into two crystal glasses. He handed one to Whitney, then sat in an armchair next to the fire.

"Sit down, young man. I'm glad we're having this meeting. I've felt for some time that you've been owed an explanation."

Whitney was surprised by this opening. No small talk; straight to the point.

Ward's eyes narrowed.

"The Provos have an informant in Los Angeles, Major, someone within the government. You've been out of the loop while we've done our best to find out who it is."

Whitney tried to conceal his surprise.

A leak in Los Angeles? How was that possible?

"I'm going to tell you what we've learned, but everything I say is covered by the Official Secrets Act. You must never reveal that we've had this conversation."

"Yes, sir."

"As a matter of fact, I have something to show you." He produced two printed pages from his left breast pocket and handed them over to Whitney.

"Please read these first, Major."

Whitney started reading and nearly dropped the pages. It was a transcript of Renée Marin's call to John Magruder, and he immediately recognized the implications of her connection to the terrorist.

"May I call you Andrew?" Ward asked.

Whitney nodded, still too shocked and confused to speak.

Ward leaned forward in his chair.

"That call was intercepted by the Americans. They were kind enough to furnish us with a transcript. It would appear that Ms. Marin has an active association with the Provos."

Whitney looked up from the pages. Ward stared at him and seemed to be waiting for an answer.

What the hell was going on? Renée couldn't be working with the Provos. It was inconceivable! But she did dismiss the case against Magruders' daughter, and apparently, she was meeting with him over here. What did she think she was doing?

"Sir, I know this woman, and I'm sure there's some reasonable explanation for this." It was all he could think of to say.

"You may be right, Andrew, but the fact remains that she mentions an understanding that she has with John Magruder. There are people on both sides of the Atlantic who believe that she may be furnishing the Provos with inside information."

Whitney was dumbfounded. "Really, Colonel, that makes no sense. Her daughter's been kidnapped. I've seen firsthand what she's goin' through. The kidnappin's for real."

"Ah, yes, but it's also possible that it's nothing but a sham; a tactic to pressure the authorities into releasing Liam Cassidy. Our American friends want to speak with her. In fact, I've been told that when she reenters the States, they plan to take her into custody."

Whitney's eyes betrayed his surprise. There had to be a logical explanation.

"By the way, Major. Do you have any idea where she'll be meeting with him?"

"Sir?"

Ward stared at him. "It's my understanding' she accompanied you on the plane?"

Whitney tried to think quickly. *Should he cover for her?*

"We flew over together, but she never mentioned who she was meetin' with or where she was goin'."

Ward managed to convey a look of disbelief.

Whitney's mind raced. Ward must know more than he was letting on. What could be coming next?

Ward took another sip of his sherry.

"I had her followed from the airport," he began, "but our people managed to lose her in the city." He placed his glass on a small table by the arm of his chair. "I suspect we'll find her soon enough when she tries to leave the country. In the meantime, Major, if she is involved, exactly where do you stand in this matter?"

Whitney felt his anger rising. She couldn't be a collaborator. *Couldn't?*

Was he starting to have doubts? He'd come here believing that something was terribly wrong within his own government, but now there were questions about Renée, and from the tone of Ward's voice, even his own integrity was un-der suspicion.

He decided that he'd better be careful, for it seemed he was walking through a minefield.

"Sir, my loyalty is to my country," he said simply.

Ward held his gaze.

"Your loyalty is beyond reproach, Andrew. Our concern is with your feel-ings for Ms. Marin."

Whitney tried to sound nonchalant. "As I said, sir, my country comes first."

Ward watched him for a moment, then seemed to make up his mind.

"Very well. In that case, I need to inform you that the Prime Minister has ordered a change in your assignment. Once again, what I say is covered by the Official Secrets Act."

What now?

"The PM has held discussions with the American President. Apparently, our

Prime Minister is deeply embarrassed by the loss of life being experienced by the Americans as a result of our internal problems with these terrorists. He's received permission from the Americans to have our own people handle the capture of these terrorists under our own Internment Act."

Whitney was confused. This wasn't making any sense.

"Sir, if you don't mind my askin', why would the Americans consent to allow us to conduct an operation in their country?"

Ward eyed him carefully, surprised by the question.

"Apparently, the Prime Minister pointed out that our situation has certain similarities with American incursions abroad when they go after foreign nationals involved in terrorist acts."

"I would think the Americans are perfectly capable of handlin' this situation by themselves, sir."

Ward smiled. "It's not really that complex, Major. If the Americans capture these terrorists, they could be faced with an unending series of attacks designed to force their release."

Ward shook his head, then picked up his glass and took another sip of his sherry.

"They don't have the stomach for such a battle, and the trials would be costly and potentially embarrassing. Their President has shown that he's a realist. He saw the wisdom of using our people to bring them back. That way, if there's any retribution, it will likely be focused on our side of the pond."

On the surface it made sense, but something wasn't right. There had to be more going on.

Ward leaned forward in his chair.

"The Prime Minister has authorized your regiment to handle the operation in the States. You'll be assisted by a member of their Delta Force."

Whitney wanted to ask a dozen questions, but Ward cut him off with a wave of his hand.

"Mind you, Americans will be there only for logistical support, so as far as the general public is concerned, we're the only ones involved."

"I understand, sir."

"Your unit has been ordered up, Major. The assignment is code named

Operation Archangel. Your people are being assembled out at Hampton, and from there, they'll be transported to the States."

"But Colonel, there won't be an operation if we can't find the terrorists. I need access to our network and we have to press our informants in Ireland." He ran his hand through his hair. "And the US government needs to be persuaded to begin to negotiate with the Provos if we're goin' save that little girl's life."

Ward smiled. "I've already ordered our networks to gather whatever they can on these people. You'll receive the raw data on the plane, and if we learn somethin' in time to save that poor little girl, then we'll be very lucky indeed. And as for negotiating with the Provos, the American's seem firmly committed to a policy that precludes negotiations of any kind."

It was painfully obvious to Whitney that the child's safety was not Wards' highest priority. If he was going to save Julie, he was going to have to make things happen on his own.

"One more thing, Major." Wards eyes narrowed. "The Prime Minister has instructed me to order you to take no prisoners during the course of the operation."

So that was it!

No extraditions and no show trials. His Commandos would end up doing the job so the Americans would not have to dirty their own hands.

"He assures me they'll be no inquiry after the fact, either here or in the States."

"But sir--"

"That's an order, Major. It would not be in the best interests of either of our countries to have these prisoners stand trial. He wants their complete elimination to serve as a lesson to others who might consider a similar course of conduct. The truce in Northern Ireland is very fragile and we cannot allow anything to put it in jeopardy."

Whitney needed time to think, to unravel what was going on.

"Do you understand your orders, Major?"

He had no choice. If he said no, he'd be out, and then what chance would Julie have?

He needed to play for some time.

"I understand, sir."

"Very good, Major."

The Colonel stood up, a sign that Whitney was being dismissed.

"Please proceed without delay and join your team out at Hampton."

Whitney saluted and headed for the door.

"Just a reminder, Major," the Colonel called after him. "I would caution you against any further association with Ms. Marin until the question of her collaboration has been resolved."

****

Ward watched from the front window as Whitney climbed into the black Citroen. Behind him, a door opened, and in walked John Carrington, the UK Secretary of State for Defense.

Carrington's height was imposing. At fifty-six, he had the bearing and appearance of a much younger man. His steel gray hair was meticulously trimmed and he sported a thin mustache that did little to conceal the size of his large upper lip.

An international banker by trade, he'd used his contacts to further his political ambitions with a posting in Defense, a Knighthood, and a seat in Parliament. Over time, he'd garnered a wide sphere of influence and he made no secret of his desire to be the next Prime Minister.

"What do you think, Nigel?" he said in a soft, smooth voice. "Can we trust him?"

"I don't see why not, John. He's an excellent soldier who's been conditioned to follow orders."

Ward walked from the window and retrieved his half-filled glass of Sherry, while Carrington made himself a gin and tonic at the bar.

"We've been very lucky so far, Nigel," Carrington said over his shoulder. "The fact that the Americans have focused on Ms. Marin has been a blessing in disguise. Did you arrange for that as well?"

Ward laughed. "I wish I could take the credit, John, but sometimes things just happen by themselves. Fortunately, it provided me with a plausible excuse for keeping the Major out of the loop."

"Do you really think she's a collaborator?"

"Does it really matter? By the time they get things sorted out, Major Whitney will have successfully completed his mission."

Carrington took a long pull from his drink.

"When do you plan to tell the Major where they are?"

"I'll tell him just before the deadline runs out. That will force him to act without time to think."

Carrington slowly shook his head.

"God help me, Nigel. I never thought it would go this far."

"Have patience, John. You've put together a brilliant plan. When the time comes, our young Major Whitney will do as he's been told."

"I hope you're right, Nigel. I certainly hope you're right."

****

Renée walked through a storage area and down a short hallway that led right past the pub bathrooms. As she entered the main room, she stood for a moment to allow her eyes to adjust to the darkness.

Heavy drapes were drawn shut and a small overhead light at the end of a long bar gave faint illumination to several booths and to a dozen small tables scattered about the room. She unzipped her jacket, stepped into the room, and found him seated in a booth, away from the windows. Their eyes made contact and he waved her over.

"Sit down, Mrs. Marin."

She slid into the booth.

"Very melodramatic, Mr. Magruder, especially the motorcycle ride."

He smiled. "We can't be too careful. Can I get you some tea?"

"Yes, please."

He stood up, walked to the bar and poured her a cup from a kettle on a hot plate.

"Will you help me get my daughter back?" she asked.

He walked back to the table, handed her the tea, and silently slid his large frame back into the booth.

"Ironic, isn't it? Not too long ago our roles were reversed."

"Will you help me, Mr. Magruder? *Please!*"

He added a lump of sugar to his tea.

"I want you to know I appreciate what you did for me daughter."

She sat without moving. His refusal to answer her question was maddening. She wanted to grab him and shake him, but the impulse quickly passed. Magruder was firmly in charge here and he wanted her to know it. It was she who'd come begging, and he was going to set the pace.

He took a sip of his tea, then placed it on the table.

"What you're askin' me to do will cause problems."

"But we had an understanding!"

"Our understandin' concerned the future plans for a bombin' in London."

"Please, don't get technical. Do you think I give a damn about some future bomb in London? For God's sake, John. They've got my daughter. You, of all people, know what that means. I just want her back, and I need you to tell me where she is?"

"It's not that easy. Jimmy Cassidy's actin' on his own. He's tryin' to destroy the cease-fire, so he doesn't take orders from us."

"I don't care about his politics. I just want to know where he's keeping my daughter."

He shook his head.

"If you'll be still for a moment, Ms. Marin, I'll try to explain what's goin' on."

Sufficiently rebuked, she held her temper in check.

"I'm listening."

"Good. You need to understand that his politics have everythin' to do with your daughter's situation. When the IRA proposed a cease-fire, it was in the belief that the Brits were willin' to negotiate independence for the North. But that hasn't happened, and there are elements within our movement who are growin' very impatient. Cassidy is one of 'em."

"Then surely you have no reason to protect him?"

"It's more complicated than that. Cassidy's decision to take the war to the

States has been a disaster for everyone. You Americans brokered the cease fire, and now the Brits are sayin' we can't be trusted. Because of what he's done, our chances of negotiatin' for independence may now be gone."

"That's ridiculous. No government is going to let the acts of a single terrorist upset the chance for peace between countries. I'm sure the peace process will continue."

"We've lost our only bargainin' chip, Mrs. Marin. Our people are tired of war, they've lost the stomach for it. Durin' the cease fire, they've grown comfortable with peace. They'll never go back to a shootin' war."

"Well, what's wrong with that? I thought you wanted peace?"

"Not if it means we get nothin'." He spat out the words as though they stuck in his throat.

"Then turn him over to us. It will be a sign of good faith. Maybe it will even get the peace process back on track."

"You don't understand..."

"No, I don't." Unconsciously, she raised her voice. "You just told me he's ruined everything you've worked for, but you won't give him up. That's what makes no sense."

His eyes narrowed.

"What I'm tryin' to tell you is that someone else is pullin' the strings. What Cassidy's done has benefited only the Brits. He's made us look like criminals, and it's weakened our position. If I give him up, he'll be dead, and the world will be none the wiser."

"Are you trying to tell me that you think the British have a hand in this?"

"That's exactly what I'm sayin'."

"Where's your proof?"

Magruder did not answer. Instead, he lifted his cup and took a sip of tea.

"You don't have any proof, do you? *Jesus Christ!* Everybody connected with this case is paranoid."

She slammed her hand on the table in utter frustration.

"It's all so simple," she said. "Cassidy has a grudge, so he takes it out on a British soldier. His brother wants him out of jail, so he kills and bombs and takes my daughter hostage. It's as simple as that. There's no grand conspiracy, and the events of our times won't be altered by the acts of these fucking bastards." She rolled her eyes and leaned back from the table. "You're all crazy, and my daughter's life is hanging in the balance."

Magruder watched in silence as she slowly regained control of her emotions. When she finally spoke again, her tone of voice had softened significantly.

"Please, John. I have to get my daughter back. This has nothing to do with politics or legitimate targets of war. She's just an innocent little girl. Please help me. She's all I have."

Magruder scratched at his two-day growth of stubble while he contemplated what to say.

"And what about our innocent children, Ms. Marin? Are they to be condemned to live forever under the iron fist of a Protestant culture that survives with the backing and support of the Brits?" He shook his head. "There's too much at stake here, and I can't let all our years of effort and sufferin' end in defeat just for the life of one American child."

Renée was tired of being lectured to and so once again, her anger quickly got the best of her.

"You listen to me, you son of a bitch. I don't give a damn about your stupid country. Those bastards have taken my baby, and unless I find out quickly where she is, they're going to kill her."

He tried to interrupt, but she yelled him down.

"You owe me nothing. What I did for your daughter I did because it was the right thing to do. She was innocent and did not deserve to be dragged through our system. Well, the same thing applies to my daughter, and I'm asking you to do this because my daughter is innocent. And if you don't..."

"And if I don't, *what?*" he asked.

Marin gave him a stare.

"For openers, I'll release the tape of your first and most generous offer."

"You taped it?" Magruder clenched his fists. His eyes, dark and brooding, never left her face.

Renée didn't speak but held his stare.

His mind worked overtime as he considered the consequences of her threat. He shook his head in disbelief. She had him over a barrel.

"Maybe you're right. Perhaps nothin's worth the life of even one more child." His face turned deadly serious. "If I tell you where they are, my debt to you is settled. And after today, we'll never have contact again."

"Agreed," she said.

"And I want your word that the tape will be destroyed."

"I want to know exactly where they are and who we're dealing with. After that, I'll destroy the tape."

Magruder cocked his head.

"Have you taped this conversation as well?"

She held his stare without flinching.

"No," she finally replied.

Magruder pulled a piece of paper from his pocket and slid it across the table. She opened it and discovered an address in Lancaster, California.

"Are you sure they're there now?"

"You have my word on it."

"How many people are we talking about?"

Magruder rubbed the stubble of his beard.

"There are three men and two women."

"All right. Tell me who they are."

He gave her the names, and when she started to get up, he motioned for her to sit back down.

"I want to tell you somethin' more about the women."

She sat back down in spite of an overwhelming desire to run to the nearest phone to call Gibson.

"The woman, Claire Harris, won't appear on anyone's list. Eight months ago, I set it up for her to become a member of Cassidy's group. She was to give me intelligence about their targets and any connection to the Brits. Basically, she's not a violent person. She just cooks and does what she's told." He hung his head. "She called me several nights before your daughter was taken, and for what it's worth, she promised me she won't allow them to harm your little girl. So if you have any say in how things turn out, do what you can to spare her life."

Renée's eyes grew bigger.

"You mean you knew it would happen in advance?"

Magruder did not answer.

"I can't believe your... *your cruelty*. You bastard!"

"This is war, Ms. Marin; nothin' personal."

"Well, it's personal to me, and it was certainly personal to you when it was your daughter's life on the line."

She stood up and stared at him, not willing to let him off the hook.

"I guess I'll never understand you people."

She zipped up her parka.

"I'll see what I can do for your friend, Magruder, but I'll tell you this. If it means so little to you to involve an innocent child in your war, then you people lack the basic human decency to ever control your own destiny."

As she started for the door, he called out to her back.

"In many respects, Mrs. Marin, we've lost our way in this struggle. There are many who subscribe to the premise that the ends always justify the means."

"Spare me your bullshit. I'm too tired to listen anymore."

He smiled. "Then perhaps you'll want to hear this. The Provos have a source in the Los Angeles Police Department. I don't know who it is, but the second female in their group, Mary O'Conner, is posing as a reporter, and she's the one who's developed the source. If you tell the police where your daughter's being held, Cassidy's group will quickly find out."

Renée tried to grasp the import of his words. Gibson's suspicions were correct; there was a leak. But if she couldn't tell the police, how would she get her daughter back?

"This Mary O'Conner? Is she using her own name?"

"No, she's got an alias and I don't know what it is."

Renée paused for a moment, then sighed.

"Thanks for the warning, John." She headed for the door.

"Don't forget to destroy the tape," he called out.

She turned back and held his glance.

"What tape?"

****

After he'd arrived at Hampton Air Base, Whitney spent the better part of an hour packing his bag and inspecting his weapons. His entire team, a group from the Second Paras Regiment, were already packed and anxious to take off. But he needed to stall their departure. He wanted to give Renée more time to make contact, so he told his adjutant he was waiting for headquarters to deliver him some documents.

When his men were settled down, he retired to an office that was not in use to review his meeting with Ward.

Nothing seemed to make sense. On the surface, it all appeared plausible, but there were disturbing and nagging questions that still had to be resolved. For one thing, Ward never mentioned Michael Kelly, and in the wake of the revelations, he'd forgotten to ask about him. And if someone believed there was a leak in Los Angeles, then why wasn't he told as soon as they knew?

It didn't add up. Something was still missing.

And what about the order to terminate the terrorists? What was that all about? If he was acting under the Internment Act, then they didn't need to kill them. There were plenty of Provos interned in England, and a few more would make no difference.

The more he thought about it, the more certain he was that Renée was not a collaborator. Her judgment might be questionable, but the kidnapping was real. Of that much he was certain.

His cell phone rang and he quickly took the call.

"Whit?" she said.

"Renée? Are you okay? Where are you?"

"I'm fine, but I can hardly hear you. I'm on a pay phone near Trafalgar Square. I've got an address where they're at, Whit. I'm going to catch the underground to the train station now. I can meet you at Heathrow if you've finished your meeting."

"No. Don't go to Heathrow," he ordered.

"Why not? There's a flight leaving in about two hours?"

"No." he repeated. "Somethin' has come up. I need to see you right away."

"What's wrong? Has something happened to Julie?"

"No. Not that. Just tell me exactly where you are and I'll send a car for you."

She was silent for a moment, then described her location near the square.

"I'm sending Lieutenant Michaels. He'll be there in twenty minutes. Watch for a black Opel and stay where you are until he arrives."

"You're scaring me, Whit? What's going on?"

"Don't worry, Renée. I've got it under control."

****

The ride to Hampton Air Base took almost twenty minutes and it gave Renée time to think about the warning from John Magruder. If one of the terrorists was posing as a reporter, then she could obviously trust Gibson, Donahue, and Elwood because she knew exactly where they stood in their dealings with the press. More than likely, since the informant had access to fairly secure information, the leak would be from someone in Headquarters Division, where status reports on all investigations were routinely discussed. That would mean they should be able to narrow down the suspects.

But more importantly, it meant that Whitney could be trusted, too.

She'd let Gibson and his suspicions cloud her initial judgment. Whitney had always been honest with her and she should have relied on her instincts. Her lack of trust had been misplaced, and she planned to tell him so.

Lieutenant Bryan Michaels stopped the Opel in front of an old beige Quonset hut right next to an aircraft hanger. They climbed out of the car and he guided her into a nearby office.

Whitney stood by the desk in a dark blue jumpsuit, and when she walked in, he quickly closed up his weapons bag. He embraced her warmly and advised Lieutenant Michaels to tell the men it was time to board the plane.

Michaels left the room and she turned to Whitney.

"What's going on?"

"Sit down, Renée. It's time we had a serious talk."

They settled on a settee across from the desk.

"I need to know what you've been up to? Some things have happened that directly concern you, and I need the truth right now."

"What things?" she asked.

"You're goin' to have to trust me. Who'd you see here in London?"

She knew this was serious. He'd never meddled before. Something must be terribly wrong. She decided to trust him with everything she knew. She gave him the details, holding nothing back, and it felt as though a weight had been lifted from her shoulders.

She told him what Magruder had said about the promise made by Claire Harris to keep Julie safe.

"He asked me to see if her life could be spared?"

"Is that what you want?" he asked.

"I don't know. On the one hand I hope they all die for the murders and what they've done to my daughter. But he says that she's promised to keep my baby safe, so I guess I really don't know?" She hung her head. "I can't help but re-member that I was the one who lectured you about letting the system work. I guess I've had my perspective broadened the hard way." She looked up. "Sort of makes me a hypocrite, doesn't it?"

"It just makes you human."

But before he could say more, there was a knock on the door.

"Come in," he said.

"Excuse me, sir," Lieutenant Michaels said, stepping into the room. "The men are on board and the Captain says we can leave whenever you're ready."

"Thank you, Lieutenant. We'll be set to go in five minutes."

As Michaels departed, Whitney walked to a closet and pulled out a military jumpsuit.

"Here," he said, handing it to Renée. "Put this on."

"What's going on?" she asked.

"We're leavin' for Los Angeles. I'll tell you everythin' I know when we're in the air."

****

TWENTY-FOUR

October 7, Tuesday, Late Afternoon

In his haste to get to his feet, Aaron Rosen sent a stack of files on the corner of his desk sprawling to the floor.

"*God damn it,* Fletcher. What the hell are you trying to say?"

Garrett Fletcher, the Special Agent in charge of the FBI's Counter Terrorism Division, rolled his eyes at the outburst of temper.

"I said we want to talk to Renée Marin about the bombing at the mall."

Rosen looked over at Kerin who sat on a couch across from Fletcher.

"Can you believe this guy?" Rosen said, pointing a finger at Fetcher. "He's gonna try to smear the reputation of my office over some bullshit interview with Renée Marin?"

Fletcher appeared to hold his anger in check. "There's no excuse for that kind of language, Mr. Rosen."

"*Jesus Christ!* Now he's gonna lecture me on the use of profanities?"

Rosen balled his fists while a pulsating vein on the left side of his face signified the depth of his anger.

"I know bullshit when I smell it, Fletcher, and this is a truckload of prime. Who the hell do you think you're kidding?"

"I'm just the messenger, Mr. Rosen."

"What a joke!" Rosen shook his head in disgust. "The last I heard—and correct me if I'm wrong—was that Marin's daughter was kidnapped." His short, nervous laugh was derisive. "But I guess that doesn't count for much with you *know-it-all* Feds."

Kerin cleared his throat; this was not going well. Rosen's reaction was out of control.

"Agent Fletcher," Kerin said, "I'm sure you can appreciate the implications of your request. Mrs. Marin is a trusted and senior member of this office. To suggest that she might be involved in some way with the very people who kidnapped her child seems absurd."

"Nevertheless, Mr. Kerin, we want to speak with her."

"This is crap!" Rosen stormed over to his desk, grabbed a bottle of antacid pills from the top desk drawer, and popped three of the tablets into his mouth.

"You won't get away with this, Fletcher. It's nothing but a cheap ploy to cast aspersions on this office, and I won't stand for it."

Rosen walked back to his desk, picked up a cup of cold coffee, and washed down the three tablets.

Fletcher, face flushed, fought to control his temper.

"I resent your insinuation, Mr. Rosen. We have a genuine investigation to conduct, and we'll do it with or without your help."

Kerin stared at Fletcher in horror. The man was completely serious. *God Almighty! What could they possibly have?*

"Agent Fletcher," Kerin began, "if someone suggested that a member of your unit was involved in some way in serious criminal activity, I'm sure you'd be as shocked as we are. Without an explanation, your request seems bizarre. If you could give us some reason why you think she's involved, it might go a long way towards helping us come to grips with the situation."

"Yeah," Rosen said. "Let's hear what you think you've got?"

Fletcher shot Rosen a withering glance.

"I have no obligation to tell you anything about our investigation. I came over here as a courtesy because my boss believes you're entitled to a little advance warning. But we owe you nothing, and quite honestly, I'm sick and tired of your attitude."

He got up to leave.

Rosen seemed mildly startled as if realizing for the first time that he'd neglected to learn what they had. He carefully changed his approach.

"I'm sorry I took this out on you, Fletcher, but this is a shot to the heart, and I can't believe what I'm hearing." He sat down heavily at his desk.

"You see, Mrs. Marin is in possession of confidential information on a daily basis. Maybe if you give us some specifics, then Glenn and I would be in a better position to evaluate the damage to our organization."

Fletcher smiled at the apology with obvious satisfaction.

"Your concerns are well founded, Mr. Rosen." He reached into his inner coat pocket. "I can't reveal the details of the scope of our inquiry, but I can show you a transcript of a call she recently made. Perhaps this will help to explain our concerns."

He handed Rosen a two-page transcript of the call she'd made to Magruder.

"This call was intercepted several days ago."

Rosen read the transcript, frowned, then asked, "Who's this John Magruder?"

He handed the transcript to Kerin.

Fletcher seemed thunderstruck.

"Are you kidding me?"

"No, I'm not kidding," Rosen said. "Who the hell is this guy?"

Fletcher shook his head in obvious wonderment.

"His daughter is Anne Magruder. You know, the one you dismissed against in the Westwood Village killings?"

"What?"

Rosen appeared to be in obvious shock.

"He's also on the Ruling Council of the IRA, a major player, I'm told."

Rosen glared at Kerin. "What the fuck is going on here, Glenn? Did you know about this?"

Kerin felt his jaw go slack.

"I haven't any idea what this transcript means, Aaron. She told me she met with Magruder's father, and that he was a leader in the IRA, but she never said they had some kind of an understanding." He looked at the transcript again. "There must be a perfectly good explanation."

"There better be."

Rosen got to his feet and snatched the transcript back from Kerin's hand. He silently reread it.

"Wait a minute, Fletcher," he said after a moment. "I'll admit the fact that her meeting with these people calls for an explanation, but how the hell do you reconcile the fact that her daughter's been kidnapped?"

Fletcher smiled thinly.

"Our counterparts in London feel the kidnapping might be a ploy to increase public pressure on you to force the release of your prisoner."

Rosen stared at him in disbelief.

"This gets more fantastic by the minute, wouldn't you say so, Glenn?"

Kerin nodded and then directed his thoughts to Fletcher.

"Since it would seem that there is some basis for your investigation, perhaps you could enlighten us concerning what comes next?"

"Actually, Mr. Kerin, since she left the country for London, we may have to seek a warrant for her arrest—just a technicality, you understand—but we might need it to get jurisdiction internationally. The British were supposed to keep a watch on her, but we've been told they lost her when she left the airport. We've notified Customs and Immigration, so hopefully, we'll pick her up the moment she tries to come back to the states."

"*Shit!*" Rosen put his head in his hands. "Has the press been notified yet?"

"Not to my knowledge, but you know how they are in this town. It's just a matter of time until the story gets out."

Fletcher gave a nod to Kerin. "You have my card, and I'd appreciate a call if she checks in with you."

He extended his hand to Rosen, but the man didn't take it. He was staring out the window, lost in thought.

Kerin got to his feet.

"Thanks for the heads up, Agent Fletcher. We'll stay in touch."

Once Fletcher was gone, Rosen stood up and confronted his Chief Deputy.

"Did you know she was going to London to meet with this IRA guy?"

"No, Aaron. I had no idea."

"*God damn it!*" He pointed a finger at Kerin's face. "How can we contain this mess?"

"I have no idea."

"Well, I for one don't plan to stand by and let this go down without a fight. The best defense is a good offense, and it's time to cut our losses." He took a moment to gather his thoughts. "We're gonna to fire her ass right now, Glenn. Take care of it."

Kerin was shocked. Rosen was on his high hobby-horse again, and no surprise, he hadn't stopped to think things through.

"We can't do that, Aaron. She's protected by Civil Service. She's got due process rights."

"Knock it off, Glenn. You're the one that recommended her to run that division. I'm gonna look like a first class fool for putting the fox in the hen house. We have no choice. Get rid of her now."

Kerin shook his head.

"Slow down, Aaron. I'm sure there's a reasonable explanation for all of this. We need to talk to her before you do something stupid."

"I'm not prone to doing stupid things," Rosen barked, "and I think I know how we're gonna handle this."

He started to pace while he worked out the details in his mind.

"We'll issue a press release describing the fact that the Feds have issued a warrant for her arrest, and due to the seriousness of the situation, we'll be placing her on *administrative leave* until the matter's resolved."

"Do you really want to move this fast?" Kerin frowned. "We're under no pressure to act immediately. We can give this time to---"

Rosen quickly cut him off.

"Absolutely not. I want the story out in twenty minutes. We'll lose our advantage if we can't beat the leaks, and if the warrant turns out to be bogus, then we can blame it all on the Feds."

"It's a two-edged sword, Aaron. If they've got nothing and her daughter is a victim, we're going to look pretty heartless."

Rosen gave him a menacing look.

"Just do as I say, Glenn."

Then, off his frown, "And you might want to remember, you too can be replaced."

Kerin shrugged. Like it or not, his own future was connected to Rosen's, and the transcript did raise some pretty troubling questions about Renée's connection to the IRA. But it was far from a smoking gun, and moving too quickly could turn out to backfire badly---but then again, what if the Feds have even more?

Rosen was probably right. They should cut their losses while they had the chance.

"All right, Aaron," he said. "I'll have a press release for you in twenty minutes."

****

Claire Harris finished making a grilled cheese sandwich on wheat bread. She put it on a plate, opened a can of Pepsi, and started to walk out of the kitchen, but Cassidy reached for her arm as she entered the hallway door.

"Where are you goin'?" he asked.

"The child needs lunch, Jimmy." She brushed off his arm and reached for the knob on the door to the bedroom.

"Hold on." He grabbed her arm again and turned her towards him. "Don't get too attached," he cautioned.

She held his glance, then opened the door and stepped into the bedroom.

Julie was on her back on the bed with a blindfold over her eyes. Her hands were secured with a tight nylon rope. She was still in her school uniform; a knee length plaid skirt and a short-sleeved white blouse. They'd taken her sweater—it was thrown on a nearby chair—and they'd placed her tennis shoes on the floor at the foot of the bed. The blindfolded she was wearing kept her from seeing where she was, but she heard the door open and knew right away that someone had come into the room.

On the bed for so many hours, she'd run through the gamut of emotions. There was little she could do to change her situation; but stubborn as she was, she had no intention of giving up. She'd struggled with the knots, but they wouldn't come loose. The rope around her wrists had also been tied around her waist, and it prevented her from pulling off the blindfold. She thought about trying to get off the bed, but decided it was better to wait. If she tried and failed, they would surely tie her legs, and that would only make things worse.

The men had all but ignored her, but the lady brought her food and tried to coax her to eat; something that Julie had refused to do. As far as she was concerned, none of them could be trusted as far as she could spit.

"I've brought ya some lunch," said a soft, woman's voice. "Are ya hungry yet?"

Julie stayed mute—her way to resist—and she was not about to give her an answer.

"C'mon, little one. Ya have to eat somethin'."

The lady put the plate and drink on the end table, then sat on the edge of the bed. She reached over and patted Julie's hair.

"This won't go on much longer," she whispered. "You'll be goin' home soon. Why don't ya eat a little somethin'? I know it'll make ya feel better."

Julie smelled the grilled cheese sandwich and her stomach growled. Her resolve began to weaken. Couldn't she cooperate just this once? After all, she would need her strength if she was going to escape.

"Will you untie my hands?" she whispered.

The lady shifted uncomfortably on the bed.

"All right, but you'll have to promise to be good and quiet. I don't want the others to know, and it can only be while yer eatin'. Okay?"

"Okay."

The woman untied Julie's hands and Julie scooted up into a sitting position. The sandwich was placed in her lap and she shoveled it quickly into her mouth.

Halfway through the sandwich, she spoke to her captor.

"Thanks for untying my hands."

The woman handed her the soft drink.

"You're welcome. Is the food all right?"

"Yes, ma'am." She took another bite, washed it down with the Pepsi, and wondered if the woman could be convinced to do more.

"Can I please take this thing off my eyes?" she ventured.

"No," the woman said firmly.

"Please? I won't tell anyone. I just can't stand being like this. It's so boring."

The woman continued to stroke her hair.

"I'll talk to the others. Maybe later we can let ya watch the telly or some-thin'?"

Julie smiled to herself.

"I'd really like to read a book, if I could?"

The woman sighed.

"I'll see what I can arrange. Now, since you've finished your food, I'm gonna have to tie your hands again."

Julie frowned. She didn't want them tied, but she really had no choice. The lady seemed afraid of the others. Better not to push her too far.

She held her hands out while the lady tied her up, and as soon as she was gone, Julie began to work the at the knots that secured her hands to the cord around her waist.

****

When the C-130 Lockheed Hercules reached its cruising altitude and the cabin lights were lowered, Whitney motioned for Renée to join him in the front of the plane.

They left the benches where the rest of the twenty-man squad was seated, maneuvering their way past vehicles and supplies until they reached a spot that afforded some privacy.

Whitney pulled her close to be heard above the engines.

"Your call to Magruder was intercepted by your government. They think you've been collaborating with the IRA."

Her head jerked back.

"What? That's crazy! How could they think that? I've got to explain--"

He cut her off. "Too late for that now. They're going to try and pick you up at the airport."

"Oh my God! They can't do that."

"There's more to tell you and we haven't got much time. My people are worried about a leak in LA; and by the way, they think it's you. So I've been chosen to take the terrorists down. The LAPD is now out of the loop."

"I'm not the leak, Whit."

"I know. I'm not worried about that. But there's more. I've been instructed to kill all the terrorists, and I'm thinkin' they want them dead because someone knows somethin' we're not supposed to learn."

Renée rolled her eyes. "Magruder told me that he thought your government was involved in what's going on."

Whitney considered her words. That was interesting, considering the source.

"What are we going to do, Whit?"

"I've got some ideas, but I'll have to tell you later. In the meantime, I think you better stay with my team until we get a few things sorted out."

She nodded and went back to sit with the troops while he moved forward to the communications room. He spoke briefly to the radioman who entered a number and then handed him a phone.

"This is Gibson," said the voice on the line.

"Gibson? This is Whitney."

"I can barely hear you, Major. Are you calling on a car phone?"

Whitney smiled.

"Actually, I'm on a military flight somewhere over Greenland. We'll be in LA in about six hours."

"Where's Renée?" Gibson asked. "Something's come up and I need to talk to her."

"She's fine. We know what's goin' on. Don't worry."

There was momentary silence on the line.

"These phones are not secure," Gibson said.

"I know, but I have to tell you somethin' that won't wait. A female reporter is the conduit. Do you understand?"

Gibson considered his words.

"I understand, Major. Is there anything else you can tell me?"

"I've got her true name, but it won't do you any good because she's usin' an alias."

"If you give me the name, I can run it through channels and get a description."

"Don't do that." Whitney was adamant. "The name didn't come from my people."

"You've lost me," Gibson said. "What are you trying to say?"

"It means nothing's secure. Understand?"

"I do. Where's she getting her information?"

"Someone on your department, but I don't have a name for you yet."

"Maybe we can work backward," Gibson offered.

"Do that. Now, I'll need to see you and Elwood when we touch down at Edwards Air Force Base. Can you be there?"

"Does that mean you have a lead?"

"I do," Whitney said.

Whitney gave him an estimated arrival time.

"We'll be there. Can you arrange a pass to get us on the base?"

"I'll take care of it."

"Okay, we'll see you in six hours."

"Gibson," Whitney cautioned, "we're goin' to have to work fast once we're set up, so don't say anythin' to anyone until we talk."

****

Gibson tracked down Donahue and the two of them found Elwood seated inside his office on the fifth floor of the Police Administration Building (PAB).

As the Captain of Robbery Homicide Division, Elwood was ensconced in a single person office that was separated from the rest of the divisional personnel who were relegated to rows and rows of individual cubicles in two large rooms that occupied half the floor in the L-shaped building.

"Tom," he said as he knocked on the Captain's doorframe. "I just heard from Whitney. He's got info for us on the leak."

"Shut the door you two and sit."

Donahue closed the door and the two of them took chairs that were in front of the desk.

"He called me from a plane over Greenland," Gibson said. "He says that a female reporter is the conduit to the terrorists and the leak is someone on our department."

"Is that it?"

"That's it. We'll have to work backwards from this end."

Elwood ran his hands through his hair. "Are you thinking what I'm thinking?"

"I sure am. Carlson's a chaser, and that makes him the likely suspect, but we've got a little problem. He wasn't privy to the info on the Valley raid."

"Yeah, I know." Elwood folded his arms across his chest. "But he could have learned about it from the Chief. He has access to info not meant for release." Elwood shook his head. "It sure would go a long way towards explaining things."

"How do we handle it, boss?"

"I'll have Internal Affairs put a tap on his phone, and in the meantime, they can pull in his adjutant and ask a few questions. We'll get the credentials list and run everyone on it through a complete background check."

"Sounds good, but we have to leave for Rosamond in about three hours."

"Rosamond? Where is it and why would we be going there?"

"Whitney's plane is coming in at Edward's Air Force Base. You know, where the space shuttle used to land? And I have the feeling that Renée Marin is with him."

Elwood sat up straight.

"Does she know that the Feds are looking for her?"

"Apparently she does. Whitney told me not to say a word, but he's got something on the whereabouts of Renée's little girl."

Elwood picked up the phone.

"Give me a few moments to get things going on Carlson. I'll catch up with you as quick as I can."

****

Tim Marcia sat at Carlson's desk and went over the afternoon teletypes. In the past twenty-four hours, two officer-involved shootings had captured the attention of the press, and just before lunch, a pregnant woman was mugged and killed for the keys to her late model Lexus. With so many reporters in town, every event seemed to garner attention, and that meant more work for him.

He smiled to himself. Ever since Carlson had hit on that reporter, he'd been flaking off on the job, so Marcia had stepped in to cover for him, which meant that he provided the Chief with the daily briefings that Carlson was normally responsible for. Not that Marcia was complaining, for the Chief was a man he admired and respected, and knowing the Chief on such a personal basis could only be good for his career. Connections were everything in government; it was who you knew that got you your promotions, so by usurping Carlson's access to the Chief, it was Marcia's big chance to make a good impression.

Brushing these thoughts aside, he'd re-read and circled the important news items that he planned to put in the briefing. He was so engrossed in what he was doing that he never saw the two men who were watching him from the hallway door.

"You Tim Marcia?" said the smaller of the two.

Startled, Marcia looked up and spotted the badges that hung on their suit jacket pockets. His gaze then shifted to their facial expressions, and both men appeared to him to be extremely tense.

"I'm Marcia," he said, putting down his felt pen. "What can I do for you?"

"I'm Lieutenant Magarian and this is Sergeant Homa," said the smaller man. Marcia noted that he was built like a fire plug. Thick, hard, low center of gravity, and not an ounce of fat. Not a guy you'd ever want to tangle with.

"We're from Internal Affairs," said Magarian, "and we want to ask you some questions."

Marcia slowly eased upright in his chair.

Uh, oh. A visit from *The Headhunters*—the nickname given to investigators from Internal Affairs—could only mean one thing. Someone was in some very deep shit.

"Is this an official inquiry?" he asked, his voice cracking.

"It definitely is," Magarian replied. "Is there someplace we can talk without being interrupted?"

"We can talk right here," Marcia told him. He couldn't imagine why they wanted to speak to him? He was as clean as a freshly bathed infant. He'd done nothing wrong that he could think of...*unless...?*

Oh, shit! Was covering up for Carlson's extra-marital affairs some sort of departmental infraction?

He was suddenly not quite so sure of himself.

"Do I need an attorney?"

His eyes darted back and forth between the two men.

Homa, the taller of the two, shut the outer door, then stood in front of Marcia's desk. His expression was hard, eyes cold and dark; a definite challenge in his tone of voice.

"That's entirely up to you, sport. Do you think you need one?"

"Aaaa...I don't know?" Marcia was confused. "What's this all about?"

Magarian slowly walked around to Marcia's side of the desk and seated himself down on the edge. He was close enough for Marcia to smell the garlic on his breath.

"I'll tell you what, Marcia. We're conducting an investigation into a possible leak of information from this office. It seems that someone's been giving confidential information to a female member of the press. You know anything about it?"

"No," Marcia said. He tried to sound confident. "I sure don't."

"That's good, sport." Homa gave him a tight, fake smile. "Then perhaps you can answer some questions for us about your boss. What's he been up to for the last few weeks?"

The tall guy seemed positively menacing, and Marcia knew that he didn't want to tangle with either one of them.

"Carlson? You guys must be kidding." He tried to smile but it came out pained. "He's the press relations officer, for God's sake. His job is to give information to the press."

"Oh?" Magarian scratched the side of his face. "And just how intimate are his contacts?"

Marcia looked from one to the other. "What do you mean?"

"I think you know exactly what we mean, sport." Homa moved closer to the desk.

Do they know about Carlson's long afternoons?

He continued to stay with his bluff.

"I don't know what you're talking about," he stammered, but fear appeared on his face as he broke off his eye contact with Homa.

Magarian got to his feet.

"Okay, Marcia. I've had enough of your bullshit. You better come with us."

He grabbed Marcia by the arm and forcefully lifted him up from his chair.

"Hang on. Wait a minute! I haven't done anything wrong. You can't take me anywhere."

"Oh yes we can, sport." Homa moved up right next to him, face to face;

intentionally violating his personal space. "The Chief told us to tell you to cooperate completely. In fact, why don't we go see him right now?"

Homa grabbed ahold of Marcia's other arm and muscled him out from behind the desk.

Marcia's mind was racing. These guys were really serious, and this was quickly getting out of hand. It was Carlson's ass on the line, not his, and he had no intention of taking a fall in order to protect that skirt-chasing, ill-tempered bastard.

"We don't need to bother the Chief," he said softly. "I'm more than willing to cooperate. What do you guys want to know?"

Homa let go of his's arm.

"Take a seat, sport. We want to know who Carlson has been seeing on the side?"

Homa took a small tape recorder out of his pocket and turned it on. "And don't hold back, sport. That would be a mistake that could cost you your job."

Now thoroughly intimidated, Marcia slid down into the chair. He loosened his tie and opened his collar to alleviate the feeling he had that he was suffocating.

He looked from one to the other.

"He's been meeting with a reporter from an English newspaper. Her name is Collins, *Lisa Collins*."

"Is she on the credentialed list?"

"I checked her out myself," he said. "She's with *The Guardian*."

"Get me all the paperwork you have on her," Homa demanded.

Marcia pulled open the bottom drawer of his desk and Magarian pressed forward to peer inside.

"Don't have a gun in there, do you sport?"

Marcia's eyes went wide and he nearly dropped the file.

"No gun," he said in a shaky voice. "Just her file."

He slowly pulled it out of the drawer and handed it over.

Magarian quickly thumbed through the file. He nodded to Homa, then fixed his gaze on Marcia.

"We're gonna need you to come down to IA so we can straighten this out."

Marcia's eyes got wide as saucers.

"But I've got a briefing to give to the Chief?"

Homa smiled.

"Your briefing's just been canceled."

He took Marcia's arm, got him to his feet, and led him out of the office.

As soon as they were gone, another detective from IA quietly slipped into Carlson's office. He pulled a micro transmitter from his pocket, placed it in Carlson's telephone receiver, and then, just as quickly as he'd arrived, he disappeared out the door.

****

The C-130 Lockheed Hercules banked sharply as it made its final approach from the east into Edwards Air Force Base.

From his seat at the communications console, Whitney gazed out the window at an unobstructed view that stretched for more than fifty miles. The entire horizon was aglow, attesting to the enormous size of the city of Los Angeles; a city so bright that it could easily be seen from the moon.

The plane dropped rapidly, and at seven fifty-two p.m., it touched down on a long cement runway that had frequently been used for the Space Shuttle landings. They taxied past a series of large, metal hangers before coming to a stop at the eastern edge of the base.

The wind swirled around and it blew in gusts—up to thirty miles an hour—leaving curtains of dust on the wings of the plane. Whitney walked along the tarmac, looking around, and once he was convinced that the FBI was not lurking in the shadows, he returned to the plane and signaled to his adjutant to take Renée Marin into a nearby hanger that he planned to use as their base of operations.

The rear loading ramp was then dropped and he watched with satisfaction as his troops began to bring out their vehicles and supplies.

Captain James Cobb came out of the hanger and introduced himself to Whitney. On loan from the U.S. Army Special Forces Command out of Fort Bragg, North Carolina, and assigned by Executive Order to assist the British

SAS as advisors and facilitators, Cobb and the members of his team were unconventional warfare specialists, and no strangers to hunter/killer operations.

They shook hands quickly then moved into a nearby office which was furnished with a table and a dozen straight-back chairs.

"Welcome to Edwards, Major," Cobb said as he gestured to his visitor to take a seat.

At six foot two, Cobb was muscular in appearance, with powerful forearms and an angular jaw. Military all the way, his sandy blond hair was cut close to his scalp and his hazel-green eyes were all business.

"Were you able to handle all of my requests?" Whitney asked.

"Yes, sir. After your call, I set up a high altitude overflight just before dark. We used a drone out of China Lake to handle the recon, and it made two passes. The digital feed is being reviewed and it should be edited down and ready for use in another fifteen minutes."

"Is the drone still on station?" Whitney asked.

"No, sir. We didn't want to risk any chance of detection until you were all set up and ready to go. But we can put her up in less than five minutes anytime you give us the go ahead."

He pulled out a notebook and flipped through a few pages.

"Intel's determined the address you have is for a single family dwelling in a residential area of half-acre parcels. One of my men found a set of plans for the structure on file at the City Planning Department. A copy is in the file on the table in front of you. It'll give you the layout of the rooms."

Whitney reached for the file and took a quick look while Cobb continued his report.

"Our contact at the local Sheriff's substation checked out the address for me and determined that the owner of the house is a retired school teacher named Flores. The house was placed on the rental market four months ago and was recently rented to a female Caucasian going by the name of Abrams. We checked with the rental agent and got her description."

He referred his notebook again.

"Let's see...in her twenties with brown hair. She gave the realtor some local references, but they never bothered to check 'em out. I was going put a man on it, but I thought I'd check with you first?"

"I'm glad you waited," Whitney replied. "It won't be necessary. Did you get the materials we'll be needin'?"

"The lumber and canvas are stacked in the hanger, and as luck would have it, we have a crew from the Corps of Engineers housed right here on the base, so I took the liberty of showing their CO a copy of the plans. He had his men start on the mock-up about an hour ago, and he thinks they'll have it finished in another forty-five minutes."

Whitney smiled.

"I appreciate your foresight, Captain. That will save us a lot of time."

"My pleasure, Major. I'm just glad we can help you take these bastards down. I've got an eleven-year-old daughter at home myself, so whatever you need, just let me know."

"We'll get her out," Whitney said.

Cobb nodded, then continued. "I've also arranged for the two helicopters you requested, and we got you three vehicles as well. I'm afraid the cars are nothing special, but there wasn't much to work with out here."

"I'm sure they'll be fine. I'd like to dispatch my recon team as soon as we review the drone feed."

"No problem, sir. Is there anything else you'll be needing?"

"Nothing I can think of at the moment, but I was waitin' for two officers from the LAPD."

"There's three of them, sir. They're waiting nearby in our commissary building. I can have them brought over if you'd like?"

Whitney nodded, and was about to return to the blueprints when Cobb cleared his throat.

"By the way," he began, "my orders are to provide you with technical assistance. However, I'm more than willing to join your entry team if you determine there's a need."

Whitney smiled. Cobb was the consummate professional.

"Tell you what, Captain. I'll see what I can do to find a need."

Cobb smiled, saluted, and then left the office while Whitney reviewed the blueprints for the house.

Within five minutes, Cobb came back with Gibson, Donahue, and Elwood in tow. While they waited near the hangar door, Cobb walked over to Whitney and laid out several rolls of contact prints, the product of a high-altitude, high-resolution still camera. There was also a digital video, shot in real time, taken from the second drone pass, but it still wasn't ready for review.

Whitney studied the still photographs, then signaled for his visitors to join him at the table while Cobb excused himself and walked out the door.

"Is Renée here?" Gibson asked.

"I've got her waitin' with my entry team," Whitney said. "We don't have much time, so let me fill you in on what I know, and maybe it will help to put things in perspective."

He described Renée's meeting with Magruder; how and why the meeting had even come about; and then he told them about his own interaction with his superior officer, Nigel Ward.

"I have a theory," he said at long last. "I think Michael Kelly may be workin' for someone in British Intelligence."

Donahue frowned.

"That raises a host of questions, Major. But even if that's true, why give your people the responsibility for taking down the terrorists?"

"I see they didn't waste any time passing that on to you," Whitney said.

"Word came down to me directly from the Chief," Elwood told him.

"Does he know we're here and what we're up to?"

"He has no clue," said Elwood. "If you've got a lead, no one's been told on our department."

Whitney nodded. That was okay with him, but if he wanted their help, he knew he'd have to tell them the truth.

"We've been given the job because I've been ordered to take no prisoners."

Gibson stared at Elwood in momentary disbelief. Only Donahue chose to speak.

"That figures."

When both Gibson and Elwood looked at her, she said, "They're using the Israeli model. No matter what they do to you, you hit 'em back harder. And because it's categorized as a military operation instead of a criminal investigation, no one can point the finger at us for a violation of their human rights."

Gibson looked over at Elwood. "Just like we do to the Taliban when we take them out in Pakistan."

"I think there's more to it than that," Whitney said, and that's why I asked you to meet me here. I've got an idea, and I'm goin' to need your help."

He outlined his plan and what he thought he would need, and when he was finished, he waited for their response.

Elwood flashed him a crooked smile.

"I'll do what I can for you, Major, but I've got to run it by my Chief."

Whitney's eyes narrowed.

"What about the leak, Tom?"

"You won't have to worry about that much longer. Our Internal Affairs folks have identified the reporter. She's using the name of Lisa Collins, and we believe she's been sleeping with our press liaison. When she calls him again, we'll have them both."

"That's a relief." Whitney smiled. "Renée will be glad to hear it. But if we're goin' to pull this off, it has to be a total surprise."

Elwood agreed. "Since the leak was discovered, the Chief and I have an understanding. Whatever I say stays with him."

Lieutenant Michaels and Captain Cobb entered the room with two members of Whitney's recon team. Together, the entire group watched the digital drone feed on a laptop, then Whitney spread out the still photographs.

Michaels studied the pictures, then said, "The point should set up just below the ridge." He pointed at a spot on one of the photos. "On this small hill just behind the house."

Whitney agreed, and passed the photo over to his two-man team.

"Set up as soon as possible. You know what to do."

When the recon team and Captain Cobb were gone, Whitney turned to Lieutenant Michaels.

"Brief the outer perimeter team on where they should go, then select a staging area. You can set one up about three klicks away. I don't want them any closer to the target. Then get the entry teams set up. I'll be goin' in with the first group, and Captain Cobb will goin' in with you. Give copies of the layout to everyone, Lieutenant. I'll expect every man to have it down by the time the mock-up's finished."

****

TWENTY-FIVE

October 7, Tuesday, Evening

The high-altitude air reconnaissance photographs had revealed a six-acre hillside about a mile to the east of the targeted house. By air, they could reach it in under seven minutes, and since driving would be closer to fifty, a helicopter was selected as the obvious transport choice.

As part of the preparations that were made while Whitney was flying in from London, Captain James Cobb had arranged for the helicopters and pilots from the 160th Special Operations Aviation Regiment, a unit that used the MH-60, now commonly referred to as stealth helicopters.

The MH-60 approached from the downwind side of their target to avoid the possibility of an accidental discovery. The buffeting of the heavy winds in the area made the landing unsafe, so the two man recon team was forced to rappel from thirty-five feet above the ground.

In the darkness of the high desert, they made their way through large un-fenced properties to arrive at a small outcropping located five hundred yards behind and above the rear of the target house. Using the natural terrain of the rolling hills, they set up their surveillance post just below the ridge line to make themselves all but invisible to those in the house below.

Dressed in their desert tuxedos—camouflage clothing that blended in with their surroundings—they settled in, made a radio check using the on-air designation of *Cloud*.

Both men were snipers by trade, and they set about the task of assembling the rifles from components that they carried in field packs strapped to their backs. Night-viewing laser scopes were mounted on the rifles which they trained on the back of the house.

"*Cloud to base*," whispered one of the men into his mouthpiece.

"*Base*," acknowledged a single male voice. He spoke from a van equipped with a unit that routed the call to the rest of the team.

"*Base, we're on station. It's quiet...two cars parked in front, lights on inside, winds up to fifteen knots from the West. Out.*"

The man in the van clicked twice on the radio send button to acknowledge receipt of the call.

****

Renée stood quietly inside the hangar. Dressed in the black combat fatigues worn by the rest of the team—and with her hair pulled up under a baseball-style cap—she was virtually unrecognizable to outsiders as anything other than a member of the squad.

One of the officers had taken the time to brief her on how the raid would be conducted. Their thoroughness was a comfort; to her, it seemed that they'd thought of everything, and for the first time, in days, she felt her spirits on the rise.

She watched with a sense of wonderment as the men and women of the Corps of Engineers worked furiously to construct a mock-up of the house. Using floor plans obtained from the Planning Department, they built the wooden frames to support canvas tarps that were used to form the walls. They assembled plywood doors, which they placed inside the model according to the plans, and holes were cut in the canvas where the windows would be.

Whitney gathered the men together in a quiet corner of the spacious hanger. They were seated on their duffel bags beneath a chalkboard diagram of the residence, and when he asked them for silence, they quickly settled down.

"Gentlemen, our objective is quite basic. The Provos have set off a series of bombs to force the release of Liam Cassidy, currently on trial for the killing of two of our mates, Sean Clarke and Paul Whitcomb.

"Most recently, they've kidnapped the daughter of the prosecutor assigned to handle Liam Cassidy's case. The child's mother, Ms. Marin, was the lady on the plane with us. Her daughter Julie is eleven years old."

The group listened intently, but more than a few sneaked a quick glance over at Renée.

"For political reasons, we've been asked to handle the rescue. Captain Cobb from Delta will provide the technical support. I've been advised that there will be no negotiations for the child's release, so we've been given a green light to take them down."

He looked around the room.

"You've all seen the air recon photos, and you've had a chance to walk through the mock-up. Are there any questions?"

A hand came up from the side.

"Sir, are we to take prisoners durin' the operation?"

"Any decision on that will be made by me when the time comes. Are we clear on that, Corporal?"

"Yes, sir."

"Good. Are there any other questions?"

Whitney's eyes swept the room, but no one raised their hands.

"Very well." He pointed to a man in the front. "Sergeant Major Harris, you will lead the support teams to the rendezvous site. Use the vehicles provided by Delta. While we work in the mock-up, it will give you time to get your group on station. Check in when you're set and hold your position until further orders."

Harris rose to his feet, gave his men a nod, and they followed him out of the hangar.

Whitney turned to the chalkboard and finalized the details—field positions, points of entry, and free-fire zones—nothing was left to chance. Once everyone knew their assignments, he ordered them up for their first dry run.

They broke into groups of three and four with their respective section leaders. Each team reviewed objectives, gathered up their weapons, and walked through the mock-up one more time.

Whitney left his group, signaled to the LAPD detectives, and they met in shadows by the hanger door.

"Did you brief your Chief?" he asked Elwood.

"He warned me my ass is now on the line."

Whitney gave him a half-hearted smile.

"Welcome to the club."

Elwood smiled back.

"I also suggested to the Chief that he might want to tell his friends at the Bureau to recall the warrant for Renée Marin's arrest. We wouldn't want them to be too embarrassed."

Whitney led them over to Renée, who got to her feet when she saw them approach.

"How're you holding up?" he asked as he gave her a hug.

"I'll make it."

Whitney checked his watch.

"Let me bring you all up to speed." He pointed to the mock-up. "We're goin' to do a couple of practice entries right now, and while we're doin' that, I've ordered the perimeter team to transport the chase cars to an area near the house. The recon unit's in place and everything is quiet. There are lights on inside the house, and if they see anyone movin' about, they'll call it in."

He put his arm around Renée's shoulder once more.

"Just a little longer," he whispered. "I'll get her back. I promise."

****

Julie finished her dinner; two bowls of cereal and a piece of whole wheat toast. The lady tied her up again, saw to her comfort, then pulled a blanket up and wished her good night.

Julie listened carefully to the noises that were coming from the front of the house. The woman was arguing with the men, but she didn't seem to be making any headway.

Twenty minutes later, when things became quiet, Julie resumed work on her bonds. She twisted and wiggled and tried to stretch the nylon---and to her surprise, it finally came loose enough to get one hand free and then the other.

Her heart started pounding. She'd reached her first goal; it was time to consider an escape. She slipped the blindfold off her eyes.

The room was pitch black, but a quick glance around disclosed two small windows, one on each side of the bed. Outlines appeared; end tables, lamps, a single, straight back chair, a hallway to her right, and a closet by the door.

She adjusted the nylon cords so she could slip them back on if she had to while she kept the blindfold up on her forehead. Once she was ready, she slid off the bed and gingerly tested the floor. When it didn't creak, she made her way slowly to one of the windows, and by gently pulling out the blind, she was able to gaze out the window onto a large back yard.

Were there other houses nearby?

It was pitch black, no lights of any kind. How would she ever find help?

She studied the window by touch. It was an eight-paned slider with a wooden frame, and all she had to do was slide it up.

She ran her hand along the sides of the casing and found the stub of a nail that protruded from the frame. She knew what it was. Her father had done it to a window at their house. It was used to keep the window from sliding up.

If she wanted to escape, the nail would have to come out.

She grabbed the nail by the head and gave it a tug, but it was solidly embedded in the wood. She moved carefully over to the other window, gave it a try, but found that it was also nailed tightly shut.

She searched around for something she could use as a tool, but there was nothing she could find that would pry a nail. Alone in the darkness and out of other options, she felt like crying, but she didn't. Instead, she crept back to the first window, and hell bent on escape, she did what she could with just her fingers to wiggle the nail back and forth.

At first, it wouldn't budge, but an hour or so later, with surprising determination and several bleeding fingers, the nail came loose and out of the frame.

There was no time to think about the pain. She had to concentrate on the window. It was her only chance to finally get away.

****

"Have you checked on the child?" Cassidy asked.

Claire looked up from her magazine.

"She was goin' to sleep the last time I looked."

"Check her again," he ordered.

"She's sleepin', Jimmy."

Nevertheless, she got up from her chair and headed down the hallway. She didn't want to wake the child; the poor thing was better off asleep.

When she opened the door, the light from the hallway flooded the bedroom.

The girl was up and standing by the window. She was trying to get away.

With a look back over her shoulder, Claire entered the bedroom and quickly shut the door behind her.

****

"Cloud to Base. We've got movement by the back bedroom window. Can't tell who... wait! Small... looks like it might be a child."

Both of the recon men used their scopes to watch the activities at the window.

"Might be our victim. Base. Are we green?"

Whitney was monitoring the frequency while leading his team through a room-to-room search of the mock-up. He blew a whistle, the exercise stopped, and since all were monitoring the same frequency, they stood still and listened to the call from Cloud.

"One to Cloud," Whitney interjected. *"What's she doing?"*

"Standing at a small rear bedroom window, One... Wait. A light came on. Someone just entered the room. The little girl is tryin' to slide the window up. Positive confirm, Base. It's her. A female adult is strugglin' with her now."

His partner sighted in on the woman.

"Request green on the female," he whispered calmly.

"Negative!" Whitney said. *"We're Red, repeat Red."*

This was not the time to intervene. The sniper could take the out woman, but they'd never get to Julie in time. It was just too dangerous for everyone involved.

"Cloud to One. The girl's been pulled back into the room. We've lost the target."

"One to Cloud. If the situation looks fatal for the girl, call for green. Repeat... request green again. Otherwise, hold position. We'll be en route in zero-ten minutes."

"Roger One."

****

Cassidy and McGarry moved through the house with speed devoid of all caution. Both heard the jarring of the window blinds, and both assumed that someone was trying to get in.

When they reached the bedroom door, McGarry pushed open the door while Cassidy swept the room from behind the barrel of his gun.

Julie and Claire were wrestling on the floor.

"Bloody hell!" McGarry yelled. "How'd she manage to get loose?"

"I don't know," Claire shouted. She was short of breath. She struggled to grasp Julie's hands.

"When I came in she was tryin' to raise the window."

Cassidy slapped Julie hard across the face. It knocked her to her back, and she quickly stopped the struggle. But she wouldn't give him the satisfaction of seeing her cry.

Claire pulled the child up against her chest, as much to gain control as to shield her from Cassidy. When he made no effort to strike her again, she lifted Julie up and placed her on the bed.

"Cover her eyes," Cassidy ordered.

Julie stared with contempt at Cassidy as Claire replaced the blindfold.

Cassidy tied her hands with the nylon cord and fastened them securely to her waist.

"Check the window," he said to McGarry.

Claire shut off the light and McGarry pulled the blinds back to take a look at the yard. Nothing moved in the darkness, so he checked the window frame.

"Nail's gone," he said over his shoulder.

"Here it is," Claire said. She retrieved it from the floor.

"Get a hammer," Cassidy told McGarry, "and this time make sure that it won't come out."

****

"Cloud to Base."

"Base," came the reply.

"Positive ID of Target 2. Repeat Target 2. He's nailin' the bedroom window

shut."
"10-4 Cloud."
"Cloud out."

****

McGarry and Cassidy waited for Claire to come out of the room. "Has she settled down?" Cassidy asked her.

"She has, and you didn't have to hit her."

Cassidy ignored the rebuke.

"How'd she get loose, Claire?"

"I don't know," she said, wiping her forehead. "She probably worked on the knots. Lord knows, she has nothin' else to do in there."

"And of course, you never untied her and loosened them up?" It was not so much a question as a statement.

"No," she lied. "I didn't."

"I warned you not to get too close. She's becomin' a problem we don't need."

"And what are you sayin', Jimmy?" The reality of his meaning quite suddenly hit home. "For Christ's sake, she's just a little girl."

"Good riddance, if you ask me," McGarry said. "We've already gone too far with this farce. And besides, she's seen our faces. We'd be crazy to give her back."

Claire turned to Cassidy.

"You're not goin' to listen to this idiot, are you?"

"Knock it off, both of you," Cassidy ordered. "We'll deal with this tomorrow."

Claire walked into the living room and sat on the couch. She watched in silence as the others moved into the kitchen. When no one was looking, she picked up a handgun from the end of the table and slid it into the waistband of her jeans and under her shirt.

In the kitchen, McGarry took several bottles of beer from the refrigerator and passed them around.

"What do you think, Jimmy?" Kelly twisted off the cap of his and took a swallow of his beer. "Do you really think they'll trade for the girl?"

"I don't know, but sooner or later, they'll have to do somethin'."

"And if they won't?"

"Then they'll learn a painful lesson and we'll do another bomb."

"That's gonna be a problem, Jimmy." McGarry took a pull from his beer. "I can't build another one until I get another shipment set up with McCrossen."

Jimmy flashed him an angry look. Up until that moment, only he and McGarry knew about McCrossen, so mentioning his name in front of Kelly was a blunder of major proportion.

This was the second time that McGarry had made a big mistake, so Jimmy decided then and there that it wouldn't happen again.

****

Lisa tried to reach Carlson all afternoon. She'd called his office several times, but a secretary had advised her he was out in the field, and when she tried to reach his adjutant, the message she got was the same.

She had dinner alone in her hotel room, and two hours later, when he still hadn't called her back, she began to get nervous. She dialed his office again.

He answered the call on the third ring.

"Mark? This is Lisa. Where've you been?"

"Lisa," he sighed. "I got tied up on a murder case. I'm sorry."

"I thought we were goin' to meet for dinner? I called and left messages."

"There was no one here when I got back. I guess Marcia must've taken off." He sat up straighter in his chair. "I'm really sorry, babe. I've been really busy."

The silence between them was awkward, and it hadn't been like that before. It had her really concerned.

"Look, Lisa. I'm not sure we should meet for a while."

"Did your wife find out?" she asked.

"No, no...it's not that. There's been talk around here that there may be a leak on the Department."

"A leak? You've got to be kidding?"

"I wish I was. Anyway, if there's an investigation, well, they might find out about us. So, I think we should just cool it for a while, you know, just to be safe."

An investigation into a leak? How close could they be?

There was no way to connect her---she knew she'd been careful---but it nonetheless gripped her with fear. What if they were monitoring his phone right now?

"You're probably right," she said in a measured tone. "I wouldn't want to cause any problems. I'm willin' to wait if you are?"

"You're great, Lisa." He was noticeably relieved. "I knew you'd under-stand. This investigation won't go on for too long. Besides, I think the whole thing's just a smoke screen to cover their asses for missing those bastards in the Valley."

"I'm sure you're right, Mark." Her voice was warm and seductive. "It's just a shame that we have to put things on hold."

"I know it, baby," he whispered, "but I just can't afford any problems right now. Can I reach you at your hotel when everything calms down?"

"I'm not sure," she said. "If the trade goes through or once you get them in custody, I will probably have to go back to London."

"Don't worry about that. This thing is far from over. There won't be a trade and we haven't got a clue where they're staying."

She smiled to herself. This was almost too easy.

"That makes me feel a little better," she said. "Is it okay if I call you tomor-row to find out how it's goin'?"

"Sure. If I'm not around, just leave me a message."

****

"You slimy little *motherfucker*."

Homa put down his headphones and turned off the recorder. He was seated at an IA console down in the basement of the PAB.

He looked over at Magarian.

"Did you get a trace?"

Magarian had a phone to his ear. "One second, John." He held up a hand to silence him, then began to write furiously on a pad.

"Thanks, Manny," he said as he hung up his phone.

"We got her! Pac Bell traced her to the Luxe Hotel, you know, the one on Fig."

"What do we do now, boss?" Homa was dying to go after Carlson.

"The Chief said to run it by Elwood." Magarian began looking through his desk.

"I've got his cell phone number around here somewhere."

****

TWENTY-SIX

October 7, Tuesday, Late Evening

The advance perimeter teams scrambled out of the helicopter into the foothills just east of the residence. By using the contour of the hillside to mask their arrival, they were able to form up and start their cross-country hike without the fear of being observed. They ran at double time, carrying their gear, and they were able to cover the mile run in just under fourteen minutes. At three hundred yards from their target, they split into groups of two men each and quickly surrounded the house. Their job would be to cover the entry teams and to establish an outer perimeter that would effectively prevent their targets from getting away.

One of the two-man teams designated Gamma, moved forward slowly and did a survey of the property for man-made or other previously unseen natural obstacles. What hazards they discovered, all minor, were called into Edwards where a support team did a careful evaluation of all the factors. Their conclusion? Nothing they had learned would effect the entry team's plans.

In full desert camouflage, the Gamma Team crawled for the last fifty yards on their stomachs, completely protected by the deserts thick darkness. When they reached the side of the house, they discovered that the walls were made of stucco and the windows were wood framed.

Both men concluded that their job would be a snap.

Gamma One opened up a pouch on the side of his backpack and pulled out some high-tech microphones. While his partner provided him with cover, G-One crawled around the house, and at various intervals, he inserted the spike-mikes into the stucco walls. Once activated, the spikes could pick up sounds from the various rooms, which were then duly transmitted back to the base.

When they were finished with their task, they carefully withdrew to the outer perimeter.

****

The MH-60 stealth troop transport lifted off slowly with Whitney and the members of the entry teams. Renée was seated in a second helicopter, an MH-60 that was modified as a gunship. It surged ahead of the troop transport to provide the entry teams with cover for their arrival.

Prior to liftoff, Whitney's men had completed two separate rehearsals. One was conducted in full-light conditions, while the second was held in total darkness. Precluded from doing live fire, they'd worked out an entry scenario designed to minimize the risk of a deadly crossfire. If it all went according to plan, Whitney believed they just might pull it off. But he was also a realist, and experience has taught him that the unexpected would always happen, and that would create the potential for disaster. Success, as usual, would have to depend on his men getting by on a great deal of luck.

He sat shoulder to shoulder with his troops as they composed themselves for the action at hand. They were dressed in black jumpsuits, carrying field packs on their backs; including armor, face shields, radios, and earphones, as well as night viewing headsets for use in the dark. Everything they carried was state of the art.

Over the din of the helicopter blades, Whitney spoke to his men through their headsets.

"We'll be landing about a mile downwind from the target. Once we're out, form up and we'll move over land. We'll make the run in under ten minutes, so keep it sharp."

There were smiles down the line because his men all knew that six minutes would likely be closer to the mark.

"One last thing," he said. "The child's safe rescue is our primary mission. Once you're inside, do what you have to do."

"Does that mean no prisoners?" asked one of his men.

Whitney looked down the line.

"You've all seen the pictures of the men. If it's possible, and only if it doesn't jeopardize the safety of the child, I'd like Kelly and the woman to be taken alive."

"And the others?" asked Lieutenant Michaels.

Whitney slammed home the clip in his handgun.

"They murdered innocent people, Lieutenant. It's time they paid the piper."

****

Elwood's cell phone went off.

"Captain? It's Andrew Magarian. We've got 'em."

Elwood's spirits soared. "What happened?"

"We squeezed his adjutant and found out that Carlson's been banging a broad named Lisa Collins. She claimed she was credentialed as a reporter for the *The Guardian*, but they say they've never heard of her. The phone number the adjutant called to verify her background came back to an empty apartment that was somewhere in London."

"Do we know where she is now?"

"Yeah. She called Carlson just about thirty minutes ago. We traced the call to a room at the Luxe Hotel. Homa grabbed a couple of guys and they're on their way over there now. Do you want us to pick her up?"

"No, not yet. Tell Homa and the others to wait for SIS. I want to know who her contacts are, so don't let anyone screw this up."

"I'll get him on the horn right now," Magarian said. "In the meantime, what do we do with Carlson?"

"That depends. What's your take on him?"

"To be honest, based on what we overheard, I think the stupid shit doesn't know that he's been taken. He can't seem to see past the end of his dick."

"Nothing new there. Did she get anything out of him tonight?"

"Nothing important. She wanted to know if the brass was gonna trade and he told her they wouldn't, but I guess that's no big news—"

"Damn it!" Elwood closed his eyes to gather his thoughts. "Listen, Andy, call SIS for me right away. Tell them to watch the woman, but don't bother with Carlson for now. I've got to make another call that just can't wait."

He hung up the phone, ran back to the hanger, and found a technician from SAS.

"Are you in contact with Major Whitney's team?"

"Yes, sir," he replied.

"Can you raise him for me? It's an emergency."

"No problem, sir." He pulled off his headset and handed it to Elwood. "You're all hooked in."

Elwood put on the headset.

"Major Whitney? Can you hear me? This is Elwood."

"Go ahead, Captain," Whitney replied.

"I just heard from IA. We've plugged the leak, and both are under surveillance. But I think we've got another problem."

"What's that?"

"Our man told the girl that there wouldn't be a trade. I'm worried that she might try to pass it on."

****

The heavily laden MH-60 landed four minutes later, disgorging its occupants on a darkened hillside slope. As soon as everyone was off, it lifted up to an altitude that made it all but invisible from the ground.

While the teams formed up, Whitney took a moment to contact Renée on a secondary line, as she was in the MH-60 gunship that was hovering in the sky, more than a mile away.

"You'll know what's goin' on if you listen to the radio," he said.

"I want to be there, Whit. What if something happens?"

"Sorry, Renée, but I've got enough to worry about. Once she's okay, I'll have them fly you in."

****

Seven minutes later, they crossed the last two hundred yards leading up to the residence. Invisible as shadows, Whitney and the Alpha team moved up until they were about forty yards to the west of the front door. The backup team, Beta, was in the process of setting up about ten yards behind.

Both teams would enter the residence, one behind the other. Alpha would do the sweep of the house, while Beta provided the cover.

The sounds from the house were monitored by a team that was parked in a van, well away from the premises. The men inside worked in controlled pandemonium; to filter the sounds, decipher their sources, and to communicate their findings to the waiting entry teams.

Whitney listened to the reports in his earphone. The back of the house was quiet, but a TV was on in the living room. There was no discernible conversation, only mechanical sounds, clicks of some type, which were overheard at various intervals. The technicians' best guess was that someone was cleaning a gun.

Whitney asked for raw data to see if he could learn where Julie and the others might be?

"Run the spikes for me in sequence," he whispered into his microphone, and one by one, in prescribed order, each section of the house was played into his headset. As he listened carefully, his disappointment increased. He could not get a fix on where Julie might be.

When the living room mike came on, the noise from the TV filled his headset. He strained to listen, concentrating his thoughts on the background noise. What he heard was very faint, almost a mumble. Was it a conversation?

"Alpha to Base," he whispered. *"Can you amplify the last one?"*

"Base. We'll try."

A few moments later, a conversation was lifted from the background noise when the technicians filtered out the television sounds. As words took shape, he focused intently on what was being said and how many people were talking.

"Beta... I make out two males," Whitney whispered into his headset.

"Copy, Alpha," First Sergeant Stephens replied. He was the leader of the second team. *"We make out two as well."*

Strain as they might, the substance of what was being said remained elusive. Whitney shut his eyes and tried to think. Julie was still in the house, probably somewhere towards the back, and two of the males were now talking in the front. That left one male and a female unaccounted for, and that spelled trouble for everyone involved. To enter now would be risky. Success was going to depend on surprise.

Should he wait and take a chance that they might all go to sleep? They didn't post sentries, so they must feel secure. But his team was pumped up and ready to go, and if he waited too long, they might lose their edge. Whitney knew what he had to do. Right now the odds were still in his favor.

"*Get ready,*" he whispered to both teams.

They pulled down their face shields, and those with night goggles slipped them into place.

"*Alpha One to all teams. Move up to station one and wait for my signal.*"

From their positions on three different sides of the house, the teams moved slowly forward. As they got underway, the ringing of a telephone came over the spike mikes and seemed to blast into their earphones.

"*Hold positions,*" Whitney whispered.

They froze in their tracks as the words of a male came drifting in over their headsets.

****

"*Yes?*"

"*Jimmy?*"

Cassidy recognized her voice.

"*What's goin' on, luv?*"

"*He wants to break it off for a while. They're lookin' for a grass on the job.*"

"*Is he on to you?*"

"*I don't think so. He told me tonight they don't plan to trade for Liam. He says they're draggin' it on and hopin' to find you before the time runs out.*"

"*The bastards.*"

"*They've got no idea where you are, Jimmy,*" she said, "*so they might still change their minds.*"

"*Fat chance of that. They're playin' with us.*"

"*What do you want me to do?*"

He thought for a moment.

"*Just stay on top of things. Press him if you have to, but be careful. Things are gonna get tense.*"

Cassidy hung up the phone and turned to McGarry.

"They're not gonna trade, Devon; they're just buyin' time."

"Bloody hell! I knew it wouldn't work."

"*Shhh,*" he cautioned. "Not so loud. I don't wanna wake the others."

"So what are we gonna do?"

Cassidy smiled grimly.

"I'll send 'em an ear. Maybe then they'll listen to reason."

He started towards the bedroom, but McGarry stepped up and blocked his way.

"Might be time to think about packin' it in?" he cautioned.

Cassidy's eyes grew cold.

"We can't turn her loose. She's seen our faces. Besides, they need to know we mean business. If we send 'em a piece, it'll drive 'em fuckin' crazy. You mark my words. They'll deal with us then."

****

Claire Harris stood in the doorway of the second bedroom. Awakened by the ringing of the telephone, she had opened the door and overheard Cassidy telling McGarry what he planned to do.

Adrenaline pumping, she reached for her pistol, slipped down the hallway, and silently made her way into Julie Marin's bedroom.

****

Whitney had heard enough. The spike mike had picked up only the kidnappers side of the conversation, but that was enough. From what Whitney and the others had overheard, their worst fears were now confirmed. The terrorist now knew there would be no negotiations, and worse than that, it sounded as if they were about to take out their anger on an innocent, eleven-year-old girl.

There was no time to waste. The child was in clearly in imminent danger.

"This is One," whispered Whitney into his mouthpiece, *"We go through the door in ten seconds!"*

The men on the perimeter scrambled towards the house, and when they got in close, several of them pulled out grenades—flash-bangs and concussive—

counted to five, then tossed them through the windows and into the house.

The grenades went off in a thunderous burst of noise and blinding light.

Whitney then gave the command to enter, and in they went.

Alpha hit the house just after the explosions. A battering ram was used to take down the door.

The first man dove in on his belly, ready to fire at any threat, while the others behind him went in standing up.

The Beta team followed close on their heels. They entered the house five seconds behind.

****

Cassidy had searched through several kitchen drawers before he found what he wanted, a serrated steak knife. He picked it up and was walking towards the child's bedroom when he was showered with glass from the kitchen window.

He knew right away they were under attack, and the first thought he had was to use the child as a shield. He ran from the kitchen and crashed into McGarry who still didn't grasp what was going on.

Both men fell to the ground in a tangle of limbs.

Cassidy somehow scrambled up to his feet and ran full speed down the short hallway just as the three grenades went off in the front living room.

Two were concussion and one was a flash.

McGarry never knew what hit him.

****

The first man through the front door had been Lieutenant Bryan Michaels. He dove head first, landed on his belly. He spotted his target, sighted his handgun, and squeezed off two quick rounds.

Still dazed from his collision with Cassidy and the concussion grenades, McGarry looked up from his sitting position on the floor just as both of Michaels rounds caught him through the forehead.

****

In the darkened bedroom, Claire Harris had dropped her handgun on the bed, scooped the sleeping child into her arms, and placed her on the floor in the closet.

"Stay here and don't make a sound," she warned. "I promise I won't let 'em hurt you." She pulled off Julie's blindfold then closed the closet door with Julie inside.

At that moment, the glass from the window on the side of the bed came crashing into the room.

My gun? Where's my gun?

She dove for the bed just as the first flash grenade went off in the room. She was temporarily blinded, but she continued to grope around for the gun.

There were several more explosions from the front of the house, then thunderous footfalls coming down the hallway.

It all was happening within just microseconds, but time had stopped and seemed to her to drag on.

She struggled to find the gun.

****

Cassidy hit the door with his full body weight which cracked the casing and sprung the door open. He was deafened by the blast of the concussion grenade, but his eyes had been closed during the flash, so his vision was not completely impaired.

The light from the hallway behind him spilled into the bedroom and illuminated Claire who was still lying on the bed.

But something was wrong. Where was the child?

His gaze quickly swept the room.

Had Claire turned her loose?

He stood with the knife in his hand, oblivious to Whitney who was now coming at a run down the hallway behind him.

****

It took only an instant. Whitney entered the bedroom, and in the glow of the light attached to his MP5, he quickly assessed the situation. He had taken them completely by surprise.

But in that brief half second of realization, he wasn't even sure who he had?

Time for him, too, seemed to have stopped, and the image frozen before his eyes was of a man staring down at someone on the bed, and he was holding something dark and pointed in his hand.

Without the slightest hesitation, Whitney fired two rounds, striking the man in the upper back and sending him sprawling face forward on the bed.

The person underneath him let out a sharp scream.

Whitney recognized the sound as having come from a woman. While she struggled to extract herself from the weight of the body on top of her, Whitney concluded that it must be Claire Harris.

When she freed herself from the body on top of her, he could see her hand, and in it was a gun.

He dove towards the bed and using the butt of his gun, he struck her hard on the side of the head.

She slumped to the side, rendered unconscious; her handgun falling from her hand to the floor.

He reached out, rolled the male over, and was pleased to discover it was Jimmy Cassidy.

Michaels came into the room and switched on the overhead light. Together they looked around, but Julie was nowhere in sight.

Whitney moved over to the closet, and with Michaels providing the cover, he grabbed the handle and opened the door.

Julie was lying on the floor, curled up in a ball, still bound and with duct tape over her mouth.

Whitney tore off his face shield, dislodged his headpiece, and scooped her up in his arms.

"It's okay, Julie. It's okay. It's me, Whit. You're safe now, darlin'. It's over."

Julie buried her head against his shoulder and started to sob with relief.

He looked over at Michaels.

"Are we secure?"

"The rooms have been cleared, but not the attic."

"Have Beta see to it. Is everyone accounted for?"

Michaels spoke into his mouthpiece, then looked over at Whitney.

"Alpha has a male in the other bedroom; the one in the hall and this one makes three. The woman in here makes four."

"Good. That's all of 'em. Did we have any casualties?"

Michaels checked using the radio.

"No, sir." He reported. He looked down at Claire Harris. "Is she dead?"

"Just a big headache, but cuff her up and get her ready for transport."

Michaels nodded. He pulled a syringe from the pack on his waist and gave her a quick injection.

Whitney tried to reattach his headset, but Julie nearly slipped from his arms. He placed her on her feet then quickly cut the ropes that bound her hands to her waist. When her hands were free, he removed the tape from her mouth, then adjusted his headset, picked her up, and carried her out of the room.

First Sergeant Stephens waited in the hallway with a short-barreled shotgun cradled in his arms. He motioned to Whitney to follow him down the hallway. Whitney reached up, pressed Julie's head against his shoulder, and covered her eyes with his hands to keep her from seeing the body that was lying on the floor.

He carried her through the corridor but stopped for a moment at the door to a third bedroom where Cobb and a soldier from the Alpha Team standing were standing over a body that was stretched out on the floor.

"Who's this?" Whitney asked. The man was face down and his hands were wired together behind his back.

"That's Kelly," Cobb said.

"How's he doin'?"

"He'll live." Stephens gave him a smile. "Got his head banged up a bit when I put 'im on the floor."

"Bring him along," Whitney instructed. "We'll load 'im up outside."

Stephens nodded. He removed a syringe from his pack and took a knee next to Kelly.

"Nighty-night," he said as he plunged the needle into Kelly's arm.

Whitney turned on his heels and walked out of the house with Julie ensconced in his arms.

****

Michaels pulled a blanket from a pack carried by one of the men and placed it over Julie's shoulders to protect her from the wind. She refused to let go of Whitney, so he continued to hold her while he waited for Renée.

"Pretty smart of you to hide in the closet," he whispered.

She lifted her head off his shoulder.

"The lady put me in there and told me to stay quiet."

He smiled and gave her a hug.

"I guess we should thank her."

"Is she all right?" Julie whispered.

"She's fine." He shifted her weight in his arms. "You just keep your head on my shoulder and relax while I let your mother know that you're safe."

He reconnected his radio transmitter.

"*Alpha to Base,*" he said. "*We're secure. Bring in the birds, and tell Ms. Marin that her daughter is fine.*"

****

Renée arrived on the gunship a few minutes later and ran from the landing zone to meet her daughter who was still in Whitney's arms. And after a tearful group hug, Julie let go of Whitney and wrapped her arms tightly around her mother's neck.

Renée kissed and hugged her daughter while tears streamed down her face.

Whitney watched the two of them with relief and satisfaction.

A few moments later, he interrupted their reunion.

"Renée, I'm going to have First Sergeant Stevens fly with you and Julie back to the base."

"Can we get her checked out by a doctor?" she asked.

"Stevens will arrange it. In the meantime, I still have a few things to take care of out here. As soon as I'm finished, I'll catch up with you."

She gave him a kiss on the cheek.

"Thanks, Whit. You've given me my life back."

"I could get used to that," he said with a grin.

As she and Julie walked off with First Sergeant Stevens, Whitney, Michaels and Cobb walked over to the house.

"Where are they?" Whitney asked

"Inside," Michaels said. "Follow me."

He led them into the front room where a team of soldiers was filming Mc-Garrys' corpse being placed in a body bag. As soon as it was sealed, they moved to the bedroom and repeated the process with Kelly.

"But that man's not dead?" Cobb said with surprise.

The soldiers looked up to Whitney for guidance, and he signaled for them to continue.

Whitney pulled Cobb aside.

"If certain people think he's dead, it will buy us some time."

"I hope you know what you're doing, sir. Do my people know what's going on?"

"Not yet, and I'd appreciate your silence. For the time bein', there are no survivors. The three men and the female were all killed resistin' arrest."

"I don't know, Major." Cobb seemed to be balking. "I've got to let my CO know?"

"You can, Captain, but I need you to wait until we've finished our interrogations." He looked him squarely in the eye. "It's really important, Jim. There are other things at play here, and we've only got a few hours."

"Okay, Major. My orders are to assist you. You're running the show. Is there anything else I should know?"

"Not at the moment, but if the local authorities or the press show up, I'll need you to run interference."

"I'll do what I can," Cobb said. He slapped Whitney on the shoulder. "Thanks for letting me go in with your team. They do nice work."

Whitney smiled. "Anytime, Captain. Thanks for your help."

****

Lieutenant Michaels came out of the bedroom.

"We're all finished, sir. The attic has been cleared and they're bagged and ready for transport."

"Alpha to Base," Whitney said into his headset. *"Bring down the transport. We're ready to move out."*

Flares were ignited to mark a landing zone, and the MH-60 transport helicopter touched down a few minutes later. The engines stayed on and a tape was made of the bodies being loaded aboard.

Lieutenant Michaels led Whitney back into the kitchen.

"Sir, we've collected their weapons—they had quite a few—and we'll be takin' 'em back by car."

"Any explosives?"

"Yes, sir. We found three bricks of Semtex under the sink."

"Have you now? Let's have a look."

Michaels opened the cabinet and moved out of the way.

"About three kilos, sir. There's enough in there to take down the house."

"Is it rigged?"

"No sir."

Whitney peered into the cabinet then got to his feet.

"I want everyone out of here now, Lieutenant. We'll turn the scene over to the locals. Have Cobb call in the Sheriff's and notify their bomb squad. Tell them to see if they can tie this batch to the blast that went off at the mall."

Michaels nodded.

"One more thing, Lieutenant. Tell Cobb to put out a story that some armed robbers were holed up in here. I'm sure the press will get involved once the locals get called out, but I want to buy some time before they find out the truth."

****

TWENTY-SEVEN

October 8, Wednesday, Early Morning

The winds from the West picked up, making the flight back to Edwards exceptionally choppy, but everyone on board was in a jubilant mood. The troops huddled together, recounting what they'd done, and in the retelling, the stories were gradually embellished. There was a great deal of gallows humor as the team came down from their high.

When they landed at the base, the bodies were carried into the hanger. Kelly and Harris, still unconscious, were left on the floor with the others.

Gibson, Donahue, and Elwood stood near the hanger door with smiles from ear to ear.

"Congratulations, Major," Gibson said, "You pulled it off."

"Without a hitch," Whitney added with a smile. "Julie's been taken to a clinic at the other side of the base for a checkup. Renée is with her, but I'm sure she's fine. She was hiding in a closet when we found her."

"Thank God!" said Donahue. "Are all your people all okay?"

"They're fine."

"Any survivors?" Elwood asked.

"Two. Kelly and Harris. They've been given a sedative. Are you all setup?"

"We are." Elwood's eyes narrowed. "I hope this works, for all our sakes."

"I hope so too. Let's get started."

Whitney entered the hanger and walked over to Lieutenant Michaels.

"We're ready for Harris and Kelly."

Without any pretense of gentleness, Michaels and several of his men dragged the two body bags into a small, empty office at the back of the hanger.

Whitney and the others followed closely behind. The office had been set up with several straight back chairs, a large wooden table, and a video camera mounted on a tripod. A separate TV monitor and a laptop computer sat on a cart in the corner.

Satisfied with the set up, Whitney turned to Michaels.

"We'll start with Kelly first."

Michaels and his men removed an unconscious Kelly from one of the bags and put him into a sitting position in one of the straight-back chairs. Duct tape was used to secure him in a sitting position while leg chains were attached to his feet. His hands were cuffed and secured to a chain that ran around his waist.

Michaels dismissed his men while Gibson adjusted the lights to prevent Kelly from seeing his captors.

"Bring him up," Whitney said to a medic who injected Kelly with a counteracting drug. Kelly came around a few minutes later and retched four or five times as his system adjusted to the drugs.

"Is he okay?" Donahue asked.

"He'll settle down in a minute," the medic replied. The retching soon subsided, and Kelly took note of his surroundings.

"Good evening, Mr. Kelly," Whitney said. "We've brought you here to ask a few questions."

"I've nothin' to say," he said hoarsely. He looked as though he was ready to sleep.

Whitney pulled up a chair and sat down in front of him, then turned to Elwood and the others.

"Leave us for a moment, would you? I want to explain to Mr. Kelly what's goin' on."

Elwood, Gibson, and Donahue exchanged glances. If they shared any misgivings, they chose not to say so. They slowly walked out the door.

Kelly smacked his lips from the dryness of the drugs.

Whitney smiled.

"I have a proposition to make mate, and I think you'd be wise to listen."

Kelly stayed mute, but Whitney had his attention.

"Here's the deal. You're still in America. They want to prosecute you for multiple murders, the bombin', and the kidnappin' for ransom. I've been told that you'll get the death penalty, and you'll spend years in prison during the appeals. That may not seem so bad to a person of your character, but you're goin' to need some protection in jail. To keep you alive, they'll put you in a place called Pelican Bay. Ever hear of it? It's a California prison for the worst of the worst. I hear they never let you out of your cell. There's no television, no privileges, and you'll be in total isolation for years. How's that sound?"

Kelly glared but he refused to answer. Whitney smiled.

"By the time your appeals are exhausted, you'll be beggin' them to let you die."

Kelly barked a nervous laugh and shook his head in defiance, but Whitney knew he'd struck a nerve.

"On the other hand, you know somethin' I want to hear about, and if you were to tell us the truth, then maybe I can work somethin' out."

Whitney held his breath. *Would the bastard take the bait?*

Kelly looked perplexed. "What is it you think I know?"

"I want to know about your deal with MI5."

Kelly's face went pale and his eyes darted back and forth.

"Think about it, Kelly. This is a one-time offer."

"I've got friends in London," he said weakly.

"Not anymore." Whitney stood up and walked over to the table. He picked up a video tape and waived it in the air.

Kelly couldn't take his eyes off the tape.

Whitney moved to within several inches of Kelly's face.

"My orders were to kill you durin' the raid. You're expendable, man. They don't want you around."

Kelly started sweating profusely.

"Then again, if you don't cooperate with us, you're goin' to have problems with the Provos. I wouldn't want to be in your shoes when they find out you turned *supergrass*."

The look of shock on Kelly's face said it all. No matter what happened, he was already screwed.

"If I cooperate with you, they'll get me for sure."

"Not necessarily."

Whitney walked over to the video player.

Kelly stared with dismay at the tape of his dead companions, and he noticeably blanched when he saw his own inert form being placed in a body bag.

"Right now you're officially dead. There's no reason for that to change unless you decide you won't cooperate."

Kelly stared in horror at the scene on the monitor.

"Did anyone else survive?"

"No," Whitney lied. "You're the only one we didn't kill."

"All right," he said, still reeling from the video tape. "What is it you want to know?"

"A wise decision, but let me give you fair warnin'. If you hold back or lie about anythin' at all, the deal is off, and I'll feed you to the Provos myself. Are we clear on that?"

Kelly nodded.

"Good! Would you like a cup of tea?"

"I don't suppose you'd make it a pint of ale?"

Whitney ignored him and walked from the room and found the others just outside the door.

"He's ready to talk. I told him he's the only survivor. Lieutenant Michaels will stay with you. He can cover any background on the PIRA's while you walk Kelly through the crimes. I've got somethin' to take care of right now, but I'll be back in a while to get what I need."

He found Michaels waiting for him in a second interrogation room. He sent him to join Elwood and the others while two of his men stood guard over Harris. She was tied to her chair just as Kelly had been, and one of the men, a medic, was ready to bring her up.

"Do it," Whitney said, and when she was ready, he sent the two soldiers out of the room so that he could speak to her alone.

"How are you feelin'?" he asked when she finally stopped retching.

"Terrible." Claire had trouble speaking with clarity. "Is the child okay?"

"She's fine, thanks to you."

She smiled thinly, then fear returned to her face.

"Where am I?" she asked, looking around.

"We took you out in a body bag. Everyone thinks you died durin' the rescue."

Her confusion was apparent.

"I don't understand?"

"I spared your life, Claire. Do you want to know why?" He didn't wait for an answer. "I know why you were with 'em, and I know you never planned to let 'em hurt the little girl."

"But how...?"

"That's not important now. The only issue we have to deal with now is your future."

"What do you mean?" she said with a tremble in her voice.

"If word gets out that you're alive, then I'm afraid I can't be responsible for what will happen."

"I don't understand?"

"Let's review the situation. First, the Americans want you for killin' their policemen. If they find out you're alive, they'll give you death by lethal injection. My country would love to give you life in prison as a terrorist, and you know what British prisons are like. You might as well be dead right now. And the PIRA's? Well, we both know they'd kill you if they find out you were grassin' on the Cassidy's."

Her face went pale and she looked as though she was going to be sick.

"Not very attractive options, are they?"

"I'm dead no matter what," she mumbled.

"Maybe not. I've decided to let you go."

He could tell by her face that she was stunned.

"We'll settle you somewhere in Britain, and you'll have to keep silent about your past, but I would think you could make a new life for yourself."

"I don't understand. What do you want from me?"

"Nothin'," he said. "Not a single thing."

"Then why?"

"The child was a friend of mine, and because you protected her, I promised her mother I was goin' to let you live."

"That's it?"

"That's it," he said simply.

"*Mother of God!*" The tears flowed freely from her eyes. "I'll do whatever you say."

****

Whitney tracked down Cobb and walked him over to Kelly's interrogation room. Michaels met them at the door.

"I don't know what you told him, sir," Michaels said. He couldn't keep the smile off his face. "He won't shut up."

"That's music to my ears, Bryan. What's he sayin' now?"

"He just finished with his stint in detention. The detective decided to stop at that point and wait for you to come back."

"Tell Gibson to go ahead. He knows what I need. Cobb and I will stay out here and watch on the monitor. If Gibson or the others need to speak to me, have 'em pass me out a note."

"Yes, sir!"

"And, Bryan, I don't want you to react to what he says or to ask any questions. If he answers the questions put forward by the Americans, it will be easier for others to believe what he says. You'll understand what I mean when it's over."

****

Gibson leaned forward in his chair.

"And while you were in prison, were you ever interrogated by British Intelligence?"

Kelly nodded. "I was taken from Ireland and brought to London by plane."

"What do you remember about the flight?"

"It was a military transport, that's all I know. They put a hood over me head."

He took a drag from a cigarette that came from a pack that Michaels had conveniently left lying on the table.

"What makes you think it was a military plane?" Elwood asked.

"'Cause there weren't any birds in short skirts offerin' me a spot of tea or a pint."

He smiled at his own joke, but when no one else did, he averted his eyes and put the cigarette back in his mouth.

"The seats were hard benches. It was a transport of some sort."

"How do you know they took you to London?" Gibson asked.

"The smell, mate. The city smells like *shite*."

"Where did they take you?" Donahue asked.

Kelly sighed. "To a room, somewhere; I was blindfolded goin' in and out, so I don't really know where I was."

"Did they ever take off the blindfold?"

"They did."

"What did you see?"

"I was in an interrogation room; lights in my face, a table. They pretty much stayed in the shadows."

"What happened?"

"They cuffed me around a bit; then they told me I had two choices. I could work with them and grass on me mates, or they'd send me back to prison and pass along the word that I turned."

"So you decided to work with them?"

Kelly laughed sarcastically. "What choice did I have?"

"What happened then?" Elwood asked.

"They put the blindfolded back on and took me to that place where I met *The Old Man*."

"What old man?"

"The one in charge. That's what they called 'im."

"Did you ever see his face?"

"No, I didn't see his face. I had a bloody blindfold on, and I don't know the name of his aftershave, neither."

Gibson smiled at the sarcasm. He was at a disadvantage in this interview, not familiar with London or the people involved, and it slowed him down.

"Okay, Kelly, I can see you're getting tired of this. Why don't you just tell me what happened in your own words."

"It's like I said. They took me to see the Old Man. Me eyes were covered, so I never saw his face; but he was cool, very sure of himself. Said he wants me to get close to Jimmy so I can work me way into his group."

"Jimmy Cassidy?" Gibson asked.

"That's right."

"And did you?"

Kelly nodded.

"After the meetin', when they took me out, the blindfold came loose, and that's when I saw the Tower through the window."

"The Tower? You mean the Tower of London?"

"That's right. We were in a buildin' just across the street."

"Do you know which building you were in?"

"No, sir, but I remember the view."

He stubbed out the butt of the first cigarette and reached for the pack on the table. Gibson lit it up for him, and after a deep drag, he continued to talk.

"They took me back to the North and arranged for me to bunk in a cell next to Jimmy. We became mates, and when I got out, he asked me to join 'im."

"Why did the Old Man want you in Cassidy's group?" Elwood asked.

"I guess he wanted me to tell 'im their plans."

"How did you communicate with him?" Donahue asked.

Kelly held her glance. "I didn't always speak to 'im directly. I'd call a number, get a machine, give 'em a code name, then someone would call me back."

"What was your code name?" Donahue asked.

"Shamrock," he replied. "Pretty stupid, eh? Makes me sound like a poof, but they were callin' the shots."

"Tell us about LA," Elwood said.

Kelly gave him a stare and shivered. Gibson could sense that they were closing in.

"I checked in with the Old Man last July to tell 'im about a delivery of Semtex that Cassidy wanted to truck into London. He told me that two Brits would be goin' to LA to give a speech and that one of 'em was named Sean Clarke. Clarke's the one that killed the Provos near Downing Street. You know what I'm talkin' about?"

Gibson nodded even though he didn't know all of the details of the incident.

"Well, one of the dead Provos was Mairead Devenny, a cousin of Cassidy. The Old Man told me to pass it on to Liam. He said Liam was a hothead who'd try to take 'im out, so I did what I was told."

"Did Cassidy ask where you got the information?"

"I told him I got it from a drunken soldier in a pub near Whitehall. Liam went for it just like that."

"Why'd he want to set up his own man?" Donahue asked.

"He never said, and I didn't ask. But Liam did it all on his own, and once he got caught, Jimmy went crazy, and gettin' 'im out was all he could think of."

Donahue shifted in her chair.

"Did you tell the Old Man what was going on?"

Kelly nodded. "He just laughed. Thought it was a big joke. He wanted me to encourage Jimmy to try and do a rescue. But, I didn't need to. He'd already made up his mind. So we tried a snatch on the way back from the courthouse, but that fell apart, so then we tried the bombs."

What surprised the three detectives most of all was Kelly's cavalier attitude about the crimes and the deaths they'd inflicted by their efforts. He showed no sign of remorse for the horror that he and his mates had caused.

"Where'd Jimmy get the Semtex?" Gibson asked.

"Jimmy and Devon brought it in by truck through Mexico. We unloaded it in a garage the first night we got here."

"Did anyone help them bring it into the country?" Donahue asked.

"Jimmy didn't say where it came from, but when he and Devon were talkin' about doin' another bomb, I heard Devon tell Jimmy that they'd have to contact someone named McCrossen to get more stuff."

Donahue sat straight up. *Could it be the same McCrossen?* She didn't want to sound too anxious.

"Do you know who he was talking about?"

"No, but the truck we off-loaded was from the United Catholic Charities Association if that means anythin'?"

Donahue wrote it down. It should be easy enough to determine if Barrett McCrossen was connected with that group.

"Okay, Kelly," Gibson said. "I think we're gonna to take a break for a few minutes. Can I get you another cup of tea?"

"Thanks, mate. Is there any chance I can use the loo?" Then off their confused looks, "The loo? You know, I need to take a piss?"

Michaels led a hobbled Kelly out the door while Gibson stepped outside to track down Whitney and Cobb. He found them standing by the video monitor in an adjoining empty office.

"No wonder they told you to take no prisoners,." Gibson said. "What do you think, Major? Have we got enough for you to work with yet?"

"I'm not sure, Gibby. He said he never saw Ward face to face."

"Who's Ward?" Cobb asked.

"Behind his back, Ward's known as the Old Man. He's the Director of MI-5 and the man who oversaw this operation."

"*No shit*!" Cobb showed his concern. "No wonder you wanted me to sit in on this."

"It's too bad we didn't—"

Whitney stopped talking mid-sentence. So far, only his team knew what had happened to the terrorists, but what if Kelly called London and Ward called him back? They could tape the call and corroborate Kelly.

"I've got an idea, Gibby." He paced for a moment to marshal his thoughts. "I'm goin' to have Kelly call his contact in London and maybe we can get Ward to call 'im back."

"You think he'd be that careless?"

"I don't know, but it's the only way I can think of to connect him to Kelly."

"Can we link him to the number that Kelly calls?" Gibson asked.

"I'm sure we can track it down in London, but chances are it'll go to a phone drop. We might have better luck if we trace the incoming call."

He turned to Cobb. "Can your people handle that for us?"

"I'll have to put a call into some folks I know at the NSA, but it shouldn't be a problem. I'll need some time to set it up."

Whitney nodded his agreement, then had a flash of inspiration.

"Gibby, you finish up the interview with Kelly. When you're done, I'll come in and we'll brief Kelly on what he should say. In the meantime, I'm goin' to have a talk with a contact of mine over at MI6. There may be somethin' else we can do."

****

TWENTY-EIGHT

October 8, London, Wednesday Afternoon

After twenty minutes of running around an indoor track, followed by a shower and a shave at his townhouse, Nigel Ward dressed in a starched white shirt and a soft, gray wool suit. Adjusting his tie, he looked himself over in the mirror, and once he was satisfied with his appearance, he walked to the window to see if his driver was waiting out front.

He was scheduled to attend a dinner meeting with several outspoken members of Parliament who wanted to know specifics about the inordinately large expenses that his units were piling up while they dealt with the problems in Northern Ireland. In spite of the supposed peace agreement, certain factions of the IRA refused to honor the accord.

Ward wasn't worried about the meeting. He had his facts and figures in hand to prove that these dissidents were up to no good. His staff worked hard to prepare a briefing package, and he was reasonably confident he could prove his case and keep the wolves at the door for at least another year.

But Ward was worried nonetheless. The LA situation was a messy loose end, one that he wanted to resolve quickly. What mattered now was a blurring of the trail, the one that could lead straight back to him.

The telephone rang and shook him from his thoughts.

"Good evening, sir," said a soft female voice. "You wanted me to call you when Shamrock checked in?"

He reached for a pen and a piece of paper.

"What's the callback number?"

****

Kelly answered the phone on the second ring. "This is Shamrock."

"Good mornin', Shamrock. Do you know who this is?"

"I do," Kelly replied.

"Good! I was beginning to wonder when you planned to check in?"

Ward had meant it as a mild rebuke.

"The peelers got too close, so we had to move fast, and Jimmy's been keepin' us in. I only got out tonight because he needs me to lift a cold car."

Ward sat down on the arm of a chair.

"What's the plan for the little girl?"

"Jimmy knows they won't trade, so he's gonna kill her when the deadline passes."

The girl's death would focus American hatred squarely on the Provos, and to Ward's way of thinking, that could prove to be a plus.

"By the way," Kelly added, "he's got another job planned before we leave LA."

"What job?" Ward asked.

"There's an exhibit on loan from the London Museum of Natural History. It opens today at the Getty Museum in Malibu. He wants to blow it up this afternoon."

"Blow up the art?" Ward was truly offended.

"Not the art. The mayor and some celebrities will be there, and since we've got a little Semtex left, he wants to blow a car in the parkin' garage."

Ward's mind raced over the plan. An attack against celebrities? That would guarantee unparalleled media attention. Cassidy was truly a madman, but this was better than he'd ever imagined.

"Where are you stayin'?" Ward asked.

"He's got us in a house in a city called Lancaster. It's out in the desert."

Ward thought for a moment. "If he does the museum today, will you be goin' back to the house?"

"We have to go back and clean it out."

Ward smiled. This was almost too easy. "What's the address?" he asked.

"For the museum?"

"No... no! For the house in Lancaster?"

Kelly was silent for a moment, then, "I think it's 4004 Avenue 26.

"Thank you, Shamrock. Keep in touch."

****

TWENTY-NINE

October 8, Wednesday, Early Morning

"Have we got him?" Whitney asked.

They were seated around a table in the makeshift conference room next to the hanger where they had just listened to the conversation between Kelly and Ward for the second time.

"Not yet," Elwood replied. "You can't prove a thing from that tape."

"But he went along with the plan to do the bombin'," Gibson told him.

Elwood shook his head.

"If you took him down now, Ward would say that Kelly was just an informant gone bad. He'd claim that he was stringing him along to set him up for an arrest. It all depends on what he does now."

Whitney realized Elwood was right. If Ward called him back and warned them about the bomb, and if he gave them the address in time to save the girl, then he could plausibly claim that he was never involved. The tape was really worthless. They had to have more.

Whitney gazed at his watch. There were decisions to make and time was running out. Soon enough the truth about what happened to the terrorists was going to get out.

Lieutenant Michaels stuck his head in the conference room door and knocked on the doorframe.

"Excuse me, sir, they want you over at the van. You've got a call comin' in on the secure line."

Whitney hurried to the van and picked up the phone. Was it Ward?

"This is Andrew Whitney," he said cautiously.

"Major? This is Wellesley."

Lord Peter Wellesley was the Director of MI-6, (Military Intelligence, Department 6), the group responsible for foreign intelligence gathering.

"I hope you have good news for me?"

"We got lucky, Major. In fact, we got more than we bargained for. We put a tap on Wards' secure line, and after he had spoken with your informant, he used the same phone to talk with John Carrington."

Whitney was stunned. Carrington was the *Secretary of State for Defense*.

Wellesley said, "It might interest you to know that the two of them apparently concocted this little scheme to undermine the peace process in Northern Ireland."

"That doesn't make any sense, sir. What could they possibly hope to gain?"

"Power, money. Maybe both. It's not a new story. Carrington wants to be the next Prime Minister, and he likely believes that if the truce falls apart, the current PM will get a no confidence vote. That would leave the job open. Carrington has always been perceived as a man of action, so he probably feels that he's next in line for the job."

Whitney shook his head. "And Ward?"

"My guess would be that he wants to keep his budget up. There's been a lot of talk recently about cutting his operation now that we've got a truce. Also, I suppose if Carrington became Prime Minister, then Ward might end up as Secretary of State for Defense."

Whitney exhaled heavily. "If I'd followed my orders, they might have pulled it off."

Wellesley chuckled.

"It's a good thing for all of us that you didn't, Major. By the way, the Prime Minister has asked me to convey to you his congratulations on a job well done. He was particularly delighted to know that the child is safe."

"Thank you, sir. What happens now?"

"I've discussed this with the PM, and he believes that we need to take Ward and Carrington into custody as soon as possible. Both of them have access to very sensitive information, so it's important that we get them before they flee the country."

For the first time, Whitney truly grasped the significance of arresting these two men. It would shake the very core of the British government, not to mention what it would do to relations with the United States.

"How do you want me to handle it if Ward calls here?" Whitney asked. "He's probably goin' to give us the address in Lancaster."

"Don't worry about that, Major. He told Carrington he'd call you and tell you where the child was only after Cassidy plants the bomb at the museum. So I suspect he won't be calling for a while, and we should have him in custody before you have to worry about it."

Whitney was relieved.

"Do you want me to say anythin' here about what's goin' on?"

"If it's possible, the PM has asked that we keep it completely quiet. He's meeting now with his Cabinet, and I suspect they will be calling the President of the United States within a few hours. I'm sure you realize that this matter will have to be resolved at the highest levels, and containment, for the moment, is paramount."

"I understand, sir."

"For the time being, the PM has asked me to oversee your operation until we get things sorted out. Can you give me a status report?"

Whitney spent the next ten minutes describing the state of their information on Collins, Carlson, and McCrossen.

"Are you asking me what to do with these people?" Wellesley asked.

"Yes, sir. I am."

"Well, Major, I would imagine that the first thing you should do is find out if there's enough evidence to prosecute them in the States? If so, then take them into custody. Or better yet, let the Americans do it."

"And if there isn't enough?"

"Use your best judgment, Major. Whatever you do, we want to wrap it up as quickly as possible. Your objective is to neutralize these people so that no more innocents get hurt."

****

Whitney shook his head slowly as he walked back to the conference room. Wellesley had given him enormous discretion—the power of life and death over the three peripheral players—but just as predictably, he'd made it crystal clear that Whitney would also have to shoulder the blame if something went wrong.

He urged himself to be cautious. He was not at war and this was not Northern Ireland. If he ordered any one of the three to be killed, he might end up in the cold—twisting in the wind—facing an inquiry or something even worse. On the other hand, his government would want to keep things under wraps, but would that happen if people were arrested?

No matter what he decided to do, he knew he was going to be second guessed.

He walked into the conference room and found the others still seated around the table. They looked up at him expectantly.

"Our problem in London is solved," he said with a smile. "Ward made a call after ours and implicated a co-conspirator. The whole thing's been recorded by MI-6."

There were applause and smiles all around.

Elwood said, "That means it doesn't matter if he calls us back?"

"That's right." Whitney replied.

Gibson sat back in his chair.

"Who'd he call, Whit?"

Whitney tried to blow it off with a sheepish grin.

"I'd rather not say at the moment. You know, national security interest and all that."

Gibson raised his eyebrow.

"Just trust me. It's bein' taken care of."

Elwood leaned forward.

"So what do we do with Lisa Collins and Mark Carlson?"

"Have you got enough to make a case against either one of 'em?"

"Not yet," Elwood said. "We've got them both under surveillance at the moment, but nothing's happened so far. Did Kelly or Harris give you anything to tie them in?"

Whitney shook his head. "Both of 'em knew there was someone on the inside feeding information to a member of their team, but both professed ignorance when it came to knowing who that was."

"Then we've got no way to tie 'em in," said Gibson. "Everyone else directly connected with this case is dead." He thought for a moment longer. "I hate even to suggest it, Tom, but what if we offer Carlson a deal?"

"To give up Collins?"

"Sure, why not? She's the heavy in this case."

Elwood twisted in his chair. "There's no way we can justify giving that bastard a break."

"Then you'll never get either one," Whitney said. "Even if Carlson told you he gave her information, you can't prove she did anythin' with it. You've reached a dead end."

Elwood set his jaw. He was truly upset. "I can't believe they're gonna get away with this," he said.

There was silence around the table as they contemplated their dilemma.

When Whitney finally spoke up, he said, "I'll take care of Collins."

Gibson cocked his head.

"What does that mean?"

Whitney's face became impassive.

"It means I'll deal with her accordin' to my orders."

"Hold on," said Elwood with a shake of his head. "I can't go along with that."

"I'm not askin' you to. She's our problem now, not yours. She's a British national, and pursuant to my orders, that gives me jurisdiction. It's Carlson that poses the problem."

"Must be Carlson's lucky day," Elwood said. There was a touch of sarcasm in his voice. "At least he's gonna get a fair trial."

Whitney gave him a withering look.

"Look, Captain, let's not mince words. I'm here to do a job, nothing more. While I'm not particularly proud of what I have to do, the fact remains that we're operatin' under a different set of rules. What I do is sanctioned by my government, and at the moment, by yours as well. So I'd appreciate it if you'd simply recognize that fact and reserve judgment for some other time."

"That doesn't make it right," Elwood told him.

"No, it doesn't make it right. But it's not a perfect world. Lettin' her go free is not right either. Remember, she's responsible for killin' a lot of innocent people. Don't lose sight of that."

Elwood nodded. "I understand where you're coming from. If you're asserting jurisdiction over Collins, then she's yours. I'll call off my people whenever you say, but Carlson's a different matter. He has to face our laws."

"Fair enough," Whitney said. "And how about McCrossen?"

"I forgot all about him." Elwood ran his hand across the stubble on his face. "We're gonna have a hell of a time connecting him to the case."

When no one said anything further, Whitney stood up and started for the door.

"You won't have to worry about him, Tom. Just forget you ever heard his name."

****

Homa sat on a couch in the lobby of the Bonaventure, a large hotel in downtown Los Angeles. He'd secreted his men throughout the hotel lobby to make sure that all of the exits were covered. The lateness of the hour meant there were fewer people around, and that decreased the likelihood of Lisa Collins getting past them.

A Cuban LAPD officer disguised as a bellhop floated around the hallway just outside her room. Shortly after midnight, he reported that she'd turned off her television. This convinced Homa that she'd called it a night.

Patience was his long suit; you didn't last long in Internal Affairs without it.

He got up, stretched his legs, and walked around a bit before moving to a table in the lobby bar where he settled in once again to wait for further instructions.

His cell phone vibrated at three-thirty a.m. It was Magarian calling him from the station.

"What's up, Lieutenant?" he asked.

"Where is she?"

"Still bedded down in her room."

"Okay, I want you to pull the team off her and report back to the PAB."

"What? Why?"

"Because I said to."

To Homa, this didn't make sense.

"What's going on, LT? We can't just let her walk out of here?"

"She's not gonna walk away, John. Elwood just called. There's a British commando team en route to your location."

"But we can take her. What do we need them for?"

"Elwood says there are other fish they're working on, and this will be done on the QT, so it doesn't interfere with their bigger operation."

Homa was losing his temper.

"Don't tell me they're gonna cut her a deal?"

"I don't think that's what this is all about, amigo. I have the feeling that something's going on that we don't want to know about. *Comprende*?"

Homa gave it a moments thought.

"Plausible deniability, eh? How soon till they get here?"

"Their ETA is twenty-five minutes."

"Okay, boss. We'll be out of here by then."

Homa found a quiet corner, took out his rover, and put out a call to his team. Within five minutes, they were out of the hotel and on their way back to the PAB.

****

First Sergeant Stephens and three of his men arrived at the Bonaventure shortly after three am. Dressed in sports coats and slacks, they looked like ordinary businessmen returning from a late night out.

Stephens opened up the trunk of their car and pulled out a large, rectangular, suitcase. He unfolded a portable luggage caddy, slipped it under the suitcase, and pulled it behind them as they entered the hotel.

The lobby was quiet, so they split up, and using separate elevators, they headed up to the eleventh floor. During the ride up, each man put on surgical gloves.

Her room was centered in the southern tower. One of the men opened a briefcase and removed a fiber-optic cable which he inserted very slowly under the door. They watched on a monitor in the briefcase as the cable scanned the inside of her room.

She'd thrown the deadbolt. There was no way they'd get in unless she opened the door. They pushed the cable in further—past the entry to the bathroom—and discovered her sleeping in the bed.

Stephens signaled the technician to withdraw the cable, and after a few moments of discussion, he opted to go to their fallback plan.

One of the men left the group and walked down the stairwell to the ninth floor. When he was sure that no one else was around, he pulled a wall mounted fire alarm, then ducked back into the stairwell. He went to the tenth floor, picked up a lobby phone, and dialed the number for Lisa Collins room.

The alarm screeched loudly in five-second bursts throughout the upper floors of the hotel. In a matter of moments, people would start to come out of their rooms.

Stephens began to worry that they'd cut it too close, and he was just about to signal the others to withdraw from the floor, when he heard the phone ring in her room.

****

"Miss Collins?" said the male voice. She nearly dropped the receiver as she struggled to get up into a sitting position.

"Yes?"

The sound of an alarm of some kind began to register in her consciousness. What could it be? Was an elevator stuck?

"Miss Collins, this is the front desk calling. We've got a fire alarm on the ninth floor and smoke is reported on some of the upper floors. We don't think it's serious, but please leave your room immediately, and for your safety, use the stairwell on the south side of the hotel."

"Who is this?" she asked. She was not awake enough to grasp the full import of his words.

"This is the front desk, Miss Collins. We're calling all of the rooms on the upper floors. Please evacuate immediately. This is not a drill."

The caller hung up, and as she listened to the dial tone, his warning finally sank in.

She hung up the phone, now fully awake. She turned on the light, jumped out of bed, and pulled on a pair of jeans. She found her shirt, and once it was buttoned, she stuffed her feet into a pair of cowboy boots and began to search for her gun.

She found it on the nightstand, next to her purse. She grabbed them both, walked to the door, and unlatched both of the locks.

****

Stephens heard the locks open and watched as she turned the knob. As the door cracked open, he used his shoulder and hit it full force with the weight of his body. It swung wide open and knocked her to the floor. The others pushed in, someone closed the door, and together they attempted to pin her to the floor.

At first, they struggled in silence. When she tried to scream, one of the men covered her mouth with his hand. She bit him for his trouble, drawing blood, and he let out a yell as he pulled his hand away.

Then someone punched her twice in the face. She was stronger than she looked. She twisted and thrashed, then brought up her knee and caught Stephens flush in the groin.

His grip on her arms relaxed, but not long enough to enable her to break free. He rolled to his side, his back to her face, and held one arm while he tried to catch his breath. His pain turned to nausea as he struggled for control.

"Hurry up!" he said between clenched teeth, and the struggle renewed with a flurry of blows.

"She's got a gun." yelled one of his men. More punches were thrown until her body went slack.

"Got it." said a voice.

Stephens used his weight to hold down her arm while someone stuffed a cloth in her mouth.

One of the men produced a syringe and emptied the contents into her arm.

Stephens rolled away. He lay on the floor, reached for his groin, and groaned. While the nausea had subsided, he knew he'd be sore for a couple of days. He got to his knees and finally to his feet. Standing up straight was a chore.

He looked down at her body. A huge crimson bruise was forming on her forehead, just above the socket of her left eye. He reached down and felt for a pulse in her neck. It was strong.

"Let's get her into the suitcase," he said.

They wheeled it over, lifted her up, and stuffed her unconscious body inside.

"She fought like a tiger," said one. "Scratched me good on the face."

"I don't know why we don't just kill her," said another.

"Enough talkin'," Stephens said. "The Major knows what he's doin'. She's goin' back to London with us, and once we get her home, she'll be gettin' what she deserves."

He glanced around at the room.

"Now, pack up her things and wipe it all down. There's to be no sign of a struggle."

****

The Blackmore Club was located in a stately old manor house on McGovern Road; a five-minute walk from Hyde Park. For seventy years it had served as a meeting place for top government officials, and the dignified atmosphere was heavily accentuated by the warm woods, rich fabrics, and priceless accessories collected for decades from throughout the British Empire.

At half-past eight a.m., Ward received a call from Carrington's office requesting a meeting at the Blackmore. Ward had been a member there for a number of years, so he quickly cleared his schedule—postponing a meeting on his budget—and hurried over to the Blackmore, arriving nearly twenty minutes early. He settled into a comfortable chair by a window in the second-floor library, a book-filled room he thoroughly enjoyed when he wanted to be alone to pursue some quiet reading.

In the last several years, with most of the domestic security funding aimed at the global Islamist threat, scant attention was being paid to the threat being posed to the UK by the successful Russian and Chinese efforts to steal British industrial secrets. The threat they posed to the nation was real, and the result of their actions took bread from the mouths of hard-working, middle-class families. The unemployment rate was still going up, and it would continue to do so unless and until the members of Parliament came to their senses and recognized the true enemies who were right on their doorstep.

Ever since the cease fire with the IRA, the PM and the Parliament had grown complacent about internal defense. Now was not the time for them to cut back on domestic security spending, but they had, preferring instead to spend the money they saved by doing so on domestic programs that doled out precious resources that kept the current government winning electoral votes.

But he and Carrington had seen the threat, and they'd done their level best to sound the warning, but those fools in Parliament had all but abandoned the country by turning a blind eye towards the pointed warnings, and by choosing instead to let slip away whatever advantage the service once possessed when it had the resources it desperately needed to deal with the enemies on so many fronts.

It was Carrington who was the first to realize that what was sorely needed was a wake-up call for the nation; a terrorist incident that would so completely embarrass the government for it's inability to gather preemptive intelligence that it would force the sitting government to rethink its current position on the most recent cuts to the defense intelligence budget.

And what better way to bring things to a head than to have an incident conducted by a hated enemy, the IRA; a group the politicos had wanted to believe no longer posed a threat. There would be outrage on both sides of the political spectrum, and with the finger of blame pointed squarely at the current government, there would be calls for quick action; action that could be expected to require a large infusion of cash.

Of course, the Prime Minister would never agree to sign off on a dramatic increase in the intelligence budget. His hold on the office was based upon a policy of fiscal austerity. That would put him at odds with the general populace, and that, in turn, would put pressures on the members of his very own party.

In the end, signing off could very likely cost him his job.

The true genius of Carrington's plan was the fact that it went a long way towards completely undermining the provisions of the Irish accord. To Ward's way of thinking, the bloody cease-fire had been nothing short of a disaster; providing the Provos with the time and incentive they needed to rearm themselves for another go. Ward smiled to himself. PIRA hatred ran deep and was now quite fresh. His budget would swell, his power would increase, and if he played it just right—if Carrington became Prime Minister—then Ward just might just end up in charge of the countries defenses.

He felt a twinge of regret that historians might never come to appreciate the true genius of Lord Carrington's tactical plan, but secrecy would be critical for their long-term success, and they were so very close to achieving their goal.

His musings were interrupted when the door to the library swung open and four large men in overcoats walked over to his chair.

Ward recognized Peter Wellesley of MI-6 and tried to conceal his surprise.

Wellesley wasted no time with pleasantries.

"Good evening, Colonel. These gentlemen are from New Scotland Yard, and I'm afraid we'll have to ask you to come with us."

Ward stayed in his chair, preferring to conceal his confusion by ignoring the request.

"Please stand up, sir," said a Chief Inspector from the Yard. He pulled out a set of handcuffs.

Ward made no effort to rise. Instead, he shifted his gaze to Wellesley.

"What the bloody hell do you think you're doin'?"

"You're being detained under the War Powers Act, Colonel. The charge is treason. Please stand up and allow us to handle this with a measure of dignity."

Ward looked from face to face but saw nothing in the way of support. He stood up slowly and held out his hands while the Chief Inspector snapped on the cuffs.

"You're making a big mistake, Wellesley. I've done nothing to warrant this type of treatment."

Wellesley shook his head. "Actually, Colonel, you've done quite a bit."

"Rubbish!"

Ward stared at Wellesley with complete disdain.

"We have a statement from an acquaintance of yours," Wellesley said softly.

"I believe his name is Michael Kelly. But of course, you know him as

Shamrock."

Ward felt his legs growing weak.

"And we also have a statement from Lord Carrington—"

Wards' heart began to pound and a shooting pain traveled outward from the center of his chest.

"—who I'm pleased to say has also been taken into custody."

Ward felt nauseous. His breath became more shallow and much harder to draw.

"We've monitored a number of your calls," Wellesley continued. "In particular, a call you made to Carrington after hearing from Mr. Kelly." He smiled again. "Do you remember what you said, sir? You advised Lord Carrington that you'd give Major Whitney the location of the terrorists only after they had an opportunity to plant another bomb. Is it starting to come back to you now?"

Ward's face became ashen. He collapsed to his knees and pitched forward, striking his face on the floor.

Wellesley reached down and felt his neck for a pulse.

"Call an ambulance," he said. "I believe he's had a heart attack."

****

THIRTY

Later That Same Day

By two that afternoon, a story was leaked to the press that Julie Marin had been rescued and all of the terrorists were dead. Local Los Angeles political leaders scrambled to issue press statements, all of them giving credit to the Special Air Service for having prevented any further loss of life.

The Justice Department, under express orders from the President, released a statement that justified the SAS operation on American soil. Cited among the reasons were international precedent, goodwill between allies, and confidential intelligence in the hands of the British relating to these particular terrorists. In the euphoria that followed the success of the raid, the reasons were accepted without serious question. After all, the only casualties were the terrorists, and to the public's way of thinking, the terrorists had it coming.

The Acting United States Attorney for the Central District held a press conference to confirm that Renée Marin had been dealing with confidential intelligence sources in London to obtain information on the whereabouts of her daughter. Under questioning by local reporters, he issued an unequivocal denial that there had ever been a warrant for her arrest. He ventured an opinion that the District Attorney of Los Angeles had apparently been misinformed.

The Los Angeles Police Department, in a statement issued by the Chief, described at length their long-term cooperation with the SAS, and the fact that three of their Major Crimes officers had assisted the SAS in the successful completion of *Operation Archangel.*

The Los Angeles County Sheriff's Department released a statement which explained that the previous night's deceptive story concerning the supposed capture of two armed-robbery suspects was necessary to enable the SAS to complete its operation without further risk to human life. The Sheriff was pleased to announce that they'd recovered kilos of Semtex from the house where the child was being held.

All in all, nearly every law enforcement governmental agency basked in the glory of victory as the city breathed a collective sigh of relief. Talk radio shows, the bell-weather of public opinion, fielded a record number of calls supporting the British intervention in the terrorist situation. Considering that there was praise enough for everyone involved, it seemed curious to many that there was no official statement coming from the Office of the District Attorney.

****

Rosen had sequestered himself in his office and bemoaned the fact that he'd acted too quickly in going to the press. He could lay the blame on Agent Fletcher of the FBI, but what good would that do? Fletcher would cover his ass by claiming that Rosen had misunderstood the situation and that the DA should've checked things out before going public with the news.

His secretary buzzed; it was Kerin on the line. Did Rosen want to take the call?

It galled him to know that Kerin was undoubtedly saying *I told you so* behind his back. He couldn't dodge him forever, so he punched up the button for the speaker phone.

"What do you want, Glenn?" he asked.

"I just heard from Renée Marin."

Rosen detected a smugness to his tone.

"*And..?*"

"She wants immediate reinstatement as Head Deputy of her division."

"I presume you told her that was fine?"

"Of course," Kerin said. "She plans to take a one-month leave of absence to spend some time with her daughter. After that, she said she would resume her work on the Cassidy case."

"Maybe we should take her off that case," Rosen said. "We could--"

"That would be a big mistake, Aaron. I already suggested the same thing. I told her that after all she'd been through, we'd completely understand if she felt the case should be reassigned."

"And?"

"She got angry and said we'd never make that suggestion to a male deputy."

Rosen put his hand to his head. This seemed to be getting worse.

"What'd you tell her, Glenn?"

"I told her to keep the case. I decided we didn't need a Civil Service hearing based on a claim of gender bias."

"It never ends." Rosen moaned. He was thoroughly dejected. "She's got me over a god-damned barrel."

"There's one more thing, Aaron. In about an hour she's holding a press conference over at the PAB."

"What? She didn't clear it with me."

"Did you expect me to tell her she couldn't do it?"

Rosen leaned back in his chair and rubbed his temples. An excruciating headache had settled in squarely across his brow.

"No, I suppose there's no way to stop her. Did she happen to mention what she's going to say?"

"She didn't," Kerin said. "But does it really matter?"

****

The auditorium at the Police Administration Building was located in a separate ground floor facility. It was able to accommodate a sizable gathering of the press.

Within fifteen minutes of the announcement that Renée was going to make a statement, the room had filled to capacity, and those reporters who couldn't get in were forced to make due with a live feed line to a TV monitor set up in a second, but smaller, nearby room.

Inside the conference room, a bank of television cameras was set up in front of the stage. Nearly a hundred reporters from all over the world milled about and waited impatiently for the conference to begin.

Upstairs, on the top floor of the adjacent building, Whitney, Gibson, Donahue, and Elwood stood together while the Chief greeted Renée Marin and her daughter in the foyer of his office.

"You're a very lucky young lady," the Chief said to Julie. "Those British Commandos did one heck of a job."

"It was scary," Julie said.

The Chief laughed. "I'll bet it was."

Gibson whispered to Renée. "Are you ready to get this over with?"

"The sooner, the better."

"Good. Here's the plan. We'll go downstairs, you make your statement, and as soon as you're tired of the questions, give me a nod. I've arranged for an escort to get you out of the building. They'll take you to the airport and get you on your way."

"I wish I was going with you," Elwood said. "My wife's been pestering me to take her to Hawaii."

"So why don't you join us?" Renee said with a smile.

"Too much to do here. It'll take me weeks to wrap up all the loose ends."

"Well, I'll be thinking of you when I lift a Mai-tai and watch the sun as it slowly sets over the Pacific."

"I hope you have better things to do than think about us," Elwood told her. He gave her a warm and generous smile.

"You ready to start?" Gibson asked.

Renée nodded. She turned to her daughter.

"Honey, you stay here with Detective Donahue. This won't take too long. I'll be back in just a few minutes and then we'll get out of here."

"We can watch your mom on the Chief's TV," Donahue said with a smile. She took Julie's hand and led her over to a couch in the office.

Gibson led Renée and Whitney to a waiting elevator, and once they reached the ground level floor, he walked them into the nearby auditorium.

When Renée was spotted, a number of still cameras began going off. The TV cameras went to live feed while the on-scene reporters made their introductions.

Renée reached the podium and looked out over the audience.

"Thank you for coming here on such short notice. I wanted a chance to say a few things before I take a brief leave of absence. So, here goes.

"During the investigation of the assassinations of Major Sean Clarke and his adjutant Paul Whitcomb, I had the distinct pleasure of working with Detectives Ulysses Gibson, Jennifer Donahue, Captain Tom Elwood, and other members of the Major Crimes Section of the Los Angeles Police Department's Robbery-

Homicide Division. Their professionalism and thoroughness led to the capture of Liam Cassidy, who is currently charged with committing those killings.

"James Cassidy, the older brother of Liam Cassidy, was a longtime member of the Irish Republican Army and the leader of a cell of terrorists in England. To force us to release his brother, he brought his group to Los Angeles and began a series of attacks which caused the deaths of many people and extensive property damage. When that didn't work, they carried out the kidnapping of my daughter, believing it would force us into negotiations."

She could feel her emotions beginning to surface, but the moment quickly passed, and she forced herself to go on without breaking.

"The responsible law enforcement officials in this state took the position that it would be a very dangerous precedent to negotiate with the terrorists, and while I'm not going to pretend that I supported that position, I've come to realize that this is a policy that must be adhered to. We must never deal with terrorists. Once you do, no prosecutor, police officer, judge or public official will ever be able to do their job without the risk of subjecting their loved ones to personal attacks."

She looked over at Gibson and gave him a smile.

"The detectives assigned to locate my daughter were forced to work against a very short deadline. You have no idea how unselfish and hard-working these people have been. They left no stone unturned in their search for my child, and it was their work that led to the first break in the search. We were privileged to have them on our side, and for all their hard work, my daughter and I will be eternally grateful."

She looked over at Whitney. He smiled and gave her a nod.

"Sources in London and Ireland provided the final break in this case, and I will always be in debt to the members of the British Special Air Service who risked their lives to save my daughter.

"I want to conclude by saying that I firmly believe the terrorist acts committed by the Cassidy's and their group should not be allowed to derail the current cease-fire agreement in Northern Ireland. Just as we should not negotiate with terrorists on an individual basis, no actions by a splinter group should be allowed to turn the tide of public opinion against any process that stresses negotiations and peace.

"Thank you again for your prayers and support."

The reaction to her remarks was immediate and loud. Photographers snapped pictures from every direction, and reporters began to shout out their questions. Renée raised her hand for silence and waited for the room to quiet down.

"I'll entertain a few questions if they're one at a time."

She pointed to a reporter near the front.

"Why did you leave the country?" he asked.

"I flew to London and met with several confidential sources in the intelligence community. They were able to come up with the address in Lancaster. Next question?"

A woman near the back shouted out, "Have you met with District Attorney Rosen yet? And if so, has he returned you to your assignment?"

She smiled. "I have not met with Mr. Rosen, but I have spoken to the Chief Deputy, and he has assured me that I have been reinstated to my former position as Head Deputy of the Organized Crime and Terrorism Division."

She pointed to a man who was seated in the second row.

"You said you were taking a leave of absence. Is that at the request of your office or the police department? And are you still in any danger?"

"I'm not in any danger, and the leave of absence is at my request. I want to spend some time with my daughter. When I get back, I'll resume my responsibilities on the Cassidy case."

"Mrs. Marin," said a TV reporter, "do you have any comment about the adequacy of the protection that was provided to your daughter?"

She thought about that for a long moment before answering.

"The fact that two investigators were killed in cold blood while trying to protect my daughter would indicate to me that there was no way to anticipate what was going to happen."

"But are you satisfied with what was provided?" he persisted.

"I'm satisfied that we're all vulnerable to determined terrorists. But when I get back, I plan to discuss with the District Attorney some ideas I have about improving our security." Her eyes swept the room. "Thanks again everyone. I've got a plane to catch."

She nodded to Gibson, and suddenly a group of uniformed Metropolitan Division officers entered the room and escorted her through the throng. A spontaneous round of applause broke out from the press corps, and when someone shouted out that she should run for DA, it was greeted with spontaneous cheers of agreement.

Renée and Julie were quickly taken to a waiting undercover car. The Metropolitan Division's Special Protection Detail had been assigned to escort them to the airport, and their vehicles were lined up to form a motorcade.

Under the watchful eye of a uniformed officer, Julie was placed into the back seat of one of the transport cars.

Renée paused to say goodbye to Gibson, Donahue, and Elwood, and when Whitney walked up, they gave him a chance to speak to her alone.

"I don't know how I can ever thank you, Whit," she started.

He gave her a hug.

"You already have."

She smiled.

"So what's next for you?"

"Can't say. I've got some loose ends to clean up, and I've been sworn to secrecy."

"Oh?" Her smile was joyless and betrayed her disappointment. "Well, I guess this is good-bye."

Whitney reached up and held her by the shoulders.

"Listen, Renée. If you can find your way to London, I'd really love to show you around."

"I'd like that, too."

He studied her eyes for a moment, then leaned over and looked into the car.

"Take care of yourself, Julie."

"I will, and don't forget you owe me a ride in a helicopter."

"You just had one," he said.

"I know, but I want to do it again."

He laughed out loud. "I won't forget."

"Whit," Renée said when he caught her glance, "if you get back to LA, give me a call."

He pulled her close and gave her a kiss.

"Take care," he said.

Once she was seated in the back of the car, Whitney slapped his hand twice on the trunk, giving the driver the signal to go.

As the motorcade moved out, Julie's head popped up in the car's rear window.

She looked back at Whitney, then smiled and waved.

****

Aaron Rosen snapped off the television. Sitting alone in his office, he felt as though all of his energy had been sapped. His heart was beating too quickly, and a line of perspiration had formed on his brow. He pulled out a handkerchief and blotted his forehead.

Involuntarily, his hand reached down, and he grabbed for his stomach; the searing sensation just wouldn't go away.

Her news conference had spelled the end of his quest for the Governorship, and would likely cost him his future as the County's DA.

She'd nailed him cold for extremely bad judgment, and she'd been given an ovation to boot. It was a masterful performance. The members of the press were eating right out of her hand.

He opened his desk drawer and pulled out a half-pint of scotch. In spite of the pain in his stomach, he needed a drink to settle his nerves.

He took a healthy swig, gulped it down, then promptly threw it up in the basket by his desk.

My God! he thought. *What a way to end a career.*

****

Barrett McCrossen was seated at his desk high above *the Miracle Mile*, a stretch of high-rise office buildings and retail stores in the mid-Wilshire section of Los Angeles. The decor was luxurious. He had a penchant for walnut paneling, red leather furniture, and *objet d'art*. His walls displayed an extensive collection of Southwestern Indian artifacts, including Navajo rugs and Hopi Indian pottery. Collecting was his passion, and he indulged himself without shame.

It was almost nine-thirty at night, and he was ready to leave the office. In the light of a Tiffany lamp on the corner of his desk, he'd been working on a set of contracts for the purchase of a sizable tract of land for the Catholic Church. The details of the purchase were laborious and exhausting, and he knew that he badly needed a break.

He sat back, rubbed his temples, and let his thoughts drift to the terrorists and their untimely deaths.

Only Cassidy and McGarry could connect him to the group; a condition he'd demanded from the start, and their deaths had insured the severance of the link. After twenty-plus years of providing financial support, he'd been flattered when they'd asked him to assist their operation. He'd agreed to let Liam use his boat in the Marina as a hideout, and he'd arranged to help McGarry get the Semtex into the States. But now he was having second thoughts about his past involvement. It was one thing to go against legitimate military targets and quite another to take part in the killing of civilians.

He stretched again. The contracts could wait; it was time to go home. He put them in a folder on his desk.

The hair on the back of his neck stood up. He could sense that there was someone in the room.

A black gloved hand placed a pistol against the back of his head. McCrossen froze in fear while someone roped him to the chair and placed a gag inside his mouth.

His eyes darted from figure to figure. There were four of them, and all were wearing balaclava hoods.

It must be a robbery! What else could it be?

One of the men went through his desk. After checking several drawers, he pulled out a .38 caliber air weight from beneath a box of envelopes and placed the loaded gun to McCrossen's right temple.

McCrossen's eyes grew wide as the hammer cocked back on the gun, and he cringed with fear as he waited for the inevitable.

But the man never pulled the trigger.

"Hey mate," said one of the men. "You pissed your pants."

McCrossen looked down at his lap. The man was right.

Amid the group laughter, another man stepped forward. He grabbed Mc-Crossen's chin and forced up his head. "The Americans wanted to take you down themselves. They know you helped the Cassidy's get their Semtex into the country. But we talked it over, and before they come for you, we wanted to give you a message."

McCrossen could feel the man's breath on his face.

"We took a vote, McCrossen," the man continued, and while some of the men want you dead, the majority of the Regiment decided you should live with a reminder of what you've sown."

He pulled a small caliber handgun from behind his back and pressed it against McCrossen's right knee. "Here's a little somethin' to remember us by."

He fired a shot which shattered McCrossen's kneecap.

McCrossen let out a scream that was muffled by the gag.

The man moved the gun to McCrossens left knee and fired a second shot.

McCrossen screamed again before passing out.

The shooter shook him roughly and brought him back up.

"You'll never walk again," he said, "and this will serve as a warnin' to others who think they can do what you did without payin' a price." He grabbed him by the chin and squeezed him hard. "Your days as a Provo are over."

The four men then started for the door, but their leader stopped mid-stride, turned around, and walked back. He untied the rope and let McCrossen slump forward against the top of his desk.

McCrossen pulled the gag from his mouth and slowly reached out for the phone on his desk.

The man stopped him with a hand on his wrist.

"After I'm gone, you can call for some help; but I'm warnin' you now. If you try to grass us out, or if you get involved with the Provo's again, we'll be back to finish the job."

****

Mark Carlson was at home when they came for him. He was dozing in a chair in his den.

"Wake up Carlson."

Deputy Chief George Taylor gave Carlson's shoulder a solid shove.

Tall and well groomed, Taylor was a man of extraordinary willpower, and it took everything he had not to slap Carlson silly.

"Get on your feet, Carlson. We're going downtown."

Carlson struggled to get out of the chair.

"Hook him up," Taylor ordered when he got to his feet, and the detectives from IA cuffed him, hands behind his back.

"What's going on?" his wife demanded as she entered the room.

Taylor turned to face her.

"Mrs. Carlson, your husband is under arrest for providing information to a member of the IRA."

"What?" Carlson looked befuddled. "I don't know anyone with the IRA."

Taylor ignored him and spoke directly to Carlson's wife.

"He's been having an affair with an IRA female who used the name of Lisa Collins. She posed as a reporter, and he provided her with confidential information which allowed the terrorists to avoid arrest."

She glanced over at her husband.

"Mark? Is this true?"

All he could do was stare, and in the face of the accusation, his silence provided the answer.

"*You bastard!*" she said. She turned away and walked from the room.

Taylor turned to his men.

"Let's go."

"You prick!" Carlson's anger took over. "You had no right to tell her that."

Taylor gritted his teeth.

"You listen to me, you punk. If the choice were mine, I'd kill you right now and be done with it, but there are others who insist on doing things by the book. Your difficulties with your wife are the least of your problems. You're responsible for the deaths of your fellow police officers, and when that news goes public,

I wouldn't want to be in your shoes."

****

Two hours later, while he continued to deny his affair, they played him the tape of the monitored call. Confronted with this proof, Carlson began to tell the truth, and as his shame increased, so did his despair.

They tortured him in hushed tones with talk about his life behind bars as an inmate; how he would constantly have to be looking over his shoulder; and how his beloved wife and children would quickly tire of coming to see him. And by the time they were finished, he was thoroughly destroyed. A man now destined to live a life that most would call a hell on earth.

They never told him they had no case; they just wanted to soften him up; to play with his mind so they could see what he'd say and what he'd admit.

But shortly after he was taken to a holding cell, Carlson suffered an anxiety attack that required his hospitalization.

****

EPILOGUE

Arrangements were made for Claire Harris to live in a village near Thurberry, in England. She was provided with a small stipend, enough to maintain a flat and to cover her food. She found herself a job waiting on tables at a tourist hotel.

Before starting her new life, she was thoroughly debriefed by MI-6 on videotape. To keep her in line, Wellesley informed her that if she ever left the village without their permission, a copy of the tape, along with her whereabouts, would be given to the IRA.

She'd been sentenced to life in the village of Thurberry, a sentence she was grateful to have.

****

After Ward's fatal heart attack, Michael Kelly was called to testify at a military tribunal in London. He gave his story to the magistrate, and along with the tape, they found John Carrington guilty of treason.

Carrington was sentenced to life in prison.

The Prime Minister, in an appearance before Parliament, advised the country of Carrington's complicity in the scheme. He apologized to the American people, and the citizens of Ireland and he vowed that the actions of the terrorists would not interfere with the truce.

****

After the Carrington tribunal had been completed, Kelly was taken to a safe house in Edinburgh, Scotland. There he was questioned for more than a week by a carefully chosen team from MI-6. He told them what he knew, and based upon his word, a number of terrorist sympathizers in Ireland were rounded up and later presented for trial.

Like other informants before him, Kelly was given a break. A military tribunal sentenced him to fifteen years of semi-isolation at a military base on the

Isle of Wight.

****

Lisa Collins was returned to London. MI-6 took special delight in breaking her down. They used chemicals, isolation, and sleep deprivation, and by the time they were finished, she'd given up everyone she knew.

She too received a trial in a military court and was convicted under the War Powers Act. She was sentenced to life in a prison in a facility called the *Maze*.

****

Liam Cassidy was escorted each day back and forth from his cell to the jail law library. His arms were chained to his waist, and the escort deputy paid him little attention; it was purely routine, day in and day out.

In the cell next door, the Sheriffs had placed an inmate brought down from San Quentin's death row. Sentenced to die for two counts of murder, Charles Freemont was in Los Angeles to appear as a character witness for a member of the Black Guerrilla Family (BGF) who just happened to be on trial for two counts of robbery and murder.

The Sheriff's were aware that the BGF liked to subpoena their own members to a single facility where they could meet and set policies that affected their group. Whenever that happened, the Sheriff's made sure that they were kept in isolation, under careful watch, to discourage any meetings between guys like Freemont and his fellow gang members. They checked out Freemont's background, but he was not a "made" member of the gang, having never actually killed on behalf of the organization. They did not conclude that he posed a threat, so he was given a one-man cell right next to the one housing Liam Cassidy.

On the first evening of his stay, an inmate trustee came by to deliver candy and books. A runner for the BGF, he slipped Charles a key that would unlock his cell door. Charles hid the key in his rectum, just in case the deputies decided to do an unannounced search.

Two days later, the trustee came back and delivered a prison-made shiv. It was nothing fancy, just a piece of metal taken from a bedspring and filed down to a point at one end. Charles slid it into the lining of his mattress where he knew it would be safe until the time was right.

He kept track of Cassidy's schedule and watched him go past his cell twice a day.

One week later, Charles was finally ready, and just before lunch, he unlocked his door but kept it pulled shut so that no one would know it was open. He palmed the shiv, hefting its feel, and waited with patience near the side of his bunk.

A little after noon, the door clanged open at the end of the module. Once Cassidy walked by, followed by his escort, Charles quietly slipped out of his own cell to come at them from behind.

They never even heard him coming.

He passed the deputy and plunged the shiv into Cassidy's' neck. He did it again and watched him struggle with the chains that bound his hands to his waist.

Cassidy fell to the floor, screaming for help.

Charles stepped back, fascinated by the spurts of arterial blood that shot from Cassidy's neck.

The escort deputy, frozen in horror, finally backed away and ran for help.

****

Sheriff's Homicide investigators spent several weeks investigating the killing, but they never established a motive. They questioned nearby inmates to no avail, but several months later, word filtered down to the street that Charlie Freemont had been hired by the Black Guerrilla Family. The money provided for the hit—ten thousand dollars—was split equally between Freemont's actual family and the BGF.

Even deep cover informants failed to identify the person who'd hired the BGF, but the source of the money was rumored to be a senior member of the IRA.

****

Renée Marin threw several towels on the deck chairs and opened her beach bag to reach for a paperback novel she'd started the night before called *Hidden Agenda.* The story had her hooked, and she was looking forward to spending the next couple of hours working on her tan, keeping watch on her daughter, while getting lost in a compelling romantic crime story.

Julie dumped her towel on the chair next to hers, kicked off her sandals, and made a beeline for the swimming pool.

"Hold on, young lady," Renée yelled. "You need to put on sunscreen before you go in the water."

Julie frowned, then slowly walked back from the edge of the pool.

The pool was quite large, non-geometric in shape, with fingers of decking that stretched out like docks. The effect was the creation of smaller pools surrounded by tropical foliage that fostered the illusion of many separate pools all feeding into one. The deck itself was covered with plastic recliners that embraced a sea of overweight bodies whose lavish spending and penchant for shopping kept the economy of Hawaii in the black.

Julie kicked off her sandals, presented her back, and allowed her mother to put on the lotion.

"There's a lot of people down here today, so stay close where I can see you," Renée told her.

Julie ran towards the pool, and without hesitation, did a cannonball whose splash all but fizzled. She'd been working on it for a couple of weeks but she still didn't have it down.

A slow, gentle breeze kept the humid air moving which made the temperature by the pool more than tolerable. Renée climbed out of her wrap, adjusted her bikini, then laid out, closed her eyes, and basked without a care in the warmth of the mid-morning sun.

"Excuse me? Is this chair taken?"

She opened her eyes.

"*Whit?*"

She sat up quickly and smiled brightly.

"What are you doing here?"

He smiled back and gave her a wink.

"I'm on vacation. Mind if I sit down?"

She laughed and directed him to Julie's empty lounge chair.

Whitney took a seat and brought his hand out from behind his back.

"These are for you."

He handed her a small bouquet of tropical flowers.

"That's so sweet," she said, but then gave him a questioning look. "These look suspiciously like the flowers that grow along the hotel's pathway?"

He grinned. "It's the thought that counts. Right?"

They laughed together while she put the flowers down on a nearby table.

"So how are things going?" he asked.

"Things are really fine. Julie seems none the worse for wear, and I'm finally sleeping through the night again, but if you want to know the truth, I think the two of us are just about ready to head back home."

"But I just got here?" he said, feigning a pout.

She gave him a smile.

"But what about you? Are you really here on vacation?"

He nodded.

"I had some time coming, and I wanted a chance to sort things out with you." He took off his sunglasses. "I thought maybe we could spend a little time together; get to know one another; discover what we have in common?"

She reached out and put a hand on his arm.

"Well, if we're gonna do that, then I need to tell you something. Back in LA, when we had our little talk about how to deal with terrorists, I embarrassed myself by lecturing you about your policy of taking no prisoners. I feel like such a hypocrite. As soon as my daughter was at risk, I was the one who was screaming for their blood." She looked up and held his glance.

"I was such a fool, Whit. You were right and I was wrong. I'm sorry I questioned your actions as a soldier, and I'm so very glad that you did what you did."

He leaned over and gave her a kiss on the cheek.

"See, the thing is, you weren't all that wrong." He lowered his voice. "In the past, I never questioned my orders. I was given a mission, and I carried it out. But this time, thanks to what you had to say, I questioned what they wanted me to do. And if I hadn't, if I *had* killed them all, I doubt that we would've ever learned the truth."

He shrugged his shoulders.

"There's no easy answers, Renée, so you've got nothin' to apologize for. It's me who should be thankin' you for openin' my eyes."

Her eyes got watery.

"Wow! I didn't expect that, Whit." She reached up and placed her hand on his cheek.

"Mind if I kiss you now?" she said.

He smiled broadly, then leaned in.

"I'd be terribly disappointed if you didn't...."

*****

OTHER NOVELS BY PETER S. BERMAN

HIDDEN AGENDA

MONEY FOR LOVE

ABDUCTED

This book and others by Peter S. Berman are available at
amazon.com
and other fine retail outlets worldwide.

ABOUT THE AUTHOR

Peter S Berman became a Los Angeles County Deputy District Attorney in 1973. After ten years as a trial attorney, he was promoted to the position of Head Deputy District Attorney, a senior administrative position. As a Head Deputy, he oversaw the daily operation of several geographic courthouses, as well as specialized divisions, including the Hardcore Gang Division, the Sex Crimes Division, and the Career Criminal Division. He retired from the office in 2002.

While working as a prosecutor, he lectured for the National Prosecutors College in Houston, Texas; the California Department of Justice; the LAPD Training Academy, and numerous other groups. He was a technical advisor on a Paramount/NBC Movie of the Week that recounted one of his sexual assault cases. His work has been profiled on a number of television shows, including CBS's Sixty Minutes.

He has received Citations of Recognition from the Los Angeles County Board of Supervisors; the United States Secret Service; the Association of Deputy District Attorneys, and numerous other law enforcement agencies and groups.

He currently works as a Specialist Volunteer with LAPD's Robbery-Homicide Division, Cold Case Specials Unit, where he investigates unsolved homicide cases. He was honored by the LAPD's Robbery-Homicide Division as their 2008 Reserve Officer of the Year.

*****

*

www.ingramcontent.com/pod-product-compliance
Lightning Source LLC
Chambersburg PA
CBHW051545250626
47157CB00001B/196